BUIL

UNIVER

Gbenga Sokefun

Adigun

europe books

Gbenga Sokefun

www.adigunnovel.com

First published by Gbenga Sokefun in 2023

This book is published by Gbenga Sokefun

Copyright © Gbenga Sokefun 2023

© 2023 **Europe Books**| London
www.europebooks.co.uk | info@europebooks.co.uk

ISBN 9791220141826
First edition: September 2023

Adigun

This book is dedicated to all the boy victims of social in-adequacies and trafficking from the continent of Africa.

Table of Contents

Acknowledgments

"In everyone, there is a writer within." These were the words of my long-lost literature teacher, Mr. Chidi Okpara. "Are you there?!". He was only a young teacher, a fresh graduate (youth corper) from the Alvan Ikoku College of Education.

It was his first time in the Western part of Nigeria. He took me into his home and gave me the best tutoring in English Literature and Creative Writing. I pray one day our paths might cross again.

The phenomenon of human trafficking, though as old as human society, is receiving global attention and considerable political effort is being applied to the fight against it. The focus of these efforts has been primarily on female children in general, including African female children trafficked for purposes of prostitution and other forms of indentured servitude. Trafficking of the African male child has received far less attention, despite the simple fact that it exists.

The pressures of poverty and the inherent psychological damage of colonialism have resulted in a brisk trade of young African boys and men under the auspices of narcotics smuggling. The perpetrators have created a pathway for the African male child, whose solution to the inadequacies of the continent is to escape to the 'greener' pastures of the Americas, Europe or anywhere away from the continent of Africa. They prey on the dreams and desires of these gullible children who seek a better life on other continents. They offer alternatives to the common avenues for illegal migration – stowing away on merchant vessels, walking miles into the Sahara, or visa violations – exploiting the reality that the coming of age of the African child has become indistinguishable from the desire to reach the western world. Therein lay the catalyst that fuelled my desire to write.

I give thanks to the almighty God, maker of heaven and earth, without whom I would not even have the intellect to write.

I give thanks to my mother, Oyedolapo Sokefun, AKA Mome, for all the love and dedication, for the gift of prayer and for introducing the book, 'The Queen Primer' into my life.

Thanks to my late father, Michael Oluremi Sokefun, who defined creativity to me at a very young age. Thanks to my wife, Laetitia Omowunmi Sokefun, who stayed up many nights whilst I wrote. Her belief & encouragement truly pushed me to finish the book. Thanks to Alexander & Anthony Sokefun, my amazing sons for spurring me on. Thanks to my editor, Maxwell Marshall for believing in me and the painful rewrites. I also want to offer sincere gratitude to Europe Books, my publishers, who have taken a chance on this first-time author. Thanks to my great friend Lady D. Agama, bless you.

God bless Dr. Ayo Osunrinade, who told me it was a great book even before I wrote the first chapter. Thanks to Harmony Osunrinade for keeping 'Salami Bababorokini' alive. Bless up Debora Anne Williams. My guys, Kevin Oluwaseun Gabriel & Femi Samuel. 'The broad in Cricklewood' Kayode and Bunmi Badiru.

To all the writers who came before me and writers who still aspire, I say, "Just keep writing."

Thanks to Mazi Okoronkwo (Ugwu Aro), Mazi Eni Kanu(Ugwu Aro), Bank Anthony (Eyimba Aro) and Princewill & Ngozi Utchay (Omu Aro) who all brought Arochukwu and the Igbo culture alive and made my research easier. Ndewo o!

The Karim Family, you have been such a blessing, big up Agbaoye.! Thanks to Dolapo Joseph.

Can't forget my siblings and their amazing halves, Folake & Sola Aina, Seun and Funto Sokefun, Toyin and Kashetu Bello; Olufemi & Blessing Sokefun,Tosin & Soji Makanjuola, Damilola & Soji Akanji.

Thanks to Subomi & Femi Daniel for the belief. Thanks to the person who gifted me the most beautiful treasure ever – his daughter, Engineer Oladipo Oyewole. I am highly grateful for the encouragement. Finally, to the foundation, the community that birthed my creativity, love to all GCKites, you all Rock!

11

The Nigeria of today speaks of several cultures breaking away to form independent countries. We forget there are people who were born into multi-tribal families. The cultural fusion of the Fulani's with the Yorubas and the Igbos inseparable.

The book, Adigun, is the author's rendition of this reality while conveying the beauty of the African tradition and picturesque natural environment; it also shows the world the disparate elements of the coming of age of the African male child.

The title character, in his mid-teens, felt constrained to head out to a foreign land and was lured into a trap by evil adults. The author clearly highlights the harsh reality of the journey and the truth that awaits the trafficked.

Adigun is an intriguing tale, playing across three continents, that illustrates the delicate interplay of diverse cultural influences in a sprawling narrative that spans several decades. This story captures the enduring power of friendship, family, and human bonding that survives (and often conquers) cultural dislocation.

Book-1

Running

Heba cofel heba ngoo foondi walaa

(You can't have both a chick and a calf – Fulani proverb)

1

New York, 1983

Adigun ran across the street and settled into a brisk trot, looking periodically over his shoulder. He felt what had to be the beginnings of frostbite on his fingertips and he sped up, still looking back now and again. His tall lean frame was clad only in a pair of jeans and the native *Aso-Oke* dashiki he had arrived with. He slowed down a bit, but the alien cold responded in an instant. It seemed to slip its icy fingernails under his skin and seize hold of his tropical bones. He began to run again, then settled back into the brisk trot. This went on for thirty minutes until he was tired and out of breath. The street was littered with bright neon lights and a puffing yellow procession of taxi cabs, the winter night thrumming with impatient horns and even less patient people.

He felt a sudden itch on one of his ears and touched it; it felt like it was going to break off his head. The frost had hit his long ears. Everyone who walked past him seemed to look at him and marvel at his dress code and bravery. It was close to 9 p.m. and the streets were still very congested. The frigid air was pierced continually by the blaring sirens of ambulances and police cars. Indeed, New York never sleeps. Adigun was too distressed to take in the blazing, modern city he found himself in, though a small corner of his mind noted that he had probably never seen so many people, cars, and tall buildings, all wrapped in this abundance of electric light. He walked up 34th street, out of breath, looking back, certain in his mind that they would find him and return him to Africa.

He got to Times Square and made a right turn onto 42nd street. The aroma from a nearby hotdog stand ambushed him and he slowed down, realizing that he was hungry indeed. This realization was accompanied by another – he had no money on him. Adigun's hands began to freeze again, and he clenched them into fists, instinctively walking faster to warm himself. He walked until it dawned on him that he wasn't going anywhere; he would run out of energy and die if he continued.

He saw a group of three men around a fire. The promise of heat called to him, and he moved toward them. They were standing next to a heap of garbage and had started the fire in a blackened barrel, using the refuse as fuel. The fire blazed high, producing a strong, sickly-sweet smell. The men took turns squeezing up paper from the dumpster and throwing it into the barrel to fuel the fire. It puzzled Adigun to see one of them stuffing some crumpled newspaper into the sleeves of his ratty coat, though a mournful longing for just such a coat overcame that glimmer of curiosity.

The man Adigun saw stuffing crumpled paper into his coat sleeve was a diminutive white man with a closed face and watchful eyes. Adigun's instinct was that this man had already seen him and was marking his halting progress toward their group. The other two men were both larger, black men in similar, shabby overcoats of indeterminate color. They all wore almost identical woolen head coverings, and, on the little white man, Adigun saw straggly wisps of blond hair sneaking out through a jagged hole and blowing in the crisp wind.

Adigun moved closer but kept a reasonable distance until one of the black men signaled to him to join them. He walked straight to the dumpster, grabbed a large handful of paper, and dumped it into the fire, making its flames leap aggressively. The men were pleased with him, and he soon assumed the sole duty as fire-feeder. Adigun climbed the tip of the silver metal dumpster and threw in paper as needed, rolling it into a ball-sized bundle each time.

"What's the crack, son? What is your name, man?" the little white man asked with a thick Irish accent. The others turned their faces to Adigun waiting for him to tell them his name. "Adigun Komaiya," he replied, throwing the balls of rolled-up paper into the fire. "Welcome," the larger of the black men said with a grin on his face. He rubbed his hands together breathing in the hot air around the barrel's fire. "What brings you to the Waldorf Astoria?"

"I just came off the plane from Africa, I'm heading to the beginning of my destiny."

"You just came in from Africa? Haha! you must be Tarzan."

"How is the motherland?" asked the bald, light-skinned, black man opposite Adigun, "I am from Africa too," he said, continuing, "from Ile-Ife! I found that out just about a year ago. I heard most of the people from Ile-Ife are albinos, so I must be from there.

"I was told that the Ifa oracle decided to slaughter all the albinos in Ife as a sacrifice and they were all put on a boat to escape the onslaught. They ended up in Mississippi! Someday I shall be back home, back home to Ile-Ife, the land of the rising sun, the foundation of the Yoruba tribe."

"No, that is not true, sir," Adigun surprised himself with the barely-restrained force of his reply. "Ile-Ife was where ALL life began! It is the cradle of civilization and the root of mankind. We all hail from two deities, Oduduwa and Obatala. They came to the world through a cord reeled down to earth by God, also known as *Olodunmare*. Obatala created the first humans from clay and Oduduwa was the first king. They named that place Ile-Ife and from that place, mankind dispersed all over the earth."

"Preach on, boy, preach on! Listen to the African kid," Bernard, the light-skinned fellow poked the old, white man next to him, his index finger sticking out from the ripped black woolen glove. Adigun noticed that he too had newspapers stuffed into his jacket. "Did I not always tell you blacks were the original humans created by

17

Dudu- whatever the dude was called?" "Oduduwa," Adigun interjected rubbing his thin hands together above the fire.

"What tribe is you from, Greg?" asked Bernard, turning to the other black man, "Your ass is too black to be from Ile-Ife!" his eyebrows rose on his forehead as he chuckled and turned to stare at Adigun. Bernard replied quietly, "I am a true Mandingo. We came to Alabama from Africa and that was our tribe. You a Mandingo, Adigun (he pronounced it *Uh-Diggun*)? I bet you is a Mandingo, the real black man, the Asiatic. Direct line of Kush, the grandson of Jesus." "Quit blaspheming, boy! Jesus never had no goddamned grandchildren!" Bernard pointed at Greg and immediately used the same hand to perform the sign of the cross. The fire sputtered and the group was silent for a beat.

Adigun, on top of the dumpster, looked into the pit. 'How did I get here?' he thought to himself, his mind casting back to the home he had come from; the home he may never see again.

2

Jobore, 1973

"Adigun! Adigun!! Adigun!! Adigun!! Iwoyi ana la soro re." A Yoruba adage meaning, 'We spoke about you same time yesterday.' The whole neighborhood would shout his name as he scaled their fences and destroyed their gardens. "Run, Adigun, run!" "Adigun, run, run, run!" The kids yelled with gleeful encouragement, each running their bamboo fence, craning to catch a glimpse of the fastest boy in the village. The event created a waving row of little heads, all lined up to watch the performance. They stood on tip-toes to get a better view of Adigun's show of adolescent athleticism.

Panting like an Olympic athlete, he ran with his rabbit ears shut to the insults from the irate neighbors whose backyard vegetable gardens he was trampling. His teeth clenched and his eyes wide, Adigun could hear the sound of his oversized khaki shorts, "Thwick-wick, thwick-wock," flapping as they slid almost to his knees. He would grab hold of the side portion of his shorts with one hand and paddle the wind with the other as though it would make him run faster. Dashing through his front door, he used his saliva to clean off the dirt stuck to his skin. Out of breath, Adigun would sit at the table, with books turned open as though he had been studying all day. Who could have guessed that Adigun was playing in the fields two minutes ago?

Adigun always made it around the block in less than two minutes. The daily dash home began at twilight, as soon as he heard the sound of his father's car, a 1962 Volkswagen beetle. The exhaust system had been faulty for about five years. The burnt-brown car sounded like a military helicopter and announced itself from a mile away. "Adigun!" His father would call, as soon as he stepped into the house, his voice sounding like it was an echo from distant hills. Adigun usually would not answer until the third call. He struggled to regain control of his skinny frame, still heaving from his exertions. "Saaahhh?" he'd answer with his frail voice, trembling underneath his skin and staring at the book, open to the same page it was yesterday and the day before.

"Okaare lai," his father would reply with his deep Yoruba accent, meaning "well done," praising Adigun for being studious and responsible. Adigun would immediately leave the study table, a few sweat beads dribbling down his thin face onto the terrazzo floor, stretching and yawning as though he had been sitting there all day.

Adigun, just a few months over 8 years old, was dark, skinny, and hairy, with bushy sideburns dropping below his rabbit-long ears, which adorned his scruffy ginger afro. He was not a big fan of academia and his years in elementary school so far were spent wondering if he and education were meant for each other. It was bad enough that he was forced to memorize verses of the Bible in Yoruba, his mother tongue, but Adigun also had to memorize The Catechism and numerous songs by the psalmists. Though a Christian, Adigun's father was also a traditional chief, with the title 'Balogun Dodondawa of Jobore'. His friends called him *Dodo*.

It was Dodo's earnest wish to educate all his kids - education was important. *"Bata re a dun ko ko ka ti oba ka iwe re,"* Dodo would sing. A Yoruba song, meaning, "If you get an education your shoes will sound elegant; *Ko, ko, ka,"* a sound proudly synonymous with good shoes and wealth. The country had just begun to enjoy the dividends of independence and there was a rash of nouveau rich pronouncing their presences in various corridors with these percussive pumps.

Dodo's father was Adolphus Komaiya, the first indigenous headmaster of the first school in Jobore, and education was very important to the family. He was distressed at Adigun's poor academic performance, especially as his first son. The success of one's first son was a thing of great import for any Nigerian man in these postcolonial times. The Biafra War (the Nigerian civil war) had ended just a few years before and the country's masses were still in the process of settling back into their lives. In primarily rural settlements like Jobore, the roadside still featured broken-down military personnel carriers, artillery vehicles, and other relics of the war. Before the Biafra war,

Adigun's father was a teacher in Arochukwu, a kingdom in the south-eastern part of Nigeria, the closest Igbo town to the Atlantic Ocean. It is believed that over half of the blacks sold into slavery departed through the Arochukwu shores. Arochukwu was hardly hit by the war as they were on the side of the rebels of Biafra against the federal government in a war to gain independence from Nigeria.

Dodo had married Obiageli, Adigun's mother, the daughter of a prominent chief in Arochukwu, a union that was highly controversial and contested by the villagers despite Dodo's long presence in the community. As the war became very fierce and several threats of recruiting his only son into 'the boy's company,' an organization that recruited juveniles into the army on reconnaissance missions into the enemy camps. Keziah Babatunde Komaiya, moved Obiageli and Adigun, his only child, to his hometown Jobore in the southwestern part of Nigeria in anticipation of the worst. When Adigun's academic performance fell well short of the desired standard, it struck Dodo as a personal affront.

"Remember the child of whom you are," Dodo would blurt out from a long silence, usually to begin a lengthy rant. "You are my crown; my pride and you will not drag my name in the mud. My father brought education to the west; through Adolphus, many were educated in this part of the country. Much is expected of you.

"All you want to do is play.

"You are playing with your future," Dodo would exclaim, slapping his hairy hand on the oak table.

"Y-y-you think I don't know you?" Dodo had a slight stutter when he was enraged, "You come into this house acting like a saint, yet one second after I step out, you are like the wind! You blow all over the village like the wind with no destination terrorizing other children. You know which family cooked beans and where the last yam was pounded."

Adigun would stand frozen with his head bowed twisting his fingers in a circular motion. His father would then proceed to trot out the transgressions of the week. "I was told you were seen again, wearing that stupid white garment." "No, papa!" Adigun would reply with his frail soprano voice, his lips rolled into a hollow form and his face all furrowed. "Shut up," Dodo would shout and always end it with the phrase, "Bastally fool!" Nobody knew what the word "bastally" meant. Perhaps he meant "bastardly" but it still didn't make sense.

"Yes, they saw you. I have told you I don't want you going to these funerals. You don't belong to that crowd! It is a disgrace to see the grandson of Adolphus Komaiya, the first headmaster of Jobore, scavenging around, *uninvited*," Dodo's voice always climbed in volume and pitch at this word, "to these funerals and functions!" As he crossed his tenth year, Adigun had begun to suspect that a substantial part of his father's aggravation was reflected in that single word – uninvited – as if Dodo was indignant that there were any functions in Jobore to which he and his were, indeed, not invited. "Your mother and I work hard to put good food on the table. We have provided for you but you continue to roam the village with these street urchins, eating at every funeral and wedding."

Adigun and his friends were known all over Jobore as the "Obituary Boys",

The gang would note down addresses on obituary announcement posters and show up in full ceremonial attire. Adigun had his white lace *agbada*, native to the western part of Nigeria, with the rest of his crew also formally dressed, and they would blend in with the guests. The objective was to get served food, drinks, and gifts. On a good day, they would get to eat breakfast, return for lunch, and would even mingle with the crowd during the dancing in the evening, picking up money being sprayed on the family of the deceased.

On one occasion, Adigun had been spotted by Dodo at the graveside portion of a burial ceremony. Adigun was right there at the graveside next to the crying bereaved, also wailing and shedding crocodile tears. Several times, he had been handed condolence envelopes by people mistaking him for one of the children of the deceased. Driving past on an errand from the school, Dodo sighted Adigun, eyes closed, teeth in the air crying profusely. After bringing the Beetle to a dusty, screeching halt, Dodo charged at Adigun, picked him by his long pixie ears, and dragged him home, twisting his ears and grinding them viciously with his colossal fingertips. By the time Adigun got home, his ears were red-hot, and certain, in Adigun's mind, to glow in the dark.

Dodo's nagging was not complete until he touched on Adigun's poor performance in school. "Adigun, Adigun, Adigun!! I have almost had it! I cannot take it anymore! It's okay if you don't want to go to school anymore. It is sad, it is sad, the son of Keziah Babatunde Komaiya, 30th position in a class of 31- including a blind child! What a shame! I have told you so many times, I have plans for you. I have plans! No son of mine will be useless; I have plans! I should have sent you to my brother, Dele all these years, I should have sent you to Dele!"

Dodo would go on and on like a broken record. He would repeat the same speech at the same time each passing school day (and often on non-school days as well). Adigun's mum would sometimes interject in Igbo, *"Ogi' muruya,"* meaning, "It is your child; the fruit does not fall far from the tree." Obiageli would often mumble the words softly to herself when she felt no wish to interfere with Dodo's rants. "I give up! I give up! I am taking you to go and learn a trade; you don't want to go to school? Fine! You will join the mechanics at Kajero's shed." At some point, Adigun had begun to wonder if being sent to an auto mechanic as an apprentice would be so bad. "I have made arrangements with Kajero for you to become his apprentice." Dodo had made this threat for so many years that it held no meaning for Adigun anymore. Many times, Dodo had taken Adigun to the mechanic's shed by the village cemetery and handed him to Kajero, only for his mother to come back for him at twilight. Taking Adigun to an auto-mechanic workshop to make him take his education more seriously backfired spectacularly. Adigun began to like the idea. He was sometimes overheard telling his father's friends how his future ambition was to become a mechanic himself. This brought utter disappointment to the heart of Adigun's father, who was usually quick to tell his friends how his son, Adigun, would go to England on a British Council scholarship to study medicine.

Jobore village was a strategic stop for vehicles moving goods from the west to the east; it had mechanic workshops scattered on every vacant piece of land that could fit in a few cars. The workshops doubled as a training ground for underprivileged kids that could not obtain a formal education. The apprentice kids, usually called "Journeyman" (or "Jolly man", by the locals), were known to be the most liberated kids on the face of the earth. They didn't have to go to school, they seldom took baths, and had uncommon sums of money in their pockets, usually tips from clients. They had more free time to play than any of the children who were trapped in conventional, school-and-family-related routines. The boys rolled around in the rich Jobore soil, covered in black oil – looking like stray mongrels – faces filled with joy and contentment. Adigun could not wait to join them. He was tired of the constant harassment by his father.

The apprentices served diligently, learning several aspects of automobile diagnosis and repair. They would serve for several years until they 'graduated', and there was a great ceremonial passing out party they called "Freedom."

Adigun would watch the kids from a distance and, in his mind, shout, "Freedom! Freedom!" He prayed liberation would come someday from the oppressive claws of Keziah Babatunde Komaiya. Freedom, yes! Freedom! It was like slavery, being restrained in the poorly lit asbestos-topped bungalow. He wanted to be free like one of those apprentices, with just a loincloth to cover his nakedness. The "Jolly man" was poorly clad; the boys, usually orphans, were handed over to the mechanic like chattel, on lease for a term. They were often badly treated and roughly used. They were given a meager sum at mealtimes and the boys didn't have much choice about what food to buy. Their default delicacy was roasted plantain and peanuts, though the jolly man could sometimes save for a few days and get a plate of rice or fufu from the few scattered roadside restaurants nearby.

In most cases. the boys only owned a single outfit; a pair of shorts or trousers and one shirt. On days the shirt was washed, they would wear only the pants, walking around bare-chested. On days they washed the pants – since their shirts were always oversized – it was convenient to put their skinny legs through the sleeves of the shirts and convert them into makeshift trousers. On very hot days, they would wash the entire outfit, and make a loin garment out of the cotton rags meant for cleaning the cars. They often looked like the typical western image of the African bushman.

At that early age, what was most important to Adigun was not his mythical *future*, though he would realize much later in life that his parents were just anxious about what would become of him. He was not a dull child, but he just didn't do well at structured educational assessments; he was wilful, self-absorbed, and usually liked to do things at his own pace. Adigun would often turn in blank examination answer sheets, simply because he could neither understand nor appreciate the purpose of the exam. He spent most test and exam periods drawing and had once made a remarkable portrait of Mrs. Gallagher, an Irish missionary nurse who had come to Jobore with the Red Cross during the civil war. The portrait showed considerable skill and might have been deserving of high praise. Unfortunately, the portrait was of an entirely nude Mrs. Gallagher (with proportions exaggerated as only a pre-adolescent mind could), who blanched on receiving the answer sheet and immediately sent for Adigun's parents. During the spirited conference that took place between his parents and Mrs. Gallagher, the nun waved the offending portrait above her head and repeated in a shrill voice that, had she been of a more violent nature, she would have delivered Adigun her very best of slaps. Her professed pacifism did not extend so far as to plead with the principal on Adigun's behalf, however, and the episode earned him a flogging, a fortnight of sore buttocks, and lasting ridicule from the entire school community.

The first time Adigun placed 30th out of 31 pupils, such was his ignorance that he didn't even realize the significance of the numbers. He had walked around Jobore with so much pride, telling people he had a high number on his report card, 30th out of 31 children, and would boast of even getting a higher position next time. Of the 31 kids, one was blind and usually took a special exam in braille, which he had not yet mastered. Adigun was, technically speaking, last. Parents would laugh at his ignorance, and he would think they were happy at his accomplishment. "Tell them you didn't get your card yet," Hadezah would urge Adigun. She was like a mother to him and loved him as any mother would. Adigun was just born when she joined the Keziah family. She was the daughter of Dodo's Fulani friend, Danladi Bako, an illiterate Fulani herdsman that had settled in Jobore. He was said to have entrusted Hadezah to Dodo's care when Adigun was born, to forge local ties and have her exposed to some education and the ways of the land. Her father was open to the benefits of formal education and would have preferred to send a son to receive this exposure but, alas, none of his male children had lived beyond the first few months after birth, so Hadezah was chosen. She became a well-loved member of the Komaiya family and had cared for Adigun all his life, while also being of immense domestic help to Adigun's mum. When she joined the family, she could not speak a word of English – she only spoke Fulfude, the indigenous Fulani dialect – and, by the age of four, Adigun could communicate perfectly in Fulfulde. His parents were not in support of this but could do little to avert it without dealing with the inconvenience of removing Hadezah as Adigun's primary caregiver. She was very sensitive and would cry even when Adigun was merely admonished for one of his numerous acts of mischief. Adigun was an only child, and his chief protector was Hadezah.

When Adigun was seven years old, Hadezah had vanished from his home for a longer stretch than was usual – he had become accustomed to her going off for two or three days every few months –this time being absent for several weeks. When she returned, it was with some furor that was just outside his understanding; Hadezah, her father, and what seemed like the entire Fulani clan in Jobore, mobbed his father's house and a tense, aggressive exchange ensued. Adigun knew it had something to do with the outsized, ball-shaped abdomen Hadezah had sported for a while, before she had disappeared, and which she still carried before her, even more distended than before she left.

Some deep part of Adigun held an inkling of what the trouble was, but the top part of his consciousness preferred not to dwell on it. So, a short while later, when Hadezah suddenly started toting a squalling infant around, Adigun took it in stride without pause to question. A bit harder to do, but still manageable, was to ignore the cloud that had descended around his mother, and which darkened the spirit of their home. Hard to ignore, but Adigun was blessed with a willful ignorance that inured him to any excess of curiosity. Thus, by this time,

Hadezah's child was an eminently tolerable (if unacknowledged) part of his home life. As long as Hadezah remained in his corner and helped him through his rough patches, she was welcome to her (admittedly) adorable brat. Despite Hadezah's residence at the Komaiyas', she always went back to Sabo and, following the arrival of her daughter, Talatu, she almost always took Adigun with her. She had taught him a lot about the Fulani culture and often dressed him up like a Fulani herdsman. Adigun was so well known in the large Fulani community that they called him *'Yaro'*, a generic term for 'boy' that delighted Adigun. He thoroughly enjoyed these excursions, and he did not question the reasons for them. He showed an aptitude for animal husbandry and became an honorary member of the Fulani clan, often joining them to tend their flock. These adventures were a welcome break from the tedium of his home life.

3

Chike

Adigun's quiet home was next to the church vicarage. It was a modest bungalow, built of mud slabs and a corrugated iron roof, with a backyard that led to an endless meadow of grass. Across the road lived the Obidikes with their only child, Chike. Unlike Adigun, Chike was of those very special children that were not only intelligent but thrived on applying and expanding their intelligence. Whilst Adigun was always at the bottom of the class, Chike maintained the top position always. Apart from the physical proximity of their homes, the only other thing Chike and Adigun had in common was their age range. Adigun was fed up with the constant comparison between himself and Chike, the geek, who always did everything right. He did everything he could to be as far away from Chike as possible, except in the mornings, when he made a show of sidling over to Chike's house to ask after him.

Chike was the most boring kid ever. Adigun supposed the more polite expression would be 'reserved'; Chike was very reserved. His family house also contained The Chemist, which was the closest thing to a medical facility in the village of Jobore. Nnamdi Obidike, Chike's father, was called 'Doctor' by all, though he was a pharmacist and not a doctor. He was the primary port-of-call for the villagers' health care, as the next medical facility was in Irede, about two villages (and half a day's walk) away. Nnamdi Obidike was always busy administering medicines to the villagers, often also performing simple medical procedures. When there were more complicated medical cases, 'Doctor' Obidike referred them to Irede village.

Jobore was a major railway depot and the Nigerian Railway Corporation had built a few houses for their technical staff. Dr. Obidike was posted to run the pharmacy and mini clinic for travelers, and his chemist was used as a medical base for visiting doctors and The Red Cross when they had immunization programs in the village. Chike's father was a British-trained pharmacist, and he spoke in what was known at the time as Queen's English. He was always dressed like a gentleman, with unforgettable grey, pin-striped trousers, and brogues. Over his pristine white shirts, he would usually wear a navy blazer and a bow tie. This attire was only altered on the occasions when he filled in as Signals Engineer at the railway station.

The pharmacy had been commissioned by the Railway company and was originally run by a pharmacist named John Akpan. Predictably, the store came to be known as John Akpan Store and the name stuck even after Nnamdi Obidike took over upon Mr. Akpan's passing. The

Obidike family had lived in Jobore long before the civil war but had to flee to the east when the war began, as did most people of Igbo descent: some to join the fight for the independence of the new Igbo nation, Biafra, others simply to escape the vilification of Nigeria's other tribes, many of whom viewed the Igbos as enemies. After the war was over, they and other Igbos, including Adigun's family, returned to Jobore. Both families had lived in Arochukwu during the Biafran war, and it was a relief for Obiageli, Adigun's mother when she found out a family was living at Jobore from her village. She immediately became fast friends with Mrs. Obidike.

Chike was the only child of the Obidikes and that seemed to suit him just fine; he was insular to the point of being antisocial. Chike never joined the other neighborhood kids to play, and his parents had to bribe the neighborhood kids (with goodies the trains brought from Lagos) to play with him. These mercenary 'playmates' all left him with his books as soon as the treats were safely consumed. Chike weathered these contrived visits with a stoic fortitude that masked his impatience for the invaders to leave. He was studious, naturally brilliant, and just wanted to read. Chike had finished the entire works of Shakespeare before the age of eight – the full versions, not the abridged ones for children. He had been wearing eyeglasses since the age of two and wore a perpetual squint that hid his eyes. His tendency to squint, stretch his neck forward, and breathe through his mouth made him look like he was using his buckteeth for sight, rather than his eyes. His glasses were as thick as the bottom of a coke bottle and they would bob up and down as Chike seemed to use his entire lower face when talking, which was seldom. All the kids believed Chike could see very far with his thick lenses and, when he sat in front of his house, they were convinced he used them as powerful binoculars... for spying.

Adigun would stretch his thin neck out of the window whenever he saw Chike, teasing him from across the road;

"Chikereuba Chikereuba,

Omo yibo, ajokuta mamomi,

Salisu wa gbobe

otu yeri yeri abaa baabaa."

Roughly translated, the song derided the Igbos. This was a severe tribal insult from a Yoruba kid, even though his mother shared tribal origins with Chike and was equally insulted by the song.

The suspicion surrounding Chike's long vision and rumored espionage made Adigun and his friends wary of Chike's location whenever they went on any mischievous adventure. Too often, their exploits were exposed to their parents, and someone had to be telling on the gang – someone with some sort of binoculars, for instance. Adigun had long wondered how his mother got detailed information about his daily activities; he would get home and his mother would know exactly what he had been up to.

Adigun was very suspicious (and resentful) of Chike's gifts, so it was not much of a leap for him to conclude that he was the likely tattle-tale. This conclusion wasn't entirely unfounded, as Chike was known to have no filters at all when relating with parents, tending to offer unreserved, excruciatingly honest responses to whatever questions he was asked. The boy had a Kodak-quality memory. He remembered every detail. *"Eyin iku,"* meaning 'teeth of death,' the kids would tease him, making fun of his dentition. Chike was indifferent. When he wasn't reading novels, he was carving wood into very interesting shapes. He had a carving knife, given to him by Ajibade, the sculptor, whose shed was on the new Lagos Road. Chike took many lessons from Ajibade on woodwork and the art of carving wood. When his father saw his love for art and sculpture, he also took him to the village blacksmith where Chike learned how to smelt and sculpt metal art. Chike developed a near-obsession with metal sculptures, but it was a costly and challenging pursuit. So, most of his free time was spent either reading or sitting under the oak tree, carving shapes into its trunk. At such times, one could observe Chike, shoulders hunched, face bent close to the tree trunk in a posture that would seem almost intimate if not for his teeth – seeing those made it seem more like he was trying to gnaw at the bark.

Despite their severe dissimilarity of character, Chike, and Adigun, on those rare occasions when they interacted, had a great time together. As long as there were no other children around (so Adigun didn't feel the need to play to the gallery), or grown-ups gushing over Chike's intelligence and composure, Adigun rather enjoyed Chike's company. He admired the boy's quality of being above the fray – not quite aloof, but unaffected. Chike, on the other hand, held a secret admiration for Adigun's capacity to seize the moment and enjoy himself; enjoyment being a concept largely alien to him, except maybe when carving. Their fraternity was short-lived, however, as Chike's family moved away after only a short time in Jobore. His father left the Nigerian Railway Corporation to pursue some pharmaceutical breakthrough he was working on, though he still came around sometimes to visit Adigun's father. At a point, news came that Chike's father went to England on a work-study program, but it was unclear whether Chike and the family went with him or not. This didn't stop Adigun's imagination from running amok, and he pictured Chike in England in some sort of special school for geniuses. He struggled with a swirling mix of emotions at these musings; pride in his comrade, wistfulness for a life he felt he could never have, jealousy, and a dark streak of forced indifference, which he nurtured. 'To hell with Chike and his genius,' he thought defiantly, 'I am a don right here! Soon, I will be a king in Jobore!'

4

New York, 1983

"Feed the fire, would you, boy?"

Adigun snapped out of his reverie! "Eh?" he asked, disoriented.

"I said the fire needs to be fed, son; more paper!"

Adigun stretched deep into the bottom of the dumpster to reach the wads of paper there.

"Oh, dude! I'm so happy to have met you, but it's getting dark, and we have to get into the YMCA, or else we'll be spending the night on the street."

"What is the YMCA?" Adigun asked.

"Oh, it's an extension of the Waldorf Astoria; a place rich people go to for a short while, just to see what poverty tastes like. In layman's terms, a homeless shelter or, should I say, a free hotel where you get served chicken soup and stale bread."

"Put it this way; we are in transit, so we are spending some time at the YMCA. It's like a monastery, we all leave the YMCA and become monks. Street monks," said Greg. They all burst out laughing hard with their jaws in the sky. It all seemed a bit maniacal to Adigun, but he was infected by the good cheer, forced though it was. He thought he had good reason to force some good cheer himself! Adigun grinned, looking into the fire, and basking in the heat.

"So where would *you* be staying?" asked Bernard.

"I have no place, sir. I will get a job to start with."

"Tonight?" Greg crowed, saying, "Oh! I love this kid. I *love* this African kid!"

Adigun ignored his mockery and continued, "I would like to work as a stockbroker. Where are the stockbrokers? I guess they must be close to the sea. I met a stockbroker once; he came to my village at Jobore and he had one of the best boats I have ever seen in my life. He seemed well-to-do, selling stockfish from his boat."

"A stockbroker? Selling fish?" the light-skinned man asked, incredulous. He peered at Adigun like he was waiting for the punchline to some joke. "Oh, young man, my name is Gerald," the little white man stretched out his mittened right hand to shake Adigun. "I used to be a stockbroker, but I went broke after the 1960 crisis, and haven't recovered since. But I know I will bounce back again. I know I will.

"If you just came from Africa and you are homeless, I think you have come to the wrong State! You should head west. It's warmer there and people are nicer.

"Speaking of nice, you've been here a half-hour, we need you to pay for the heat. We accept only cash, and all payments go into the hat. Please start reaching out for your wallets now." Adigun had no money on him, he reached into his pocket, and he felt the bag of plantain chips he bought at the harbor.

"Okay guys, pay up now; pay your energy bills." There was a pregnant silence as Adigun remained crouched on the garbage can. Greg looked at him and the other men. "Psych, Kunta Kinte, Psych! Nobody pays for heat at the Waldorf. We do have to go, though. If I were you, I would head south and catch the train at Union Station to Washington DC, and then on to the Great Canyons. Get off at the Canyons and you can hitch a ride with the tourists to California. At the Canyons there is a lad there called Axel Folly; he sells roasted nuts and dried vulture guts. Disgusting as it sounds, this gruesome delicacy has the highest concentration of iron and other vital vitamins of all. It can keep a man alive, should they get lost in the hot canyon.

"Tell him you met Cricky Greg. Tell him you met Cricky Greg at the Waldorf.

"Take the red-eye train from Grand Central Station to DC. It leaves at 11 p.m. Go straight into the first-class cabin.

"The conductors never check for tickets in the first-class cabin. And sit by the window because you may need to jump out. Fare evasion has just been voted into law as a crime. It used to be a 'slap-on-your-wrist' misdemeanor.

"You may bruise a little, but you can hop on another train. Better than going to jail, boy!" Greg reached out for a rusty bucket of water under the tree and emptied it into the hot barrel. The dying fire hissed like an old locomotive, releasing thick, smelly smoke.

"That's it, bro, we got to bounce, we have to get a bed tonight."

The men grabbed their blankets and began to walk away from the fire. They crossed the road briskly to the opposite sidewalk. Adigun followed them. Greg glanced over his shoulder, stopped abruptly in front of a red fire hydrant, turned around, and glared at Adigun. "Man!! Why is this kid following us?" shouted Greg. He moved closer to Adigun. "Dammit! Why are you following us?" "I don't know how to get to Grand Central Station, sir," Adigun replied, scratching the middle of his head. Greg replied through gritted teeth and it amazed Adigun that this was the same pleasant fellow he'd been with just minutes before.

"You need to head east on 42nd street. Walk fast, as you're running out of time."

Adigun ran, through the rainy night, down 42nd street, which was still cacophonous at that time of the night. He ran past rows of gleaming shops. He looked up, for the first time since he arrived, at the tallest buildings he had ever seen in his life. The road was a wide river of yellow taxis and, in the background, it seemed there was the permanent blare of sirens. He saw the massive sign on a huge building that read, 'Grand Central Station,' and Adigun ran towards the sign, wiping dribbles of rain from his face. He saw a black boy who was also running, and Adigun ran faster to catch up with him, He blurted out, "I'm going to Grand Central Station."

"So am I," said the boy. "Are you catching the DC night train?"

"Oh, yes!" Adigun answered.

"Follow me!"

Adigun ran behind the boy, who took sharp turns, narrowly avoiding collisions with the numerous display racks in front of the many different shops. They ran through a huge hall and got to a row of stainless-steel turnstiles, at which the boy pushed through on the heels of a man going through one. Adigun stopped.

The boy looked back to the other side of the turnstile shouting, "Come on!"

Adigun rushed in with a man wearing a brown coat, beating the barrier, and realizing that they had pulled off some sort of cheat. The man in the brown overcoat glanced at Adigun with a sort of distant disdain and kept going.

The train was about to move when the boy jumped in, and Adigun followed. It moved slowly, graffiti-covered walls sliding past on both sides of the car. They waded through the packed cabins to the last coach, where it was quiet and had only a few passengers. Signs on the headrests read, "First Class." Both boys sunk their bodies into the soft velvet seats. Adigun peered out of the window, looking at America, finding himself able to feel a good sort of excitement again. He smiled at the boy, "Thanks. Wow! That was a run. My name is Adigun, I'm from Jobore. The grandson of Adolphus JP, the first Village Court Registrar and a recipient of the United Nations award for humanity. Which village are you from?"

"Oh, I don't live too far from The Village; about a few blocks by the NCP parking lot on 5ᵗʰ Ave. My name is Shannon. Shannon Buck, born Jamerican!

"Hundred percent yardie, you *kian tes*! A rude boy! A Dangerous Animal. Cruiserweight Champion of Rikers.

"Jamaican ambassador of licking." He threw a quick punch in the air and gave a stern look with his nose scrunched up, then he continued, "Me lick spots of a leopard with a left uppercut. Left hand sting like a scorpion!

"Me like ya garb, still." He said as he ran his hands over the embroidery on Adigun's Dashiki. "You got that at The Village?" Shannon reached out to Adigun's dashiki running his hands over the yellow embroidery again.

"Yeah, man! Thatta dope man!" he said in Jamaican patois.

Then he flipped to a pure American accent. "It must be one of those exclusive 'Mashood' pieces."

Adigun was lost, as he didn't know the source of the garment at all. It was handed to him at Diokpa Obidike's office and he had changed into it in the toilet.

"Is Mashood good? Who is Mashood? Is he a Nigerian?"

Shannon looked at him and sighed, "You live in The Village, and you don't know Mashood?

"Lying Tod! You aren't from the village – you can't be from the village and not have a train ticket!

"Where do you live in The Village? Under the railway arches, *a-blood clat*?" He shifted again to Jamaican patois. This time Adigun saw his gold teeth. *"Me haff direk you wrongly, make you miss da blood-clat train, African boy!*

"The Village? Yeah, right!! You too lie, man! African people too lie!!

"Ya know Segun?" Shannon glared at Adigun. "I-and-I put de scar on his face for lying. Him too lie! We call him Chicken pum-pum," he laughed. "Chicken pum-pum, a ras clad." He laughed louder and louder, coughing intermittently and holding his belly.

"The Village! Jesus Christ, Lord o' mercy! The Village? Two-thousand-muthafreaking-dollars-per-square-foot Village?

"Blood clad!! What's your name again?"

"Adigun."

"Adigun from the Village, a ras clad! Nigga! You probably from Farocaway, or right there at Flat Bush with all the other lovely Africans. Quit lying!"

Adigun's face compressed into an expression of disgust. Pointing at Shannon Buck, he yelled, "Stop! Stop! Stop," in his strong western-Nigerian accent. He leaned closer to Shannon's face, absent-mindedly noticing the long scar around his neck, like the result of a botched decapitation. "I am from Jobore! South-West Nigeria, three miles from Kiyesi, right next to Irede, the land with the golden lakes, the land with sixteen masquerades, where love falls like raindrops.

"I don't know which 'Village' you are talking about, but I am from Jobore village in Nigeria.

"I just came off a plane at some John Ken or Animal Johnson something airport and I'm on my way to find my destiny.

"I am happy to be in America, the land flowing with milk and honey. The land of Christopher Columbus, apple pie, chicken ice cream, Werewolf, and Bigfoot."

"Chicken Ice cream?" Shannon was astonished.

"Yes, Chicken ice cream! I heard about it in my country! Look! I have no idea where this train is taking us; I ran after you, and you brought me here!"

"I met some men at the fire thing roasting and wearing newspapers. They advised me to go to the city where the sun shines – ooh, I don't remember the name, something like Calistus… Fonicalistus or Caphonica - anyway, the sun shines there."

Shannon interrupted Adigun's rant, "California! God-damit"

"Ehen!" Adigun gushed, "Dassit! I'm new here, my good friend, and I need your help; I have no family, no money, no house to sleep in.

"Where you go, I go; until I find my own destiny."

Shannon seemed to have a momentary discomfort. "You mean you just got into this country from Africa? You come from the motherland?

"Wow! Welcome from the motherland, brother. Asalam Aleikum. Peace and peace descend upon you. I get it now.

"I don't know about sunshine in the winter, but I am also going to Washington DC to reunite with *my* destiny.

"I am a boxer, a fighter. I am going to DC to meet with a new coach, Lucious Waterman. He's the biggest coach in America! He made George Forman.

"He has invited me to join his camp. I just got out of Rikers Island, see? Been incarcerated seven years.

"Was in for a bullshit GBH and attempted murder bid.

"I was the boxing Champion at Rikers Island five years straight and I have been invited by this great coach. He heard about me winning the Federal Prisons Boxing Championships and we have been communicating from Rikers. This is my ticket, man; out the ghetto!"

"Where is Rikers?" Adigun asked.

"Ummm, Rikers?"

Shannon raised his face to the ceiling for a drawn-out moment, "Rikers?

"Um, Rikers is the real hell, man. A time-share apartment complex belonging to The Devil!

"State Penitentiary. The most violent, the most notorious passageway to hell!

"You don't want to go there; you don't want to know Rikers. It has been home for me for the last seven years.

"I have been boxing almost every day for seven years. The first five years, I fought to survive. Last two years, I was training inmates to box. I was released on parole for good behavior."

"Really?"

"Yes, bro. Adigun, you don't want to ever visit Rikers; you are better off dead."

"Dead?" Adigun blurted out.

The train had attained its highest speed and it rocked the cabin aggressively. The green headrests on the plush first-class seats swayed as the train raced towards a dark tunnel. It had begun to rain. Adigun's face was pressed against the thick glass window as the rain beads drizzled down forming webby patterns on the glass. His tired eyes were blood red. The cabin was warm and there was a strong aroma of freshly baked bread and coffee.

Adigun was unaware that he had drifted asleep until a short-bearded man, with a machine strapped to his body, tapped his shoulders and startled him awake.

"Ticket, please."

Adigun stared stupidly, looking around for Shannon; he was nowhere to be found. The man tapped Adigun's shoulder the second time, "Ticket, please."

Shannon appeared from the hallway on the north side of the coach.

"Raising his hands, he shouted "Yo!! Delroy, King of boys, what's up buddy?"

"Yeah, yeah, the one and only Shannon, Rikers's Nightmare, Kick-ass Shannon!"

Shannon got up and threw a few punches in the air and the conductor ducked them playfully. Shannon Buck hugged the middle-aged black man.

"Himma one of us, blood. Lef him, blood. Him just come from da motherland."

"He straight then, bro, he straight," the conductor replied, leaning away from Adigun, who watched the exchange with a mix of consternation and confusion.

"You heard from Rakeem?"

"Yeah, bro, I was at Rikers on Saturday, visiting my nephew. Rakeem is good, bruv. Twelve years to go."

Adigun stared as the ticket man walked away and disappeared through the hallway.

"Yes, that was Delroy. By the way, the second first-class cabin of every train belongs to ex-convicts from Rikers.

"It has been like that for decades. We paid our dues in prison, and it's like our retirement benefit; an unwritten, unofficial gift, you see. Most of the ticket agents are ex-cons from Rikers Island, and they help enforce the rule."

"Delroy was in the B-Wing with me, and we worked at the prison Library."

"Oh, sorry," Adigun looked sheepish, "Was I sleeping?"

Adigun had nodded off several times during Shannon's speech.

"You must be very tired. Why don't you take a short nap? We should be rolling into Union Station in about thirty minutes."

Adigun drifted.

5

Jobore, 1975

Adigun heard his mother crying and the family elders from her village, Amakpofia, all speaking in Igbo. His father rested his head on his left hand, which was propped on his knee, scratching intermittently. He did not say anything. The walk from the Jobore village school, situated two kilometers outside the village on the one-lane, eroded clay road to Irede, felt longer than usual that day. The sun was out in full force and the humid air was oven-hot. The tarred stretches of the road seemed to shimmer in the heat, and the unmoving palm trees drooped in the stagnant heat. The sub-Saharan dust made the view look like an old piece of art painted with a worn-out brush. Skinny, uniformly dark-skinned children walked in a trance-like procession toward Jobore. Paramount in their minds were the sumptuous meals that awaited them in their different homes. Many of them walked in pairs or small groups but Adigun walked alone.

Tired and hungry, he had dragged his feet in the dust as he took the last turn by the derelict mud house behind his family compound. Nearing his compound, he had heard the loud voices for the first time. As he walked through the entrance into the yard, the mother hen panicked, and her new chicks scattered in different directions on the hot, red sand. He saw some men sitting on the low bench under the cashew tree (the locals called its fruit, "Cajew"). The voices grew louder as he stopped and greeted the elders in Fulfulbe. They were old Fulani men from the Sabo neighborhood of Jobore; seven of them, seated outside on a long wooden bench.

"Sannu, yaro," they all said, almost at the same time. They exchanged a few sentences with Adigun in Fulfulbe as Adigun walked past them. They all wore identical, stern expressions, their hard faces sitting in their palms, framed by the cone hats they wore over their white attires. There was a group of younger Fulani men at the east side of the yard arguing about something. These were dressed in sleeveless beige tops with slight embroidery on the chest portion. The tops were fitted, and they mostly wore tight-fitting trousers. A few of them had on jeans. They each had a short cane balanced behind their necks, with their hands dangling over each end. Capping off their outfits were the purple, cone-shaped headgear that tapered at three angular tips, two of which covered their ears. The hat was called Noppire. They looked furious as they railed loudly, making the sheathed daggers hanging from their rawhide belts menacing to Adigun, who was otherwise accustomed to their garb.

'Sabongida,' the small Fulani community that migrated from the northern part of Nigeria many years back, was like a small country of its own. Jobore was a stop-over for travelers carrying goods from the North and the Fulani settlement, often called 'Sabo' had evolved naturally. They had a very organized quasi-governmental structure, led by the '*Giwa*' and a strict hierarchy of officers that administered their rules. There had always been a longstanding peace between the people of Jobore and the Fulani. That did not seem to be the case on this day. Adigun walked towards the house, and he met another group of Fulanis dressed in green and red traditional attire. "Sannu, Yaro," they greeted him with familiarity; he knew all of them from his regular visits to Sabo with Hadezah. Adigun had earned some notoriety at Sabo, largely as the leader of the 'Obituary Boys', as well as for the mini-employment agency he ran. He was known all over Jobore to assist in procuring laborers at Sabo because of his language advantage. Adigun and his boys charged a meager fee per laborer and were highly sought-after for unskilled jobs.

Adigun tried to gain access through the main door but there were too many Fulani men by the main door, and he could not get in. He went to the window by the giant clay water pot on the side. He peeped in and saw some more Fulani people inside the house. Adigun climbed the window and jumped into the house. He dusted off the sand from his green khaki shirt as he walked across the grey concrete floor towards the crowd. There was some commotion with several people speaking in the Fulani language whilst others spoke in Igbo. Adigun listened attentively and tried to make out what was afoot but there

53

were too many people speaking at the same time. Some of his mother's relatives were in the gathering: Uncle Emeka, his mother's brother that lived in Irede, *Mazi* Okoronkwo, and some other Igbo men.

Adigun caught a glimpse of his mother in the crowd. Her eyes were red, and her face was pale as she cleaned the tears off her face, with her thick biceps wrapped with the old, green 'George' wrapper. There was an abrupt break in the clamoring and silence took over. A gust of wind blew the oak door in and then out again, the rusty hinges' squeaks interrupted when it slammed into the burnt clay wall. Adigun saw Hadezah standing in front of the elders. Her hair was plaited with black cotton thread, and she wore a beige *Ankara* sleeveless blouse, revealing her local tattoo, a scorpion, on her right arm. She had her palm covering her chin and her right elbow resting on her left arm, which hugged her side. The henna art on her hand seemed livid and alive.

Hadezah was twitching and blinking faster than even she usually did. She had a chronic nervous disorder that made her blink uncontrollably. In his earlier childhood, this had put Adigun in a considerable amount of trouble for lying. It was common practice when being questioned by a grown-up about another child's conduct, for that other child to hang just out of sight of the interrogator, blinking pointedly whenever the child being questioned was required to get creative with the truth. Adigun would lie about anything as long as Hadezah was around. He lied thinking Hadezah's blinking was a demand to tell the opposite of the truth and gained quite the reputation as a perpetual liar. He hated Hadezah for always getting him into trouble with his parents, but he loved her too. He had missed Hadezah, during her long absence, when (he now realized) she had been pregnant with Talatu.

Adigun's mum shouted "God will punish you, evil man!

"God will punish you, useless Yoruba man!

"You have gone even further in your shamelessness than I could have feared!!

"Not enough that you made Hadezah with child right under my nose! She was like your daughter! She became your marriage of shame! I endured that for all these years, and this is how you repaid me?

"Keziah, this is how you pay me back?

"Keziah Babatunde Komaiya, see your life!!

"Her parents trusted you!!

"Hadezah! *Chai*, Hadezah, *anwolamee*," she shouted, stamping her feet on the ground. She continued lamenting in her native tongue, Igbo.

Adigun felt more compelled than usual to pierce the mystery behind his mother's cries. Some instinct warned him that this was not a matter he could ignore. The matter of Hadezah's pregnancy was long-past and her child was almost 3 years old, so what was today's fuss about?

"Will you not honor our agreement?" Adigun recognized the voice as that of Hadezah's dad.

"Why would a brother do this to a brother? Answer me Keziah; is this what we discussed? Now he offers us money," he turned to the gathering as he said this, raising his voice. "*Kai*! We have suffered!

"We are not from here; We come from far away.

"*Shege*," he shouted, meaning 'Bastard.'

One of the old relatives of Adigun's mum, Mazi Okoronkwo brought out his snuff box and put the powder in his nose with his thumbnail. He had a haughty countenance and seemed unaffected by the cacophony around him. He sneezed in that loud, theatrical way that old people seem to have, and then he spoke. "My brothers from far, I greet you from the bottom of my heart.

"I am *Mazi* Okoronkwo, the leader of the Aro community in the whole of Jobore and Irede combined.

"This man is my brother, he is married to Obiageli, my niece.

"What has happened here is regrettable but there is nothing new on Mother Earth.

"Our forefathers say '*Anaghi ekwo ihere elo asu'* – 'One must not swallow phlegm out of shame.'" His voice had gone from a deep baritone to tenor as the spicy powder penetrated his brain and stimulated his sinuses. His bushy mustache twitched like he was expecting a second sneeze. One of the old Fulani men looked at Mazi Okoronkwo with disdain and turned to the oldest of the Fulani men. "*Dan Giwa*, please, let's focus on what we came to do here."

The old Fulani man signaled to the group of cone hats outside and about four of them rushed in and roughly grabbed Adigun's dad. Two of the young men held his hands as he struggled and the other two held his legs and stretched him, suspended face-down. The drawstring from Adigun's father's traditional trousers dangled as they stretched him, and he moaned in pain. His brown dashiki had been pulled up and was almost covering his face, exposing his back and the top half of his buttocks. The old Igbo men jumped up at the same time to intervene and all the Fulani men unsheathed their daggers and swords at the same time.

"Allahu Akbar," they all shouted as some of them raised their sticks and the others pulled out their sharp, shimmering daggers. The Igbo men were unarmed, and they sat down immediately. The oldest of them pulled up his sleeves and raised his thick walking stick amidst the Shiny daggers and sticks.

"Abomination!" Mazi Okoronkwo shouted at the top of his voice.

His thick beard was stiff and sweat rolled out from the bushy mass of black hair. "He may be a Yoruba man, but he is married to our daughter; that is enough to qualify him as an Aro man! You all know an Aro man cannot be judged outside Arochukwu.

"You will NOT give judgment to an Aro man outside Arochukwu.

"Flog an Aro man? It is impossible!

"We will all die here –" He stamped his wooden walking stick on the concrete floor.

"– And after you kill us, more will come from Arochukwu, and we will slaughter all of you from Jobore to the *Futa Jalon* where you all came from!" He said this last through gritted teeth.

"You want to flog an Aro man? You want to flog an Aro man? *Ngwanu*, flog him and see bloodshed!"

At this point, Keziah was already sweating profusely and groaning in pain as the young men stretched him harder. Hadezah's father raised his sword higher and spoke. He started with a long incantation in Fulfulde, then said, "This man is my friend. We are not judging him. This man, I have taken as my brother. I put my daughter in his care. He has violated me and brought pain to my household, but my daughter had told me she was not raped.

"In the Fulani tradition, sex before marriage is not a new thing; in fact, it is accepted. If not, 3 years ago, we should have come with war and a lot of blood would have been shed.

"Instead, we came to an accommodation; Keziah would take Hadezah in as a wife, which he has done, and he would turn over his only son, Adigun, to us as restitution, WHICH HE HAS NOT DONE!"

"When?" Obiageli screamed, "When did you sell off our son in slavery, Dodo?" But even as she asked, she thought she now understood what had happened without her knowledge on that dark day; when she became the first of her husband's two wives, the second being barely a woman herself. She knew that, when she had been ushered out of the gathering to "allow the men speak on matters of bride price," part of that bride price had included her only son. "So, you sold off our son for the pleasure of bedding a child?"

Hadezah's father spoke, "This was a very serious breach in our tradition, and you had to pay for it dearly. Allah saw this before today; Allah knew this was going to happen.

"Your son is always in our *Lungu* at Sabo, he speaks our language and eats our food. I even gave him his first set of goats and rams, like a son.

"At this point, I demand you hand over your son, Yaro to be my own as you have stolen my daughter." Adigun jerked in the shadows beneath the window, stunned to his marrow. Could he be hearing what it sounded like he was hearing?

"As we leave today, we will be leaving with Yaro.

59

"*Walahi*, that is only fair, and as we have agreed.

"You have gained a wife and we will gain a son."

Obiageli sat on the floor and put her hand on her head, wailing and crying, "Over my dead body! Over my dead body!

"Keziah has ruined my life, eeee!

"Keziah has finished me, oooooh!" She rolled about on the floor, slapping at her head.

"My only child, Keziah, my only child!"

On hearing his mother keening like her only child was lost, something broke in Adigun and he leaped out through the window and bolted across the backyard.

The Fulani men ran after the little boy.

Adigun climbed the mud fence and as he attempted to jump, he spied three Fulani men on the other side of the fence to receive him. Shocked, he jumped back into the compound, narrowly avoiding the hands of the pursuing men and bounding over the cassava-drying porch. There was chaos in the compound as Adigun ran towards the main gate. He saw the gate was blocked, made a quick turn, and ran towards the fence adjoining the church. A large crowd of spectators had gathered, and they shouted as Adigun ran around the compound.

Adigun was shouting as he ran.

"Nooo, nooooo! Mama, eee! Papa, eeee!"

The cone hats scrambled after him but couldn't catch Adigun; he jumped on the wooden chicken house and scaled the fence, landing on the tombstones in the yard of the church next door. He raced through the vicarage and entered the forest behind it. As he ran, he heard the sounds of something large crashing through the woods behind him and realized that Emeka, one of his uncles, was in hot pursuit. After about three minutes of running (that seemed like hours to him), Adigun screeched to a halt at the bank of the river and Emeka caught up with him. "Uncle Emeka, they want to take me away," he blurted, gasping. "What are we going to do, Uncle Emeka?" Adigun's chest heaved and hitched as he doubled over, placing his hands on knobbly knees for support. "Don't worry," Emeka replied, "we will go to Molajoye; there are no Fulanis there. Don't worry, Adigun, all will be well. Follow me."

Adigun and Emeka walked uphill through the bush until they arrived at the little village of Molajoye. Adigun had never been through this route and was struck by how short it was. They both walked down the narrow country road into the village and arrived at a small house sitting by the thin river. The house had all its windows open. Emeka opened the door and they both entered. "Wait here, boy. I'm sure you must be hungry. I will arrange some food for you when I get back, but there are some bananas on the table – help yourself." Adigun's jaws stretched in a wide yawn. He was tired and hungry. "What is going to happen, uncle Emeka?"

"Don't worry; I have to walk back to the house to take instructions from the elders."

Emeka walked back to Jobore, but used the long route through Old Aba Road, as it was too dark to use the bush path. When he got to the Komaiyas' house in Jobore, the Fulanis were just leaving. He hid behind a large tree until they had all left. He walked into the house and found Keziah, sitting on the wooden bench.

"Where is my son?"

"He is safe at my house in Molajoye. How did it go?"

"They insisted on taking my son but, thanks to my in-laws, we were able to plead that they let him finish his secondary education. That at least gives us some years to plan.

"They took the girl; thank God, as they said I must come to Sabo to be flogged!"

Obiageli bolted out of the room.

"Thank God? Thank God?

"Do you know God, Keziah? Do you know God?

"Emeka, where is my son?"

Keziah started to talk, and his wife cut him off.

"I'm not asking you!

"I am not asking you, shameless man!"

"Sister, your son is in my house in Molajoye. He is really tired and traumatized. I will bring him in the morning."

That night was the quietest in the entire fifteen years of the Komaiya's marriage and Keziah sat outside for most of it, fearing that his wife would kill him in his sleep – *if* he could sleep at all. There was no electric power that night and when the oil lamp burned out, no one rose to restore its light. The household was swathed in a dark, seething, pain-filled silence. Even the usual chorus of night creatures seemed subdued that night.

Daybreak took forever to come.

6

Adigun came back to the house early in the morning. The Komaiya residence had undergone a complete change. His mother had not slept all night. She had in her hands her small, black bible, and she paced back and forth with her chest leading the rest of her in the manner she had when she was extremely upset. Her head tie knotted around her waist, Adigun's mother walked past the entrance and hugged Adigun, rubbing his head absent-mindedly, then continued pacing around. Adigun still struggled to comprehend what had taken place the day before, the notion of his being traded somehow for Aunty Hadezah, and how he was supposed to feel about the situation or about her; she who had nurtured him from his infant years but was conspicuously absent now. Adigun had no way of knowing that these considerations were pointless, as he would not see her again for decades.

He sat on the floor with his back resting against the wall. The house was as quiet as a graveyard. After a while, he got up and paced around the house, hungry – he had only had bananas the night before – but nobody offered Adigun any food. When he realized food wasn't coming, he made his way to the kitchen in the backyard and helped himself to some cold, left-over yams with some oil. He could tell they were from the day before and, as he wolfed them down, he almost felt like he was eating part of a past that could never be regained.

Keziah sat alone in the front room. Adigun had tried to ask questions about what had transpired but was always told, "This is not for children." It didn't seem to be much of a matter for adults either, and his mum and dad spoke even less after that day. The previous evening's silence stretched out for weeks. Many nights, he would find his mum alone in the room, weeping.

One thing was for certain though; his father had agreed to exchange him for Hadezah and they would be coming for him after he finished secondary school.

Adigun frequently had nightmares of Fulani herdsmen chasing after him. He saw cows in his dreams, fleeing anytime he saw the herdsmen grazing their cattle, and would not go anywhere near Sabo. He felt betrayed and unwanted.

Washington, 1983

The train ground to a slow halt with a loud hiss and grinding of steel underneath. Adigun's eyes were half-closed as he noticed that they seemed to have arrived at their destination. His body was thrust softly forward as the train came to a full stop, and the passengers hurried out of their seats to disembark. Shannon was gone! Adigun's head whipped about in panic until he briefly sighted Shannon on the far east side of the platform. He sprang up hurriedly and jumped off the train, running in that direction. He lost sight of Shannon again and panic rose in him like gorge. He scanned the thick crowd and once again spotted Shannon at a distance – he was running. Adigun saw Shannon hurriedly push himself against a passenger that was about to go through a turnstile, cross over the silver barrier and speed off. Adigun scaled the turnstile and raced after Shannon. He was Adigun's only hope of making any headway in the quest for destiny in America!

His heart hammered in his chest as he ran through the crowd in pursuit of Shannon. The railway terminal was a huge concrete building with a beautiful domed ceiling designed to replicate the sky. Shannon was running even harder, looking back intermittently; it was clear that he was running from Adigun. Adigun kept the chase close though he was running out of breath. Shannon took a sharp left and ran through a group of green taxis parked outside the train station. He ran towards another huge building and, looking back again, realized Adigun was catching up. He took a left turn by an old, abandoned church, sped toward the traffic light, and then shot to his right, scaling the red fire hydrant (which surely would have ended the chase had he not cleared it).

Adigun followed close. They came to a densely populated residential area; seemingly all black. Shannon ran through an alley and stopped. His head bowed towards the ground, chest heaving as he panted.

"What the fuck! What the heck!" he gasped. He swung at Adigun, almost falling against an overflowing steel dumpster of indeterminate color. "Dude, can you just let me go my way? Can you just leave me alone? You are meant to be heading to California; this is Washington DC; don't you get it? Why don't you head back to the station and catch your train to the West coast? You can't come with me, man, you can't come with me!" Shannon spoke with a thick winter mist puffing out of his mouth. It was a frosty evening, dark and gloomy, and the harsh wind scoured their exposed skin. Adigun held onto the metal mesh fence of an abandoned house in the south-eastern DC neighborhood. He glared at Shannon. Silence spun out between them for a long moment. Adigun grabbed his green *Aso Oke* dashiki with both hands and wrapped it tighter against his cold chest. He was trembling violently.

"Go away, dude, go!!" Shannon shouted with his hands up in the air. He took in Adigun's watery eyes and chattering teeth with a mixture of exasperation and pity. "Here!" He threw his red woolen scarf to Adigun. "Wrap this around your neck before you freeze to death. I don't know who wears a dashiki in winter."

Adigun caught the woolen scarf, tucking it into the neck of his dashiki.

"No, dummy, wrap it *around* your neck; you have to cover your neck all the time."

This single act of charity seemed to bring the rest of their exchange home to Adigun; it was as much as Shannon could (or certainly *would*) do. He grudgingly accepted that he was on his own again. Adigun's eyes teared up further with emotion as turned and walked away from Shannon. He had walked about 30 meters before he looked back and waved to Shannon. Shannon waved back.

"See you soon, brother Shannon. Next time you see me, I will hit you with a surprise. By the grace of God, I will surprise you."

8

Adigun could barely remember his way back to the train station as he ran. He stopped in front of the abandoned church and looked to the west and east, not knowing which way to turn. He wandered for almost 40 minutes and was not able to find the train station. Some deep instinct warned him against asking anyone for help or directions even when he knew he was lost in the cold night. Adigun kept walking until his feet began to hurt. He felt a tingling in his right ear and, when he tried to rub it, it crackled like a piece of it had flaked off and fallen to the pavement. Adigun looked down, expecting to find the fallen piece between his howling feet. His teeth chattered in protest against the cold. He saw a long trail of bright yellow streetlights as he reached a double carriage road at a lonely junction and made a right turn onto this bright road, walking in the middle of the wide divider that split the dual carriage road. His feet felt some relief as they sank into the cold, springy grass. He walked this way for half an hour until he saw the red neon sign of a fast-food restaurant called 'Popwalis'. It began to drizzle again, and he ran into this restaurant without a second thought. He was relieved to find it warm (and almost empty) inside.

Adigun sat in an obscure corner booth, soaking up the warmth until he began to feel drowsy. He was exhausted and hungry, and the night had arrived fast, bringing with it a near-delirium that prompted him to peer out of the window in search of the missing piece of his ear. He reached up with thankfully warm fingers to touch his ear and was relieved to find it intact. Nobody bothered Adigun and he simply sat by the window even after it stopped drizzling, though the restaurant began to fill with customers quite rapidly. Adigun sat in the busy restaurant by the window, blankly observing a trash can by the green pillar to his right. He sat in dazed confusion watching people empty their leftovers into the trash. His belly rumbled as he agonized at the chunks of chicken being emptied into the bin and wished someone would hand him a piece. He fell asleep with his head on the table. The sleep was like a black hole that swallowed him; no dreams, no thoughts, nothing at all. Just blackness. It was the sweetest slumber he had had in a long time.

9

"Wake up, yo! Wake up!" Adigun jerked awake to a black lady, wearing a red apron, tapping him on his shoulder.

"Where do you think you are, dressed like a summer carnival dancer?

"We are closed; you gats to go! You gats to go. We closed! Beat it, Tarzan!" She punctuated her exhortations with repeated taps on his shoulder.

Adigun struggled to clear the cobwebs of his hours-long sleep out of his muddled mind. His feet ached and, though Adigun had no idea about such things, he was also suffering the effects of jet lag. The restaurant was empty again. He got up from the chair and heard a loud flap as he took his first step; the sole of his right shoe had peeled off from its upper. Adigun considered the shoe absently for a moment then he walked out. The street was awash with streetlights and the colors of the traffic lights outside the restaurant, which were reflected in its mirror-like windows. Adigun walked the lonely street through a small row of shops. The sole of his right shoe flapped noisily as he walked. He attempted to pull it off, but his fingers hurt too much when he bent them. He walked until he hit a crossroad and kept walking until he came to a freeway underpass that was well-lit. Adigun shivered, and he began to blow warm air into his frozen fingers. By the time he emerged from the underpass, the wind was gusting. He saw some activity on the other side of the road and, with scarcely any thought at all, he crossed into the densely populated black neighborhood. As he walked through the street, navigating between more black people than he had seen at any one time since getting to this cold country, Adigun began to feel like he was safer.

The unholy alliance of stress, hunger, jet lag, and general physical abuse took its toll on Adigun. His vision was blurry, and his movements were weak. Though he knew it must be quite late, there was a lot of activity on the street, and no one seemed to notice him. He leaned against a huge, battered, boat-like car moldering in front of a shabby brick bungalow and he saw a heap of garbage piled by the side of the house.

"Well," he thought to himself with delirious glee, "*e be like say Waldorf get annex for dis side of town!*" Adigun staggered into the garbage and tumbled into the mound of black bags. It was soft. He laid in the redolent heap and relished the relative warmth of it. He was very weak and felt incapable of any further movement.

"Who is this on my bed?" A voice barked out of the darkness, splintering Adigun's newfound ease. "Stanley, have you brought another one of those YMCA shelter guys over again? Hellooo, hellooo, buddy, you are sleeping in my bed."

Adigun squeezed his eyes tightly shut, trying to negate the intrusion by simply not seeing it. He buried himself deeper into the garbage pile for a moment before being seized by a sudden sensation of vertigo. In that instant, he recalled the feeling when the plane that brought him to America lifted off the Lagos tarmac – a feeling like he had left his stomach beneath him. It was as much as his flailing mind could manage before he went sailing through the air and crashed into the narrow road. Stanley, a burly six feet, four inches of dark-complected humanity had picked up Adigun and flung him across the narrow road. Adigun narrowly missed having his spine dashed by the silver fire hydrant that stood on the other side of the road from the garbage heap, but he didn't have the presence of mind to ponder this drop of good luck in his ocean of woes. He fell asleep where he lay – for an indeterminate period – until the cold began snaking through his bones. He came reluctantly awake, his face cold and hard, realizing that to lie there was to die.

He held on to the fire hydrant and helped himself up, walking silently away from Stanley and his gang, who chattered together, enjoying what seemed to be a pleasant evening on their hill of trash. As he staggered off, Adigun spotted a little alley across the intersection to the east and he crossed the road, aiming for the large, silver-coated garbage cans that stood like sentries along its walls. As he shambled between the cans, Adigun realized that, somehow, it was warmer here – some sort of defilade from the brutal wind that howled through the street. There was steam hissing out from the vents into the alleyway and from the manhole covers he walked over. There were black metal emergency stairs in every house. On the left of the alleyway were garages probably belonging to the houses above. They were all shut but for a single one, which Adigun walked into with no consideration at all. There was some cardboard on the floor, and he noticed some padded mats in the corner. They were made of soft leather and had the name, 'Everlast,' printed in white. There were quite a few of them and Adigun buried himself beneath them. It was the first real warmth he had experienced since his train ride from New York, and he was unconscious within seconds of closing his eyes.

10

Adigun had been asleep for less than five minutes when he was roused by the sound of a large engine. A massive American car eased into the garage, the noise coming to a stop just in front of the padded mats where he lay. The warmth from the engine had an immediate soporific effect on him, but he stayed awake and still underneath the stack. He heard three heavy thuds as the occupants of the car got out, obviously carrying on a conversation they had been having inside. From the voices, Adigun could tell that they were all men.

"Nobody talks to Bobby Brown that way – nobody! I done started this gym decades ago." The voice was high-pitched but, somehow, Adigun was certain that the chest it emerged from was cavernous. "I make champions – read my lips – champions! I won't take it, man! I won't take this mess, never!"

"Yo, Bobby, chill out, man! You lost Alonzo because you could not pay the price. The game has changed, Bobby." This voice, raspy and deeper than the first (Bobby's, it seemed to Adigun), seemed deferential and almost pleading in its tone – like he was reluctant to say what he felt to the aggrieved party. "You only know how to *train* champions," voice 2 continued, "but you don't understand the new game. Training is only a part of the game now, Bobby. You also gotta know how to wheel and deal. These guys know how to do that, AND they got money to wheel and deal. You want a champion in your gym? You gonna have to buy a champion. The game's changed, Bobby; the game's changed! Look, we have a shipment coming in, right? The Thanksgiving drop-off? We take that, we flip it, and we go poach boxers from the other gyms."

Adigun clutched the Everlast padding tightly and stifled a cough as the garage filled with the pungent smell of marijuana smoke. He heard the whistle from the drag and, for the first time, became aware of another sound in the background.; a not-quite rhythmic series of thumps, punctuated here and there by grunts and sharp, hissing expulsions of air. The exchange he had just overheard made helped Adigun make the connection: It was a boxing gym. The garage door rolled down, and the room darkened. Adigun realized the men must have left the garage and he moaned as his body was seized by severe hunger pangs. He felt like he had not eaten in days as he clutched feebly at the padded Everlast mat. He began to slip into unconsciousness again when the garage door rolled up, letting in a gust of cold air. He heard approaching footsteps and felt a tug on the cushioned mat he held over himself. The mat began to rise, and Adigun rose with it. His unseen discoverer hefted the mat (and Adigun) clear of the floor, grunting with the effort and letting out a snort of wide-eyed surprise when he spotted the skinny bundle clinging to its underside.

In shock, the man skipped back, and shouted, "Jesus! What the heck? Who the fuck are you? What are you doing here? How the hell did you even get in here?" The questions were spat out in rapid-fire succession and Adigun's addled mind stalled, then gave up on trying to answer any of them. His dashiki shimmered in the dark as he raised his hands and tried to talk. He was too weak; he squeaked out in a whisper, "Waatterrr."

The tall man was already calling for help. "Pookie!! Pookie!! Come here! There's someone in the garage! He's dead… or dying or somethin'!"

"Oh my God!" Another man joined the first. "Who put this here?" Adigun lay motionless. He was tired and all the sounds seemed to be coming from far away. His vision was blurred as he tried to take in the new arrival; a light-skinned black man with a black net bonnet of sorts, holding his dreadlocks in place. He wore a big, blue plaid jacket, the pattern growing in Adigun's eyes as the man bent down and put his ears on Adigun's chest. "He's breathing! He's alive. Hey, dude, wake up! Can you hear me?" He scooped up Adigun and placed him on his shoulder, then walked out of the garage. He made a left and took Adigun through a stairwell and through a black door that opened into a well-lit hall. The gym was bright, and the equipment and punching bags cast multiple shadows on the gleaming wood floor. More of the ubiquitous

Everlast bags hunched in corners and against walls and there were blue mats scattered on the floor.

Pookie took Adigun into an office where an old man sat in front of a table festooned with trophies and award plaques. When he saw Pookie walk in with Adigun on his shoulder, the old man swept the trophies and plaques against the wall to make room. Adigun was placed gently on the table, arms at his sides, looking half dead. "Get some water fast, Pookie, get some water." The old man flapped his hands at Pookie in a shooing gesture. "We don't need another murder investigation around this gym. Hurry! Where did you find this?"

"In the garage."

"Did we knock him down?"

"I dunno. Maybe we should call the ambulance."

"Are you crazy? Ambulance? We still have the case of the Jersey Cartel corpse bringing the heat and you want to call an ambulance?!"

Adigun felt water splashed around his face and squirted, through a tube attached to a plastic bottle, into his mouth. He winced as the cold stream of water was squeezed through his parched throat, but eagerly swallowed every drop. He opened his eyes and was vaguely surprised to see six faces staring down at him.

"Who are you?"

"Why have you come here?"

"How did you make it into my garage?"

"I'm hungry," Adigun whispered weakly.

"Go across the road, Pookie, and get this boy some fried Chicken from Rosco's.

"Matter of fact, tell Phoebe, next door, to bring a plate."

Pookie ran off and soon returned with a young white lady carrying a shiny, stainless steel banquet tray.

"Should I lay it out as usual?"

"No, Phoebe, it's not for me. Serve it to Africa here before he dies. At least, I *think* he's African, from what little I've heard from him so far. Notice the way he said he was hungry? 'Ahm hongree'." There were scattered, nervous chuckles at this mimicry. "We just found him in our garage, lifeless. Please feed Africa." Phoebe opened the silver lid, revealing the sumptuous spaghetti Bolognese prepared earlier for Bobby Brown, the gym owner, and began to fix a plate for Adigun. Phoebe Kruger was the new chef at the Italian restaurant, also owned by Bobby Brown, next door to the gym. Phoebe had only been working there for a few weeks but had gotten familiar with the gym crew. It helped that she also enjoyed the privilege of using the gym, totally gratis, so she worked out with the gym crew as well.

"I brought some salt; you know we don't make your food with salt."

The aroma of hot food brought Adigun fully awake, and he watched in stunned anticipation as Phoebe dished out the spaghetti Bolognese and roast chicken. When she was done, Adigun sat on the wooden table, with his skinny legs dangling over its edge, and ate. He accepted the mug of water that Phoebe handed him, not catching her bemused expression, subtle interest, or the way she stared at him while using her left hand to sweep her blond hair from her face. Adigun just ate. He sucked greedily at the spaghetti and grabbed at the large chicken thighs on the side.

"Easy, boy, easy," said Phoebe as Adigun crammed his mouth so full of food that choking was almost a certainty. "Drink some water, sweetie, drink some water." Phoebe took the mug Adigun handed back to her and set it down away from the table's edge. Then her hands glanced over the shiny embroidery of Adigun's dashiki, fascinated by the way its threads shimmered in the dull light of the room, their colors bouncing off the ceiling and walls like Adigun was some low-hung disco ball.

Adigun picked up a drumstick and devoured it like a hungry hyena, crushing the bone and sucking the marrow from it. "Easy now, easy," Phoebe soothed, picking off the dirt from Adigun's woolly hair. He was not able to eat the spaghetti well as it kept sliding off when he tried to eat it with the spoon. He gave up and helped himself with his fingers. He looked at Phoebe and said, "This is my African fork," showing four fingers. Phoebe chuckled, blushing at the same time. There was a little chunk of coleslaw in the corner of the bowl, Adigun dug in with his fingers and licked it all up. Buoyed by the food, the warmth, and the kindness of strangers, he told his story, taking the group through his ordeal at Tuke and his experience with the Obidike brothers. He would be talking long into the night.

Book-2

Home

Oke oshimmiri anokataghi rie onye obula nke o na-ahughi ukwu ya anya

(The ocean never swallows a person whose leg it does not come in contact with - Igbo proverb)

1

Jobore, 1976

Adigun now had trouble at home as well as at school and he realized that getting into secondary school and out of Jobore was the smartest move he could make. Jobore was a coastal village adjoining the Atlantic Ocean, the waterfront coconut groves giving way to the lush, green forest the further one traveled inland. The air offered that salty freshness unique to coastal areas and the dependable ocean breeze was a constant balm to its humble, happy inhabitants. Nature had certainly blessed Jobore. Adigun was born into a small family, and he was an only child. They lived in Jobore's middle-class railway compound with a few chickens, some goats, and, around Adigun's fifth year, a dog-called '*Riro ni teniyan*', meaning 'let the humans do the thinking' – Riro for short. Riro was a mongrel, a mixture of a mutt and stupidity, yet people marveled at Adigun's ability to train it (young as he was) to become a form of transportation. He rode his dog, like a horse, on the dusty streets, like the Lone Ranger. The other kids would watch him through their wood-shuttered windows. They were mostly forbidden to associate with "Adigun Ologun", who was widely considered to be trouble incarnate. You never played with him without coming home with either a broken ankle or a nail on your forehead. He was involved in every bit of mischief that occurred in the area. Most of his age mates had stopped associating with him long before they got admitted into secondary schools – a feat Adigun himself could not manage when his mates did. His dismal performance in the secondary school entrance exams meant he was held back to attempt entry again the following year. As a result, the few of his peers that would still interact with him had been away for the entire term in their new schools.

It was December, a festive time for the community, and most of Jobore's indigenes came home for the season. Of course, no one could miss '*Odewole*', the hunting festival in which all the masquerades came out, carnival-style, to celebrate the return of Jobore's hunters from their month-long hunting expedition. During this time, Jobore attracted visitors from all of the surrounding towns and villages. Their numerous drum ensembles alone were a spectacle, the Talking Drums maintaining their conversations for days on end, the *Iya Ilu* and the *Omo Ilu* (the Mother of Drums and Baby Drum), bringing up the rear of every drum troupe. The hunters were dressed in red *Aso Oke*, with several charms adorning their wrists. Some dressed their dogs in the same, red *Aso Oke* material. The hilly topography of Jobore made it possible to watch several troupes simultaneously. The kids would sit on the trees to watch, while the older teenagers preened, vying to win the competition for the best-dressed youth. Many families went to bizarre lengths to dress their teenagers, as the prize included a large gourd of palm wine from the King's very own wine tappers. This was also the beginning of the new wine season – the palm trees had been untapped for a full year – and the trees were ready to bring forth the sweetest and most intoxicating palm wine. Amid the hunting competitions, parading youth, and various dance displays by the hunters of Jobore, the elders engaged in some serious drinking.

During this season, Jobore moved to an almost frantic rhythm, the continual thudding sound of yam being pounded blended with the drums to provide a percussive soundtrack to every activity. It was amazingly musical and the whole village seemed to dance to it; the red-necked agama lizards' nods seemed in synch with the pounding, as did the songs from the birds, frogs, and crickets. Even the snap of slingshots, as children used the lizards for target practice, seemed dictated by the beat. Their happy cries provided a chorus for the music as they tried to impress the hunters, they sought to emulate with their hunting prowess.

The highest point of the *Odewole* festival was the last day. At the King's palace, Jobore's well-dressed citizens cheered as the different groups, known as *Legbe Legbe*, marched past the Oba's canopy. Each *Legbe Legbe* represented a particular age group of the community, but the most eagerly awaited was the toddlers – a disorderly, tottering band of children, two to five years old, clothed in their ceremonial *Aso-Oke*, dancing to the drums and waving their raffia flags when they got to the king's royal pavilion. It was the only part of the march-past in which the king would rise, showing respect to the children. It was believed that the spirit of the ancestors resided in these toddlers as they were pure, innocent, and without sin.

Jobore was known for very colorful masquerades, which usually followed right after the toddlers. The *Abe* masquerades always led, followed by the *Gelede* masquerade. Things would rise to a climax when the *Alapanshopa* reached the royal canopy. They had a distinct dance routine in which the masquerades energetically palpitated the air before them, elbows alternately flaring and straightening as they popped their hands back and forth. This was the grand finale, bringing the entire crowd to a frenzy of cheers, dancing, and drinking, during which the *Oba* would usually take his leave. The entire village went to sleep for about 3 days after the festival. The markets were closed, and everyone stayed in to recuperate from the week-long fiasco.

So, as Christmas approached, Adigun awaited his peers' return from secondary school with barely contained excitement. He could not sleep on the eve of their arrival from boarding school. Will they be the same? He wondered, trying to figure out whether they would remember how to climb trees and set a chicken's tail on fire. He missed them. Morning came, the rising sun setting the Neem tree alight like a Christmas tree, and the cocks crowed louder than they usually did. The Yellow Robins chirruped, singing their welcome song. In the years before they had become secondary school students, the routine was for his friends to congregate at the village square and await Adigun's arrival. He was like the mafia don, and the officers would come and pay homage at the beginning of the day. On this day, Adigun got to the square and there was no one there.

He waited patiently under the statue of the prominent old chief of Jobore, the historical "Kakanfo of Jobore", a memorial statue that had stood for ages.

"They will soon be here," Adigun said to himself, with his hands in his pocket and his little belly protruding. "They probably were tired after the long bus ride from school." A while later, no one had shown up and Adigun walked away from the square in disappointment and deep sorrow. Adigun decided to swallow his pride and go out to find them. Adigun Oloogun, like a wounded lion, ran through the morning mist left by the cold harmattan night. He got to the Arikawes' (the Arikawe twins were his favorite friends) and whistled the secret tune he had with them that meant "Come out, immediately." He stood in front of the window and whistled again, louder. His whistling echoed back, as though there was nobody in the village. He whistled repeatedly, harder and harder until one of the twins walked out of the front door. Adigun's face lit up like the dawn. His adrenaline started pumping. "Orisbakosta," he shouted, and continued the praise, "*Alalanlulu, anomutepa, ko bere ri ko ma gbe nkan e, gbe nkan e, ju sile!*" This was his nickname for Taiwo Arikawe who always had his hand on his head as though he needed to support his neck. Though they were identical, it was possible to tell the Arakawe twins apart by Taiwo's tendency to tilt his head to the left, like it was just a bit too heavy for his neck.

As he came closer, Taiwo seemed different from the guy Adigun had seen off to the motor park nine months ago, when the twins left for boarding school.

Adigun could still remember him shouting from the bus, "Look after my tree for me; don't let anyone else climb it!" Adigun had looked after the trees; he never climbed any of the trees designated to the Arikawes. He came closer, with a pen in his hands and, in a newly deepened voice, said, "We are back from school now, but we cannot play your elementary school games anymore.

"We are mature now," he said, "and we have holiday projects in Chemistry, Biology, and Physics."

Those words gave Adigun a headache. 'They must be new games played in boarding school,' he thought. "I can play those new games with you," Adigun replied. "You only have to teach me." Taiwo scowled and drew a deep breath, "We can't be friends anymore, dummy; we are your seniors now! We don't climb trees anymore and we don't play in abandoned vehicles anymore and we don't hunt lizards either." The scowl on Taiwo's face morphed, as he shouted, into a runny mixture of disgust, glee, and wistful longing. "You can still find some kids in primary school to do that with you." As Taiwo concluded, the runny mixture of expressions settled into one of haughty disdain and dismissal.

Adigun had never felt so rejected in his life. He recoiled like a worm that had crawled into a mound of salt, turned, and went back home. He brooded in the corner, wondering at how cruel life was. "If this is what secondary school does to you, who needs it?" Adigun thought aloud. Restless, Adigun erupted from the house and, as the outdoors beckoned, he started running. He accelerated toward the hill, running past the sawmill and scaling the wooden fence to the meadows. The wind sent his tears streaking past his ears as he sobbed harder and harder, talking to himself. "I want to go to secondary school too! I want to play biology and chemistry and all the big games in boarding school!" Admitting this truth to himself seemed to suck all the air out of Adigun and he staggered to a halt in the tall, dry grass. This time of the year always came with a lot of dust and, as he bent over, gasping, a mustard-colored cloud whirled about him. He plucked sour berries and decided that he was not going to bother checking on any of his other friends that had returned from secondary school. Still soliloquizing as he turned back home, Adigun turned to a small herd of cows in the meadow and mused, "They are different now. They think they are better than I am." The cows responded with an indifferent "moo." This was the only time, since the debacle with the Fulani, that Adigun didn't once think of the herdsmen that usually tended the cows. He focused on the bovine indifference instead, becoming vaguely depressed.

Adigun's vague melancholy lasted for a few days, during which he stayed at home until he witnessed events that crystallized it into a harder, sharper set of emotions. The straw that finally broke the camel's back was the breaking of the cardinal rule amongst his erstwhile peers; a couple of days after they got home from school, Adigun watched from his window, as the Arikawe twins played with girls from the other side of town. Girls! Adigun watched in utter disbelief as they touched each other and made weird noises. The girls ran around the flowerbed, with the Arikawe twins chasing after them. That did it. They had sworn *never* to play with girls! Adigun's heart hardened as the sadness bled out of it and was replaced with rage… and a cold resolve. "Won't you go out and play with your friends?" His mother often asked. Adigun stayed home, running his dog around and around in circles until the poor dog got dizzy and fell to the ground in the dusty yard. Dizzy himself, with bitter relief, Adigun accepted that the reign of the 'Adigun Oloogun' was over.

2

Victory

It was a long wait and a longer ride on the stagnant boat.

After a few months facing the humiliation of being left behind by his primary school classmates, Adigun couldn't take it anymore. He stopped going to school. Instead, he made his way to the harbor each day and sat in an abandoned boat. Initially, he simply needed to avoid school and his shame but, as he settled into the peace and solitude of his harbor-side escape, he also began to develop a firm determination to change his situation. People would walk by and wonder what ill the "Adigun Oloogun" was up to in an abandoned boat. They would have been surprised to find that he was memorizing English literature in this boat and practicing algebra like he never did at school.

It was unclear to Adigun's parents why he was always failing exams. They had no way of knowing that the key to unlocking their son's academic potential lay in motivation. Adigun had never had a sense of the use of school and was not at all inclined to apply himself to it. It was ironic that it was the collapse of his social life, which he was invested in, that sparked his internal motivation to do better. His competitive streak pushed him to strive, and he strove like mad.

Adigun continued to study in this abandoned boat, fuelled by the zeal and determination to leave the Jobore school for greener pastures; away from a lonely class and a school community that was terrified of him. Adigun became the captain of the stagnant vessel, the proverbial "boat of life," studying so hard that he always got home late at night. He would sometimes get punished for coming home late but that only made him stronger. Ignoring the constant accusations of truancy and delinquency, he self-tutored in an environment that was less intimidating. He would come home from his stagnant boat ride, filled with knowledge and the determination to succeed.

When Adigun finally took the common entrance exam, he could not wait to, hopefully, be admitted into secondary school. He had studied so hard, that on the day of the examination, it took him barely an hour to finish an exam scheduled for two hours. "Wake up! Wake up!" The proctor shouted; Adigun had fallen asleep in the hall. He walked up to the front of the hall, accompanied by a loud murmur from the other candidates, and submitted his answer sheets. Adigun's eyes were bloodshot, and he was groggy, wondering if he was still asleep. Perhaps he hadn't completed the exam in real life but had only fallen asleep and dreamed that he had.

The results usually came during the rainy season and the fear of failing was a cloud that hung over Adigun's anticipation. He was happy that he didn't have to participate in the public spectacle at the school notice board – the education council now had results delivered by mail. His heart froze in his chest when the postman rang the bell of his colonial bicycle. The wheels of the steel bicycle squelched the sodden dead leaves on the ground, spraying water from the rear wheel. The bicycle bell sounded, in Adigun's ears, like church bells. Running to the door, Adigun snatched the small, twine-bound packet of envelopes from the postman, who looked weary and shabby in his baggy khaki shorts and shirt, with the logo of the Post and Telecommunications Department emblazoned on his matching pit helmet. Curious and afraid, Adigun pressed the envelopes, having already identified the one bearing the insignia (and unmistakable green typeface) of the Education Council, which was right on top of the small stack of mail. He held the envelope upside down, sideways, and up to the light, even holding it to the lit firewood in the backyard trying to get a glimpse of its contents. The letter seemed as heavy as a clay pot. He was forbidden from opening any mail in the house, so Adigun had to wait till his father returned.

The wait was interminable. As soon as the sound of "The Helicopter" rose in the distance, Adigun dashed to sit at his reading table, books open of course, momentarily so flustered that he forgot he had nothing to study for. He sprang up as his father walked in and, ignoring the normal welcome protocols, handed the letter to him. Time seemed to stand still as Adigun watched his father open the envelope with the cap of his Bic biro, take out the result slip inside, and peer at it closely. A smile blossomed on his father's face as he softly said, "That is my boy." Adigun did not realize he had been holding his breath until that moment, when all the air rushed out of his straining lungs, doubling him over, and forcing him to place his hands on his knees for support. He'd not only passed but had excelled. Adigun had admission prospects in just about any secondary school he wanted (and that his father could afford). Dodo hardly believed that Adigun wrote the exam himself.

Passing his entrance exams with flying colors changed things for Adigun. He transited from notoriety to fame and received many congratulatory messages from the entire community, along with gifts of pillows, buckets, hoes, and towels – all the little things he would need in boarding school. Jobore did not have a local secondary school, the nearest being several villages away, so boarding schools were the only option for its students.

Dodo decided to send Adigun to a boarding school, about 120 miles from Jobore, on the other side of the river. This humble community school was established by the regional government to educate the children of its farmers and hunters, as it was a community primarily reliant on farming and hunting. It was in a quiet village called, Tuke.

Boarding school was an ordeal of intrigue, labor, and confusion that forged Adigun into a young man. He endured the humiliations that were to be endured and learned to triumph regardless. He built fragile friendships and the beginnings of a solid character.

He grew. It was a time that, later in his life, he would always look back upon with a mixture of longing and relief for having put it behind him. Still, as seemed to be the pattern of his life, it was to end even less smoothly than it had begun.

3

In 1982, during Adigun's fifth year in Tuke, his world was shattered once more.

"Adigun! Adigun!" Bayo shouted, running towards Adigun and scaling the farm's ridges, knocking down the stakes holding the growing yam stems.

"Your name is on the list!"

"Which list?"

"– So is mine and Saka's! And Jewerimi!!"

"Which list, Bayo?"

"We have all been asked to leave the school for non-payment. The principal and the officers are on the way to the hostel." Bayo panted. "I just found out that the bursar had been sacked a week before he took all our money."

"Whaat?!?"

Adigun sat on the ridge he had just made. He was in his final year and had a reasonable chance of passing his school-leaving certificate exams. His hands floated up to cradle his face and he began to cry.

"My mother will kill me this time."

"Oh, I am a dead boy.

"Oh, I am dead.

"What will I tell my father?

"Two terms fees.

"My father had to sell some of our farmland to put this money together."

He left his wooden hoe and other farm tools and, with Bayo, raced to the hostel. They were met by the principal and two security guards busily herding a group of students clustered around their belongings. The principal informed Bayo and Adigun that they had five minutes to pack. Adigun went to his room and, hands shaking, stuffed his things into his suitcase. He had noticed that most of the boys in the same situation were the ones he met with the bursar when he handed his fees to him. In single file, they were escorted to the school gate by two teachers and the security guards, each handed a letter and some transport money to get home. They walked out of the gate and onto the single-carriage road. Casting about in confusion, one of the boys, Igbinedion, spotted the bursar, some distance away, in a palm wine bar on the other side of the road.

"Shukwutey!!!" Igbinedion shouted the bursar's name, pointing, as the boys ran toward the bar. The bursar was sitting at the palm wine bar, a calabash cup of palm wine in one limp hand, drunk. There were other patrons, being served by a short, light-skinned lady with pronounced tribal marks on her face, a few of whom glanced up at the approaching teenage stampede. Igbinedion pounced on the bursar and held his shirt. The other boys held his trousers and began to drag him back and forth. Adigun, with no thought at all, grabbed the big gourd, filled with palm wine, heaved it high, and brought it down on the bursar's head. The calabash shattered on the floor, splashing palm wine all over the bar, and the bursar collapsed to the floor, bleeding profusely. He lay motionless on the floor and the boys gaped in horror. They erupted at the same time.

"Aaaaaahhh!"

"Adigun has killed the bursar!"

Adigun put his hands on his head and watched, dumbfounded, as the other boys ran back towards the school gate and through it into the school, right past the gateman. His paralysis broke after a moment and he ran after them, then seemed to think better of it and halted after a few meters. They all ran to their hostels, terrified, and the news spread through the school like a wildfire in harmattan. In Adigun's dormitory, the boys gathered next to the box room. Bayo was the first to talk. "Adigun, you are in trouble! You killed the bursar."

Igbinedion interjected, "Shut up! Who told you Adigun killed the bursar?"

"We all killed him, and we are all going to jail for life. By tomorrow morning the principal would have heard we are back in the hostel. The news of the bursar's death will be all over the town and we will all be wanted for murder!

"We need to plan tonight."

It was Adigun's turn to talk.

"My brothers, this is really sad. I thank you, Igbinedion, for letting them know we all killed the bursar together. The bursar was half dead by the time I lifted that calabash. You all started it; I just finished it!"

"That is nonsense!" protested Wasiu, "You hit him with a heavy calabash!"

Adigun slammed his palm against the box-room door and hissed, "We are all criminals, and we have to stick together and plan fast! The only place that we can run to is the United States of America! Many of its original inhabitants were criminals; we have to run to America!"

"How do we get there?" Igbinedion asked, dubious.

"By ship, of course. The harbor is not too far from here and there are many ships from America. We will all get a ride on one of them!"

Thus, Adigun and his friends decided to leave the country; their young minds all turned to America. Adigun stretched out his hand and snarled through clenched teeth, "America, we go, together, forever, the land flowing with milk and honey, the land where God lives!" They all put their hands over their thumping young hearts, chin up.

It had the semblance of an initiation pledge they looked solemn as they repeated the words.

"America, we go, together, forever, the land flowing with milk and honey, the land where God lives!"

4

They agreed to stow away on one of the American ships at the harbor. In the abandoned room behind the hostel, they hid and plotted. They deliberated deeply on the plan and Bayo climbed into the school library one night and smuggled out books about the United States of America. The group spent their days at the barn about 100 yards from the hostel and would come to the old housemaster's house at night to sleep. The barn was behind the pit toilet. This was a good place to meet as the smell ensured that nobody came there unless they had to use the latrine (which they did as hastily as possible). The smell hung over their plans like a poison fog, seeming to pollute their cohesion. They talked of stories of kids that stowed away and were never seen again. Sunday expressed his dissent on the stow-away plan.

"Let us just run to the north and nobody will ever find us."

"Shut up!" Adigun said, "You want to compare Kano to Massachusetts or Chicago?"

"If you are not coming, let us know now."

Igbinedion was silent, shedding tears and shaking his head. Bayo was very much in favor of the American plan, and the debate often grew heated.

"America is the land of no return."

"People get there, and the country makes them swear never to return home, but of course in exchange for riches."

"Everyone in America is from somewhere!"

"– Have to put our courage on when I get to America."

"I shall represent Kunu, my village," said Sunday, a village boy from Warri. He had not said much, he was overwhelmed by fear. The boys began their research about America from the books Bayo stole from the library. They ate food Bayo obtained through raids he led on the kitchen and the nearby hostel. They ate these scraps as they read books on Napoleon and Christopher Columbus. Igbinedion seemed to have a lot of information about America from an older friend called Johnson; 'Ol' Sojah Nevah Die' they called him. He was the security guard at the health center in town. He claimed to have fought in the Second World War. He looked like he was about thirty years old and if the children knew when the Second World War was fought, they would have doubted Johnson a little bit. Johnson claimed to have first-hand information from American sailors who berthed at the harbor. Some stories had it that some kids had attempted to stow away but they were caught hiding in the cabin. He had told Igbinedion the best place to hide is in the engine room.

Bayo brought books on ships and shipbuilding and within two days they had studied the entire functional layout of a cargo ship. Igbinedion told them a story of one of the village kids that had made his bed in a room; his bed was made on the blade that propelled the engine. The kid was cut into so many pieces that they couldn't identify him. His bone was stuck in the engine and the shipowners had to dock the ship to remove particles of the bones in the engine. He told stories of kids who stowed away and were made to 'walk the plank'. To be fed to hungry sharks on the high seas. They concluded, however, that the engine room was the safest place to hide. The only problem was the heat. People who had made it to America had sent messages to other stowaways to utilize the engine room but stay naked because of the heat. In their research into the anatomy of a ship and how to identify the engine room, they found out that the engine room was in the front. This information was also confirmed by Johnson in the village.

They decided to leave on a warm November night. The bell had just gone off for the dormitory lights to go out. The boys listened to the bell from the abandoned barn – they'd had to move permanently into the barn after one of the students discovered they had broken into the old housemasters' quarters. Adigun and his friends would have to go through the bush path that led into town from behind the dormitory. The night was well-lit as the moon was at its fullest fluorescence. The stridulation of crickets blended discreetly into the midnight serenity, while the wild dogs' howls seemed to punctuate the crash of waves coming ashore. The night made its quiet music with the full moon as its conductor. As the boys walked, the lush foliage of the swaying trees broke up the moonlight, making the procession look like an assembly of disembodied limbs and torsos, emerging from shadow into silvery light and back into shadow again.

They had taken off their clothes by the Iroko tree. Soon, they smeared their bodies with mud from the stream, believing it would act as a cooling agent in the hot engine room of the ship. The three boys moved on through the bushes naked. Their determination and urgency of purpose had overridden any fear of the night, so they moved fast, and, in no time, they were at the harbor. Adigun noticed that the other boys were unusually quiet, and the pace had dropped. Bayo, who usually was the most talkative, said nothing. Igbinedion's pace was also lagging. At a point the silence from behind him seemed to deepen, forcing Adigun to stop and whirl around. He saw only dust, hanging in the air where his comrades had been. The three naked kids, scared to their teeth, ran back through the bushes.

Adigun shouted, "Why?!?

"Come back!!

"Don't leave me alone!!" Adigun's chest hitched twice, and he began to cry.

"Igbinedion!!!!" he shouted, "Together forever, the land flowing with milk and honey, the land where God lives!

"Together Forever!!" Adigun wept, wailing at top of his frail voice, alone, at the dark edge of the thick forest.

5

Adigun got over his initial shock and shook his head in subconscious rejection of the impulse to run after his friends. He was determined not to turn back. They had walked for forty minutes, and he was tired, his naked body sore from insect bites and scratches. He could faintly hear the voices of workmen unloading one of the ships. He moved closer to the ship and his mud-smeared nakedness made him invisible. He succeeded in making his way onto the ship, where he hid behind a black shipping container before running through the gangway. He made his way through the ship, ducking into the shadows whenever he thought he heard footsteps approaching, looking for the engine room.

The ship was different from the one he had studied in the school library book. Adigun climbed many stairs in the dark looking for the engine room. He kept following the sound that came from the forward part of the vessel. He could hear the sound but could not locate the room. The ship was massive. He saw sailors and dock workers busy doing several chores. At the gangway, men were loading boxes from a large trailer onto the ship. Several forklifts drove from one end of the ship to the other moving heavy pallets. Above was a giant crane that was moving bulk goods with a cargo net. Adigun observed these things as he scurried from shadow to shadow. Ol Sojah's description and map were very helpful and, after wandering naked for about an hour on the large cargo vessel, he finally located the room at the lower level of the giant hull. Adigun was overjoyed. He quietly crept into the noisy room, and immediately sat in a corner. He sat there for what seemed like hours until this big blast of smoke came toward him from a large pipe. Adigun smiled and he clenched his fist.

"Thank you, Jesus!!" he whispered.

6

It was a routine procedure for the chief engineer to check all the gauges before the ship moved. Adigun was sitting on the oil gauge, where the oil pressure readings were taken, looking like a kid taking a shit in his potty. Crouched low he sweated profusely. The temperature in the room rose unbearably and Adigun swallowed saliva intermittently as his mouth dried up from the hot air. The room was very dark, and it smelt like smoky palm oil. The initial blast of smoke had covered Adigun and left a residue of smoke and oil over Adigun's entire body, including his face. He looked like a carnival character. Behind the gauge was a door that led to the chief engineer's control room. Adigun sat on the oil gauge supporting his frame with the wall, not realizing he was leaning against a closed door. Just as Adigun started wondering if the boat would ever move, the door opened, and he tumbled backward onto a metal floor.

The chief engineer roared, taken aback by the soot-covered imp in front of him. Adigun screamed in fear, looking up at the six feet and seven inches of the Irish chief engineer, his entire lower face obscured by a thick, bushy beard.

"Jaysus!!!" the engineer growled through his beard, "What are you doing here?" Adigun's bladder let go and a stream of hot urine ran down his legs and mixed with the black engine oil to form a slowly swirling puddle around his bare feet. He barely registered this bit of shame as he focused on the behemoth in front of him, momentarily paralyzed. Then the paralysis broke and he closed his eyes and started counting in his native tongue, "*One – ookan, two – eeji, three – eeta…*" Adigun counted on in this English-Yoruba litany as the captain watched, trying to figure out what kind of black creature he had encountered.

Igbinedion had distributed some native charms among the band of would-be stowaways before they left the school that night. He said he had got them from Ol Sojah Nevah Die and asked them to swallow one each. Ol Sojah had told him it was special juju, from some medicine man, that would make them invisible if caught. Eyes squeezed shut, Adigun had counted to fifty-six, and was beginning to think the charm might just be working, when the captain grabbed his hands.

"What are you doing here? Who are you?"

Adigun wriggled free and ran further into the room but there was no way out. The room was poorly lit though and he hid behind a barrel of oil.

"Jason!" the Irish engineer called, "Stowaway on board! Stowaway on board!!"

Adigun heard cries as those three words echoed around the ship and realized there would be no sliding out of the situation – he knew that he was done for. As if to confirm this thought, Adigun was bathed in a sudden glare as all the engine room lights flashed on. Squinting, he stepped out with his hands up in surrender.

"Jason!!" yelled the engineer, as another white man barged in with a group of deckhands. There was a brief silence as Adigun approached them, naked and trembling, despite the heat, which had turned the mud and oil on his skin to a dripping sheen. His privates dangled between his skinny legs as he was walked by the men to the captain's office. He used his hands to cover his crotch as the dockworkers all fell on each other laughing and shouting, "Stowey! Stowey!" It was an amusing break from monotony for them. Adigun was handed over to the Captain, an Indian gentleman, dressed in his full white uniform. The captain and the chief engineer escorted Adigun through to an inner room where the captain handed him a towel to cover himself.

"What are you doing on my ship, this fine morning?" The voice sounded like three people were talking at the same time. The three-voiced individual was the director, Diokpa Obidike, brother to the richest business tycoon in the country. At the window were laborers looking into the room, curious about the fate of the skinny fellow. Diokpa Obidike shouted, "Away! Away! You lazy under-educated dogs. Get back to work!" The workers walked briskly away, accompanied by the slapping sounds of their flip-flops. Diokpa Obidike pulled out his pipe and emptied the old ash into a stone ashtray, knocking it hard. He pinched tobacco out of its pouch and sprinkled it into the chocolate-hued pipe bowl. When he flicked open his gas lighter and pulled at the pipe, the room was soon filled with the strong smell of fresh tobacco and a hint of roasted coffee. The smoke blasted out of his mouth and nostrils simultaneously. He slipped his right hand under his tan suspenders and sat with one side of his buttocks on the mahogany table. Dragging the pipe passionately, and with a quiet, fatherly voice, he repeated his query.

"What were you doing in my engine room?" Adigun lowered his head towards the ground, his hair dripping with oil from the ship. He slouched, gripping the towel around his waist and staring at the pool of black spreading on the cream floor tile beneath his feet.

"Okay, what in the world were you thinking about?"

As Adigun looked up, glistening tears rolled down his oily face.

"I didn't mean to kill him," he blurted, "I didn't know he was going to die."

"Who died?

"Who did you kill?"

7

He narrated his story from when he was born to how his parents sold him to the Fulani community. He explained why he needed to flee as his time was coming to an end and his father was going to hand him over to the Fulanis to be enslaved. He also told them about the incident with the school bursar. How he was caught up in a murder case and wished he could get to America.

"I don't want to spend the rest of my life as a Fulani slave, nor do I want to go to jail. I will love to go to America; I will do anything, sir. Please don't let them send me to jail."

"Young man, I have heard all you have told me. It is all rather unfortunate; and I truly feel very touched by your story.

"Boy, I will help you. I will help you."

He paused for a long moment and with a soft voice assured Adigun, raising the boy's chin to look into his face.

"You will help me to help you."

"If you follow instructions and do as you are told, I will get you to America.

"Go now and come back next Monday. I will have a plan for you.

"Just remember, boy, nothing goes for nothing." Obidike grinned and Adigun was too numb to properly register the fact that the smile didn't seem to rise to his eyes.

"Call me Victor," Obidike barked, "Tell him to bring the camera!"

A young man came in with another towel, dampened it, and cleaned off Adigun's face. Directing him to turn his head this way and that, Victor took a few photographs of Adigun.

"You should not smile, but do not frown either," said Diokpa Obidike, "You need the pictures for your passport."

Adigun signed some American visa application forms and he thumb-printed a few documents, perhaps for his passport data page. Still mostly covered in oil, he was given oversized blue overalls and black work boots, then let loose. The walk back to the school through the forest was longer. The boots were heavy, and the chemical composition of the engine oil had begun to inflict some tingling pain on his skin. He did not go back to the part of the school he and his friends had left from but took a different bush path that brought him to the school gate. He stretched out behind a large concrete slab, some distance from the school gate, and slept.

Morning came and Adigun sat on the concrete slab by the bush in front of the school gate, scratching at the spots on his arms and legs where he had been bitten during the night. He wondered how he would spend his life if caught. He worried that the Obidike man may not be sincere and may just hand him over to the police on the agreed meeting date. But that didn't make much sense – why release him at all then? In any case, he truly had nowhere to run, and Obidike's offer was the only hope of any escape, unclear as it was. He sat on the slab, dwarfed by the backdrop of the thick tropical forest, and watched the comings and goings along the road that ran in front of the school gate.

Late in the afternoon, a grey car turned into the school entrance. The suspension of the car squeaked and grated against the chassis as it labored to support the old vehicle over the uneven surface. As the car slowed, Adigun saw Ahmed Effiong, probably returning from another suspension. Ahmed was always in trouble with the school authorities, seeming to spend more time on suspension than he spent in school. He saw Adigun and gave him a thumbs-up as the car passed through the gate and into the school. Adigun knew that was the beginning of trouble. Ahmed was a light-skinned, medium-height student from Lagos Island. He was of Calabar origin and spoke both Yoruba and fluent Efik. He had come into Tuke a year before Adigun. Ahmed was not the brightest student and had performed disastrously in the last promotion exams, forcing him to repeat the class. He was much older than the other students but was childlike and playful; he was also obscenely loose-lipped. Adigun was certain his presence at the gate would be broadcast within minutes.

The grey car drove out of the gate having dropped off Ahmed. The sun had dropped low on the horizon and a cool evening breeze sighed from the harbor. The day was fast disappearing, as it usually did at this time of the year, grey evening turning to pitch-black night in a matter of seconds.

Adigun sat on the concrete slab, and with the light that was left of the day, doodled on the ground with a short twig. Glancing up toward the school entrance, he saw a group of boys pointing at him and making frantic gestures. In the failing light he could not quite make out what the gestures meant, and he certainly could not hear whatever they were shouting, but he recognized Bayo among the boys. Without hesitation, Adigun spun around and fled.

"Come back home, Adigun, he didn't die!!!"

"Welcome back Adigun!!" Bayo was shouting and crying, "Come back, my friend, come back! You didn't kill anyone!!!"

"The bursar was drunk; he collapsed; he didn't die. come back home, Digs, come back!"

But they were too far off, and Adigun thought they were coming to capture him and hand him over to the authorities. Awkwardly grabbing at the sagging bottom of his khaki overalls with one hand, and gripping the pole that hung his belongings over his shoulder with the other, Adigun raced toward town. with the lace of his big black heavy boots whipping the red soil, the boys surged, as if to pursue Adigun, but made an abrupt stop at the gate. They could not go past the gate as it was prohibited. Heedless, Adigun scampered, like some ungainly insect, to the railway crossing, where a slow-moving train trundled. Adigun threw his belongings and the pole on the train, keeping pace with it, then he accelerated and hopped on, through an open portal. The railway tracks ran parallel to the road in front of the school gate and Adigun gazed in grim silence at Bayo and the other boys. From this vantage point, he could make out Ahmed Effiong, who threw him a solemn wave. Adigun found himself waving back, seemingly in slow motion. Everything about the scene seemed to be in slow motion, he realized as he closed his waving hand into a fist and raised it towards the gaping boys. The train went slowly past the school, now bending coastward along its tracks, and Adigun craned his neck to catch a last glimpse of the gigantic school sign. 'Government College Tuke', it proclaimed, then it passed out of his view.

Minutes after, Adigun was still looking back. When the wind moved over the skin of his face, he realized he was crying.

8

The horn blasted as the train stopped at the harbor to pick up more passengers. It was the same harbor in which Adigun had tried to stow away just yesterday, and Adigun was struck by a thought; the Obidike man had asked him to come back the next Monday – why not just wait? Grabbing his things, he hopped off the train as it began moving again. The black laces of his oversized work boots flailed and lashed the concrete pavement of the harbor as Adigun wandered. When he got too tired and hungry to roam about further, he simply sat on the pavement at the pier, throwing pebbles into the water until night came. Then he walked away from the harbor front towards the bridge behind the railway track.

Adigun sat and leaned against the brick column that supported the bridge, listening to the sounds of vehicles driving in and out of the nearby motor park. Beginning to nod off, Adigun realized that this was going to be his second night sleeping outside, this time under a lonely bridge by the motor park that served the harbor. The same motor park that his school principal always talked about as that historical spot that accommodated dropouts and "ne'er-do-wells," as the principal called them.

Just as he began to get comfortable, using his belongings as a headrest; Adigun noticed there was a group of people walking toward him. They were loud and all spoke at the same time, though Adigun noticed that there was a fat boy among them who was the loudest. The boy looked like an overweight teenager but had an adult voice. He wore a brown shirt (that looked like it once was white) that sported twin holes in the armpit area, over an over-sized pair of blue denim pants that were kept aloft with a brown rope. He had very bushy hair like he hadn't seen a barber in years. Looking over Adigun with utter scorn, he sneered, "That's my spot." Adigun ignored him. The boy produced a nasty-looking, dull-bladed dagger and tapped Adigun's forehead with its tip. "That's my spot," he said again.

Adigun stood up and moved a few feet away.

The boy said, "That's my spot too.

"And that, and that, and that, too.

"I own this place. If you've come for trouble, you just met him. Pleased to meet you. What is your name?"

Adigun mumbled his name.

"Odukun, or whatever your name is, if you want tomor-row to meet you alive, I'll suggest you find your own bridge.

"It took me months of war to get this one and I am not sharing It… unless you are willing to pay rent like the other boys."

Adigun had no money and was too tired to plead or argue. In his mind, if he'd had any, he would have eaten with it long before. He moved away from the vicinity of the bridge, stumbling over heaps of rubbish. The only light came from the oil lamp of the old lady that sold fried yams and fish a few yards from the bridge. Adigun stumbled again and fell into something soft and warm. He just lay there in the dark until he felt some movement and found that he was lying on the torso of a huge nursing pig with its piglets all curdled around him. Adigun shouted and jumped up.

The fat boy ran towards Adigun and saw what had happened. He took Adigun back to the bridge and provided a few blankets for him. Whatever made this big bully have compassion for Adigun went further to make them fast friends. "My name is Salami. Salami Baba Borokini, they call me, last born of Satan, Shaolin fighter, *Borokini wole Iya re Busekun*!

"*Whos Wobi*!

"Call me SB."

He spoke with the coarse voice of a 40-year-old smoker and Adigun found himself drawn to the under-bridge 'boss'. He stayed up all night narrating the story of his life to SB and had only been asleep for a short while when the prayer call from the mosque across the motor park pierced his slumber. As if a switch had been flipped, the motor park roared to life.

Adigun woke up to this noisy motor park, where everyone seemed to be talking, at the top of their voices, at the same time. The morning was still dark, but the darkness was alive with the screamed names of various bus destinations and the sounds of vigorous engine-revving. Quiet as a graveyard moments before, the motor park had become a seething den of Barbarians.

SB reached out to Adigun with a piece of newspaper, wrapped around a large piece of yam he had woken up earlier to roast. He had made a fire with some firewood and had placed on the fire a thin asbestos slab, on top of the asbestos slab was a fish. SB used his knife to cut the yam in two and passed the smaller portion to Adigun. The yam was scalding, and Adigun blew on it to reduce the heat before taking a bite. It was vile but, apart from being careful not to offend Salami, Adigun was hungry. "Thank you, SB," he mumbled, "This is tasty." SB came back with the head of the fish. This was even worse than the yam, and it seemed to have gone off, but Adigun had to eat this fish. He closed his eyes each time he swallowed.

"Hahahahaha!" Salami blurted laughter as he recalled a nugget from Adigun's late-night story. "You killed the school Bursar, and you want to go to America?" SB paused for a moment, peering at Adigun (and completely ignoring Adigun's apparent difficulty with his meal), smacked his forehead, and continued his laughter. He laughed so hard that the other kids came around and started laughing too, rolling on the floor and clutching their bellies. Whatever it was that made him laugh, they did not care to know. SB was laughing, so they laughed too.

Absurd as the scene was, the laughter was contagious, and Adigun himself began laughing. Salami picked up his blankets, still laughing, washed his face with a cup of water, and walked off. Adigun then heard his manly voice at a distance shouting the names of different destinations. SB was a bus conductor; responsible for attracting customers to the bus by shouting out the bus's intended destination. They were also responsible for collecting the fare from the passengers and loudly announcing each destination they approached. The role of the conductor was a very important one. It involved some high-risk skill sets too. They would usually have to stand for long stretches of the ride, when the bus was full, to cram in as many passengers as possible. They sometimes would hang with more than half of their bodies outside the buses' open doorways to create even more space inside. They had to be aggressive to ward off – and, sometimes, to fight – irate passengers. Always with a torn-off collar or otherwise ripped garment, fighting was a strong point in a conductor's job description. They traveled all day in buses shouting different destinations at the tops of their voices and collecting money for their exploitative employers who operated outside the bounds of fair business practices.

Adigun spent the rest of the day at the harbor, watching the ships dock and disembark. Activities at the harbor were intriguing to Adigun and, as he roamed, the day went by in a flash. Adigun went towards the Obidike brothers' office, tempted to go in to inquire about his fate, but he felt he might look too desperate and piss them off. In the clear light of day, Adigun's resolve was strengthened. He would not weaken and turn away from his chosen course. He could not go back to Tuke and his old life where, even if he could avoid jail, he would eventually be a slave of the Fulanis. His only option was to either make it to America or spend the rest of his life as a fugitive living with the stinking SB, sleeping under the bridge, and eating spoiled fish heads with roasted yams.

SB returned late at night, took off his dirty singlet, and slipped out of his trousers revealing his polyester multicolored underwear with the colors of the rainbow and its untied drawstring. The night was dark and stifling. Adigun was already asleep.

"Hey, you! America! America!

"Wake up!! Wake up from your dream!

"This is life, if you think you're going to just be sleeping here while we all go to work and you can live here rent-free and also expect us to feed you, you must be joking!

"So, I advise you to take your high-class, 'daddy-give-me' buttocks back home or get yourself a job. Nothing is free here.

"If you want, I can talk to a few drivers; they might let you become a conductor.

"But you don't have any experience." SB mused, "It's a very dangerous job without any experience. I don't want you falling from a moving bus.

"You have to be able to hang off a bus with one arm for at least two hours. One wrong move and you will be killed by oncoming vehicles.

"*Sho daamo*?" He asked; street slang for "Do you get it?"

In one of his hands was a corn cob and, in the other, a huge piece of coconut.

SB dismembered the corn and intermittently took bites of coconut. Adigun stared at SB, thinking he could at least offer to share some of the food (the foul breakfast had been his only sustenance the whole day). Instead, SB reached into his box and threw Adigun a blanket. Adigun stayed awake late into the night; the dull glow thrown by the *akara* lady's lamp was put to shame by the darting fireflies, and he zoned out while watching the little insects. Every so often he would be snatched out of his reverie by the high-pitched whine of a mosquito streaking by his ear. He thought about America; how he would end up either on a ranch, to become a cowboy in the 'wild' west, or maybe end up in some movie in Hollywood. He thought of how worried his mum would be by now. He knew his family would be distraught to know he took the life of another man. He had nightmares every day since the dark episode and saw the Bursar in his sleep. The previous day, it had been a dream about the Bursar's funeral.

Day broke fast and the sounds of cocks crowing in the distance were continuous. Adigun woke up to the smell of yams being roasted on the fire. Nastiness forgotten, this had become the most anticipated meal of his life. Adigun had not eaten anything since the previous morning. He sat up, pretending to ignore SB devouring the huge piece of yam, wilting as the yam became smaller by the minute. SB paid him no mind at all, blowing the steamy hot yam while holding a morsel in his mouth. In abject misery, Adigun watched him throw the last piece into his huge mouth, licking his fingers. He stared at SB with naked disappointment.

"Let's get you a job," SB growled, opening a wooden cabinet and pulling out a rumpled, white, silky shirt.

"Ah, you see this shirt? Silk shirt. It was given to me by my *oga*," SB paused reflectively.

"Princewill.

"You know Princewill?

"*Ah, na the highest boy for Lagos!*

"*He get yellow Fiat convertible; the only one for Lagos!*

"*I be him housebodiguardboy!*

"*I dey follow am enter the Fiat convertible go Kakadu. From Kakadu, we enter Nucancan. From there, go*

Batakoto, then we go end up for Hot Sport. Once we don enter, the light inside dey make my silk shirt shine like disco light.

"Na so I go make my hand dey follow Oga Princewill.

"You go dey hear the gbedu, 'shekem che shakaran cha shakaran cha'.

"Na so the gbedu dey sound!"

The little boys had gathered around, eyes bright, listening to the tale like they were hearing it for the first time. "America, get up make we go hustle." SB seemed to have deflated a little bit, like his reminiscences had drained him, and he scowled as he put on the fabled silk shirt.

Adigun got up and staggered like a drunken monkey. Famished as he was, he could hardly walk straight. He walked behind the big fat boy in the rumpled silk shirt and oversized khaki shorts like a convict following his executioner. Adigun knew he couldn't lean out of a speeding bus on an empty stomach. His vision was blurry too. He became weaker by the minute. The noise in the motor park seemed to pile up on his slumped shoulders. Adigun was led to the side of a yellow bus, which he leaned against while Salami argued with the man inside about Adigun's ability to be a conductor. Adigun was six- teen years old, but his weakened condition made him seem much younger. He was rail-thin, his clavicle pro- truding noticeably from the open neck of his oversized overalls. He was summoned into the bus and his eyes

126

made a jarring connection with a scary-looking man in his late thirties, with about six tribal marks on each cheek. Adigun, weak from hunger and holding the metal seats as support began to swoon.

He looked into the man's eyes and said, "I'm dying . . . I'm hungry."

Adigun held fast to the seat, his vision fading.

"What makes this one think he can be a conductor?" The man asked.

Adigun in his hypoglycaemic state slumped forward, face-first, onto the floor of the vehicle.

S.B raised his eyebrow in disappointment, twitching his cheeks as though to communicate, "You blew it, sucker."

The man stood up in a panic, carrying Adigun and looking at SB.

"You have brought this *ogbanje* of a boy to die in my vehicle." *Ogbanje* was the name given to children who supposedly are possessed by some evil spirit, with the tendency of dying young, only to be born again to the same mother.

"Hey! Hey!" Slapping Adigun's cheeks. Adigun began to clench his jaws and the man forced his mouth open and put in his keys to keep the lips and teeth apart.

"Hey! Have you eaten?" the man asked as Adigun regained consciousness.

"No, I have not eaten.

"I ate the day before yesterday, Sir, but I'm not hungry now. I just want to sleep."

Adigun's head fell back, and he lost consciousness again.

"Bring water!" the man shouted, and SB raced inside the office to get some water.

Adigun was closing his eyes slowly and the man hit him on the chest.

"Wake him up! Wake him up."

SB poured some water on his face.

"The boy is dying. He is dying.

"What is this you have brought to my business Salami Baba Borokini?

"What is this SB?"

Adigun slumped again in the arms of SB as they tried to feed him a morsel of bread.

"Feed him!"

"Feed him"

"You say this kid is your friend; you make decent money here and you couldn't buy him food?

"How wicked can you get?"

Adigun's teeth had clenched again, and they could not feed him. After a moment, he spat out the small bunch of the bus driver's keys and opened his eyes. As they laid him on the floor beside the table of a roadside canteen, a small crowd gathered to watch.

"He is fine now, he is fine."

"Thank you, my people, thank you."

Adigun woke up to the smell of real food as the bus driver sat him up and handed him a plate of fufu and hot soup. Adigun attacked this food with his bare, unwashed hands.

"Eat up, son."

"Eat, boy."

"We thank God."

"Finish up."

"What is his name?"

"Adigun," replied SB.

"Eat up and let us go, you will start work right away!

"No sleeping in Texas!

"No free lunch in Toronto!"

Adigun was immediately employed as a trainee conductor back at the van where he had fainted. The vehicle revved off leaving a trail of thick black smoke.

The driver introduced himself as Bashy and began Adigun's orientation as he drove on.

"You will borrow yourself a brain, boy; you have to learn fast!

"Every day you sit on this seat as a trainee costs you money!

"You better learn the work fast so you can start to pay for the training!

"Since you are occupying a seat that could have been occupied by a paying passenger, you will have to pay for each ride from your salary."

Adigun learned fast and, by the second day, his yells were loud enough to attract customers.

"Kunu! Kunu! Kunu! Nnewi, no change, oh! One Naira, Fifty Kobo!"

Adigun soon memorized the tricks of the trade. Bashy traveled back and forth to Kunu, stopping, on their way back, at Nnewi for a cool calabash of palm wine. In fact, by the second day, Adigun had learned all he needed to about the job. He had to now leave Bashy's vehicle to serve in another, and he was assigned to Osaro.

They got along right away. Osaro was a middle-aged driver, a little on the fat side; the lower buttons of all his shirts had long since lost the battle with his midriff, where their absence served to reveal his bulging belly, which was only outshone by his large, bald head. Adigun bonded quickly with Osaro and soon noticed that he dipped directly into the day's takings to purchase palm wine when they stopped at Nnewi. Adigun hated the palm wine stops. They brought back memories that made him uncomfortable. Still, he kept his observations (and reservations) to himself and remained friendly with Osaro; enough so that he even told him of his plans to travel to America. Coincidentally, he discovered, Osaro had worked for the Obidike brothers a few years before.

"Be careful," Osaro warned Adigun, "Those men are evil."

He was not too happy to know Adigun would be gone in a few days.

9

Adigun was given a permanent sleeping space under the bridge, close to SB's cluster. They both left for work each morning and returned very tired at night. The days came and went. On a sodden Monday morning, Adigun and SB got to the motor park, as usual, at dawn. SB set off almost immediately, but Adigun had to wait for Osaro, who was late that morning. Adigun ordered a bowl of pap and some bean cake from the park food vendor. He was just finishing up when Osaro lumbered into view.

"Uncle Osaro, good morning. Hope nothing."

"Oh, don't worry, we will make up. I had to go and organize another conductor – did you forget that today is your day?"

"Oh, yes, Uncle Osaro! Thanks for remembering."

The morning was cool and there was a steady drizzle. In another few hours, Adigun's fate would be decided by the Obidikes. They ran the western route, picking up and dropping off passengers for a few hours while training the little boy they had picked up to replace Adigun.

Osaro dropped off Adigun right in front of the white bungalow occupied by the Obidike shipping line. He drove away in the beat-up Volkswagen Combi bus with the little boy hanging from the side of the bus. Adigun waved to the departing bus slowly. He turned around and walked through the swivel doors like a priest at the beginning of a catholic mass, making the ubiquitous sign of the cross.

"Come on in my boy, we have been waiting for you."

Adigun was hit with the thick smoke from Diokpa Obidike's pipe. They went straight to business. Adigun felt a strengthening of his faith in the Lord, and the power of the sign of the cross when Diokpa Obidike presented a slip of paper he called "the tickit", which Adigun surmised to be the airline ticket. "This is the tickit to New York. You shall be leaving on Friday. There is a church choir group; they have a slot to have an expedited visa service, as they will be performing at Times Square." The man paused his clipped, efficient delivery to glare at Adigun as if to ensure that he was being properly attentive. He continued, "You will go quickly with my assistant to take your passport photo. Your passport will be ready tomorrow and you will accompany the choir to the American embassy in Lagos. You will be given two hundred dollars whatever happens after that is your own business." Adigun's eyes widened and his face lit up. He went down on the floor, prostrating flat, as it was done to elders in his tradition.

Diokpa Obidike's face darkened in rage and his hand flashed out and snatched the ticket from Adigun's hands before he could get off the floor.

His tone changed too, "You young men always want everything for free! I've spent half of my life working for my kid brother, sweating and slaving for my rich sibling, and the wimp thinks he can deprive me of all I've earned.

"Over my dead body," he shouted.

Adigun trembled from the blast as Diokpa Obidike's large fist came crashing down on the solid oak table. Adigun squirmed helplessly in the corner of the huge sofa, listening to this bitter soliloquy. It referred to a 'wimp'. Whomever this wimp was, Adigun didn't want to be in his shoes.

"Get inside! Get inside!" Diokpa Obidike shouted at Adigun, as he pointed into a large room visible through an open doorway. Adigun, taken aback by the brutal rage Obidike suddenly displayed, did not think he wanted to go into that room (or any room) with this thundering man. This thought was barely formed when he found himself swept into the room and the door slammed shut behind them.

"You will do as I say," Obidike hissed.

"Yes, Sir," Adigun whispered, staring at the terrazzo floor.

"You will be on the bus to Lagos with the Holy Trinity Church Choir. A man called Tiroko will meet you. Say nothing to anybody. Tiroko will tell you what to do.

"After you have collected your visa, you shall go to the *NsonsoSoronsonso* and do as instructed."

Adigun puzzled over the word, "*NsonsoSoronsonso*", repeating it under his breath.

"Why are you looking at me that way? You mean you have never of *NsonsoSoronsonso*?

"Didn't you tell me your mum was from Arochukwu?" Obidike sneered, "Our people allow our women to marry these *Ndi ofe mmanu*," he intoned, using the native expression for 'oily food people', "then totally forget to teach their offspring about the rich culture and history of Aro. *NsonsoSoronsonso* is the short form for the Arochukwu phrase, '*Sososoronsonso-Sonsosoronsonso*'!

Back in the day, there was a code language called the *Nsibidi*, our secret mode of communication used during the slave trade era. It was the language used to communicate between the Arochukwu people and could not be understood by anyone else. It was further symbolized by the *Omu*. The *Omu* was a special palm leaf used to send messages to Aros across the nation and the way the leaf was knotted had a unique meaning to the recipient of the *Omu*.

How do you think the Aros were able to go to war with the British troops and defeat them?

"Yes!!! Disgraced them. I wish we had time I will tell you a lot about the unique Aro people. By the way, we are like Jews; there is no city in the world you won't find an Aro. Even in Ijebu, Aros are living there. So, when a confused outsider asks for an explanation we usually explain by telling them '*Nsonsosoronsonso-Sonsosoronsonso*' which represents the Aro's intent to make certain conversations secret.

"My brother named his castle accordingly, giving a clear answer to curious elements seeking the source of his wealth.

"Okay, back to business!" Diokpa Obidike produced a small pistol and thrust it into Adigun's hands.

"This here is the safety catch." He clicked on and off the small switch, pushing the pistol closer to Adigun's face.

"Once you click it here, you are ready to fire."

Adigun gaped in wordless, uncomprehending horror, at the object in his hands.

"You will go to *Sososoronsonso*, my brother's castle, one of a kind, a unique architectural edifice. There you will find a young man by the name of Chike. He is only sixteen years old – just about your age – you can handle him.

You shall kill him!!!!" he shouted, and Adigun squealed, his heart jumping to the back of his throat.

"If you don't, we will find you and kill you! Remember what I said, we are everywhere." So saying, Diokpa Obidike fell silent, twitching his nose and lighting his wooden pipe with a short match.

Adigun felt his recently renewed faith dissolve into nothing. knowing his life ended right here, in this room. Barely a week ago he had accidentally killed the bursar, and now, to escape punishment for that deed, he was required to deliberately murder a teenage boy with a gun. He had never seen a gun before. He closed his eyes and took a deep breath, then looked up at the huge old man with a foul breath, looking placidly back. Obidike measured Adigun with his eyes and dropped the little envelope on Adigun's lap. "This is your *tickit*. Your flight leaves on Friday. You will be out of the country before anyone finds the corpse. You're happy and everyone is happy.

"Make sure nobody sees you. The same driver that drops you there will be waiting at the gate to pick you up and take you to the airport, where you will board the flight with the rest of the choir.

"Tonight, you rest and feel relaxed at the Memuna Inn. You have a busy day ahead of you, so sleep early."

Adigun was neither given the space to refuse nor comment on the assignment.

The weight of the pistol felt unbearable in his shaking hand. His big eyes bulged in his head, as he looked up at Diokpa Obidike.

"Why are you looking at me like that? You think America is easy?"

An elderly gentleman walked in, dressed in a white French suit with big front pockets. He also wore white shoes. He had a bushy, but well-groomed, beard. This was Diokpa Obidike's younger brother Chibuzor, though he preferred to be called Ogbuagu. He looked older than Diokpa and was gentler, more understanding, and soft-spoken. The gold-plated toe-caps of his white shoes flashed as he walked, the sunlight bouncing off them and rebounding off stained-glass windows to create a disco effect. He began a long conversation with his brother in thick Igbo. The only thing Adigun could understand was his constant use of the phrase, "New York City" (he pronounced "city" as "sirry") and a constant query of "*Ighotago?*", which Adigun knew to mean "Do you understand?"

After the dialogue, Ogbuagu came closer to Adigun and raised his eyebrow pushing his face closer to Adigun's face. "Young man, you are already a wanted criminal. I can make just one phone call, and you will be arrested by the authorities."

"You planned to stow away on a ship," Diokpa interjected, "where you would have been discovered and fed to the sharks, as it could cost the crew a big fine if they arrived at the shores of America with an illegal immigrant."

"We have been so kind to you. We have procured a passport and your visa will be ready by tomorrow morning."

"If you are already going to hell for murdering your school bursar, another death on your hands will not increase the heat in hell."

"I advise that you cut out the drama, complete the work and go and try asking God for forgiveness when you get to America."

"This time it won't be on a boat, it will be on a big bird. In less than two days, you will be taking a bite of the big apple. Our associates will pick you up at the airport and you shall be properly settled into your new life in America."

Adigun lifted his hand, pointing his index finger to the sky like he was in a classroom requesting permission to ask a question.

"Isn't there any other way I can earn this ticket, like working on the boat or washing your car every day till the ticket is fully paid?"

"Look, boy," Diokpa's soothing voice was replaced by a low growl, "it's a done deal. You do it or you die!" Twitching his nose continuously, he looked to Adigun like a tiger that was trying to home in on its prey. Adigun gave up trying to reason his way out of this insane situation.

Adigun was led to a black Mercedes sedan. The leather interior smelled brand new. Even with his trauma, Adigun could register the massive difference between this car and his father's Beetle. The wiper swiftly glided across the windscreen, in a very smooth rhythm, helping calm Adigun's pounding heart as they drove through the slip road parallel to the harbor.

"My name is Uche," the driver announced, "I shall be picking you up tomorrow morning as well. I will check you in at your hotel. Memuna is a very comfortable hotel, and you will enjoy it. How old are you, boy?"

"Seventeen," whispered Adigun.

The Mercedes pulled up in front of the purple neon sign of the Memuna Inn. It was a low-class motel in the seamier part of the town. Uche helped him check into his room, hugged him, patted him on his skinny back, and said, "You are going to be all right, son."

Those words echoed in Adigun's mind long after Uche had left.

He sat alone in this nasty room that smelt like cod liver oil and damp. It reminded him of his residency under the bridge, though his abused body would rejoice in the comfort of an actual bed. He contemplated running away; then banished the thought when he remembered what still awaited him at home. His mother would kill him before the hands of the law got to him for killing the school bursar. The killing at home would be a more humiliating death, right in front of the whole family. And if it didn't end up that way, he'd probably be handed over to the Fulanis immediately anyway.

Adigun laid face-up on the hard bamboo bed; the room was painted in glossy army green. The squeaky rotating sound from the ceiling fan disguised the occasional whine from the mosquitos. He slept on his back, from which position he could see the palm trees and hear the owl hoot. The floor was carpeted in red, with stains that made a leprous black and red pattern.

Adigun could hear his heart pounding and his stomach rumbled continuously. It sounded like a conversation between his heart and stomach. Adigun's body disagreed with what he was about to do.

His spirit was low. He got up from the bed, walked in circles in the room, and then knelt beside the bed and, with his eyes closed, began saying a prayer. "Good merciful Lord," Adigun intoned, "you have said 'Thou shall not kill', Father Lord. you have specifically laid down the rule not to take another's life.

"Father Lord, I want you to know my life would be taken if I don't take this boy's life.

"Lord, you know I'm not the real criminal here. Help me not to do what I should not do. Show me a way out."

Adigun stared at the wooden window and found himself falling asleep. He got up, stretched, and laid down on his back. He slept fitfully, snapping awake every time he dreamed of the bursar. This happened several times throughout the night and, eventually, Adigun sat up, sweating and weeping, engulfed in fear, the image of the bursar seeming to linger behind his tightly closed eyelids. A door in the hallway slammed and Adigun's eyes opened. He took in the pale light filtering through the cheap curtains and the cooing of the pigeons confirmed

141

that it was morning already. The temperature in the room was cool but he still was drenched in fear-sweat. He was startled by the sudden blast of a car's horn, and he jumped out of bed. Looking out of the window, he saw the Mercedes that had brought him here last night. He stuck his head out of the window and made eye contact with the driver, who stood beside the open driver's side door looking pointedly at his watch. Adigun rushed into the dark bathroom and washed his face. He used his palm to scoop some water into his mouth, gargled, and spat into the broken sink. After scrambling into his clothes, he dashed out of the room and made his way into the waiting car.

They arrived at the Obidikes' building and Adigun took a seat in the little room outside Diokpa Obidike's office. The seats were made of wood and there were soft rectangular cushions on them. The place was deserted, the silence broken only by the sound of Diokpa on the phone, shouting at the top of his voice. He was soon done, and Adigun heard the clink of the phone as he replaced the receiver.

"Uche!"

"Uche!"

"Whoochay!" Diokpa Obidike yelled for the driver.

The driver answered from the three-storey building at the back of the office, "Sah!"

"Did you pick up that boy?"

142

"Yes, Sah, he is here now."

"Did you drop Chike at *Nsonso* yesterday?"

"Yes, Sah, I dropped him off and he is alone."

"You opened the back gate, right? Did anybody see you?"

"No, Sah, the place is always empty. The cleaners were leaving when we arrived. They all were paid, and they will not be coming to work today, as planned."

Diokpa's phone rang, and he picked up the black bulky phone.

It was a Motorola with a black rubber antenna.

"Chukie? Yes, Chukie. Absolutely, Chukie, by tomorrow morning all will be done.

"The lad's passport was done at record speed.

"Thanks, Reverend Amaechi was amazing, his passport was included with the group and off he goes with the choir group to the Kennedy choral competition in New York." Diokpa Obidike took a long drag of his pipe, twisted his upper lip and bushy mustache sideways, and blew smoke.

"Good stuff, Good stuff," he continued, "All well done! My driver is ready to take him to *Nsonso*, where the boy will complete the job.

"No, not at all, no previous experience; he's just a kid." A pause as Diokpa listened, then, "But he desperately wants to be on the flight to America, so he has to do the deed, or his sorry ass is in jail for life.

"I will personally deliver him to the police if he plays any pranks.

"Yes, Sir. Oh, it's all set. They should clear immigration by Thursday, and he will be giving Charley a ride.

"Charley, all dressed up. And he has put on weight, too; 10 kilos!

"It's a big one, but don't worry, the boy will get Charley to his destination. He'll meet Okpanku and the other boys in Brooklyn. He would be a good runner for Okpanku – a good replacement for the Haitian guy."

Adigun listened to the entire conversation in silence, unable to make head or tail of most of it.

"Who is Charley, Sir?"

"Shut your trap, boy, you are not a part of that conversation. If you piss me off right now with your silly questions, I will personally hand you over to the homicide department of the police.

"Jail for you, American Boy!" Diokpa smirked and repeated, "American Boy! Don't you know you are now the American Boy? In 48 hours, you'll be in Brooklyn, living the American dream.

"Here is your luggage," Diokpa chuckled as he rolled out a grey Samsonite suitcase from behind his desk. It was new and still had the sales tag on it.

"We have packed some Nigerian foodstuff for our friend, Okpanku, in New York. He will receive you at the airport and you will hand over the suitcase to him."

"I have also added some clothing for you, a toothbrush, comb, and also some underwear; I packed it in a blue nylon bag."

Adigun reached for the suitcase and pulled up the handle. He looked at the case again and smiled.

"Thank you, Sir."

"When you get to Brooklyn, stay close to Okpanku. He will settle you into America. Okay? But don't thank me yet; you will leave these things here until you return from your mission. You can leave now. Thereafter you would be singing amazing grace into the big apple. A smile began to form on Adigun's face again, then froze when he remembered the gun in his pocket. The steel was cold and heavy, against his thigh, and sent shivers up his spine. He was about to commit a second murder within a couple of weeks of his first.

"American Boy!" Diokpa Obidike chuckled again.

"Off you go to *Nsonso*; the driver is waiting. The body should be disposed of in the river behind the mansion.

"The balcony on the east side overlooks the river, be careful with the crocodiles, those monsters would have you for dessert if you fall over the railings."

"Thank you, Sir."

"Thank *you*. Now, go."

"Thank you, sir."

Adigun walked out of Diokpa Obidike's and climbed into the black sedan. The heavy doors thudded shut and they sped out of the premises. They drove past the harbor and continued for almost forty minutes down a lonely single carriageway. The car turned off at a rubber plantation and Adigun looked out of the window, seeing the endless rows of rubber trees as the car raced along the dusty, un-tarred road. At length, they approached a huge black gate that bore, at its top, the legend, "NsonsoSoronsonso".

The driver was dead silent for the entire trip. He was an albino with a galaxy of orange freckles on his cheek. His neck was red and folded into rings. His hands were an angry red and looked rough and cracked as he gripped the steering wheel. He squinted his eyes and stretched his head close to the windscreen, suggesting some problems with his eyesight. Adigun decided to hold his tongue, as silence seemed the only appropriate attitude for the situation.

They came to an abrupt stop in front of a huge oak door. The door was decorated with intricate carving and its handle was made of gleaming brass. The albino made a head gesture, signaling Adigun to exit the car.

"You can piss off now," the driver said, and Adigun wondered what the reason was for his sudden hostility.

Adigun got out of the car and looked about him. Shivering with fear, he opened the ostentatious oak door onto breathtaking opulence. The foyer boasted an enormous painting of a man wearing a red hat and a long white feather. He was on a beautiful white horse. Past the art was a short flight of marble stairs and all around was white velvet wallpaper. This *is* a castle, Adigun thought, walking through the hallway and across to the fishpond, according to the instructions earlier given to him by Diokpa Obidike. The pond seemed out of place, infested with algae, and featured a broken stone statue of a cupid. The murky water had long grass growing out of it. Adigun took in the discordant scene of neglect through the tall glass doors to the courtyard. As he opened these doors, he heard a voice.

"Ugo! Ugo! Is that you? Who is there? Ugo! Is that you?"

A young man looked down from the balcony and asked, "Who are you?

"How did you get here?

"What do you want?

"Who let you in?"

He spoke in crisp Queen's English. His accent was so polished, that Adigun didn't know how to start.

He replied, "My name is Di… I mean, Lekan! Olalekan."

"I have a message for you."

"Message from whom? How did you get in here? How did you know I was here?" Chike had been moved to this property after there was a failed kidnapping attempt in the city. He was only meant to wait there for his flight out of Nigeria. Military personnel usually guarded the castle, but his uncles had done everything possible to make them disappear for this period.

"I asked who let you in.

"Rupert? Rupert!!" He yelled at the top of his voice. When He did not get an answer, he took a few steps backward, snatching up the intercom to the security gate. The phone was dead, he tapped at the transparent breaker in the cradle of the black rotary phone but there was no sound.

"Your uncle's driver brought me here; the albino."

"Oh, that's Yellow," said Chike, as he continued to click on the phone looking for a dial tone, "Is he here too?"

"No, he dropped me off."

Chike marched to the window and pulled back the heavy velvet curtain, peeping out.

"Where is everybody? Okay, wait in the living room downstairs. I will be with you in a few minutes."

Adigun turned from the courtyard doors and walked into the expensively furnished living room, redolent with the smell of supple leather. The floor was made of the highest-grade marble and its luster was blinding. An imposing black Steinway and Sons grand piano hulked in the far-left corner and there was a life-sized statue of David, sheathed sword in its scabbard, carrying the head of Goliath under his arm, made of pure marble.

The ostrich-leather sofa sported a tag on the seat cushion; 'Roche Bois-Bois' it read (the name held no meaning for Adigun, but he figured the Roach Boy-Boys, whoever they were, made exquisite sofas). The 3-storey-high ceiling was dome-shaped and painted to resemble the sky, with puffy, white clouds. Beneath angels holding hands, gold-lettered text proclaimed, "*Nwa Aro Icho Nkpoola Icho,*" a popular phrase amongst the Arochukwu people, depicting their desire to distinguish wealth from the rest of life. Spiralling behind the piano and statue of David was an expansive staircase with intricate gold banister rails. The marble steps were blotted out down the middle by a wide strip of lush, green carpeting, held in place by gold paneling in the center of the room, a massive white shag rug sprawled, with a discrete inner border of gold bearing a circular inscription in turquoise; '*Ogbiti Nsosonsoronsonso.*'

Adigun was out of breath looking around this beautiful living room the Aros call *Ogbiti*. He heard footfalls on the staircase and immediately sat on the sofa. The young man came down the stairs, looking regal in his velvet robe and black, soft leather bedroom slippers. He was only a teenager, but the robe made him look older. The huge brown air conditioner breathed out a frosty mist.

"I am Chike. Please feel at home.

"I don't know where all the maids and the housekeeper disappeared to, or I could have offered you something." He grabbed the thick blue blinds coming down from the cathedral ceiling and called again even louder. "Ugo! Ugo!"

Utter silence. Chike sat down opposite Adigun on the large sofa, crossed his legs, and grabbed the newspaper that rested on the stool beside him. He adjusted his thick glasses on his nose, looked up at Adigun, and scratched his head.

"You look really familiar. I don't know where I've seen you before, but you certainly do look familiar. Did you attend Jobore Elementary School?"

"Chike!" Adigun sprang up. "Oh, my God! My God, you lived right in front of us at the Railway Compound at Jobore!"

"How are those twins?" Chike asked.

"Oh, the ones with the big heads? Oh, my God, they moved out of Jobore as well."

"So, you are now Lekan Olalekan? You! Oh, my God, Adigun Oloogun; the boy with the magical powers.

"Ugo! Ugo!" Chike called again. "Shoot! I forgot Ugo is not here. Where is everybody?"

Chike walked to the window and dragged the enormous curtain aside on its rails, then looked out and yelled again, "Ugo!!!"

He walked back to Adigun, looked at him closely, and embraced him. Adigun blurted, "Everybody missed you at the village. All we heard was that your father invented something and became rich!

"Oh, look at you! *Chikereuba Chikereuba Omo yyibo, Salisu wa gbobe Otu yeri yeri aa baa baa baa.*"

Chike giggled, letting go of Adigun and clutching his abdomen. Doubled over and gasping, he extended his right hand to Adigun, palm outwards, as if signaling him to stop.

"Oh yes, you are right; I went to school in Ghana for a year and returned to Lagos for the rest of my secondary school. There were some threats to my life and I almost got kidnapped, so my father moved me secretly to this property whilst I await my travel arrangements.

"I will be going to school at Harrow school for boys in England.

"I'm so happy to see you, Digs; how's your mum? And… oh! *Riro*!! Your amazing dog.

"Oh my God, you were such a crazy kid – now look at you! You look like a man."

Adigun burst into tears.

"What's the matter, Digs? What is it? Are you okay?"

Adigun reached into his pocket and brought out the pistol. He placed it on the oak table and narrated how he met the Obidike brothers.

"Obidike?" Chike shouted, "At the harbor? Those are my uncles – my father's BROTHERS!

"They gave you this gun to kill me?"

"Yes, that is why I was sent here, Chike." Adigun outlined the story of the school bursar and failed stowaway plan. Chike was moved to tears.

"Oh, my friend you have been through so much. But what do we do now, Digs? I don't want to die… I mean, I know you want to get to America…"

"Stop!" Adigun shouted. "Stop! I am not a killer! I don't even know how to fire a gun.

"Chike, you are my childhood friend. I've known you since I was little. I cannot and will not kill you. Please, I need you to calm down and let's draw up a plan. I have an idea." Adigun looked up to find Chike slowly backing away up the spiral stairs.

"Why are you scared of me, Chike? Why are you backing up?"

Chike's skin puckered with goose pimples as he stared at the gun on the table.

"Let's call the police, Digs. Let's go and report to the police."

"No! We cannot do that. We cannot, I am already wanted by the police for the murder of the school bursar. I just need to get out of this country. I don't want to go to jail, and your uncles are my only way out!"

Adigun collapsed into the white leather sofa and held his head in his hands. There was utter silence in the room. In a flash, he sprang to his feet and lunged at Chike, grabbing him by the lapels of his robe.

"Listen, Chike," Adigun's eyes were wild, "listen to me carefully. Do as I say, and we will both be fine.

"You will bring one of the goats in the backyard; we slaughter it and use its blood. If we carefully cut a hole into your shirt and singe its edges, it will look just like damage from a gunshot.

"We smear the shirt with the goat's blood, and I shall return with this to the Shipyard. I shall tell your uncle you were shot, and I dumped your body into the lagoon at the back.

"We would create a trail of blood to the lagoon to show you were dragged to the balcony overlooking the water.

You disappear and lay low till you can fly out of the country – no one can know your whereabouts, apart from your father. This would give me time to board my flight to America."

"Soooo… *don't* call the Police?"

"Shut up, you dummy, you can't call the police. Don't you get it? I am in a bad situation here and I am trying to avoid having to use that gun! With this plan, you get to live, and I get to go to America; everyone is safe, and we continue our lives." Adigun was glad to see Chike nodding thoughtfully.

The boys went out to the yard and grabbed a goat that was, fortunately, tethered. Chike held the goat down, with his eyes closed, while Adigun slit its throat. The goat stared up at Adigun with placid eyes, then kicked as the wound produced a splash of crimson.

"Please open your eyes and hold the goat well," Adigun snarled at Chike. "I don't want to be soaked in blood; that will look suspicious since I am supposed to shoot you, not cut your throat." The little black goat stretched as the life left its hairy body.

Adigun let it bleed out a little more, then dragged the goat through the living room, Chike walking behind him and carefully avoiding the trail of blood. They conducted the trail to simulate Chike's post-execution journey into the crocodile-infested lagoon behind the castle.

The muddy waters outside the castle fence showed no sign of the fabled crocodiles and Adigun was nervous as he threw the carcass of the goat over the balcony's railing. He was just thinking it would not do to have anyone find a goat carcass floating near the castle when he saw a dark shadow streaking through the water toward the still-floating carcass. Soon he saw two more shadows converging on the same spot and the water soon boiled as the crocs tore at the ill-fated goat. Adigun flung the knife into the lake and exhaled.

"So, this is the deal, you can not disclose who ordered your killing, or else I would be in danger.

"You will disappear for a sensible period and never tell anyone what went down. Do not EVER reveal my own identity to anyone… please."

"I guess this is where our paths divide again, Digs."

"So long, my friend, so long."

Adigun gave the neighborhood whistle code from Jobore and Chike replied, "*Eyin iku wonu igo jeyo,*" the old jest of Chike's buck teeth in Yoruba.

"Wow, you still remember that too?" Adigun pulled Chike to himself and hugged him hard.

"Thanks, Digs Thanks for saving my life. I wish you all the best in America."

"Thanks, Chike."

"I wish I knew where you would be – my father would surely want to reward you someday."

Then Chike handed Adigun his shirt and ran, robe flapping, into the thicket behind *NsonsoSoronsonso* out through a little pedestrian gate at the back. He waited in the shadows of a back road until he saw the yellow and black markings of a taxi cab, which he hailed and rode to a nondescript motel about ten kilometers away.

10

Bang! Adigun fired into the air, carefully holding the heavy weapon with both hands. The sound echoed through the air as a flock of birds erupted from the trees at the back of the deserted castle. Adigun took Chike's shirt and examined the hole he had burned into it with the lighter from the kitchen (he had found that burning the hole into the shirt worked out much better than trying to cut one into it). He smeared a generous amount of goat blood on Chike's shirt and put a modest amount on his own. He walked briskly through the estate entrance, struggling not to break into a trot as he approached the waiting driver in the Mercedes.

Adigun slammed the door behind him, and the car eased into the dusty road.

He sighed in relief as the scene of his second would-be murder fell behind them, happy he did not have to commit a second murder. The gun was still warm in his pocket, and he could feel it against his thigh. Once they hit proper, tarred highway, the albino gunned the engine, driving fast until he reached the harbor, then screeched to a stop in front of the Obidikes' office building.

He rushed into the office, looking around furtively. Diokpa Obidike was in his office with two other men. One was his brother and the other was an old man dressed in the traditional Igbo garb, with the red velvet hat. His black tunic, also velvet, had a pattern of gold lion heads all over it. Following behind the albino, Adigun entered the room through the thick smoke. Diokpa stood in front of his table with his ever-present pipe in his mouth. After clapping quietly, he pulled the smoking pipe from his mouth and set it on the wooden stand.

"Job well done my boy; I am so proud of you."

Chief Obidike collected the gun from Adigun and sniffed the muzzle. Adigun dropped the bloody shirt on the table and the chief jerked back like it was a snake. "Are you stupid? Why did you bring this here? You might have as well brought the dead body here." Then understanding dawned in his eyes and he nodded, "Smart boy! You brought proof of the deed. Body all fed to crocodiles?"

Adigun nodded.

"Then make sure you clean yourself up well, and you will head to the airport right away. You just earned your trip to America! Your Choir group awaits you, Choirboy! Well done! Job well done!"

It would be a two-hour drive from the harbor to the airport. Adigun went into the bathroom and had a brisk, cold shower, washing off the goat's blood he had smeared his hands with. When he had changed and returned to the office, Diokpa was on the phone.

"Yes, *Ndewo, Ndewo*, the boy has been erased.

"Yes, absolutely perfect. Send the security back to position.

"Did you ensure everybody got paid?

"Yes, we move unto the next plan, right away."

Diokpa handed Adigun his passport and ticket and gave him a plastic bag containing a bright green Aso Oke dashiki with very elaborate embroidery woven around its neck and down its front; it had a pair of matching trousers. "Put this on quickly, boy; your flight for America leaves soon." Adigun hurried back into the bathroom and changed into the bright green dashiki outfit. He walked out as he tightened the trousers, tying the fabric rope into a strong bow. Diokpa then rolled out the grey Samsonite suitcase and handed it over to Adigun without a word. Then they walked through the small reception and out to the tarred driveway.

Diokpa patted the Adigun on his back and led him to the Mercedes, which appeared to be attended by a different driver. He instructed the driver to place the grey

Samsonite suitcase in the boot and gave Adigun a stern warning to take good care of it. Adigun couldn't believe he was on his way to America. He kept looking back at Diokpa until he was out of sight. It seemed a long drive through the wooded old road from the rural south-western suburb into the freeway that led to the city of Lagos but, exactly two hours after they departed from the harbor, the car pulled up at the Murtala Muhammed Airport in Lagos.

There was a crowd at the airport and Adigun had a hard time keeping up with the driver while toting the suitcase and his meager personal effects. However, he soon noticed a distinct group of people, dressed just as he was in bright green, and he realized where they were headed. They were the young boys and girls on their way to the choir festival and contest in New York. They were all gathered together, with clasped hands, and heads bowed towards their leader. A mixed-race girl of about 16 said a prayer. They were being led by a middle-aged priest dressed in his white clerical outfit. The priest had no direct history with their church, nor was he familiar with the group, but he had been informed about Adigun, and his role as a substitute chorister, by the head of the church, a fellow priest. Adigun was uncomfortable and scared that the law enforcement agents would recognize him. He looked away as a group of policemen passed. Adigun held his suitcase and personal effects firmly with one hand and held the envelope that contained his passport in the other. He walked away with the group, and it didn't take long before a member of the group began to get curious about Adigun, stealing numerous obvious glances in his direction.

They passed through immigration and followed the leader towards their gate as boarding was announced for their flight.

"You are not a member of this choir." Adigun jumped and turned to the owner of the accusatory voice. She was the smallest of the group, with dark skin and a chirpy attitude.

"Who are you? Why are you dressed like us?" She looked into Adigun's face as she grabbed the hem of her burgundy Aso oke blouse, sitting on top of a skin-tight little skirt made from the same material.

Adigun did not say a word.

"I'm talking to you, boy – don't you ignore me!

"How can you sing with us when you never attended any rehearsal?

"Which section do you sing in?

"I'm speaking to you!"

Adigun ignored her and walked into the aircraft. The air hostess assisted him in locating his seat and, as he busied himself with the unfamiliar seatbelt, he saw the diminutive girl looking back at him repeatedly. Her periodic spot checks were interrupted by the safety instructions and, as the aircraft cycled up for take-off, even she was a bit too excited to concern herself with Adigun. When they took off, Adigun clenched his fists in equal parts fear and elation; it was his first time in the air and he was in a state of terror. His eyes remained squeezed shut for a long time after the plane stopped its climb, banked widely, and leveled off. He opened his eyes when he felt a tentative tap on his shoulder and realized for the first time that he was seated beside the priest.

"Are you okay?" asked the priest, and Adigun nodded, eyes downcast.

"So, you are a member of the choir," the priest continued, "What section do you sing?" He asked.

"Uhmmm, center-forward sir."

The priest looked at him.

"Center-forward?"

"Um, s-s-sometimes I sing at the back sir . . . in the middle."

"That's rather strange," the priest stared at Adigun, "How long have you been in the church choir?"

"Sir, I'm just a substitute singer. I'm new."

"What is your name?"

"Adigun. Adigun Komaiya. Sir, I'm very scared of flying! Can you pray for me?"

The priest, who had been regarding Adigun with considerable skepticism, suddenly relaxed and, with a small smile, held his hand and said a short prayer. Adigun was gratified to see that this new tack had been a brilliant stroke; seeming to explain away his nervous and nonsensical responses to the priest while ending the unwelcome interrogation. He made the sign of the cross, closed his eyes, and soon fell asleep.

It was a 12-hour flight to New York.

About 3 hours into the flight, Adigun was woken by a soft tap from the beautiful Nigerian Airways hostess.

"Chicken or beef?"

"… Chicken, aunty."

The lady passed him a tray with a roll of bread and several small plastic containers, and Adigun quickly located the chicken, sitting on fluffy white rice.

The food was sumptuous, the best Adigun could remember ever eating, and only the proximity of the prim priest beside him stopped him from wolfing it down without decorum. The roasted yam and fish head he'd been eating mere days ago seemed like relics of an ancient, dim past.

The cabin lights were eventually dimmed, and Adigun began to play the last two weeks over in his mind. He wondered how worried his parents would be when they found out he was missing from Tuke and what would have happened to the other kids. They probably would be arrested for the death of the bursar by now. Adigun flipped through the pages of his passport and stared at his American visa. He feared he may be asked difficult questions at the border and the other members of the choir may give him away, especially that little 'Nosey Rosie'. He soon fell into a deep, and for the first time in ages, dreamless sleep. He slept through the next two rounds of cabin service and had no idea when the priest assisted the air hostess to put a blanket over him. When he was awakened by the short tone of the PA system, Adigun was groggy and disoriented. When the pilot's calm, competent voice announced that in a few minutes they would be landing at John F. Kennedy airport, he may as well have been reciting the periodic table in Farsi. It wasn't until he registered the bustle of activity amongst his fellow passengers, fastening seatbelts and raising their seatbacks into the upright position, that Adigun's cobwebs cleared. *I am in America*, he thought, awestruck.

Some of the other kids raised their hands and chattered in excitement and it soothed Adigun somewhat to learn he was not alone in his exhilaration.

There was a sudden big bang as the tires of the Nigerian airways DC 10 made contact with the runway, then the rush of air as the flaps were lowered to curb its speed. Adigun held tight to the armrest as the plane exhaled pressure and rolled to a gentle stop. The choir gathered at the door of the aircraft, having had to wait for other passengers to disembark, and were then ushered to immigration by a member of staff of the airline. He was Indian,

164

with a carefully twisted mustache, wearing a black turban atop the same uniform as the cabin crew. He also had a remarkable red dot on his forehead. He led the group along gleaming, glass-partitioned corridors until they got to the immigration desk, where he placed all of their passports in front of the black immigration officer. The immigration officer stamped the entire batch of passports and showed them through the little corridor on his right side.

"Welcome to America," he told them.

The group walked, single-file, behind other passengers, towards the baggage claim area. Once there, the Indian airline staffer called out each member of the group and handed them their passports. They identified their luggage and pulled them off the black conveyor belt. Adigun spotted and retrieved the suitcase given to him by Diokpa Obidike; the one containing foodstuff for their friend Okpanku. He still did not speak to any of the kids and deliberately avoided the nosey little girl who kept staring at Adigun and nodding her head.

Once more, in single file, they followed their guide into the arrival hall, appearing like an over-decorated bridal train. The line of bright-green-attired choir members surged through the automatic doors and broke formation, splintering into a rough constellation as they looked around for their handlers. People were waiting to pick up their guests, some with placards bearing the guests' names.

Adigun noticed a tall black man, carrying a placard that had 'Nigerian Choral' written on it.

"Yes! Here we are!" shouted Nosey Rosey.

The Indian crew member approached the man with the placard and had a short conversation with him, following which the man performed a roll call. The kids all responded to their names, shouting, "Present, Sir."

Adigun's name was called last, and he silently raised his hands. The man led them towards another set of automatic glass doors, above which the sign read, 'Shuttle Buses and Taxis'.

When the doors opened, the group was hit by a blast of cold air and, as they stepped out into the frigid night, their breath puffed out of their mouths and nostrils in little white clouds of mist.

"Look! We are smoking!" said Nosey Rosie.

A white bus waited under a concrete cantilever across the road and the kids filed after the tall man into the bus (Adigun got the lone seat in front beside the driver) and they set off, leaving the airport and merging with the highway. "Van Wyck," Adigun managed to catch on the road sign that flashed by. The bus raced along, while the choir kids had their faces glued to the bus windows, trying not to miss anything, their subdued chatter not quite masking their nervous excitement. Adigun simply watched as the bus turned off, following the sign that read, Queens Midtown tunnel, pondering the words on the road sign and wondering if there was a Queen's Uptown and Downtown. This far from the airport, they now passed through a city that seemed entirely covered in snow. Adigun stared, with his eyes wide, as he had never seen anything like this. The kids at the back were mesmerized too as they shouted to each other.

"Snow!"

"White snow!"

"This is snow," they shouted with their faces pressed flat against the glass of the windows.

The bus driver spoke over the PA system on the bus. "Welcome to America," he said, "My name is Bob, and we'll be arriving at Grand Central Station in exactly forty minutes." The bus finally entered the tunnel and the kids' babble rose a notch as they shouted over one another. The tunnel ride was long and serpentine, and the passengers quieted down as if the scenic deprivation compelled them to look inwards for a while. The bus finally exited the tunnel into a large, brilliant avenue, guarded on both sides by a parade of skyscrapers. Traffic lights were hung high above the street, and flowing through it was a river of yellow taxis.

"Your host pastor will be at Grand Central Station to meet with you."

The bus was noisy again, now that they had escaped the monotonous tunnel, and nobody paid that much attention to the driver's speech. "Thanks for riding with us and thanks for being such an attentive audience." The driver's voice dripped with sarcasm. The bus glided through the white-coated night, across a large bridge, and into a narrow street. An enormous sign, "Welcome to Grand Central Station," beckoned.

The choristers got off the bus, each carrying their bags, and walked through the marble arches, now following Bob. There was a sea of people in the massive hall, and the choristers clutched hands as they followed their guide. Bob stopped and checked his watch, then pulled out a folded sheet from his shirt pocket and studied it. He asked the group to wait where they were and stalked off towards the bank of pay phones. While the group waited in the middle of the colossal hall, Adigun felt a tap on his shoulder; Nosey Rosie on the warpath.

"I'm watching you. I'm watching every move you make," she sneered.

"Who gave you our uniform? I know impostors like you. I'm just waiting to see any policeman and I will raise the alarm on you."

Adigun ignored her.

"You did not bring a coat? How will you survive this cold in that dashiki?

"There is something funny about you, guy, really funny. You have not said a word to anybody since we left Nigeria. I have asked all our members, and no one knows you; nobody saw you come to choir practice. Who are you?"

Stoic silence from Adigun, who was suddenly preoccupied with what she had said about a coat. He noticed for the first time that she had on a woolly turtleneck sweater under her dashiki, and there was a bulky coat in the crook of her elbow.

"I have to call the authorities. I'm not comfortable, for real. I'm getting uncomfortable."

Her voice had begun to rise in pitch and volume and Adigun spun away from her and walked off, leaving his suitcase.

"Hey! Mr. Man! Where are you going?"

"Hey!!" she shouted louder.

"He's running away, oh!"

"He's running away!"

"*Gbomo Gbomo!*" Yoruba for kidnapper. "*Gbomo Gbomo!!*" She started shouting clapping and pulling the jacket of the priest and pointing in Adigun's direction as he fled.

"He left his suitcase," she wailed. "*Gbomo Gbomo!*"

Adigun walked into the crown towards the exit, looking over his shoulder and seeing the girl and others pointing at him. He picked up his pace, instinctively following the exit signs.

Shortly before Adigun walked off, a certain gentleman, by the name of Okpanku, had been asking after Adigun on the other side of the cluster of choristers. No one seemed to know him and Okpanku drifted toward Nosey Rosie when she began calling after the swiftly departing fugitive.

"I am looking for Adigun," Okpanku said to her.

"He walked that way." said the skinny little girl, pointing at the exit. Okpanku peered into the crowd in confusion as the girl's escalating cries attracted wide attention. When he heard, "He even left his suitcase," Okpanku attempted to snatch up Adigun's case, but he was thwarted by the steely grip of a policeman who had arrived to see what the fuss was about. He had barely a moment to sputter in protest before he was surrounded by a large group of cops and forced to the ground at gunpoint. They were the Drug Enforcement Agency; their dogs at the airport had sniffed out the ten kilograms of cocaine in Adigun's suitcase and they had trailed the group from the airport to determine its destination.

Bob and the priest were pulled aside for preliminary questioning, while Okpanku remained on the floor, with his hands handcuffed behind him. His face was flat on the concrete floor as spectators began to gather. A few policemen peeled off and ran towards the direction where Adigun left but he was gone.

The supervising officer immediately put out an All Points Bulletin on Adigun but described the *Aso Oke* dashiki as a green overcoat.

New York's finest swung into action, looking for an 'adult male black, wearing a green overcoat.'

Adigun was already in the cold streets, on the run.

When Adigun got to his ordeal on landing at JFK airport, Pookie raised his eyebrows and blurted, "Damn! This African kid is GANGSTER! I love this kid!" His sentiment was echoed amongst the enthralled audience.

"This sounds great!"

"Couldn't make *this* shit up!"

"I love this kid!"

Adigun concluded, "That is how I came to this land. I'm heading to California where the weather is just like in Africa. I also heard many of my fellow Nigerians live there."

Bobby Brown twitched his nose, pulled at his long mustache, looked at Pookie, and said, "I'm so grateful to God it wasn't another dead body on the premises."

Phoebe removed some more dirt from Adigun's hair and Pookie and Bobby looked at each other.

"Okay Phoebe, you can leave now."

"Thanks for the food, please put the bill on my tab," Bobby told her.

"Will he be having some dessert?" Phoebe asked. "No, the boy is fine; you can leave now, Phoebe." Bobby's voice had turned steely, and Phoebe packed up and left without another word.

"Pookie, please get this African boy out of my office and give him some money and lead him back to Union Station so he can be on his way to California to meet his fellow Africans." They all burst out laughing.

"Pookie?"

"Yes, Bobby B."

"Did the old Puerto Rican lady come back?"

"No, Bobby B."

"She didn't?"

"She said she found another job in Jersey and had to move."

"So, we don't have a cleaner anymore?"

"Yes… I mean, no, Bobby B, we don't have a cleaner, no more."

"So, give Africa her job. The gym is filthy. We need someone to keep it clean. Give Kunta the job. Maybe he can work his way to California. No free lunch in America and all that."

"But he has no papers to work."

"Forget the papers! Did we have papers when we got off the boat?

"We came on a boat, Kunta came on a gaddem plane.

"Give the boy a damn job and let his American dream begin!

"Call Terrence Lily at the State Coroner's office. Ask him to look for an identity for Africa; the last thing we need is immigration on our ass. We need to keep everything legit here, you feel me?"

"I hear you loud and clear, sir."

Pookie took Adigun into the main exercise area and gave him a thorough orientation on how to clean the gym. It was nice and warm thanks to the white radiator, the exercise machines arrayed in the small room at the side, and a professional-standard boxing ring in the middle of the main hall. Around the boxing ring were several punching bags hanging from thick chains and the grey walls were adorned with pictures of boxing champions. The street-facing portion of the gym was a curtain wall of sound-proof, one-way glass.

"Come with me, Africa," Pookie said, leading Adigun toward the changing rooms.

"Sir, my name is not 'Africa'; my name is Adigun Komaiya, of Jobore village, the land with a thousand rivers and sixteen masquerades. The…"

'Shut up, dude! One hour ago, you didn't know *who* you were. We done fed you and brought you back to life and you complain about what we call you?

"Sheeyit, you look like one of the migrant farmworkers at the Ocheebokee labor camp; ashy and dusty!" Pookie chuckled.

"Sixteen masquerades, my ass! Seriously, Africa?"

"This will be your bed – it's very comfortable. Nice and toasty in here. The controls to the radiator broke, so it's full-on or full-off, if you know what I mean. Gets real hot in here in the summer, though – fucking sauna!"

Adigun was too tired to give any attention to Pookie's rambling. He collapsed on the brown sofa and went straight to sleep.

The next morning, Pookie brought over an assortment of old clothes and a red winter jacket. Adigun tried on the 'American' clothes with a self-conscious smile on his face. He left his green Aso Oke dashiki hanging from the window.

"You may want to get rid of this green junk hanging here, now you have cool gear. That's a classic South Pole jacket – I'm coming back for that one."

"Thank you so much, sir, I'm very grateful."

"Damn! Stop calling me 'sir'."

"Okay, sir."

"I said stop flippin' calling me 'sir'! Like I'm a massa from the slavery days."

*Adigun looked at Pookie, tall and broad, rough and regal at the same time, his narrow face framed by the mass of dreadlocks he wore long.

"You… were a slave?"

"I am still a slave, dude. We all slaves. Enslaved to the American dollar!

"…Oh, sugar! I forgot to bring you a towel. Here, use this; It belonged to one of the customers, but he ain't never coming back for it, so…"

Pookie grabbed a pink towel off one of the wall hooks and tossed it to Adigun. "Settle in, brother. Looks like you're home."

Book-3

The Ropes

Alla andinaay gujjo de bangi munaafiki

(God didn't tell the thief he was marrying a gossip – Fulani proverb)

1

Adigun was holding the mop stick, the tool of his new trade, and had on his new South-Pole jacket, and the seemingly oversized denim trousers. He pulled the trousers to his belly and tucked in the woolly green plaid shirt he had also received from Pookie.

"Oh no, Africa, you can't dress like this."

Pookie grabbed the shirt and pulled it out of the baggy denim trousers.

He also pulled down the denim to hang low on Adigun's skinny hips.

"You got to sag this one, man! These are Dickies – you got to sag 'em."

Adigun walked out of the changing room, with his oversized clothing, holding his bucket and mop. He was bare-footed but unconcerned as he got to work and got lost in it. He cleaned the gym like his life depended on it – in his mind, it did – and this became his routine for the next several weeks.

One morning, as he cleaned the ladies' toilet next to Bobby's office, Adigun heard the raised voice of Bobby

Brown, yelling into the phone. He paused the swishing motion of his mop when he heard his name. "Where is that African boy, Diggun? Did I pronounce his name right? Get him."

Adigun walked out of the ladies' toilet almost strutting in his baggy outfit. In his time at the gym, he'd rarely said more than 'hello' to Bobby and had never been to his office except to clean it.

"Pookie, you fucking crazy, man! You hooked the boy up with some street duds; got him looking like a street dealer or sumthin'. You trying to take away his identity?"

Adigun was already sweating from the stifling heat and his warm clothes.

"Africa! Ebolebolooooolebooo!" Bobby made an approximation of what he considered 'jungle talk', flapping his hand over his mouth as he ululated. "Hope you slept well. You've been doing a good job taking care of the gym."

Adigun nodded shyly.

"Pookie, this boy can't keep sleeping here. It's . . . what's the word… inhumane!

"Call me Alagba. I need to tell him one of his homeboys just landed from Africa and I want him to take him in. The boy can be dropped off in the morning by his wife; she works not too far from The Capitol. I'm sure she'll be happy to have him; someone else to eat all that spicy food she's always cooking. No one else can eat it, that's for sure!"

Pookie got on the phone immediately and Bobby fell silent, waiting.

"Hey, buddy.

"No, I dropped that off myself.

"Yes, got the money right here.

"Yes, I made sure he paid!

"Yo, the boss needs to speak with you; that's why I called." Pookie handed over the phone to Bobby Brown.

"Hey, amigo, we rescued one of your peoples from freezing to death in my garage a few months back and I gave him a job at the gym." Bobby paused for a full minute, his eyes occasionally slitting as Alagba spoke on the other end of the line.

"Cool your jets, my friend. I didn't get where I am today by rushing into things without checking shit out first. And my business is *my* business until I make it *your* business, comprende'?" Bobby leaned back and nodded as he listened to Alagba's response, satisfied.

"He's been sleeping here in the gym.

"You know how it can get here, plus, I ain't trying to draw no attention from social services folks – I can't have him sleep here any longer! Not safe at all.

"He's from Nigeria. I need him to stay with you until we can figure out a permanent place for him. Meanwhile, I am working out some paper for the kid . . . some I.D.

"I reckon he should be done cleaning around the same time Dee is leaving work.

"She can pick him up, right?

"Cool.

"Perfect."

Adigun leaned on the high grey file cabinet as his accommodation was being arranged. He stood facing the window and saw how high the snow had piled up. Last night's storm, no doubt.

"Africa, I just got you an African home!" Bobby declared cheerfully.

"What religion are you?"

"Christian, Sir."

"Perfect; they practically live in church . . . matter of fact, they own the church!" Bobby chuckled, "So, you can join the whole white-gown-wearing African gang."

"Pookie you remember when he invited us to the church?"

"Bobby, that's not a Church; it's a set-up!"

"They must have taken fifteen offerings."

"In one service – jeez!"

"I knew we were had the moment we walked in. But guess what; I made him pay me back every dime I dropped into that offering basket."

"Damn!! They kept calling the offering until I raised my hands – all my cash was gone."

"Yes, I remember."

"And they offered to drive us to the freaking ATM!"

"Alagba won't ever change! Who invites their business partner to a church to rob them?"

Pookie was in hysterics, holding the table with one hand and his midriff with the other while he laughed.

"I got all my money back Pookie," Bobby mused, "Every dollar put in that basket.

"Africa! You will be going to stay with a Nigerian brother. He has a lovely home in the suburbs of Maryland. His wife, Dorothy will pick you up in front of the office."

"Thank you, sir."

Later that day, Dorothy stopped over at the gym to pick Adigun up. When Adigun climbed into the car and gave his tentative greeting, she held her palm up to his face, placed a finger to her lips in a shushing gesture, and pointed at the cassette player in the console. She was listening to a tutorial in French, and they did not speak until it was over.

"Where in Nigeria are you from, my son?"

"I'm from Jobore, ma."

"Where is Jobore?"

"In the south-west of Nigeria, ma. Not far from Kiyesi."

"Oh, yes! So, you are Yoruba?"

"Yes, ma. But my mother is Igbo, from Arochukwu."

"How interesting" Dorothy had been married to Alagba for over twenty years but they did not have any children. She was from the Eastern part of Nigeria, Awo Nma Nma to be precise. "I went to school there – St. Margaret Model School for Girls. *Igbo oyin Igbo*?"

"*Eee*," Adigun answered her question about whether he could speak the Igbo language.

They continued their conversation in Igbo for a while, endearing Adigun to Dorothy. "It is so nice that you can speak the language; your mum has done so well. Does your father speak Igbo?"

"No, ma."

"That is so great that you are Igbo. Do you remember which school your mum went to in the east?"

"I don't know, ma."

"If she schooled in Arochukwu, then it must be Our Lady's or St. Margaret. I used to play netball... we did a lot of sports with all the girls' schools in and around Arochukwu.

"What's your mum's maiden name?"

"Kanu, ma."

"Hmmm, Kanu," Dorothy raised her chin slightly, frowning and tapping her index finger against her lips, "I know the Kanu family. Did your mother have a brother or cousin called Callixtus?"

"No, ma." Adigun was becoming uncomfortable with the discussion about Nigeria and his family. The last thing he wanted was for this lady to turn out to be a friend or relative of his... someone who would end up contacting his parents. His father had sold him out to the Fulanis, he was a fugitive from the law, and he planned never to the land of his parents again.

Dorothy seemed to sense his misgivings and she changed her line of inquiry.

"How do you see yourself – an Igbo boy or Yoruba?"

"I'm a Nigerian, ma. A Nigerian. I speak some Hausa and even Fulfulbe, the Fulani dialect."

"Wow! How did you learn this?"

"Can we not speak about that, ma?" Adigun had an unpleasant flashback of the incident in his family home with the Fulanis.

"Oh, so sorry to be intrusive. To me, you are an authentic Aro boy, not Yoruba."

Adigun looked at her with his misty eyes. "Nigerian, ma."

They drove along the snowy freeway and Adigun kept his eyes glued to the window. It was like a dream that he made it safely into America, but he had been confined to the gym all this time. It was good to be out, under the sky, really seeing the city. Dorothy's phone rang.

"I'm almost home, Dim'.

"Be patient, now. There is some *banga* in the freezer if you cannot wait.

"*Biko*, I'm almost home, *iwuatago*?"

They drove another thirty minutes until they reached a farming community. There were corn plantations on both sides of the narrow road.

Adigun figured they had reached their destination when Dorothy took a sharp turn off the quiet country road and onto a private driveway. He was amazed to see how large their home was, and he gaped as he and Dorothy exited the vehicle. They walked in through the large front door, Adigun in front.

"We are home," Dorothy called.

A muffled voice responded from somewhere in the upper part of the house, but they couldn't quite make out the words. The entire foyer was white, from the granite floor to the pristine walls and blinding, plush carpet.

The curtains and furniture were also white, but there were subtle highlights of red and gold. Adigun looked up and around him.

"Don't mind my husband; he just loves white. Please take off your shoes – we don't wear shoes in the house."

Adigun slipped off the battered sneakers he had obtained from Pookie before leaving the gym.

"What would you drink before I show you to your room?"

"Water, ma."

"Call me Aunty D. Sparkling or still?" Dorothy had already started moving off in the direction, Adigun presumed, of the kitchen.

Adigun didn't answer; he couldn't tell the difference. He had only known water to be water all his life.

Dorothy called from the kitchen, from somewhere seemingly far away, to the left side of the colossal mansion.

"Is sparkling okay?" Her voice drew closer.

"Yes, ma."

Dorothy walked in with a glass and a big bottle of Sparkling water. The glass had a lemon in it. Adigun opened the bottle and was surprised at the hiss of escaping air, wondering if she had accidentally brought him a fizzy soft drink, or 'mineral' as it was called back home. He was even more surprised to find that, while it was indeed fizzy, it was just water – but made glorious with the carbonation and that hint of lemon. He downed the first glass, and then another, enjoying the sensation as the gas burned down his throat.

Alagba came down the white marble stairs.

"Halleluyah ooooh," he bellowed.

Adigun stood up and immediately went face-down on the floor, fully prone and arms stretched out in front of him, as was customary when greeting an elder in the Yoruba culture style.

"Ah, Halleluyah! *Omoluabi, dide. Dide, omoluabi, dide!*" Alagba expansively encouraged Adigun to rise in their native tongue. He was dressed in a white flowing gown, with sleeves so long that his arms and hands were not visible.

"*Omo ibo ni ire?*"

"*Jobore ni, sir.*"

"*Jobore? Hmmmmm, Jobore Adubi. Omo Jobore Adubi onile ire! Jobore alagemo merindinlogun.*"

He continued to eulogize Jobore, Adigun's village.

"Welcome to my home and your home from today on.

"Baby D!" he called Dorothy. "Come and let us pray!"

Dorothy opened the kitchen door onto the expanse of soft, bouncy white carpet and the foyer and living area were immediately awash with the aroma of fried plantain. "*E ku ile*," she said, in poor Yoruba. She reached out to her husband and knelt in front of him. "How was your day, dear?"

"Let us pray now; we will discuss that later."

"Please don't be long. I have plantain frying."

"I've told you, my dear; prayer is never too long."

"Thanks for bringing… errmmm, what is your name again?" Alagba turned toward Adigun.

"Adigun, Sir."

"Yes, Adigun," Alagba returned his gaze to his wife, "Thanks for bringing Adigun home."

The prayer was short indeed. Dorothy raced to the kitchen as soon as it ended, and so began Adigun's stay at Alagba's house.

2

Large as Alagba's home was, Adigun had gotten himself acquainted with it by his third day there. It had jacuzzi baths and a sauna on the third level, with an indoor pool on the second level of the house. There was also a larger swimming pool outside right next to the tennis court.

The house was like a holiday resort. It confused Adigun somewhat because this was the first domicile he was settling into anew since he made his first trip to secondary school in Tuke. Some perverse auditor in his mind kept laying the two scenarios and experiences side-by-side, as if to compare them or, more likely, simply to come to terms with the contrast. Adigun couldn't help comparing his ride to Alagba's home with Dorothy and the ride he had taken with his father all those years ago.

Adigun had sat in the car quietly. His father was quiet as well, looking like an executioner leading his prisoner to the gallows. The journey to Tuke was a long one, starting at about 5 a.m. Several of the community's earlier risers were out to bid Adigun farewell as he and his father set off. Five hours later, the silence in the old black Volkswagen beetle was thick. To the left and right of the lonely road were miles of deep, green forest.

At this point, Adigun was tired and uncomfortable. He'd had to sit for hours on one side of his skinny butt as some sharp metal springs stuck out of the opposite side of the front passenger seat. The heat produced by the engine of the old Volkswagen was excruciating. The vent oozed out hot air and the yellow doll hanging from the mirror was spun around like a ballerina.

The exhaust of 'The Helicopter' changed its sound, the rear-engine vehicle mimicking a giant, epileptic cricket. Adigun's father, stoic as ever, kept driving.

Adigun began to console himself; to see the good side of leaving home. No more daily one-hundred-meter dashes when Dodo came home; no more lonely days at the harbor to study for an exam; no more unending insults from Dodo and derision from neighbors that thought he would never amount to anything; no more terror at the thought of spending the rest of his life in Jobore, doing nothing. It was a great relief to leave the village of his youth.

Finally, they took a bend that was so quick and sharp that it made Dodo lean far enough to the right to bump shoulders with the sleeping Adigun, who woke up to see the signboard of Government College Tuke Ajose. He leaped in excitement. Dodo, with a sigh of relief, navigated the loud smoky car through the sudden bend. Embossed in concrete, in a white arc above a black gate, was the name of the school and, in red paint, "Labour and Serve with Probity".

This last dampened Adigun's excitement, making entry into the new school seem, for a moment, like admission into a correctional facility. "Labour and Serve with Probity". Adigun's usually uncurious mind began to process the possible meaning of this motto, then all thought was halted and submerged by a sudden realization: this was the beginning of his last five years as a free man! He remembered his father had traded him and he would be adopted into slavery by the Fulanis after he finished school. Five years. This brought instant sadness to Adigun's soul.

He fell into one of the trances he had been experiencing lately. He saw the same cow each time he slept and, each time, he ran. A loud explosion from the exhaust woke Adigun. He was shaking. The 1962 Volkswagen Beetle stopped at the gate and the wrinkled, ancient gate-man ambled over. His trousers were tucked into his long black socks, and he wore a pair of brown rubber sandals with thick black soles made from old tires. He had his brown 'buba' tucked into his brown pants, over which we wore a thick woolen ski sweater. Under a black wool beanie hat, his gnarled face drooped. In his mouth was a huge chewing stick. As he leaned into the car's driver-side window, frowning as though he was trying to identify the occupants, they were struck by a strong blast of Eucalyptus Tiger Balm, mixed with the deep stench of stale sweat. He spoke to Dodo in Ijebu, a common dialect spoken very widely in that part of the country. Dodo showed him the admission letter and he pointed Dodo to the hostel area.

There was a long red-earth stretch of untarred road, with deep gullies created by erosion from the rains. Under the sound of the loud, busted exhaust were piercing squeaks from the wheel, and occasional clangs when the chassis made grudging contact with the rocky road. On the left was a large structure of unplastered block-work, surrounded by towering stalks of grass. A small path led from it to a raised concrete water reservoir, about four feet high surrounded by dark green algae and filled with filthy green water. Beside it was a squat grey building with perforated walls. Emerging from the top of this structure, like a giant finger admonishing everyone to be silent, was a charred-black exhaust pipe. The building housed the giant Perkins generator that was visible from the exterior. The green water in the reservoir was what was left of the last rains, and there were shirtless kids, in brown khaki shorts, washing their clothes in silver buckets. They were loosely clustered around a free-standing tap. Attached to the faucet of the rusted tap was a little boy, sucking hard at it for a few seconds and then pausing to catch a breath. It looked like some demented sort of reverse mouth-to-mouth resuscitation. On about the third or fourth pause, the faucet would spit out a short gush; perhaps enough to fill a standard teacup. This meager bounty was collected in the bucket hung over the back of the tap's valve. The boy continued sucking pausing with dogged resolve, while Adigun gaped from the car, wondering when that bucket would ever be filled. Dodo looked at the boy and turned back towards Adigun, shaking his head slightly. He whispered, "Welcome to reality.

This will be your home for the next five years. There will be no light and there is no potable water here."

He paused and, with his teeth mashed together by his clenched jaws, sucked in air. "Mtscheeeew!" Dodo's eyes were wide. "This is where leaders are created."

'Well,' Adigun snapped back to the present, taking in the splendor of Alagba's home and thinking, 'I can certainly see how leaders could be made *here*.' Clearly, this palace was owned by a leader and Adigun felt sure it would be the foundation of a better future for him, or, at the very least, a better present than he could remember lately.

3

Alagba had told Adigun he owned a large pharmaceuticals distribution company, but he spent more time in his church, about forty minutes' drive from the house. Adigun had to leave home early with Dorothy to beat the morning traffic and he was picked up each evening from the gym. Adigun was well-treated in Alagba's household, and he was doing well at his cleaning job at the gym. He got paid in cash and had converted an old biscuit tin into a safe under his bed. The little box was reaching its capacity.

Adigun enjoyed the steady rhythm of his new life, including the church services, where he was able to display his proficiency with the conga drums.

He soon became a star attraction at the church where, though the congregation had several diverse West African members, Nigerians were the more highly represented nationality. While Adigun enjoyed the adulation, he was careful to avoid any undue intimacy or closeness with anyone. The church reminded him of Nigeria, a place he was desperate to erase from his memories. The church was a staunch, Pentecostal, 'white-garment', music-loving church. They spared no expense when it came to their music and paid the best session instrumentalists they could engage. They sang more in Yoruba than in English, but Adigun liked it just fine. He blended right in.

One morning, Adigun – fed and ready for work – was walking out to join Dorothy in the car when Alagba came down the stairs to tell him he would be going out with him instead. He ended up sitting around all day until evening came and, with it, some Nigerian guests. Dorothy had not returned from work.

The visitors, who had arrived in the same vehicle, were in the large living room. Their discussion went on for about an hour, after which Alagba called Adigun from his room. He met the party in the living room, but no introduction was made.

Adigun was asked to ride with three gentlemen, two of whom he knew from church. They drove to the airport in Baltimore and picked up a Senegalese man who had just come in from abroad, as Adigun gleaned from their conversation.

They drove a few miles from the airport to a motel off the freeway, where the unfolding events would shake the foundations of Adigun's idyllic new life – and his perception of Alagba – forever.

Adigun returned to the house in utter fear. He could not meet Alagba's eyes, and he could not sleep that night. He wondered if Bobby Brown knew about this side of his much-praised associate. The Senegalese visitor was a drug mule from somewhere in Africa. Adigun remembered the horrible scene and felt his gorge rise. Eyeing the toilet bowl through the bathroom door, he made a desperate attempt to blot out the slow-motion replay of the motel room events but failed. He remembered the Senegalese man squatting, with his genitals loosely cupped in one hand, and defecating on a white towel; in front of them! How one of the men he had ridden with to the airport pulled out black balls from the feces and rinsed each ball in the bathroom sink, pointedly leaving the door open. The smell was still fresh in Adigun's mind hours after. He bolted to the bathroom and vomited, retching mightily as he recalled the balls being rinsed off and then deposited in a nondescript backpack.

After that, everything had happened fast. As they had walked out of the hotel there was a crowd gathered around the poorly lit foyer. They gawked as some sort of major police operation was being conducted. The motel walls seemed to dance as the blue and red lights pulsed from the fleet of police cars outside. Adigun saw a group of people being led away by cops in handcuffs. As soon as his own group walked out of their room, Adigun was handed the bag with the black balls. He strode past the cops and the drama, through the gathered spectators, to the waiting vehicle. He got in and watched his cohorts following in his steps, noting the loose grouping they had assumed; like they were molecules of a substance that was changing from liquid to gas. They all got in without incident and he almost heard the men breathe out a collective sigh.

"Ha! Those cops rolled up without sirens, men – I didn't hear a sound!"

"For real! Maybe it was a sting operation. That crew is fucked!"

The men seemed delighted with Adigun for some reason he could not quite fathom; he didn't understand why he had been handed the bag, nor why the driver kept praising him and saying, "You are a star boy!! You are a savior!!!"

They returned to Alagba's mansion and, just as he was getting out of the car, the driver twisted around in his seat and snagged Adigun's red sweater. All Adigun could see in his eyes was amused malice. "You just completed your first drug deal. Congratulations."

Realization and horror had dawned on Adigun simultaneously. A drug deal! That was what he had just participated in.

Now, in his bed, Adigun grabbed the pillow and curled into the fetal position. The understanding of how close he had come to being arrested, again, weighed on him. He had no desire to spend one more minute in Alagba's house and decided he would go back to the gym and live there in the cloakroom. His stomach was sore, and he was tired and afraid. He knew the morning was close as the country birds were beginning to sing. he knew he had a few hours to sleep before heading to his job at the gym. He was determined he wasn't coming back. Then he heard footsteps approaching his room and his door opened. It was Alagba. "We will be leaving early this morning. Go and take your shower and get ready." Adigun drifted back into a deep sleep. They usually prayed very early in the morning and there was a bell from Alagba's room that signaled the prayer time.

Adigun waited for the usual call for prayer, but it never came. He had just finished his prayers when he heard Alagba call for him. He had not taken his shower, but he sprang up, grabbed his jacket, and walked down the stairs. He was terrified and prayed he would not have to do anything like the night before. Adigun walked through the large hallway, out the main door and hopped into the quietly humming truck, where Alagba was already seated.

"How was last night?"

"Fine."

Adigun was fatigued and mute. They drove for about forty minutes and parked in front of a large red brick house.

"Wait here for me, Adigun." Alagba slid out of the tan leather seat and walked into the house. Adigun fell asleep, as soon as Alagba was out of sight, only to be jerked awake shortly after by the muffled thuds of heavy car doors.

He looked to his left and saw Alagba at the front of the brick house receiving two men. Adigun's heart thumped fast, and the blood roared in his ears – they were the men from the night before. The Senegalese, Chloe, joined them at the entrance. They seemed to have arrived in two cars. Alagba spread his hands and his big round belly expanded the woolen red turtleneck sweater under the sleeveless black jacket.

"Hey, what's up? How are you? All in order, I guess?

"Why don't you park over here? Remember it's Thursday; you can't park on that side of the road."

"No, I can't park here. I have to go to Baltimore when we are through; another shipment arrives today from *Naija*... ladies."

"Really?"

"I have to be there. I will ride with you people and Segun will drive my car after us." The man walked to Adigun in the car, but the window was up and Adigun had no clue how to bring it down. The man opened the door.

"Sorry I didn't introduce myself yesterday," he said, "my name is Ojo. You can call me Bros Ojo. Job well done yesterday." With that, he walked back to Alagba and they continued their conversation, Alagba gesturing twice towards

Bros Ojo's car – a burgundy Bentley Arnage with vanity plates. '0J0 YWG3', the plates declared. The Bentley was facing the opposite direction to Alagba's black Range Rover, and Adigun recognized it as the car they had used the night before, when Chloe, the Senegalese, was picked up. The horrors of the night before washed over Adigun, and he shivered. He could not wait to get back to his cleaning job and away from this enterprise. He was aghast at the source of Alagba's wealth and wondered again how much Bobby Brown knew about him.

Bros Ojo went back into his car and leaned over to have a brief chat with his driver, Segun. The twin exhaust pipes produced wisps of fine white smoke as the car idled. When he concluded his instructions to Segun, Bros Ojo walked towards the Range Rover where Alagba already had the engine running. Bros Ojo got in the front passenger side and immediately began adjusting the seat. Chloe was also in the car and sat beside Adigun in the back.

From the back seat, Adigun offered a subdued greeting to Bros Ojo, observing for the first time the man's distinctive Yoruba tribal marks, which distinguished him as being from Nigeria's south-western city of Ibadan. Adigun remembered him driving the night before. Alagba seemed to have forgotten about Adigun and jerked his head up to peer into the rear-view mirror when he heard his voice. "You know what," Alagba turned to Bros Ojo, "let's ride in your car." He tapped on his car horn, waving Segun over from the Bentley as he exited the Range Rover. Bros Ojo also got out of the Range Rover but, before walking over to his car, he went to Adigun's window again.

"Adigun *baba*!!"

"*Okunrin ogun*!!

"*Adigun mi, Adigun mi, Adigun mi o,*" he sang in a style similar to that of Islamic clerics during a prayer call.

"*Twale, baba,*" shouted Bros Ojo, sticking both hands through to the vehicle's interior as he praised Adigun. Then he straightened up and walked off with Alagba towards his Bentley. Segun had already got in behind the wheel of the Range Rover and was adjusting the mirror and seats. Adigun mumbled in greeting, then fell silent. Segun waited for the Bentley to pull out before falling in behind it.

As Bros Ojo drove, Alagba pressed a button and smiled at the muted electric hum as his seat sank lower. While fiddling to adjust his headrest, he declared, "I love this car! Maybe you should ask James to drop one for me. I want this same one, but in white."

"Your boy, Adigun is sharp! I love him! He acted very sharp yesterday.

"They didn't tell you?

"Ol' boy, come and see the police presence! And your boy just carried the matter right through the nostrils of the police! Fearless!

"I can't believe nobody told you – there was a drug bust in the motel we used."

"Which Motel did you use?"

"It was the Motel 25. We wanted to avoid that one by 26th street we used to use; *eye don dey enter am.* Adigun drove with me to the airport as you instructed. He sat in the car while I went into the arrival hall. The Nigeria Airways flight came early and the cargo came in swiftly.

"As I saw Chloe pass through the silver barrier, I knew there was no *yawa*.

"We immediately went to the hotel. *As Chloe bend down sugar the abunna for towel, na him di smell hammer Adigun; e vomit quick.*"

"*E no know say na inside sugar money dey,*" Alagba smirked.

"All of a sudden *as we dey come down the stairs, na him we see police light dey flash, dog dey bark. I think say alarm don blow.*"

"*Tell me! Di boy no tell me anything, oh!*"

"*Na hard boy! Chai! I look everybody, carry di load, give am to Adigun.*"

"Why did you do that?"

"*You no say him face no strong like our own. Dem, just bust some people. DEA wey dey for the lobby, dem reach two thousand!*"

"No way!!" Alagba exclaimed.

"*Police siren dey blow; everybody run commot for the hotel; sniffer dogs full ground! Adigun pass all of dem, carry matter enter motto, no shaking. Na there I know say di boy get liver.*"

"E be like say na him go accompany Chloe enter bus go deliver di matter to Barry. "

"I too like the boy. Where you find am?"

"Oh boy, you remember that Akata man, Bobby Brown? Wey I tell you say we start together for Columbia with our Oga Edguardo?"

"Wey dey that gym?"

"Yes, you don remember now."

"Him just come from Nigeria, na him Bobby say make I help am, take am for my house. E don reach two months now wey e don dey stay with me." Alagba looked at Bros Ojo. *"De tin complete? You count am well-well?"*

"All correct, sir, all correct. I even spoke to Barry this morning; they are already in Chicago waiting for us."

Alagba took a deep breath. "Barry? I thought we decided not to use Barry again."

"But, Alagba, Barry has the best price"

"Perhaps, but he cheats in the counting of the money."

"You don't worry; I already replaced the broken counting machine. It will be arriving in Chicago with us."

Bros Ojo made expansive hand gestures as he spoke, his cuffs often pulling back to reveal his huge gold watch and diamond bracelet. Combined with the diamond-crusted gold rope chain sitting on his hairy chest, they produced a dazzling effect.

"*When be di next flight from Lagos?*" Alagba settled back into pidgin English.

"Sunday."

Segun kept pace behind the Bentley. In the back, Chloe fussed with his clothing, while Adigun sat still and gazed intently at the headrest in front of him. The soft, customized red leather seats of the luxury vehicle emitted a blessed heat as Segun had left his window open. The cold air blew in as he lit a cigarette. Chloe had on a white crushed linen shirt, with buttons made of glittering stones. On the left breast pocket, its logo bore an inscription that boasted, 'Billionaire'. Chloe adjusted his wrinkled sleeves, which were rolled up to the elbow, his slender left wrist encircled by a diamond-encrusted, gold Rolex Oyster Perpetual. Around his waist was a black snakeskin belt with a huge golden Medusa head Versace belt buckle that was almost certainly unnecessary to hold up his tight orange sherbet pants. When he had got into the back seat beside Adigun, he preened, delighting in his finery. All Adigun could see was the image of him cupping his dangling balls and shitting on the floor; no amount of jewelry nor designer ensemble could wipe that image from his mind.

Bros Ojo's Bentley cruised along the freeway, using the high-occupancy vehicle lane. The car was silent for a while as Alagba got into one of his prayer trances. Then

Bros Ojo started again in pidgin. *"Ehen, the boy! Na correct boy. E no too know this awa game, but we go train am!"*

"Na so. Him go join dem Barry for Chicago. I want make e be our eye there for Chicago."

The driving conditions had deteriorated as the snow came down, and the convoy dropped speed. "Hey, the bus leaves at nine a.m. We need to drive faster!" Alagba protested as Bros Ojo slowed the car down. Bros Ojo looked at his Rolex and stamped his foot down on the accelerator, throwing Alagba's head back against the headrest. The heavy sedan swayed slightly, for the briefest of moments, then settled in a steady line again. The sleet came down harder visibility through the snow-caked windscreen dropped to just several feet beyond the Bentley's probing headlights.

"We still have to stop at the church for prayers."

"Church?" Bros Ojo shook his head in disbelief, his tribal marks thrown into sharp relief as they caught the light. "Please let's move; the traffic starts to build up at eight."

"But it's a holiday; there will be no traffic."

"Did you book the hotels?"

"Yes, I did all that last night."

"I sent you a message with our new guy's details."

"Yes, I booked him in the same hotel."

Bros Ojo sped up and the Range Rover matched pace with the Bentley, keeping three car lengths behind it. Segun was a more-than-competent driver and the gap between the two cars hardly ever varied. The stereo in the Range Rover played Senegalese music, and Chloe bobbed his head in delight. Adigun pondered how a man could be so wretched, so full of himself, and so happy at the same time. After about half an hour, they exited the freeway and came to a stop in front of a warehouse at a very quiet business park.

Four doors thumped as all but Segun exited the two cars, with Alagba carrying the black roll-along bag from the night before. He pressed a code into the digital access panel and opened the large entrance door. Alagba walked into the warehouse and immediately made the sign of the cross, then bowed. Chloe followed and did the same. Bros Ojo followed suit. Adigun walked behind Bros Ojo towards what appeared to be an altar. Approaching the altar Ojo immediately went into a spiritual frenzy, making duck-like quacks and jerking back and forth with his shoulders elevated and his neck stretched out.

Alagba disappeared through a doorway and, moments later, the lights came on and the fans picked up speed. The altar stood on a stage of deep green carpet and was draped with pink silk, on top of which sat baskets of fruit. Overlooking the stage was a massive painting of Jesus, with his right hand up, the first two fingers pointed together upwards. Flanking the altar (and facing the congregation area) were elaborate, throne-like wooden chairs and, at the front were six microphone stands. Off to the left and towards the rear of the stage were a drum set and two keyboards. At the far left was a Beringher sound mixer with a mass of writhing black cables dangling to the white floor. The rest of the church glowed with highlights of yellow. It had plenty of half-burned candles all over. The congregation area was arranged with white, monobloc plastic chairs, on a blinding white tile floor, making the stage area look like a lush, jungle island in a frozen white sea.

Adigun, with barely any thought at all, went behind the two conga drums and began rolling his fingers on them, delivering an entrancing percussive rhythm. Alagba turned and shouted, "Halleluiah! Ojo did you hear what Adigun played last Sunday during Thanksgiving? Oh, the boy can play!" Adigun continued jamming on the Conga drums, bopping his head to the rhythm, eyes closed and jaws clenched. Alagba went into the room behind the altar and emerged shortly after in a white flowing gown, barefooted. He had a blue sash tied around his waist, with three crosses embroidered on both ends. He fired up the incense basket and, in two minutes, the entire warehouse was engulfed in the strong-smelling smoke of the myrrh. Alagba checked his watch, then shouted in Yoruba, "*E je ki a gbadura!*" Let us pray.

Bros Ojo joined Alagba in a raucous prayer session. Alagba held the black bag containing the narcotics up high during the prayer, facing the altar. Chloe hung back in the congregation area, looking upon the unfolding scene with a bemused expression, also stealing glances at his watch. The prayer session lasted about twenty minutes, during which Alagba sprinkled some lavender-scented water around. The water was cold as it touched Adigun's skin. Alagba looked at his watch again and raced into the back room. Seconds later, the fans stopped, and the lights went out. Alagba returned to the main hall, and they all filed back into the cars still running outside. They quickly climbed into the cars and drove off.

In a few minutes, they re-joined the freeway, then exited once more after a road sign with the Greyhound symbol pointed them to the right with its stern arrow. The convoy pulled into a Wells Fargo car park and Alagba got out to use the cash machine. He returned to the Bentley in short order, with the grim pronouncement, "Wow! There was no cash in the machine."

"I hope we can pay '*Ike*'." Yoruba slang for credit card.

"*Haba!* We can't do that; nothing should be traced to us."

"I have some cash," said Ojo, pulling away.

The black Range Rover rolled behind the Bentley through the streets of South-East Washington DC. They drove through shadowy 123rd Street straight into the car park of the Greyhound bus station. Bros Ojo lowered the volume on the reggae music he was playing before the cars were parked, and the crew filed out of the cars into the greyhound hall. It was like a market; an array of people with different designs of rucksacks and other assorted items of luggage, a lot of them left on the floor in a roughly circular pattern. The smell of hotdogs and burnt popcorn wafted through the air.

"So, when is the bus arriving?" Bros Ojo turned to Alagba with suppressed irritation, "We really should have done the night bus. The night bus goes straight to Chicago, non-stop. This one has to stop in Cleveland!"

"Come on, it's only a two-hour stop – two hours. Don't worry, they look good; nobody would suspect a thing."

Alagba was still dressed in his white prayer garment and was still barefoot. He stood like a mafia don with his wide belly and his blue sash almost touching the floor. Bros Ojo and Chloe negotiated at the counter and Adigun followed them.

"Hey, you," Chloe called to Adigun, "bring your ID." Adigun began to respond that he didn't have any ID when Alagba gently pushed him aside and spoke to Chloe. "Leave the boy; his ID is with me," Alagba said lifting his robe and extracting Adigun's passport from one of his pockets. Adigun hadn't even thought about his passport and realized with mild surprise that Bobby Brown must have given it to Alagba when he'd started living with him.

The black roll-along was checked in, in Adigun's name and the attendant gave Bros Ojo two tickets. Adigun's heart skipped a beat as it dawned on him that he would be travelling to Chicago, with the bag – the bag with the smelly drugs – and it was checked in his name! Bros Ojo came close to Adigun and grabbed him around his shoulders. *"Adigun mi, Adigun mi o,"* he sang again in the Islamic Fuji style – My Adigun, my Adigun, o. A playful man, he had sung the same song on the night they went to the airport to pick up Chloe. Chloe was rubbing his palms together and blowing hot air into them. It looked like he was travelling too, and Adigun sensed the nervousness in his demeanor.

Alagba picked up the bag and handed it to Adigun, who trembled.

"You will catch the nine-a.m. bus," he instructed, then handed a piece of paper to Chloe, and another one to Adigun. They were handwritten, in red ink.

"These are your hotel reservations. The address is on it; the Best Western on Grand and 15th, downtown Chicago."

Adigun's lips were dry; another hotel, with that same bag. The day felt colder, and his teeth chattered.

"Good luck. Be careful and stay low. Jesus help you, we'll meet you in Chicago." Alagba walked away with Bros Ojo and Chloe walked towards the greyhound bus door. Adigun struggled to hold his head up as he fell in behind Chloe.

They moved towards the back of the car and Adigun lifted the black bag into the overhead compartment.

"All aboard!!!" shouted the greyhound staff. "Nine a.m. to Chicago. All change at Cleveland, Ohio."

It took about another thirty minutes for the bus to be fully loaded and ready to go, then it set off and traveled through the streets of DC, into the beltway. It was a wet morning with a drizzle pattering against the cold, dimly lit bus. The large greyhound windows were fogged over and light from other vehicles was broken up by the beads of rain running in rivulets as the bus picked up speed.

Adigun was tired and sleepy, falling into short, trance-like naps, before snapping awake in a fit of shaking. He was not experienced, but he knew how serious it was to be transporting narcotics. He knew how terrible drug trafficking was. It wasn't murder but, in his mind, it was only one step lower on the crime ladder. His every fiber screamed at the frying-pan-to-fire trajectory his life seemed to be taking.

Over the next several hours, Adigun arbitrarily assigned seven years to each state line they crossed but, being unfamiliar with the US geography, he could not distinguish between states and cities. The bus crossed Maryland to Virginia, through Philadelphia, and, for every sign he saw welcoming him into new territory, Adigun sank into an even deeper state of trepidation. By this time, each time he napped, his dreams featured prisons and bars... except when they featured Fulanis and cows. Heart racing, Adigun couldn't stop himself from stealing glances at the overhead compartment, where the black bag rested, filled with all that heroin. Almost five kilograms of heroin with a market value of about two million dollars. The smell of human feces bloomed in Adigun's memory as the air got warmer on the bus. He began to have flashbacks of the hotel ordeal two nights before – the black balls, the feces, the police. A fine sweat broke out all over Adigun's skin as his stomach heaved. The long chain of narcotics, tied together, end-to-end in their condom sheaths, had looked like the intestine of a goat.

The Greyhound bus roared down the wet road for hours. The light of day began to fade and, in the dim coach lights, Adigun looked around in envy at those passengers snoring the trip away. To him, they seemed to have no worries at all.

4

They ran into some traffic as they entered Pittsburgh; the snow was heavy here and the flow of traffic on the highway was slow. Adigun had finally fallen into a deep sleep and, when he woke, ten hours had passed since they began the journey. He looked at Chloe, who was still fast asleep, then looked up at the overhead compartment, the edge from which the strap of the black bag hung innocuously. The engine of the big greyhound roared and there was a loud blast from the horns as it pulled into the greyhound bus station in Cleveland.

Adigun kept staring at the bag and he kept his tired eyes open. "Good evening, ladies and gentlemen, boys and girls. Thank you for riding the great American Greyhound." The voice over the PA system had a thin chirpiness that did nothing to lighten Adigun's sense of gloom. "We are in Cleveland, Ohio. We will all disembark here for two hours before continuing to Chicago. For those whose final destination is Cleveland, we hope you had a pleasant trip and wish you an even more pleasant stay in Ohio. For passengers going on to Chicago, please check the scheduling boards and move your luggage to the correct docking bay."

The passengers filed out of the bus, snowflakes settling on their faces as they emerged. As Adigun walked into the hallway, he immediately put the black bag in the queue of luggage that snaked along the floor. He realized with horror that he was the only passenger standing next to his luggage, and he made a swift beeline for the men's toilets. He made his way through a tide of men adjusting their zippers, looking back to ensure that the black roll-along with the mustard stain was not tampered with. From his vantage point at the slightly elevated entrance to the men's toilets, he saw the long lines of bags and suitcases, varied in color, size, and shape, all leading to exit bays, at the ends of which buses were parked. He cast his gaze over the crowd, trying to locate Chloe. No luck.

He looked back over at the Chicago line, where his bag stood, and took in the other lines of luggage for other destinations. He observed the way departure announcements over the PA system prompted passengers to herd over to their lines, standing around their bags. Some were already boarding. It was 8 p.m. according to Adigun's steel Casio, which tallied with the clock on the wall above the swivel doors. The station was well lit and the area by the entrance doors smelled strongly of fresh paper from the large newspaper stand. The newspapers were clipped on rope lines on the wall at the stand. Past the newspaper stand, the smell of coffee and freshly baked pastries wafted down from the small diner on the mezzanine. Classical piano tinkled from the red speakers suspended from the ceiling, looking modest amidst the enormous brown chandeliers hung by lengthy chains from the six-storey-high ceiling. The upper tiers of the building were separated from the outside by curtain walls, which looked upon the bridge and its parade of streetlights. The bridge was close enough so you could hear cars speeding by.

Adigun's mind idled for an indeterminate period until an announcement over the PA system of another departure sent passengers scurrying to stand next to their luggage in the line leading to their designated loading bay. Some were already boarding their buses. Adigun looked to the far left and saw two dogs being led by two uniformed men. The dogs were Doberman Pinschers, straining at their leashes as they sniffed at the bags in the lines. Adigun felt an icy fog settle around his heart as he realized that the sniffer dogs were only two lines away from the one that his bag was sitting in – the line of bags for the bus to Chicago.

His mind went blank as he acted on pure instinct, stalking over to his line, picking up his bag, and walking out of the nearest open door. He found himself in a repair area and realized he had picked up the wrong bag; the mustard stain was not there. Panicking now, Adigun returned to the Chicago line, noted how much closer the dogs were, then spotted the black bag with the mustard stain and made a swift switch. Adigun exited through the open side door, with his heart racing, and crossed the busy, snow-covered street.

5

Adigun was just happy to get the bag away from the sniffer dogs and he walked at a brisk pace, without a destination in mind. Worried that he may have been followed, he glanced over his shoulder every few seconds until he noticed a police car approaching. Without thinking, he threw the bag in the green dumpster at the side of the road. He watched the patrol car closely as he walked, breathing a little easier when it stopped, and he saw the driver have a casual-seeming conversation with a security guard. Adigun remembered that the bag still had the tag with his name on it and he spun on his heels and ran back to the dumpster as the police car drove off down the east freeway. He pulled the bag out of the dumpster, tearing off the tag as he did so. He tossed the tag in his mouth and chewed on it as he resumed walking, beginning to feel the cold and the weight of his damp sweater.

He made a right turn and picked up his pace until he found an alley in which he could lay low for a while. How long he crouched there, Adigun could not tell, but some instinct told him he ought to move, and he emerged from the alley, mentally rehearsing his story should a police car come towards him and ask questions. He saw one of the Greyhound buses approaching, clueless as to where it might be headed. he reflexively looked at the windows at the back of the bus and froze there was Chloe at the back window, staring back at him with a tense expression. The Chicago bus – it was departing, and he wasn't on it! Chloe started to make frantic gestures that Adigun could not read then, as Adigun stood open-mouthed by the dumpster, the bus passed and drove out of view. Adigun realized he was all on his own.

He walked hastily to the taxi stand; he was determined to deliver the merchandise. To stay alive. He had to. It would be better to walk to Chicago than to arrive in Chicago without the merchandise. Approaching a taxi driver at the stand, a middle-aged Ethiopian with very curly black hair, Adigun asked, "Sir, how much is it to Chicago?"

"We don't go to Chicago brother. We can get you to the airport."

Adigun walked away from the taxi stand as he noticed more police cars approaching the area. The flashing lights intensified as the group of police cars converged at the Greyhound bus station.

The wheels of his bag growled on the rough road as Adigun found himself heading deeper into an unlit stretch. It wasn't quite pitch-black, but in Adigun's frightened mind, it might as well have been. Wet and cold, he picked up the bag by its side handle and began to run toward the freeway. He heard sirens and imagined they were blaring for *him*, the policemen coming after *him*… probably with their dogs! He neared the highway and heaved the bag over the giant pipes that separated him from a frosty field. He could feel the cold of the steel through his clothes as he crossed over the pipes and into the grass. Emerging from the field, he crossed the six-lane freeway onto the dark, concrete slipway on the other side.

Police lights still pulsed in the distance, from the direction of the bus station and Adigun, trembling in the aftermath of his adrenaline rush, felt certain the police presence must have something to do with him and his cargo. Behind him was a thick cornfield and he could hear croaking frogs and crickets. He pondered how they could sound so cheerful in this weather. The hard, heavy snow was falling harder now, pelting Adigun's face and impairing his vision.

Unknown to Adigun, after he made off with his bag, the sniffer dogs at the station had scored a hit on a piece of luggage in the line (just before his roll-along) and the suspect had tried to flee before being brought down by security and police. Cleveland was a notorious hub for overland drug smuggling into Chicago and the Drug Enforcement Agency had a bustling office just next to the greyhound station. The station was soon crawling with police and DEA agents and Chloe, having no clue as to Adigun's whereabouts had quietly boarded his bus when the call for Chicago passengers went out over the PA.

Adigun shivered by the highway with no idea of what to do with the black roll-along bag. Cars sped past as he walked along the freeway shoulder, away from the grey-hound station. He was lost in thought when one car, a white Ford Capri, came to juddering halt on the shoulder slightly ahead of him. As he approached, Adigun noticed that the car had a huge gash on the dirty passenger-side door and flakes of rust on the roof.

"Hey, boy, where headest thou?" The driver was a bearded white man and spoke with a strong southern accent.

"I'm heading to Chicago."

"Jes' a little help with the gas bill and you can ride with me to Chi-Town if you like."

Adigun hesitated. He was unsure but a glance toward the Greyhound station, still awash in red and blue lights, decided him. In his mind, some of those lights appeared to be moving in his direction – coming towards the freeway.

"Can I put this in the boot?" Adigun held up his bag.

"Boot? You want to put that in your boot? I ain't quite catching yer drift there, son."

"Boot, Sir, the back of the car… for luggage.!"

"Aahhh, the *trunk*! Why didn't you say so, boy?"

The man got out and went over to the rear of his car, strained, then jerked the boot with a grunt. Adigun took in the contents of the man's trunk, still clutching his roll-along.

"Oh, never mind my trunk; I collect waste wool from big factories and sell it to some smaller factories in Chicago."

Adigun placed his bag in the trunk, and they got into the Capri, pulling off to the sound of loud country music from the radio. The car cut through the rain, wipers thumping a steady rhythm to keep the windshield clear, with surprising stability and speed. Adigun would not have expected the performance he was experiencing from a car that looked the way it did. A blue rosary dangled from the mirror, but Adigun had neither the exposure nor presence of mind to ponder the strangeness of a Catholic southerner. The dashboard was dark grey, and the seats were black and very old. The cabin reeked of stale tobacco and the ashtray by the long gear stick was open and filled to the brim with cigarette butts.

The passenger seat was very low, and its backrest was faulty, making it difficult for Adigun to sit upright. Adigun kicked through the mass of branded paper bags and covered cups with straws in the footwell, making room for his feet. He let out a small cry when his backrest gave off a hollow bang and fell into the back seat so that Adigun found himself lying on his back. Smoke from the exhaust was finding its way into the car from somewhere under the back seat and Adigun was overcome by a fit of coughing. He got the backrest back into an almost upright position with the driver helping him out with his free right arm.

"Sorry 'bout the old rust bucket, my friend; the seat ought to hold for another twenty minutes or so before she tanks again," the driver chuckled, "Temperamental is this baby of mine." Adigun found himself infected by the man's good cheer and he smiled.

"Howdy diddly doo, partner, my name is Douglas. Douglas Callahan." He held the steering wheel with his left hand and offered a handshake with his right. Adigun shook the hairy hand and introduced himself.

"Pleased to meet you, Mr. Douglas. I am… Andrew. I'm going to the Best Western hotel at… at…"

Adigun reached into his breast pocket and for the small piece of paper Alagba had handed him in DC.

"The Best Western at 15th and Grand, downtown Chicago."

"Oh, I know where that is. The good old Best Western."

Mr. Douglas reached into the center console and pulled out a tin box from which he extracted a hand-rolled cigarette.

"You want one?"

"No, sir."

"There are some bottles of water somewhere on the floor."

Adigun looked at his feet and saw the load of junk he had placed his feet on. The car was filthy indeed.

He didn't mind though; it had started snowing again and he was just glad to be sheltered, moving, and reasonably warm.

6

Three hours later, a large road sign indicated that they were entering Toledo. "Time to pay up son. We'll be stopping at the gas station up front; jes' ten bucks from your kind self would do the magic."

Adigun squirmed to retrieve his wallet from his back pocket. He brought out an old ten-dollar note and handed it over to Douglas.

"Much obliged… umm, what did you say your name was – Andrew, was it?"

"Adigun, Sir; Adigun Komaiya."

"Hm, maybe I *should* just call you Andrew, eh?" The driver chuckled. He made a sharp turn into a small gas station on the outskirts of Toledo and stopped by the old pump. They both got out of the car and Douglas walked to the thick glass window to make payment. Adigun spotted the sign for the toilet by the side of the white building and the snow crunched under him as he headed off to relieve himself. He came out of the toilet and Douglas was waiting right behind the door to use it as well. Adigun got back into the car and sat leaning forward. Soon after,

Douglas returned and swept off the snow on the car roof before getting in and pulling back out onto the freeway.

The duo rode along the lonely highway. The heat coming from the engine progressed from pleasant to uncomfortable. Adigun found the window crank on the floor by his right foot and fitted it onto the knob in the door. He rolled down the window but soon rolled it back up; the blast of icy wind and snow was much worse than the heat. He eventually managed a paper-thin slit that let in a thin, whistling stream of air and called it good.

They exited the freeway onto a rural, single-lane, unlit road and Adigun noticed for the first time how dim the Capri's lights were. The radio stopped working, all of a sudden, and Douglas hit it several times until it came back on again. After about another hour of driving, they merged with the freeway again. They had driven past a stationary patrol car and Adigun noticed Douglas checking his mirror intermittently.

"Is there any problem?"

"Oh no, it's just the pig."

"Pigs? I didn't see any pigs."

Adigun turned his body and looked back trying to catch a glimpse of the purported pigs.

"Not actual pigs, buddy; the police. How long have you been in America? Not long, I'll reckon. Here we call the police pigs – 'cos they be dirty to a man!"

Adigun noticed there was a heavy police presence on the freeway, and they passed several cars that had been pulled over by the cops. His heart thumped in his chest as he thought of the cargo he had in the trunk of the car. He resented the slick way Alagba had used his identification to check in the bag of drugs at the bus station – the way he had been roped into this mess. He recalled the appearance of the sniffer dogs at the station and his heart skipped at how close it had been.

"Aaahh!" Adigun was jerked out of his deep thoughts by his own cry.

"Are you ok?" Douglas looked at him. "You were zoned out there, buddy. is everything ok with you?" Adigun mumbled a non-response and turned to look out of his window, noticing that they had turned onto one of those dark country roads again. He preferred not to talk. The duo sat silent as the car cut through the darkness.

After several minutes, Adigun could no longer hold his peace. "We had to come this way?"

"We buy about forty minutes from going off the freeway here." Douglas sounded casual enough but kept looking in his rear-view mirror. He seemed tense, and Adigun looked back. There were headlights about six car lengths behind them and approaching fast. Adigun twisted all the way around in his seat and saw that it was a police car. As he hastily returned to the front-facing position, the surrounding countryside and the interior of the Capri were lit up by flashing blue and red lights. Douglas

Callahan pulled over and the emergency lights remained flashing as they sat in the car waiting.

Adigun realized that he was sweating, and a sudden uncontrollable shiver seized him. Douglas was looking at him with concern. "Are you okay brother?"

Adigun's teeth chattered as he replied, "It's the police, Sir - I don't like police."

"It's only the pigs, buddy," Douglas soothed. Now that they had been pulled over, he didn't seem tense at all. Adigun muttered something that sounded like, 'Yes, pigs', but it was hard to tell the way his entire jaw was shuddering. Douglas was surprised that the boy didn't jump out of his skin when the cop tapped on the driver-side window.

Callahan rolled down the glass and said nothing.

"You're producing a hell of a lot of smoke, Sir. Bit of a hazard to other motorists. Can I see your registration and driver's license?"

Adigun looked and saw the gun on the waist of the Police officer as he received the documents Callahan handed him. The cop barely looked at the papers, strafing the Capri's interior with the beam of his flashlight instead.

"Bit of a mess in here, isn't it? Looks like you've been on the road a while." Callahan looked up at the cop blankly, not responding to his conversational gambit. The cop's eyes narrowed, and his jaw clenched; "Would you be kind enough to open your trunk, Sir?"

"Why, of course." Douglas Callahan sounded cheery as he unbuckled his seat belt and got out of the car. Adigun was frozen in his seat and could not look back. He strained to hear the conversation outside the car but couldn't. The repeated squawks from the cop's walkie didn't help. The flashing lights seemed to multiply, and Adigun felt his terror grow as he saw several additional police cars approaching in the side mirror. Moments later, they whizzed past, sirens howling. The officer spoke briefly into his walkie-talkie and turned his attention back to Callahan.

"Let's take a look in the trunk then, shall we?"

"Oh, sure. It's only some waste wool and a case belonging to my passenger," Douglas replied, "I hitch-hiked this route twice a week when I went to college in Chi-Town, and I swore to always give a ride when I got a car of my own." Douglas chatted pleasantly as he opened the trunk of the car. The black, six-foot-five police officer looked down on Douglas, chewing gum, with his hands hooked into his thick leather belt – the right one close to the holster of his gun.

"What's in the bag, Sir?"

"Oh, that's not mine, officer. It belongs to the young man."

The policeman walked around to Adigun's window and tapped the glass. Adigun made frantic efforts to find the crank for winding down the window. He felt cold sweat rolling down his ribcage and pooling around the waist-band of his trousers.

"Hey, boy, I need you to step down and show me the contents of your bag," the cop called through the slim slit at the top of the window. Adigun stammered, trying to explain that he was trying to find the window winder, but the officer couldn't make out what he was saying. He took a single step back, with his right hand now firmly on the butt of his service pistol, and ordered, "Step out of the vehicle, boy." Douglas sidled over, hands raised to shoulder level, talking fast. "Easy, officer, that door gets jammed sometimes." He carefully stretched his right hand to the door handle and tugged on it with some force. The officer relaxed his posture and took his hand off his weapon but held his position. Callahan thumped on the door with a closed fist, then resumed jerking it.

"Sorry about the door.

"Let me go around and push it from the inside, okay? Then, when I tell you, please just pull on it from out here."

The police officer regarded Callahan with wary eyes while he considered the situation. He seemed to arrive at decision, then he sucked air through his teeth and thrust Callahan's documents into his chest.

"Here is your license and registration. You can go on about your business, but make sure you fix that door as soon as you get to Chicago. And sort out the smoke too!"

"Will do. Thank you, Sir."

The cop made a swift beeline for his car and sped off, pulling in after three additional police cars that roared past them. Adigun sighed in relief.

"How long to Chicago, Sir?"

"Oh, we are already in the suburbs. Once we get back on the freeway, it will be 'bout thirty minutes to downtown Chi-Town."

They returned to the freeway and Adigun could see the Chicago skyline in the distance. As he caught sight of his destination, his mind balked at the thought of what he was supposed to do next.

"I still have another forty minutes' drive, but I will drop you at the Hard Rock Café, bang in the middle of down-town."

"It's a few blocks walk from there to the Best Western on Grand."

He lit another cigarette. Adigun was gratified that, this time, Callahan rolled down the window on his side.

True to his word, Douglas dropped Adigun off at the Hard Rock and gave him solid directions to the Best Western before continuing on his way. At the Best Western, Adigun walked through the lobby and went straight to the reception desk, where he checked in. When offered help taking his bag to his room, Adigun refused, telling the porter he needed to wait a while for a guest.

Adigun sank into one of the plush sofas in the lobby and promptly fell asleep, unaware of the men observing him from the mezzanine area.

Chloe sat with his crew and watched Adigun for a full hour, not daring to approach him for fear that he was being surveilled by law enforcement. After a further hour, they relaxed a bit, certain that they would have identified any tails by that time.

Adigun had been sleeping for the entire two hours when he felt a nudge on his side. He opened his eyes without moving his head and his brain registered the Best Western sign on the white wall in front of him. His eyes drooped shut then popped open again when he felt another nudge. This time, he tilted his head down enough to see a white child, seven or eight years old, dressed in blue denim dungarees. He had a white shirt under the dungarees and the strap hung off his left shoulder.

"Hello, sir."

"How are you, boy?" Adigun stretched and looked at the reception, where two new guests were checking in. Outside, the snow came down with renewed vigor. There was Asian music playing from the speaker in the ceiling.

"How can I help you, son?"

"Can you please get me some ice from the ice machine, sir? The table is too high, and I can't reach."

"Oh, certainly."

Adigun got up and followed the boy, taking several steps towards the deserted corner by the lift before realizing he had left the black roll-along by the couch. He whipped around in a blur and grabbed the bag, then followed after the little boy, through the lobby, pulling the bag along the brown carpet with the blue flowery design. He made a left after the kid to the array of tables in front of the lift. As he reached out for a cup in front of the ice machine, the elevator doors opened and revealed Chloe who, without a word, stretched out his hands for the black bag. Adigun, noticing that the little white boy had vanished, gave it to him. "Walk out of the hotel and meet me across the road in the Indian Coffee shop." The elevator doors closed, and Adigun watched as the lift floor indicator changed one number after the other and stop on the thirteenth floor. He turned around and walked out of the hotel, glad to be rid of the hideous millstone he had been burdened with since DC.

Chloe, got out of the lift, made a right, and headed through the exit into the stairwell, then climbed down to the third floor. He strolled with exaggerated casualness to room 306 and tapped on the door. "Hey, Frenchies!" He called as the door was opened.

"The chicken has finally come home to roost."

"What a guy!!"

"What a guy"

"He wasn't followed."

Two men were sitting on the bed and another on the chair backing the window. Chloe dropped the roll-along on the dresser-drawer and unzipped it.

He pulled out ten parcels, placing them on the table.

"*Mission accompli. S'il vous plait, tester et laissez l'argent.*" Chloe exhaled with relief.

"Speak in English, man, this is America," said one of the men on the bed, a giant of a man, as he stood up. He wore a Dallas Cowboys jersey and had on baggy jeans, held up by brown leather suspenders over a brown plaid shirt. He was close to seven feet tall and had left a ditch-like crater behind him in the mattress. The wooden floorboards under the pink carpet creaked in protest with every step he took. He affected an American accent, but any Nigerian would recognize him as a Yoruba man – from the cadences that lay underneath. He brought out a penknife from his pocket and cut through the parcel. He took a pinch of the white powder and rubbed his gums and teeth with it. He paused for a second and then picked up a small portion with the knife tip and put it into his nostrils. He inhaled the substance with a long sniff, closing his eyes as they teared up and wagging his head in approval. Then he exhaled through his mouth, revealing his two gold incisors.

"Carry go, baba, carry go!"

"Yeah?" Chloe regarded the behemoth with an exaggerated look of pleading that suggested his question was rhetorical.

"Super, duper, kosher, my brother. Firebrand." The giant put the parcels back in the roll-along and signaled to the other man on the bed – a bald fifty-something African, dressed in a white crushed linen suit, with his chest buttons all open to reveal a thick gold rope chain. His skin was an odd orange-pink color with black, soot-like patches on his neck. This pattern was also evident on his pale pink hands, with unsightly black knuckles. He slipped his uneven-colored feet into his expensive-looking crocodile slippers.

The man reached out to the table in front of the window and brought out a black briefcase and flipped it open on the bed; it was packed with crisp dollar bundles. He handed it over to Dallas Cowboys, who passed it to

Chloe. There was a counting machine on the bedside table and Chloe took out the bundles of hundred-dollar bills, inserting one after the other into the counting machine. The next several minutes were punctuated by the aggressive whirring of the counting machine as it raced through the crisp hundred-dollar bills.

"All counted and all good," Chloe declared after the last bundle was counted.

"Lovely baba, lovely. It has been an eventful day."

"But I told you the boy won't run away with the goods."

"I must confess, the boy did well."

"I watched him run to the line of bags before the dogs got there," Chloe recalled, continuing, "He grabbed the bag and I watched him from the greyhound hall, running off in the rain. *Le garcon a bien fait, il doit etre indemise.*"

"There we go again!"

"Oh, sorry. I meant the boy did very well, I think he should be compensated."

"Oh, definitely."

"Anyone else would abandon the cargo. . . or disappear with it."

"We plan to keep him here in Chicago."

"Yeah, I spoke to Alagba and he talked about us taking the new boy on. We can use a fresh, unknown face on the street." The bald man had a pensive expression as he said this, one green vein pulsing in his florid forehead.

"Yes, once we touch base with him, we will regulate that. I already booked him a room here. You will love the kid; he's as unassuming as you could want."

"Great! When is the next delivery?"

"Don't know, boss. Only Alagba has that information. I shall be returning to Lagos, and I know there is a group scheduled for this week, they come in through Miami."

Chloe shook hands with the men and walked out of the room.

"Bring the boy to my house – you know my house, right? On 56th? The bald man looked satisfied when Chloe nodded in affirmation, walking off down the hotel corridor without another word, in the broad shadow of Dallas Cowboys, who ambled behind and slightly to the right of him.

Chloe walked down through the stairwell – it was forbidden to go into elevators with payment cash – he gripped the black briefcase tight as he descended. The hotel lobby was deserted, except for the reception staff, and he pushed the swivel doors into the dark winter night without having any interaction. Chloe crossed the road and walked into the 24-hour coffee shop opposite the hotel. Adigun sat by the window looking morose. He had covered his head with the hood of his black sweatshirt.

"Hello, sir."

"Big boy, you did well. you did very well. I will be catching the bus back to Washington DC, but I have to deliver you to your new host."

"Host?"

"Alagba has arranged that you move in with them to work in Chicago. They have agreed to take you on, with a fat compensation.

"You have no idea what you just did – you are a hero, boy, a hero!"

Adigun looked at him with a frown, then licked his chapped, bleeding lips.

"So, you mean I am not coming with you? I will be staying here in Chicago... *to work*." There was an unmistakable sneer in his voice when he landed on the last word.

"Work as what? Work where?!!!"

"Shhhhhh! you are shouting!" Chloe's eyes darted as he hissed his admonition.

Adigun paid him no mind. "Did you even ask me how I got to Chicago from where you abandoned me? You guys just put me on a bus not thinking I had a say," he seethed, "Do you know what I went through to get here? You better take me back to where you brought me before I shout for the police to come and see what we cooked that the roof caught fire!

"Who does this? They asked me to come and live with my countryman, so I don't sleep in the gym anymore, and before I knew what was happening, I'm in possession of drugs and I'm fighting for my life." Adigun was weeping as he ranted but could not have cared less. "Me, I'm not staying here, ooh! Compen-what?! I don't want any bloody compensation!"

"Chill, boy! Lower your voice; you are creating a scene here." Chloe was glad the coffee shop was empty.

Adigun shouted, "French man, I don't want any compensation! I don't want any part of this! I'm the son of Dele Komaiya of Jobore! I didn't come from far to come and die or enter jail!

"You abandoned me at the station to get here on my own," he seethed, "I delivered your drugs safely. Now, please just take me back to Bobby Brown!

"I don't want your drug money and I don't want to stay here with any stupid 'host'!

"If you don't take me to the bus station now, I will lock your shirt and only the police will release my hands from your neck after I choke you!"

"Bro, you are creating a scene here!" the exasperated Chloe was now pleading.

"Scene? You have not seen 'scene'!"

"Okay, okay, okay, let's head to the greyhound station – stop fucking shouting!"

The duo walked out of the coffee shop into the dark street and Chloe flagged a taxi. They got into the taxi and went directly to the Greyhound terminal.

Chloe got them two direct tickets from Chicago to Washington DC. It was a silent trip.

8

The bus pulled into the Greyhound station in Washington DC and Adigun got off, sprinting down the concrete stairs at Union Station and into the Metro, without sparing Chloe a single word. He made his way back to the gym and walked straight into Bobby Brown's office.

"What are you doing here? Alagba told me you decided to stay in Chicago."

"Daddy, I did not decide to stay in Chicago. That Nigerian man is into drugs; he made a drug mule of me and wants me to continue in his narcotics trade in Chicago.

"You did not tell me you sent me into slavery there! You said I wasn't comfortable here – did I complain? I have never been used like this in my life!

"Bobby B, I am from a very humble family in Nigeria; I did not come all the way from Africa to go to jail. I was doing very well as your cleaner here.

"I don't know if you know," Adigun's babble was picking up speed and volume, "but your pastor friend, Alagba, is a drug dealer – a kingpin!

"I saw everything – I mean everything! How they ship in drugs ingested by human smugglers; how they shit it out – disgusting, Sir!

"This is not the life I want here in America. A good name is better than silver and gold, my mother always told me, and…" Adigun halted.

"Daddy Bobby, what are you smiling about? Don't you hear what I've been saying to you? I said your friend – your Nigerian friend – is a drug dealer!"

"And what do you think we are here?" Bobby Brown looked both amused and sorrowful as he asked this question in a soft voice. "What do you think we do here?"

"Boxing."

"Ha ha ha ha ha ha!" Bobby Brown erupted in laughter, sputtering and coughing as he did.

"African boy, wake up!! We are all immigrants like yourself; nobody is going to hand you the American dream. You have to fight for it on the streets." Bobby Brown's demeanor turned grave as he spoke. "I like you and I have taken you as my son.

"Son, your 'father' sells *Yeyo*!

"You will get your African ass out of here, back to Alagba, and apologize to him for disobeying his instructions!

"We are one family and, in this family, there is no room for slackness. What you have just done is pure slackery!

"You see all these people around me, they started like you. You need to chart your own path.

"'Alagba is a drug dealer'," Bobby Brown chuckled mirthlessly, "then who am I – the pope? Kiddo, I appreciate everything you have just told me, but you need to wake up from your slumber. America is a jungle. We are all squirrels scrambling after very few nuts – the American dream! Everybody has their strategy.

"Millions of people arrive in America daily in search of that American dream. What is your American dream? Sweeping the gym?"

"Daddy, I don't want that dream, sir, I want to be like you, a good man. I did not come here to go to jail, daddy. I want to be here with you.

"I can work. I can work harder. I don't want to live with Alagba, Sir; I never want to see them again!" Adigun wrung his shirt, nearly hysterical.

"All right, okay! Step out for a minute, son." Bobby Brown waved Adigun out with his left hand while he unlocked a drawer in his desk with his right. He rooted around in it for a few seconds while Adigun left the office. As Adigun shut the door, Bobby Brown and Pookie shared a look, then burst out laughing.

"He wants to be like me!"

Bobby Brown held his stomach laughing and coughing at the same time.

"Where did you find this kid?"

"I love that guy."

"He wants to be like me."

Pookie, at this time, was on the yellow couch, laughing out loud and almost choking.

"Kid came to the devil for holy communion."

"He wants to be like you, Bobby B," Pookie's veins stood out on his forehead, "I guess it's a good thing you had me work a new ID for the boy, huh?"

"Damn right, Pookie. You don't get where I have without using your head. Call the boy back in."

When Adigun came back in, he looked at Bobby Brown with such apprehension, that Bobby's expression went from one of stern hostility to grumpy compassion.

"Here," he said, handing Adigun a sheaf of papers, "this is who you are now. I can't have you bringing immigration or whatever in on my affairs, so you are American now.

"I knew this season will come. Sign here; your name is now Adelaide Fernandez. We have our boy working at the mortuary downtown. Some bodies are abandoned when there's no family to claim them.

"Adel Fernandez died almost a year ago. You will be taking over his social security number and the papers in front of you are the passport forms.

"In one week, you shall have your passport and you can function in the States – within reason, of course. You Dig?"

Adigun signed the documents as directed and he stood up, reached out to Bobby Brown, and hugged him.

"Thank you, daddy," he said.

"You welcome, Mr. Fernandez. Just remember, your name is Adelaide Fernandez – that's what you tell anyone who asks – you have a social security number and everything. Be smart, don't talk too much. No one can pronounce your real name anyway, so just call yourself Addy or something. Go get your mop and beat it!" Pookie snickered at this, and he and Bobby erupted in laughter again as Adigun left the room.

Adigun ignored the raucous laughter coming from the office and wiped down the entire gym like he had never before. He scoured the boxing ring, removing all of the black scum on the puffy red leather on the corner buckles. He cleaned out the toilet and, in a few hours, the gym was spotless.

As the customers came in Adigun realized how much he had been missed after just a few days.

"When are you going to wear your shiny green Danjuju?"

"Dashiki, Terry, Dashiki."

Terry was the old man that supplied towels. He was from Pennsylvania originally but had lived in Washington for a long time.

"Your girl, Phoebe's been asking looking for you."

"My g-? Come, stop teasing, Mr. Terry."

Terry snorted and started to reply, then his gaze drifted over Adigun's shoulder and his wrinkled face twisted into a sly smile. "Oh, talk of the Devil!"

"Hey, Diggy Boo. Where have you been? They told everyone you were not coming back anymore." Phoebe had walked up to Adigun while he was talking with Terry, and he was a little ashamed of how fast he spun around at the sound of her voice. The shame didn't have any time to settle in, however, as Phoebe soon seized him in a tight, unabashed embrace. Terry's smile was much comelier as he walked off with his pile of towels, saying in an exaggerated whisper, "Told ya!"

"Hey, hey, hey, dirty old man, what are you telling my Diggy Dear?"

Terry was walking towards the bathroom, "Oh, nothing. Just that some people missed some people more than everyone else is all."

"Piss off, you dirty old man!" Phoebe chuckled as she said this, with no trace of embarrassment. She was still hugging Adigun, who wore a comically shy expression, not quite sure where to direct his eyes or his hands.

"Hey, Phoebe, what are you doing here again? It's not lunchtime!" Bobby Brown shouted from the door to his office. "Let the man work!"

Phoebe looked up and rolled her eyes. "Don't be such a wet blanket, Bobby B.

"See you at lunchtime, Diggy Boo. The usual spot."

Aware of Bobby Brown's gaze, Phoebe walked away provocatively swinging her hips. She walked towards the exit, brushed her long blonde hair to the back, and looked back. She made eye contact with Bobby and then, with a twinkle of mischief in her eyes, turned and blew a kiss at Adigun. Adigun returned the wave with a hesitant smile, relieved that the exciting, but uncomfortable, episode was over.

He resumed cleaning and exchanging pleasantries with the customers as they came into the gym for the next few hours until lunchtime came. Phoebe had prepared lunch for Adigun every day since he began work at the gym. It was often his only meal and on days when Phoebe was off, he would not eat until she returned the next day. Phoebe had come to like Adigun, and she was enthralled by his stories of Jobore and the surrounding villages. She recognized and respected his passion for his roots, going so far as to press him for recipes for several African dishes, which she began experimenting with and, periodically, giving him to sample. The lunch break had become the high point of the day for chef and cleaner alike, and Adigun was looking forward to their rendezvous on this day.

He walked out through the back door that opened into the alley. He was carrying two trash bags filled with garbage. Phoebe had already arrived and sat on the black metal railings next door with her feet dangling. She had the top button of her chef outfit undone and was still wearing her chef hat.

"I will be with you in a moment, Phoebe; I have to drop this in the dumpster."

"Take your time, Diggy Boo. I made you your favorite – J rice."

"Oh my God, Jollof!"

Adigun dropped the bag on the dumpster and hopped up the black metal stairs in front of the garages. "Please give me a second, I have to wash my hands." Adigun opened up the squeaky metal black door, disappeared for a minute, and returned, cleaning his hands with a paper towel. He held the elevated metal railings and walked to the left side towards Phoebe. He sat next to her and she brought out a Tupperware container from a black cooler back.

"Open it yourself."

Adigun pulled off the flexible plastic lid of the transparent container, revealing the pepper-red jollof rice, strewn with slivers of chicken.

"Oh, wow, Phebes, this looks authentic! You are getting to master this jollof matter."

She passed a fork to Adigun, and he spooned some of the rice into his mouth. His eyes widened and his nostrils flared as his taste buds were assailed by the familiar flavors. It was not quite like home (understandable since he knew how hard it was to find ingredients like dried crayfish), but it was a delicious reminder.

"Oh my God! This is so good!"

Phoebe's face became pink, and her broad forehead glowed as she shook her blonde hair away from her eyes. She pulled out her own lunch, the same meal in a similar container, and they ate quietly for a while. Adigun was scraping up the last of his food when he spoke at last.

"I'm so grateful, Phoebe. This is awesome. Please consider my offer of giving you some of my wages monthly. You have fed me for free for too long."

"Oh, Diggy Boo, I told you not to mention that anymore; it is not a problem. I'm a chef and I love to feed people. When it's your turn to look after me, I'm sure you will." Phoebe's face fell as she went on, "I was really sad when Bobby Brown told me you would not be coming back. It bothered me, not even being able to say goodbye."

"I don't know where to start, Phoebe." Adigun lowered his head for a long moment and when he looked up, he was struggling.

"Come on with it, Diggy Boo. You can trust me."

"I was taken to Alagba's house, and I was happy. His wife was amazing! She even went to school in the same town as my mother. They lived in this very lovely, posh mansion and they received me well. The wife brought me to work and took me back home in the evening."

"I know this part, Diggy, I was here, remember?"

Adigun continued, trance-like, as if he had not been interrupted. "Until this day, when I was made to go to the airport to pick up a French drug mule, who had arrived on a flight from Nigeria."

"Which airline?"

"Pan Am."

"What time did it land?"

"I don't know."

"Was the mule alone or were there others?"

"How am I supposed to know that?" Adigun was irritated by the questions; they were interfering with his unburdening.

"Anyway, we got to this hotel where the mule defecated in the white hotel towel, and they picked up the stuff with their bare hands and rinsed it in a bowl of water. Oh, did it stink! That was the most disgusting thing I've ever seen in my life.

"There was very huge police and DEA presence at the hotel – I think there was a drug bust in another room – but they gave me the bag containing the drugs, as we walked out to the police-infested lobby. Can you imagine?

"I carried it through the lobby, and they walked ahead like they did not know me. We got home and Alagba never said a word to me. The next morning, I was all ready to go to work, when Alagba informed me I wouldn't be coming in. Instead, they drove me to the Greyhound station, took my ID, and I became the owner of a bag filled with drugs, on my way to Chicago with the French mule."

"What is his name?"

"Chloe."

"Chloe who?"

"He didn't tell me."

"Doesn't matter anyway. Eat your chicken; don't you like it? I seasoned it with dry smoked cayenne pepper, the way you like it. Does it taste like party rice?"

"You know I always finish my food before I eat the meat. Yes, it tastes like party rice. In fact, I don't know how you can handle these spices – are you sure you are *Oyibo*?"

Phoebe gasped in delight, gushing, "Oh my gosh, I've forgotten the song – "pepper-pepper-eaty-eaty-pepper, yellow, yellow, something, something."

"Wrong. It's 'Oyibo pepper, Oyibo pepper, if you eaty pepper, you go yellow more, more.'"

Phoebe shrieked, "Yes, that is it."

"Anyway, we got to Cleveland to change buses and big dogs were sniffing all the bags. I quickly picked up the bag and ran into the rain and walked in the rain till I found a good Samaritan that gave me a lift to Chicago. His name was Douglas. He's into some sort of waste wool business or something."

"Douglas Callahan?"

"How did you know his last name?"

"Oh, I used to go to Chicago to visit my grandma and Douglas has given me rides a few times. It's the waste wool that tipped me off."

"The police presence on that road was scary. We even got stopped and the policeman asked me to open my bag in the boo-... trunk, sorry, but my door was jammed, and the driver could not open it.

"My heart was in my mouth, I was shitting myself, but anyway, we made it to Chicago and I delivered the cargo. Then I found out Alagba had made plans for me to wait in Chicago and live with the buyers. I was so mad, that I had to force the French guy to pay my way back to DC. That's how I ended up back at the gym."

"Oh, wow!" Phoebe exclaimed, leaning closer to Adigun and dropping her voice, "I'm going to tell you something, but promise me you'll keep it to yourself and that you will not freak out."

"I cross my heart, Phoebe."

"You are working with the biggest drug cartel on the East Coast. Bobby Brown is the head."

"Nooooo, I won't believe this; not from you, not from BB himself! All I know is he runs a gym. He trains boxers."

"Ok, African boy, guess you know it all.

"Whatever you believe, eat your chicken; you will find out, soon enough. Just keep your eyes open and tell me when you start seeing anything along those lines.

"Oh no! We are way past break time. Will I see you for a minute after work?"

"Oh yes, I'm back here now. Live here now. I will not be going back to Alagba's house."

"I don't know why you are so stubborn; I told you I have two spare rooms. You really don't have to sleep in that uncomfortable changing room; you could stay at mine."

"I know Phoebe, but I hate to inconvenience anyone. I'm fine here in the gym."

Adigun's friendship with Phoebe would bloom into a love affair but he would never take the step to move into her apartment.

9

Over the next two years, Adigun kept his head down and cleaned, becoming something of a minor celebrity at the gym. He still wore his dashiki over his regular wear, and it was an unfailing attraction to new gym members, as well as a conversation starter for regulars. Adigun was often asked about where he came from, often just so the person asking could hear the proud response that always followed; "I am American, but my ancestors come from Jobore, the land of a thousand rivers, the envy of the people of Irede, the land of sixteen masquerades."

Adigun slept alone in the gym, showering in the changing room and sleeping on the sofa in the lobby. He had gotten into the swing of his job as a cleaner but, within a year, also settled into a routine of heavy bag workouts after closing time. He found that he had a natural aptitude for the training exercises he watched others perform and came to depend on the therapeutic benefits of the physical exertion. At night, when the gym emptied and the lights went out, thoughts of illicit drug deals, cartels, and police tried to crowd his mind and steal his peace. Adigun did not want to face those thoughts, and hitting the bag helped him to purge them. Each night, after working up a sweat punching his knuckles raw, he could shower in a zombie-like trance and fall into a deep, blissful sleep.

The years passed and, one Friday night, Adigun walked down the black metal stairwell from the gym to the back alley. Phoebe was waiting for him. She had had to cater an event that day and hadn't made it for lunch earlier in the afternoon. As they kissed, Adigun took a quick look at his silver Casio and realized it was closing time for the gym. He mumbled that he'd be back and began pulling away when Phoebe grabbed his head again and kissed him again. She looked straight into his eyes and whispered, "I adore you, Diggy Boo. No one in my life has ever made me feel this way. We need to spend more time though; I crave your company all the time. Are you spending the weekend at mines?"

"Umm, not sure. We'll see. I have a sparring bout tomorrow." Adigun's night-time workouts had revealed a natural talent for pugilism that had inevitably led to his moonlighting as a sparring partner for a small number of the members of the gym. One of them was a real contender and Adigun was now learning a great deal about ring craft.

"You have to be very careful, Diggy," Phoebe frowned, "There are only so many blows a man can take before he starts to lose his marbles."

"Oh, my Phobia."

254

"I told you I don't like you calling me that!" Phoebe snapped, her face darkening.

"Sorry. Oh, now I've ruined the mood. Forgive me, Phoebe."

"I've told you over and over again, I don't like you putting yourself up to be another boxer's punching bag."

"Don't worry, Phoebe, it's because I am hard to hit that they love training with me. Very soon, I will become the most sought-out sparring partner in the gym."

"More like the most brain-dead, retarded, human punching bag," Phoebe's face lost some of its tension, "Are you coming to my place tonight or not?"

"I have some errands to run in the downtown area."

"At least let's spend Friday night together, Diggy Boo."

"Listen, I will try, but I have to close up." Adigun raced through the metal doors and into the brightly lit boxing gym. There was hardcore hip-hop music playing on the large boom box on the floor and a constant thudding as gloved fists met the heavy bags and speed bags, which, along with the boxers' grunts and exhalations, seemed to sync with the beat.

"Move it! Move it, guys! Move it," Adigun called out cheerfully, "Beat it champs. The gym is now closed." Adigun's Nigerian accent was still present, but it was faint and hard to catch. He walked to the corner and flicked the switch for the main lights off, on, off, then on again to drive his message home. The gym had expanded within the last year, as Bobby Brown had bought the property next to it and merged the two. Adigun now supervised a small team of cleaners and he wanted to ensure that things got done properly.

"Come on, guys, we have to lock up," he urged, as the members started packing their bags and switching off the exercise machines, "Pack up, please, we have to go."

It took roughly thirty minutes to empty the place. Adigun gave instructions to the cleaning staff and stripped off his sweatpants as they began working. He wrapped his hands with practiced ease and began skipping to warm up. He had spent almost every day of the last two years performing the boxing exercises he observed during his workday, and he had filled out his frame with lean, corded muscle. His stamina was phenomenal, and his discipline was unshakeable. Despite what he had told Phoebe, there were no 'errands' to run downtown – Adigun was not going to let anything interfere with his workout.

He had mastered the boxing fundamentals and had an instinct for the craft. He was also blessed with natural power that had laid out a number of his sparring partners. It was not yet a fully-formed thought in the front part of his mind, but Adigun had a notion he had found his calling in the ring.

10

Adigun and Bobby connected from the first day they met – at least as soon as Adigun had got his wits about him enough to narrate his ordeal. Bobby Brown was originally from the Colombian village of Palenque de San Basilio. Its inhabitants were descendants of escaped African slaves and they took fierce pride in their roots, considering themselves Palenqueros first, Columbian second. Bobby Brown still held to the traditional beliefs of the Palenqueros and felt a certain kinship with Adigun, believing there was a deep spiritual element to their paths crossing.

Now, Bobby Brown stood in the shadows by his office, watching Adigun train. He noted the way Adigun would alternate between intense, powerful combinations and lighter, attacks; how he would work on the heavy bag until his arms and shoulders were sore, then skip while they recovered, before returning to the bag. His power shots were frightening in their speed and apparent power; they sounded like thunder cracks. Though he tended to telegraph his big punches a bit (a common rookie mistake), Bobby Brown was shocked to see how much skill Adigun had acquired in his time as a cleaner. He knew the kid was messing about with the equipment and had even heard he clocked a couple of experienced boxers in sparring, but his prowess was unexpected – especially considering he wasn't being formally trained. No coach, nothing.

The boy was pleasant enough, but Bobby Brown had noticed he preferred to keep to himself and attributed it (correctly) to his fear of deportation. On this night though, watching the oblivious Adigun pound the leather, Bobby Brown thought he could also sense a deep rage in the kid. Adigun had gained weight and had built up a chunk of hard muscle, thanks to his friend Phoebe, no doubt. While she still treated Adigun to Nigerian native dishes now and then, he had urged her to feed him like she fed Bobby's fighters, combined with his exercise routines, the result was striking; washboard abdominal muscles, narrow waist, broad shoulders, and powerful limbs with thick, ropey muscles. His jaw was strong, and his neck was corded. Bobby Brown shook his head and returned to his office, choosing not to turn the light on. As he picked up his phone and dialed, he could still hear Adigun's punches tearing up the leather bag.

"Yo, Pookie! Pookie, are you there? You need to see what I just saw. That African kid, Dig'un," Bobby fell silent for a moment as he considered his words, then he went on, "our cleaner boy from Nigeria… that boy is something special." He fell silent again as he listened to Pookie on the other end of the line, then he erupted in a hissing whisper, "Really, you've been watching him? He knocked out Alonzo? And nobody said anything to me about it?" Bobby paused as Pookie blurted out an explanation then cut him off.

"Have him join the kids from Virginia on the road walk early in the morning. I'm going to make a monster of that African kid.

"Five a.m. See you in the morning." Outside the office, the sounds of Adigun's punches were punctuated by snarls and grunts as he launched a series of vicious hooks. He was startled when Bobby Brown's voice floated to him from the shadows around the office, "You're looking, good kid. If you want to get serious, gear up by 5 a.m. Let's train this beast, son." Without another word, Bobby Brown left the gym. Adigun stared after him, panting. The notion that he had found his calling became a harder, more substantial thing in his mind; a round stone with a comforting weight that was already making its way down from his mind to his heart.

The next morning, Adigun was in full gym gear and doing roadwork with three young men from Virginia, the top talent being coached by Bobby Brown himself. Bobby was behind the wheel of his grey 1975 Cadillac, strolling it through the hazy dawn behind the four. His Rottweiler stretched its neck out of the back window, its tongue lolling. It was not quite five a.m. and there were no other cars on the road.

"Come on, quit dragging your feet! Come on, you lazy piece of black sugar, it's only been three miles!

"This is the secret to the belt. You do it because your opponent isn't doing it. The air is clean and unpolluted – your body loves it. Lift your feet, boys, lift your feet!"

Adigun ran, shadowboxing simple 1-2 combinations every few steps.

"Kill 'em, son, kill 'em!"

They ran through Massachusetts Avenue and entered George Town and came back through Adams Morgan to link up with U Street, at the tail end, close to New York Avenue.

This became Adigun's life for the next seven months; running in the morning, drills and pad work in the early afternoon, sparring in the evening. Before long, word got out about the dangerous cruiserweight prospect in Bobby Brown's stable, but details were scarce – people in Bobby's circles knew to keep their mouths shut.

When he wasn't on the phone or taking meetings, Bobby Brown devoted his full time to Adigun. By the second month of training, Bobby Brown moved Adigun from the gym into his home, which, to Adigun's surprise, was right opposite Phoebe's apartment block in Bowie, Maryland– he ended up spending most of his free time at hers. He completely cut out fast food and his diet became even stricter, though he would indulge in a small portion of jollof rice every couple of weeks. He was as fit as a bull.

Bobby Brown's wife was a white, but Afro-centric, beauty in her late sixties. She had become fond of

Adigun, often pressing him for information about his homeland and culture. They got along well in the short periods they found for interaction. It was a thirty-minute drive to the gym, though Adigun would usually run there if the weather allowed.

Adigun became the most talked-about boxer in the gym; the name, Adelaide Fernandez was on everyone's lips and Bobby Brown's Gym was the most popular in the district. Champions had been made there and Bobby was known to have a winning formula, but membership was like joining a cult. It was not open to everybody, and the selection process was inscrutable. Still, boxers from other gyms (and trainers as well) would visit to watch him train.

Bobby Brown's biggest problem with training Adigun was sparring; he couldn't get anyone in the ring with him to last more than 10 minutes. Worse, he'd had to treat three of Adigun's past sparring partners for concussions and he would soon have to look elsewhere for candidates. Sure, it was great to be grooming a knockout artist, but Bobby needed to build the boy's grit and stamina… to make him a real monster.

Book-4

Leaning in

Bernde feewa teppeere feewa kaa walaa

(You can't have both a cool heart and a cool heel – Fulani proverb)

1

Washington, 1987

Adigun became a bulky cruiserweight – closer to border-line heavyweight – with thick arms and a neck like that of a horse. His power was legendary but, better still, he was learning how to avoid being hit, tucking his chin in, guard discipline, and head movement. His footwork was near-perfect, and Bobby Brown was certain he was championship material. It was a hot, sticky Washington DC afternoon and the still air was like soup. Adigun had completed his training for the day and had gone into the showers. Bobby had not noticed how long Adigun had been in there until steam from the shower room started seeping out from under the dark blue door. He ran down the stairs to the shower room and found Adigun lying motionless on the brown leather massage bed. He was face-down, and it was impossible to tell if he was conscious or not. Bobby Brown grabbed his shoulder and pulled at him. Adigun jerked up in shock and Bobby recoiled from the pain he saw on his face.

"Are you ok, Shango? Are you ok?" Bobby could not see properly; the steam was too thick. He reached for the tap and turned off the shower.

"Talk to me?" Bobby shouted.

The steam dissipated in seconds, revealing Adigun, whose eyes were red-rimmed and swollen from crying. His shoulders shook as he sobbed, and Bobby leaned over with concern. "Talk to me, champ, talk to me. Is it money? You need a break?"

Tears rolled from Adigun's eyes and merged with the rivulets of sweat and condensed steam on his face. He had cut his hair, leaving a patch in the middle, Mohawk style, in preparation for his maiden fight in a few days. He was booked to fight the South-East DC champ, Shanny Rikers. He had never met him, but he'd heard a lot about the havoc he was wreaking within the boxing circuit. Shanny Rikers was the undisputed champion in the district, having fought all over the neighboring states, and had a perfect record. Adigun had never fought outside the Bobby Brown gym but had knocked out all the sparring partners that ever came into the boxing ring. He had no amateur experience and was being thrust into the pros on the risky premise of his talent alone.

Bobby reached for a towel to clean Adigun's face. "Sorry about this coach," Adigun struggled to keep the tremor out of his voice, "I miss my family. It's been four years now and I can't even reach out to my family. I don't know anything about the welfare of my parents, and I can't even associate with Nigerians here in America. I feel like I came here to avoid jail only to still be locked away from so much that's important to me. I've tried to vent all that frustration through boxing, but I can't shake the sadness." Adigun's fragile composure dissolved, and he bowed his head again as he was wracked by sobs. Bobby slapped him on the back and said, "I got you, son. Meet me in my office and let's talk."

Bobby walked away leaving the changing room door open. Adigun shut the door, unwound his hand wraps, stripped, and showered, gathering himself as he did so. Dressed again, he raised the hood of his grey sweat top over his head, counting on the shadow it cast to hide his puffy face and swollen eyes. He would have preferred that the gym was empty, but decided that the warm greetings the stragglers called to him made him feel better. Still, he did not linger to chat with anyone as he made a beeline for Bobby Brown's office.

Bobby Brown was a known and respected player in the local fight scene and his fights were as big as any in Vegas. He also had a registered betting company that turned out to be a lucrative side earner for him. Adigun's upcoming fight was highly publicized and the entire District of Columbia, as well as the states of Maryland and Virginia, were talking about it. Adigun was kept out of the publicity events for strategic reasons. He only focused on the fight. He was banned from watching any television and he wasn't allowed any unsupervised trips during the six-week training program. The extreme isolation had brought deeply buried emotions bubbling up to the surface and Adigun had found himself in the unexpected agony of homesickness.

Now, he walked up the stairs and into Bobby Brown's office, working hard to retain some control over his rioting emotions. Bobby was talking to a bulky Latino, leaning forward and making energetic, agitated gestures with his hands. He paused when Adigun walked in, looked pensive for a moment, and then waved Adigun in. He turned back to his visitor and resumed his conversation.

"Dude, listen to me, boy, we were doing this shit before your parents even thought about making you, so don't question my instincts on shit like this."

"There are too many pigs on the street, man, AND we are being watched! Something is happening, but I don't know what it is. Word is there is some sort of special unit working to bring us down – a crew that is not on our payroll – and we all need to be worried about it."

"What makes you so sure?" The Latino man seemed unconvinced.

"How can you even ask that? Six of our runners arrested in the last month alone? The narrow escape with Alagba's guy, Chloe? You know he was picked up by customs on his last trip? Lucky for them he wasn't carrying 'cos they switched mules last minute.

"It's like they know what we are about to do before we do it. We already knew that I was under surveillance but I'm telling you, we have a snitch!"

"You are right," the Latino man shifted his weight in the seat, "can't be a coincidence, all those busts. We should have seen that."

"Damn right, you should have seen that! We have so much product and we can't move it! I have the Columbians breathing down my neck for their money, not you, so you and your crew have to fall in line with what I say on this one, Hector."

"My people don't like to change a winning formula, Bobby B, but I take your point. How do you want to do this?"

"All right, good. We just have to change the arrangement – at the fight, the buyers wear the Shanny Rikers colors and our people wear the Shango, I mean, Fernandez colors. We occupy all the VIP seats.

"Our people have the products under their seats, your people have the money under yours. When the fight is well underway, our guys simply switch seats. Your guys leave before the fight ends, and we stay till our boy is done mopping the floor with Shanny.

"We finish the deal and there are no police problems."

"We cannot sell on the streets anymore 'cos we are being watched, but we use that to our advantage. Set up a dummy transaction… a decoy to keep the cops busy in the streets – we bag up talcum powder and simulate a huge cargo arrival and transaction with a distributor. The attention of the Feds is focussed on the talc powder, and we go ahead with the fight."

Hector lit up, "The street team gets busted with talc powder, they get locked up! The narcs are jerking each other off, celebrating the bust until they realize they just broke up a talcum powder cartel. Brilliant."

"Yeah, it's brilliant all right. Know what else is brilliant? Apart from Pookie and me, now only you know about this plan. If anything goes wrong, then I have a much smaller bowl to fish for our snitch, you catch my meaning?"

"Hey, that's a low blow, Bobby B. I'll keep a lid on it until fight night, then I only tell my people the deal when we are at the venue."

"Dude, you have to move this product; my warehouse is full to the brim."

"I hear you Bobby B," Hector rose to leave, "you just leave that shit to me, okay?"

"Okay, buddy. Speak to you later. Remember, no phones about nothing that's business!"

As Hector passed through the doorway, Adigun replaced him in the visitor's chair. He focussed a questioning glance at Bobby Brown, who gazed back with a serene, almost resigned expression. "Okay, son, your episode in the shower or the meeting you just witnessed, which one do you want to talk about first?"

"Well, neither, frankly. I'm okay now. Tell you the truth, I'm a bit embarrassed you had to see that. Just homesick, I guess." Adigun wore a petulant look and Bobby Brown looked worried for the first time since the encounter in the shower room. "You don't ever need to be embarrassed about nothing with me, son, you hear? Whatever happens, you are family, and you can come to me if you need to talk." Bobby spoke with such undisguised emotion that Adigun felt his resolve slip and his eyes misted over. He bowed his head so he wouldn't have to look in Bobby Brown's face and replied, "You are a good man, daddy. That is part of the reason I am so mixed up.

"I understand what you and that man were discussing – you want to use my fight for a drug deal! I don't like this drug business, but I cannot see you as a bad person; you have been too good to me for that. I am beginning to see that the world is not black and white; that good people do bad things and 'bad' people are not only 'bad'.

"My father in Africa is a good man, but his bad deeds are part of why I had to run away; my father in America does bad things but is a good father to me! It is impossible to make sense of it and I am too tired to try.

"I will accept life as it is, but I beg you, for now, to just let me concentrate on boxing, daddy. I don't want the weight of anything else!"

Bobby Brown passed his once-more placid gaze over Adigun's features then he smiled. "You have wisdom beyond your years, son. I already know I can trust you with my life! Let us speak no more of this for now. We will focus on your fight." He lifted his eyes above the head of the silent, brooding Adigun and fixed on the door. Pookie marched in.

"Hey, boss, everything is set; the money is right. Jerome Engli's guys were trying to be funny, and they didn't want to increase the fight purse."

"For God's sake! It's a bigger venue and we can fill it."

"The county has agreed to put some money down for adverts in the fight brochure."

"I wonder why Lucius is being greedy."

"Sir, I told you we shouldn't mess with the Irish. They feel they invented this game and own every dime that comes out of it."

"Pookie, listen to me; we have done this before, and we have to make sure it works now. We have come up with this new way of getting our product to the street wholesale; *without* the feds tailgating us all over the district. Once Hector's crew pays us, street trade is their headache."

"Sir…" Pookie looked uncomfortable to have these thoughts aired in Adigun's presence. Bobby Brown registered his discomfort, looked at Adigun, then back at

Pookie, to whom he raised his hand, palm outward. The gesture told Pookie to hold his horses – that it was okay.

"The streets are too hot, Pookie!"

"Tell me 'bout it, sir."

"DEA has decided to shift the focus from the small-time cats to the wholesalers. Man, I miss Edguardo; he had a knack for sorting out shit like this."

"The great Edguardo! If he was still alive, he would have sorted this out in a jiffy."

"Well, fuck you very much, Pookie! What do you think we are doing here? We are handling it! We have to hold this boxing bout whether Jerome Englis likes it or not. It is our only chance of moving anything, Pookie. I will ensure Jerome comes to DC, so we can talk, move our product and get the goddam Columbians off our backs."

"We have the dopest boxer in the circuit, and we have the dopest dope." Pookie's apprehension was gone. "This kid ain't even ever fought and his story has circulated all over the region. Everybody can't wait to see him fight."

"We will make mad money from the gates and also move out products. This kid will fight from DC to Oregon, and we will move our products at every match."

"This is the best business plan since the second world war."

"We keep the streets quiet, and all transactions take place at the boxing arena. A few seconds of darkness and all exchanges take place."

"Lights come back on, we continue the boxing and everybody goes home happy." Pookie seemed giddy at the prospect.

"No police interference, no DEA problems. He kills anyone in the ring it's the boxing authority's problem." Bobby Brown chuckled at Adigun's gasp when he said this.

"Relax, son. It's just a contingency – you don't know who might be climbing into the ring with some condition that is just waiting for a light tap to turn out their lights for good."

"How is it the boxing authority's problem?" Adigun was perplexed.

"We pay a hell of a lot to the authority, son. It's insurance for any accidental death. The moment the boxers step into the ring, they are the boxing authority's burden."

Adigun wore an expression that Bobby could easily interpret as exasperation at the never-ending complications of life. To Pookie, the kid just looked nervous. He was clenching and unclenching his jaw muscles while stretching his neck from side to side. With an unkempt, matted beard under his chin and the muscles bulging through his clothes, he had the aspect of a cornered animal. Adigun looked dangerous. Bobby Brown looked at him sternly.

"All set for your rumble in the DC jungle Champ? You are about to show America what you are made of."

"Be careful," Pookie chimed in, "that Shanny Rikers guy is a monster. I have watched all his fights, he wears his opponent out with body shots and takes them out, usually, around the 5th round. His left hook is what you should watch out for. Give him the two steps, you open it up, he goes for it and you lick him with your mighty right. You need to take him out on the first round, son. He has never fought you; take him out while he's still trying to study you."

"Hey," Bobby Brown cut in, "you just let *me* handle fight strategy, Pookie."

"I'm ready, Sir," Adigun piped up with the first hint of animation since he went into the office, "I'm ready. I ask only one thing, Sir; that you allow me to wear Nigeria's colors into the ring."

"A lot of Nigerians in Montgomery County and Silver Spring. They'll get a kick out of that. "

"Coming out into the arena, I would like the music of Fela Anikulapo Kuti to be played. Precisely, *Unknown Soldier*."

"Pookie, put the street publicity team on Montgomery County and Silver Spring. Make sure you cover Howard University and Georgia Ave."

"It's on, partner; Rumble in the Jungle, baby!"

2

In a few days, the city was lit up with posters of the fight and the Nigerian colors of green and white dominated the visuals. There was even a billboard on New York Avenue that Adigun noticed on the way to the gym and the word was that there had never been a promotion like this one in the history of the district. Bobby Brown had sent complimentary tickets to the Nation of Islam and the NAACP, while the congressional black caucus also paid for twenty ringside seats. The District of Columbia was ready for its biggest boxing bout, which, unknown to its illustrious audience, was providing cover for its largest drug deal. Ever.

Adigun's training altered as he entered the countdown to the fight; he now did primarily steady cardio work mixed in with light ring strategy and sparring sessions. No heavy weight-work or explosive muscle training. Nothing that posed a risk of injury or that would stretch him too much and cause long-term fatigue.

The routine lightened up and Phoebe was a major part of it – always available to give Adigun a massage after training or to help him with his stretches, which he loved. He spent much of his time across the road from Bobby's, in

Phoebe's apartment, ostensibly because he did most of his swimming in her apartment complex's swimming pool. Bobby Brown figured Adigun had some other incentives for spending so much time at Phoebe's. He wasn't thrilled by the development, but, as long as they weren't bumping uglies the night before the fight – something Bobby intended to make sure of himself – he wouldn't upset his fighter just yet.

It was spring. The evening air was redolent with that heady, fragrant mix of coming rain and blooming flowers. Adigun, fresh off a two-hour roadwork session with Bobby Brown, was doing laps in the pool at Phoebe's apartment complex. He was in a trance-like state as he performed a languid backstroke back and forth along the pool's 25-meter length. Phoebe walked and watched from the edge of the pool, counting the laps, taking in the fluid motion of his muscular arms and legs as he cut through the water. Her pager beeped. She checked the number on the display and ran for the bank of payphones by the changing room door. She dialed and waited a couple of beats before she began speaking to the party at the other end.

"Yes, sir, I will be there.

"The other team has been following TC from Delaware, yes… I'm getting updates on their status."

The phone call went on for almost twenty-five minutes, Phoebe was backing the pool and didn't notice when Adigun climbed out and padded over behind her.

"In case you are interested, I did twenty laps after you started your phone call," Adigun grumbled. Phoebe whipped around, holding up a finger to him and saying she would call later to the speaker at the other end.

"Twenty? Sorry, darling, I know I am supposed to keep count. It's just work stuff intruding; don't be mad."

"These strange phone calls always ruin my routine, with your 'TC's and 'BB's and 'rows' – what the hell is a 'row' anyway? These coded conversations make me uncomfortable, Phoebe."

Phoebe's face arranged itself into a mask of exasperated amusement that Adigun found hard to interpret, or trust, for that matter. "Relax, Diggy, 'row' is just an easier way to say 'RW', which is an easier way to say 'Romeo Whiskey', which is chef code for Refrigerated & Wet," Phoebe giggled, "Don't go getting jealous on me, boy."

"Yesterday Romeo Whiskey went down," Adigun pouted, "today it's 'TC'…"

"Oh, Diggy Boo, it's just Chef talk, okay? Forget it."

"You are always on the phone, Phoebe," Adigun persisted, "it's only a week to my fight and I need you to focus. You're my fight physiotherapist; you need to focus, babes."

"I'm so sorry, Diggy Boo. I promise I won't let the chef business get in our way. But you seem a bit stressed, dear. Nervous about the fight?"

"Maybe, but it's other things too! I don't understand some things about you, Phoebe. Last week I saw some weapons – firearms, phoebe – in your laundry room one day. The next day, they were gone. I haven't brought it up because I just don't want distractions right, but I am worried, Phoebe. Assault rifles and ammo and shit in your flat? What in the blue blazes?!"

Phoebe's genial mask slipped for a moment then her expression resolved itself into one of genuine compassion and regret. "Oh, I didn't realize you saw those, Diggy – I wish you'd told me! Those firearms were from the rifle club I belong to. The armory was being renovated and some of the members volunteered to split up the weapons cache in our homes until they were done, that's all. I got to hold the five ARs and a few handguns and some cartridges. You know I used to be the president of the riffle club."

"Sister, me, I'm from Africa, oh," Adigun's new American accent was replaced by his Yoruba accent as he said this, "not used to guns around me. This is exactly the sort of thing that makes me not want to move in here,"

Phoebe froze, and when she spoke there was ice in her tone, "You think living with Bobby Brown is better? 'Cos you have your head in the sand about what he does?" Adigun turned from her, not wanting her to see how much this question affected him – his head had been dragged out of the sand already, but he hadn't confided that in her… yet. He was surprised when Phoebe didn't press her

278

point, saying instead, "No guns, Diggy Boo, anything you want. But you do know I'm from Arizona, and guns are a great part of our culture."

"Let's not talk about this anymore, Phoebe, I have to get dressed. Say, did I leave my blue jacket here? The one with the gold pocket?"

"Yes, you did, my dear. It's so lovely that I wore it to a restaurant in Adams Morgan, though I forgot it there because I had to leave in a rush. But don't worry, I've already called and told them to hold it for me."

"You wore my jacket?"

"Mmhmm."

"You know that's my warmest jacket and I always wear it."

"I will get it for you over the weekend when I go there."

"Which restaurant?"

"The Ethiopian one. I'm so sorry, Diggy Boo, I will get it back this weekend."

3

For two days after the poolside conversation, Adigun didn't do any swimming and confined himself to Bobby Brown's home gym. At first, he had serious misgivings about Phoebe's conduct, but these were eased by her open manner and seeming imperviousness to offense. He was disarmed by her complete lack of ego – the more he stayed away, the more she came after him. Now, she had taken to showing up at Bobby Brown's home to see him, whenever he didn't visit her at hers. Adigun began to relax again around her and his spontaneous flashbacks to his boyhood troubles with Adjua began to fade.

He had finished his workout that morning and was making his way past Bobby Brown's study to his room when he heard a scraping noise from within. Adigun knew Bobby had headed out to attend to some of his other fighters that morning, so his guard was up as he stalked silently into the study. He stopped in mid-step and stared as Phoebe, her back to him, pulled out drawers in Bobby's desk and rifled through the papers she saw.

"What are you doing here?"

"Oh, there you are, Diggy Boo! I have been looking for you all over the house."

"Did you try the gym? What the hell, Phoebe! Why are you opening these drawers? What are you looking for? This is wrong, Phoebe," Adigun seethed with barely contained rage and disgust. "You come to a man's house, and you are ransacking his study? What's this obsession with opening people's drawers, and reading files? What is wrong with you?"

Phoebe bore the admonitions with patience and a neutral expression, replying, "I was just bored, and I felt like reading a book. I had borrowed a book from Bobby a while back and was hoping I could find the sequel here."

"No, no, no," Adigun barked. How could she do this? How could she so casually make him seem like he was being ridiculous? "Phoebe, you can't be opening drawers here; the man trusts me, and he has taken me into his home," Adigun's voice was rising with his soaring emotions, "and how do you think he would feel to know you are going through his personal stuff?"

"Come on sweetie, I just was getting to know the house." Again, with the casual dismissiveness, "I'm just fascinated by its size and beauty. When you become the world champion, promise me we'll get a large house like this," Phoebe reached between Adigun's legs as she spoke, squeezing gently. His body's reaction was immediate and evident in his loose sweatpants, and Adigun's attention was forced in the direction of another concern that was

281

now more pressing than Phoebe's snooping – his pre-fight discipline.

"Yes, I promise," he gushed, "please let's get out of here. Bobby should not meet us here."

"I say let's make love right here in this study."

"Are you out of your mind? You know I have a fight coming up. Bobby has warned me not to drain my vital energy before I get in the ring."

 "But it's been so long, Diggy Boo, I'm going crazy!"

"You are going on too much about this sex thing. I have to keep my focus right now and I have to follow Bobby Brown's instructions to the letter; no sex till after the fight!" As he spoke, Adigun backed out of the study, pulling Phoebe, who still had a grip on his crotch, out with him. When they were out in the hallway, Phoebe let go of him, saying, "Whatever."

"Okay, so, now we are back to whatever again."

"Whatever, Diggy, whatever!"

Book-5

Complications

Bangaado e mo fowru naangi Nganaa bojji gooti

*(A bride and a hyena victim do not shed the same tears –
Fulani proverb)*

1

Later, in her apartment, Phoebe waited with tense nerves for her phone to ring. Her pager had beeped as their argument ended and she turned away from Adigun. She already knew who was reaching out and the routine was that, at this time of the day, when paged, she would wait ten minutes for her superior officer's call. She had given Adigun a baleful stare, then spun around and ran down the stairs, through the large oak door, and across the street.

She got into her apartment with time to spare and tried to gather herself before the call came in. She was glad she had the time for this; her nerves were frayed, and she might have gone off on her supervisor if she didn't cool down a bit first. The phone rang and, breathing in deeply, Phoebe picked it up on the second ring.

"Yes," She paused, listening, then continued, "It's not looking good, Sir – I literally just came from there and I had a nasty run-in with Fernandez." She winced at the raised voice on the other end of the line but remained calm as she waited for the storm to ease up. Phoebe was in a delicate situation with her undercover operation; her targets were under surveillance so, technically, she was too. Her handler was aware of her thing with Adigun, but she made it seem like she was just stringing him along to gain a foothold for her investigation. Whether the higher-ups suspected that there was more to it than she let on or not, they were too invested in bringing the crime syndicate down to scrutinize her dalliance closely. However, her direct supervisor was irritated by how little she told them about this new guy in the mix that she called Fernandez – for reasons even she could not discern, Phoebe never gave her agency Adigun's full story, and they only knew of him as Adelaide Fernandez, the up-and-coming boxing talent.

Now, her boss was ranting that she was supposed to have this Fernandez guy in the bag, under control. "Why the fuck are you letting him interfere with our shit, Phoebe?"

"Sir, you have to let me work this right – I'm the one on the inside, you know. I am taking all the risks. The guy is already suspicious, and I don't want him to raise his suspicions with the big man. He lives in the bloody house for now and he is super-protective of BB. Gratitude, I suspect, more than anything else. Loyalty.

"Listen, I checked the study and it's not there. I will find a way to keep looking, but this guy is sharp, Sir; I doubt he'll have it sitting on his desk at home. He already suspects something. There's some chatter about a snitch."

Phoebe paused again to listen. Her handler had calmed down and was better able to appreciate her situation. He gave her a fresh set of operations signals for emergencies and instructions in case her cover was blown.

"Please, Sir, can I have the jacket tomorrow?" Phoebe implored. "It's taking too long and it's going to be vital in the next few days. It shouldn't take this long to implant a listening device in a garment.

"Yes, the top button – the lower buttons keep coming up with distortion – top Button!

"You need to find a matching one, Sir, come on!

"Yes… this evening? Thanks so much, Sir. I told him I left it at a restaurant on Adams Morgan; the Ethiopian one."

Her caller asked her if she had any other requests. Phoebe knew he was being sarcastic, but she did have one more thing, "When are you moving the weapons cache from my crib? I can't even begin to get into how I explained that away when Fernandez saw them – speaking of which you ought to give me more credit for controlling my subject, Sir – but it is a ridiculous situation and I need them moved out, pronto!

"Okay. Thanks. Talk later."

2

The day arrived. Mrs. Brown knocked and opened the door to Adigun's room. He was on his knees, with his face buried in the bedding, saying his morning prayers. Mrs. Brown looked at him for a moment, then turned and walked away, leaving the door ajar. The smell of fresh coffee wafted into the room, followed soon after by the smell of freshly baked blueberry muffins. Adigun got up and entered the bathroom through the door barely a foot from his bed. He looked in the mirror and stroked the top of his Mohawk hair as he grabbed his blue toothbrush and cleaned his teeth. Then he gargled to clear his throat before taking a quick, steaming shower.

Back in his room, he quickly put on his sports gear, grabbed his white Nike gym bag, and stepped out. Bobby Brown was on the front Porch reading a large newspaper.

"Good morning, daddy."

"Good morning, champ. This indeed is the day the Lord has made; the day Shanny Rikers will get an African ass-whooping."

"Dig-un," Mrs. Brown called as she came out to join them. She was too enthralled with Adigun's African roots to pick up the Fernandez moniker and completely undaunted by her inability to pronounce his name properly. "Would you like your breakfast on the porch, darling?"

"Umm, yes, ma."

She grabbed the large tray from the marble tabletop.

Adigun was seated on the brown cow Hyde Chaise lounge.

"Daddy, I wonder why I'm not nervous."

"Maybe because you have made every day seem like a title fight."

"I feel good, Daddy. I feel good. Truly, I can't wait to get into that ring,"

"You bet, Shango! You bet! There's a lot that can go wrong in a fight, so don't go getting cocky, son. You can be confident that there's no way he can out-work us – that's for damn sure – but he's got good ring sense and he can punch. You've been a real soldier and you're strong, but this ain't sparring, so don't leave your chin hanging out."

"Sounds like you are saying I should respect him, daddy."

"Not him, son! Respect the craft and respect the ring. Respect the fact that a great boxer can get clocked by a tomato can with power. Respect yourself and make that sucker respect you too, got it?"

"This Shanny Rikers kid, is he African too?"

"I told you not to think about him as a person; only think of what you will do to him, boy."

"Sweetie," Mrs. Brown piped up, "You're not making him run this morning, are you?"

"No, my dear, he checks into the Li'l Ceasar this morning for the prefight mental conditioning program." Bobby paused to look at Adigun, then continued, "This is where we work on his mind – music, words, and physical stimulation to get his mind right and his blood up! You know the drill, sugar; you have been with me since the days of Rue Rawlington."

"Yes, I remember, hon, the late, great Rue Rawlington." Mrs. Brown now turned to Adigun as well, saying, "Rue was twice welterweight champion of the world. The Asian Storm, they used to call him. He lived with us for a while too, just like you, Dig-un." Bobby chuckled and said, "That's right! Back when we had the old house in Bethesda. The kid was little but ate like an elephant. And he fought like a lion!" As he listened, it occurred to Adigun that his mental conditioning may have begun already.

The drive to the airport was odd. Bobby Brown seemed paranoid, constantly checking his rear mirror and conducting coded phone conversations. As they turned into the Little Caesar hotel, Adigun was startled by an enormous billboard with his face on it, and it took him a moment to recognize it as publicity for his upcoming fight. He realized, as the surprise wore off, that this was the first time he would have a chance to really look at his opponent, but the billboard had already slid out of view; all he could register was a face with its lower half covered by a mask (or perhaps paint) in the colors of Jamaica. Bobby Brown pulled into the hotel entrance and a bellboy was at the window in an instant.

"Valet, Sir?"

One of the bellboys collected the keys from Bobby Brown and another removed Adigun's bag from the trunk of the Caddy. The two men were soon settled into their rooms and Adigun found the view outside his window dominated by the billboard with his pictures. He soaked that view in for some time before taking in his immediate surroundings within the room. The well-lit room was spacious and featured a King-size bed with a huge velvet headboard. Across the expanse of pinewood floor, opposite the bed, was a massive recessed TV framed within a dark oak console.

There was a knock on the door.

"It's me Pookie. Can I come in?"

Adigun opened the door.

"Hey, champ, here are your Nigerian pants. The seats are sold out, bro. The Nigerians bought it all! Un-fucking-believable, man! It's gonna be a Nigerian ass-whupping tonight, Shango!" Pookie was gushing with excitement. "Ooooooh, my oh my, we also got the Nigerian flag, and guess what! We were able to get the green and white gloves!

"I know you are the underdog here, but you know what? You are the one bringing the entire crowd. We have never had sales like this at any of our events. It's crazy."

Adigun stared, bemused, as Pookie left then he fell to his knees and prayed. He spoke to God in his native Yoruba language for the next hour until the phone began ringing. Adigun picked it up and spoke with Bobby Brown with a surreal feeling of clarity and serenity that bordered on numbness.

"Yes, sir.

"Yes, sir.

"Thank you for the opportunity, daddy.

"No.

"Correct.

"I will proceed to the changing room downstairs.

"Yes, Pookie was here – the gear is better than I could have hoped for."

"Will start my stretches as soon as I get down."

Adigun's phone rang again as he put it down. He could hear Pookie before the receiver even made contact with his ear.

"Dude, the place is crunk man! The Africans have arrived. They came in big buses. They have arrived,

Shango. They filled up the hall already. It's on, bro, it's freaking on."

Adigun hung up, grabbed his gym bag, and proceeded to the bank of elevators. The calm of the elevator, with its soft jazz muzak, was shattered once the lift doors opened and Adigun was mobbed by a hysterical crowd of green-and-white-clad, chanting supporters.

"Shango!"

"Shango!"

"Shango!"

"Shango!"

Some of them wielded plastic axes, trying to depict the Yoruba deity, Shango, after whom their hero had been named. Pookie materialized and ushered Adigun through the throng, cutting through with a seasoned combination of firm strength and politeness that impressed Adigun. They broke free of the jubilant crowd and made it to the locker rooms. Before being swept into the white corridor, Adigun caught a glimpse of the arena through an open service door; it was packed! It seemed like the entire Nigerian and Jamaican communities had shown up. Once in the corridor to the locker rooms, he noticed a white door with 'Shanny Rikers's scribbled in black felt on a piece of card. Two hefty security guards stood outside with wide stances and their hands clasped before them. Adigun stopped, put his index finger in his mouth, and raised it to the sky. They had on black bow ties like the Nation of Islam foot soldiers.

Several meters further down, he and Pookie came to a door with the single word, 'Fernandez', written on another piece of white card. Adigun almost passed the door, for a moment forgetting that he was Fernandez until Pookie opened the door and ushered Adigun in. Sitting in the corner, with the phone glued to his right ear, was Bobby Brown, wearing a black satin shirt with grey trim. By a gleaming massage table, stood an elderly man dressed in similar attire. Recognizing these men as his ringside team caused a small flutter of nerves, which Adigun crushed with iron resolve.

Turning to the right, Adigun was stunned to see Phoebe dressed in a white and green Nigerian attire. She even had a green head tie to match. He sat on the leather bench on the side by the window and grabbed the green high-top boxing shoes, lacing them up in swift, mechanical motions. Springing to his feet, he tested the shoes to ensure they gave him the grip and nimbleness he needed. The old man signaled to Adigun to get on the already prepared massage table where Phoebe waited, and she began his massage routine on his back and arms. He reached for the green and white shorts, taking in the embroidery stitched into the back in red and gold. Over a gold lightning bolt, the word, 'Sango' blazed in red. Adigun glanced at the Nigerian flag in the corner of the room and then up at Bobby Brown who was speaking in hushed, but animated, tones on the phone. Their eyes met and Adigun mouthed a silent "Thank you, sir." Bobby nodded and continued his phone call. Adigun turned his face down on the table and closed his eyes for the rest of the massage.

When Phoebe was done with her ministrations, Adigun sat up and the old man grabbed his right hand and began to wrap it. "My name is Steve Harris. Folks call me Pappy. I'm so happy to meet you, boy. I've been hearing about you from Philly since last year. Everybody's been talking of this strong African kid that sends all his sparring partners to the emergency room.

"It's your debut fight, but it has more buzz than the Rumble In The Jungle. It's all over the TV. I even heard it's being beamed internationally."

Pappy was in his late 70s, but his coal-black hands whipped, stretched, and looped the hand wraps with practiced efficiency. He would only occasionally glance down at the work he was doing, switching Adigun's view of him from his bushy salt-and-pepper beard to his bushy, all-white hair. His hands seemed to work independently of the rest of him, as he babbled non-stop, and Adigun was a little surprised when he felt Pappy patting his knuckles and calling the match commission officials over to inspect the wraps and the gloves a final time before he put them on.

Once the gloves were on, laced up, and signed by the officials, Adigun turned to Pookie and began doing some pad work and shadow boxing. He needed to get warmed up. He figured the noise of the gloves striking the pads and his cries would pull Bobby over for some words of instruction, but Bobby stayed on the phone. His aspect was tense and hunched as he spoke, but he gave little away to anyone in the room that may have been trying to figure out what he was discussing. All anyone could hear was his terse, ominous pronouncements:

"It will be done as we discussed, and ONLY as we discussed!

"All the pieces are in place except for yours – nothing happens until ALL the pieces are in place, understood?

"Are you out of your goddamned mind? Listen, *my* fighter, *my* fight – nothing begins until I have what I want! If the fight starts a little late, so be it, but nothing messes with my sequence, got it?

"Just bear in mind what I have already put up on press and publicity for this thing. You better come through; you hear?" Bobby hung up and stalked out of the room.

There was a two-hour delay before the fight could start and the spectators were being distracted by local bands and loud music. Adigun's team worked with care to keep him warm without tiring him out, but he worried that the long wait would give rise to another case of nerves and was relieved when Bobby rushed in and raised his two hands. "Now, let's go kick some Jamaican ass," he yelled. Adigun jumped up and began to stretch and hop, warming up and shadow-boxing until the time came for him to head out to the arena. The hallway was wall-to-wall with bodies and Adigun spotted Shanny's entourage up ahead, led by a tall man toting a large Jamaican flag. Pookie led Adigun's train with the Nigerian flag and the entire team, clad in green and white snaked and pushed through the crowd. The Arena was filled, with some of the spectators sitting on the carpet stairs. Bob Marley's "I Shot the Sheriff" filled the arena as Shanny Rikers made his way to the ring, with a ten-thousand-strong chorus singing along. The crowd roared as Rikers climbed into the ring, bouncing around with his arms raised to greet his fans. Shortly after the reggae music stopped and there was a brief hush.

Then came the creeping, insidious sound of Fela Anikulapo Kuti, over the speakers, chuffing, like a steam engine, and setting the signature rhythm of his Afrobeat style. By the time the subtle keyboard intro of Unknown Soldier came on, an electric current seemed to crackle through large sections of the gathered crowd. Several audience members stood and began to clap and sway as Adigun made his solemn way to the ring, face obscured by his hood, seemingly oblivious to the hysterical cheers. Some clever work by the DJ spliced over the typically lengthy instrumental intro of the track and cut to the chorus of "Unknown Soldier" just as Adigun ascended the ringside steps and the Nigerians in the audience went berserk. It was un-rehearsed but seemed choreographed to perfection. Then came a bright flurry of fireworks and the hall erupted again.

Steve Pappy climbed into the ring with Adigun, disrobed him, and toweled him intermittently while trying to talk him through final prep. Adigun could hear nothing but shouts from the spectators. The hypnotic rhythm of Fela's music had him in something close to an electric trance. The crowd seemed to groan as the entrance music cut out and Adigun began to register the limits of the ring and focused on his opponent as he began skipping and loosening up. There were several groups chanting war songs in Yoruba, talking drums and all. On the other side were the Jamaicans – it was a huge display of Jamaican flags – their voices loud, but not quite matching the Nigerians.

The fighters were called to the center of the ring for the referee's final instructions. Only when his opponent stood face-to-face with him did the light of recognition spark in their eyes. "Bloooood! What the heck is you doing here, you African bastard?" Shannon yelled over the referee's terse monologue, drowning out everything but odd snatches about "… the dressing room…" and "… obey my commands…"

Adigun gaped in disbelief. "Is this you, Shannon?" Adigun nearly lost his gumshield as he yelled. The referee frowned, "You better pay attention, gentlemen; I won't hesitate to deduct points OR disqualify you if you get it wrong!" The fighters nodded absently as the referee droned on about rabbit punches and kidney punches, all the while staring at each other with mixed emotions. They touched gloves and each walked back to his corner when the referee ordered, preparing for the start of the first round.

Adigun fell on his knees to pray and, above the rest of the crowd came a shout of, "Praise the Lord!" "Halleluiah," came the deafening response. A disembodied cry of "Bismillah Rahman Rahim!!!" floated across from the Rikers side, where there was a huge contingent of Nation of Islam adherents. A chorus rendition of the Al Fatiha proceeded with a solemn undertone of fervor and the air crackled. The hot dog vendors, seeming to have waited for the spiritual battle lines to be drawn, invaded the aisles to sell their food.

The noise was deafening, and few heard the referee yell, "Seconds out!" However, everyone heard the bell signaling the start of the first round when it came moments later. The tone of the crowd noise dropped from a roar to a seething white noise, like the change from a thundering waterfall to a white-water river. The fighters approached each other, flicking out jabs and seeming to jostle to claim the center of the ring. Adigun ducked under a looping overhand right and clinched with Shanny Rikers. "Fancy this, eh, village boy?" Rikers thumped at Adigun's ribs as they wrestled, grinning through his gum shield. "Where have you been?"

The referee stepped behind Rikers and tapped both fighters, shouting, "Break! No punching!" Adigun pushed back from Rikers, muttering, "I went to hell and came back . . . with a present for you!"

Adigun leaned on his back foot and twisted his head away from a vicious right cross, which whistled past his cheek. He realized that, acquaintance or not, Rikers wanted to knock his block off and, with this realization, a cold resolve filled him. He stopped responding to Shanny Rikers's non-stop verbal jabs and just let his training take over. He feinted a cross of his own and tagged Rikers with a glancing jab.

"Oh, sugar, what is this? Looks like someone can actually box a *likkle* bit!" Rikers had good head movement, but Adigun already had a decent read on his patterns of movement. He toe-shuffled in a wide circle around the lunging Rikers, leaving his left guard slightly low, inviting his opponent to take advantage of the gap. Rikers took the bait and launched another dangerous overhand right, but Adigun had already stepped off the line and it swept harmlessly through the air.

As the first round drew to its end, Adigun was content to pepper Rikers with jabs to the head and body, while he processed what he had learned about his opponent. Rikers fought in the orthodox style and showed an aggressive right, but he telegraphed his punches. He seemed to be holding his left in reserve and Adigun's instinct was that he wanted to distract from it. The bell ending Round 1 sounded and Adigun turned around without acknowledging Rikers's quips.

"You slick, you quick, but I'ma lick, village boy."

Back in his corner, Adigun was serene. His team reapplied his grease and the ice at the back of his neck felt good. Bobby Brown muttered in his ear, "You're gonna get a few extra seconds of rest, Champ..." The lights in the arena blinked off as he said this and there was near-total darkness. A nervous rumble began in the crowd and Adigun was able to make out a number of the spectators standing and seeming to switch places. Some sat back down, but others made for the exits, following the emergency lights on the floor. In less than fifteen seconds, the lights came back on, and the crowd cheered.

"You've given us all we need, son. Now go on and cream this mouthy fuck!" Bobby Brown sounded almost merry as he spoke. He and the rest of the team climbed out as the referee ordered and Adigun stood, ready for the second round to be rung in. The svelte young lady with the round number card was barely through the ropes when the bell rang and Adigun advanced on his opponent, who was already almost at the center. "*You know me a fi lick you well and eat you fi dinner, as clad,*" Rikers seemed almost giddy with joy as he said this, "*Me ha fi hurt your blood clad village ass.*" He flicked out a double jab as he spoke (the first time he'd done that so far) and Adigun had a flash of understanding – the jab was now being used as a decoy and a blinder – Rikers intended to go for the kill in this round. Adigun slipped the jabs and landed a decent left hook to Rikers's body. Rikers grunted but turned his body into the punch, reducing its impact. He almost surprised Adigun by unleashing a straight right from that slightly awkward position but, again, it was

300

clear to Adigun that the punch was meant to distract him. Even before his right hand reached full extension, Rikers had begun to twist his shoulders and hips, positioning his left arm out of Adigun's line of sight. To Adigun, life took on a slow-motion quality, and, as Rikers's straight right grazed his ear, he watched with fascination as his left shoulder dipped and his entire left arm vanished from view. Adigun had a flashback, remembering Rikers's words on the train long ago.

"A rude boy!

"A Dangerous Animal.

"Cruiserweight champion of Rikers. Jamaican ambassador of licking. *Me lick spots of a leopard with a left uppercut.*

"Left hand sting like a scorpion!"

Adigun had already begun ducking towards his right in reaction to Rikers's straight right but, with memory and instinct, he suddenly straightened and pivoted on his right foot, guard held high around his temples. This move put Adigun at a right angle to Rikers and completely off the line as he unleashed a monster left uppercut at thin air. Rikers was still trying to register what had just happened when Adigun dipped slightly and used power from his legs to drive a short-left hook that connected solidly with the bewildered Rikers's right temple.

Shannon dropped like a sack of potatoes and bounced his head off the canvas. His mouthguard was on the floor next to his head. The referee didn't even bother counting and waved the fight off before frantically waving in the ringside medics. The press went ballistic as camera flashes went off. The arena went quiet for two beats as Rikers's corner crew rushed into the ring. The referee was shooing Adigun to a neutral corner when the crowd erupted. Chants of "Shango, Shango!!" echoed as a stretcher team raced to attend to the fallen fighter. Once they had a collar, Rikers was stretchered out of the ring and directly to a waiting ambulance. While this was going on, Adigun was being mobbed by his team and others. Journalists crowded the ring, angling for a comment or a picture. Bobby Brown gave a signal to the lightbox and the lights in the arena went off once more. The crowd went ballistic in the dark, still chanting, "Shango!", while shadowy figures rose from their seats with duffel bags and melted into the darkness. The crowd's chants morphed into wild cheering as the lights came on again moments later.

The ring announcer declared Adigun – or Adelaide Fernandez – as the winner and the referee raised his hand. The Nigerians went berserk, straining the security team, who were stretched thin trying to contain the madness. Cops moved in, brandishing their billy clubs and helping to restore order. Fortunately, the general spirit was one of celebration and there were no fights to break up. Even Rikers's fans seemed euphoric. The press crowded around Adigun, all wanting a piece of this new cruiserweight contender. Bobby rushed to him and whispered,

"Remember, your name is Adel Fernandez. Speak as little as possible."

"Mr. Fernandez, did you plan to go for the knockout before entering the ring today?"

"My trainer always said to knock 'em down and take it out of the judges' hands, so I was definitely looking for the opportunity, yes."

"Would you say it was a lucky punch or…?"

"No, not really. We didn't have tapes to study Rikers's style ahead of the fight, so my trainer, Bobby Brown, told me to use the first round to study him, take it easy, read the fight, then decide. Round 2, I saw an opening and I took it."

"But, Adel, tell us about yourself, where you're from – you wore Nigeria's colors and had a massive following of Nigerian fans, all calling you Shango – are you representing Nigeria."

"Shango is the Nigerian god of Thunder and Lightning; I guess my knockout shows you why people call me that. But to answer your question, I represent the Bobby Brown Gym. Bobby Brown has made me the fighter and the man that I am, and that is all I can say to you about that.

Bobby Brown grabbed Adigun around his shoulders and walked him away from the ringside, left hand raised as if to ward off more questions, looking silent and grim until one of the reporters yelled out, "Hey, Bobby, you think this kid is championship material?" Bobby turned to where the question came from, zoomed in on the reporter who asked it, and replied with a smirk, "Think? Larry, I don't think, I know! Fernandez here is the next cruiser-weight champion! And you know it too unless you're blind or batty." The reporters laughed at that, as Adigun's entourage resumed their walk to the dressing room, Bobby Brown patting his back all the way. While the boxing match he had just won was at the club level, and not likely to be broadcast outside of local channels, there had been a considerable media presence and Adigun was a bit nervous. It would only take one of the syndicated networks like ABC to use the footage and his match might end up featuring on a show like ABC Wide World of Sports – a well-watched show in Nigeria. Bobby Brown had assured him that he looked too different now from the way he did years before when he first arrived in The States, but Adigun was worried that his parents might see him on TV and recognize him. His only comfort was that they were not likely to go to the authorities, but it would complicate his life if they decided to seek him out. He now fretted over the sentiment that had led him to sport Nigeria's colors and to court the Nigerian community, which he had actively avoided before the fight.

Adigun made it into his changing room but didn't find the blessed peace he had hoped for; the room was packed with people who had somehow made it past the security guard, who causally high-fived Adigun as he went through the door. The people inside the dressing room were the local elites – a councilman here, a talk show host there – and they congratulated Adigun with a great deal more decorum than the throngs that thrashed outside. He still had to sign the odd glove and promotional flier, but he was able to retreat to the showers within less than ten minutes. In this private space, Adigun knelt and prayed before letting the stinging jets wash away his sweat. As he stood under the shower, he chuckled, realizing that he had spent more energy making his way back to the dressing room than in the actual fight. He was unmarked and his tank was close to full.

Shower done, Adigun changed into a pair of snug, ash-grey sweatpants, and a matching sweatshirt. As soon as he opened the door into the main dressing room area, he could tell that the crowd in the room had grown. It was certainly not as genteel as it had been earlier, and the atmosphere was raucous. A buffet of hors d'oeuvres had magically appeared in the room and champagne was flowing. Several teenagers and young adults pressed toward Adigun, pushing their gloves and other paraphernalia toward him for autographs. Adigun gave in to the festive spirit and began signing with a black marker. He signed them as Adel Fernandez.

A slight commotion caused him to look toward the entrance door and he saw a short, light-skinned man pushing his way through the crowd. One of the security staff was running the man down when Pookie intercepted him and greeted him warmly. He turned to the security man and said, "Let him through; he's family."

The man wiggled through the ring of hefty security guards.

 His bare feet made intermittent appearances from beneath his flowing white garment as he walked. He lifted the skirts of his robe, just below the wide blue sash at his waist, as he struggled through the crowd. "Halleluiah, oh!!!" The man shouted as he approached, and Adigun looked at him, motionless. It was Alagba. He was with his wife, who proceeded sedately in his wake.

Adigun greeted her politely when she got closer and began to speak in Igbo.

"Congratulations! We missed you, my son – we missed you!" Alagba drew closer to Adigun as well and, all of a sudden, there wasn't enough air in the room. He said, "Bros Ojo is here as well, and the entire choristers from the church. We have been fasting and praying for you to win this fight for weeks now." Adigun dipped his torso forward slightly, in Yoruba fashion, as if trying to touch the floor with one hand. It was a gesture of respect for the elder man that he performed by reflex, without thought. Alagba placed a regal palm on Adigun's dipped shoulder, saying, *"Dide, omo mi,"* Yoruba for, "Get up, my son." Adigun's trancelike state broke on hearing this slimy creature refer to him as his son and he shot up, making Alagba's hand almost fly from his shoulder. Alagba read the expression on Adigun's face, and he took a half-step backward, his face betraying serene acceptance, rather than alarm. "I have learned much about you since you left my home – "*Omo Ekun, Ekun ni jo,*" meaning "The child of a Lion is a Lion." Alagba turned away from Adigun and surprised him by starting a conversation with Pookie in Spanish. Pookie responded to Alagba in Spanish, and he backed away from Adigun, who was also drifting off in another direction, once more signing knick-knacks for ardent supporters. His ring of security staff moved with him like a ripple that couldn't escape its bond with the pebble that formed it. At length, Bobby Brown came in with a smile on his face, hugged Adigun, and declared, "It's a wrap, guys. It's a wrap. We did it. The cars are outside waiting. We head to my house for dinner."

3

The group marched out of the dressing room through the hallway to the exit doors on the side of the arena. There was a brisk breeze outside and Adigun pulled his blue jacket tighter around him, glad that Phoebe had finally retrieved it from whatever restaurant she forgot it in. She was right by his side, her arm in the crook of his, when Bobby Brown called her aside and whispered to her. "I'm having dinner with my business partners and it's going to get a little rowdy if you know what I mean – not the kind of setting for a decent young lady. I don't want to cramp their style and I definitely don't want to expose you to their shenanigans, so why don't you leave Shango with me, and you ride in the white limo?" Bobby Brown looked at Phoebe with an apologetic expression, continuing, "You can celebrate your man's victory with him tomorrow night, okay?"

Phoebe gave him a polite nod and then kissed Adigun, before walking off toward the white limo sitting in the glare of the arc sodium lights of the parking area. Three police cars and two fire trucks sat on the east side of the hotel about 200 meters away. A fleet of black Town cars pulled up, one after the other, to pick up Adigun, Bobby

Brown, and the rest of the crew. Phoebe, already in the white limousine, made a phone call.

"Follow them; I'll be across the road at my place."

Adigun rode in the same limo as Bobby Brown, who was fussing with a bottle of Ace of Spades. He peeled off the transparent orange wrapper, popped the cork, and poured two glasses.

"Here's to you, boy. Drink up.

"Tonight, you will get to know who Bobby Brown really is. Whatever you see, take it in and be a man about it. Your life is about to change – we are about to bring you into the most exclusive, elite organization."

"In boxing?"

"Not boxing. We trade in special commodities with a very interesting demand curve. Drink up!

"We are the largest narcotics distribution organization on the continent, and we keep away from the law by being the most sophisticated. Your boxing career is closely linked to our current strategy, so you've already earned your stripes with the organization. Tonight is the beginning of your success story in America.

"Boy, tonight, you will meet my family – my real family! Do not be afraid; You have proven yourself and you have passed every test. Since Chicago."

Adigun sat in the dim limousine with his mouth open. "You knew what happened?"

"Yes, we also followed you all the way."

"Wait a minute! Even when I hooked up with Douglas Callahan?"

"Douglas Callahan," Bobby chuckled, "is in one of the other limos in this convoy!" He laughed again as he cracked his window and lit a cigar. He took a long draw from the thick chunk of dried tobacco and peered at Adigun through the smoke.

"That wasn't no Douglas Callahan, son. That is the richest real estate mogul in Chicago, Jerome Englis! He followed your bus from Washington to Chicago and, when you had some problems, he was there to give you a ride to your destination.

"We are very meticulous. We have been running this for over thirty years and the law hasn't been able to get anything on us."

Adigun blurted out, "Douglas Callahan is part of you?"

"Drink up Adel. Tonight, we celebrate. Forget about Douglas who or what! Cheers, my son, cheers!"

The white limousine was last in the convoy and, within its plush cabin, Phoebe took the car phone out of its cradle and punched in a series of digits. While it rang, she made sure the privacy partition was up between her and the driver. Satisfied that it was, she returned her attention to the receiver just as the party at the other end picked up. "How's the sound for the boys in the van? Not muffled, I hope. Yeah, I was worried he'd put an overcoat on top of the blue jacket, but we got lucky with the weather." Phoebe paused for a moment, listening, then replied, "The entire clan is heading to Big Boy's place, so we don't have to worry too much about keeping up – we know where they're going. I'm sorry, but I have to get off this call. I will hit you back in a bit."

At length, the convoy snaked through Bobby Brown's gate, except for the white one, which peeled off and parked in front of Phoebe's apartment.

"Phoebe waited for the Chauffeur to open the door, then stepped out holding her black shimmering gown with one hand and her high heels in the other. She walked bare-footed through the courtyard of her complex, shoulders squared, chin thrust forward, face intent.

4

At Bobby Brown's mansion, the party coalesced around a huge, elaborate, expensively laid out banquet table. Adigun drifted to where 'Douglas Callahan' stood talking to two fat Latinos. He glanced up at Adigun and, once more, showed no recognition whatsoever. If not for the braided plait at the back of his hat, which Adigun recalled vividly from their first encounter, he would have doubted his own recognition. He jerked as a voice at his shoulder said, "You can hang your jackets here." It was Manuel, a long-time fixture in Bobby's home.

"No thanks, Manuel. You know I am still not used to the cold here – I'll just keep it on for a bit, okay?"

As he said this, Adigun slipped his hands into the pockets of his blue coat and was instantly reminded of why it was his favorite – the fur-lined pockets gave immediate relief to his hands, which had begun to tingle.

"Leave him be, Manuel," Bobby called from across the room, "Champ is always cold. He was freezing the night I met him, and he's hardly improved since then. Boy's only hot when he's in the ring!" Laughter and scattered applause broke out and then escalated when Mrs. Brown came out from the kitchen and, with a large smile, invited everyone to the table. She had prepared an elaborate dinner with a sprawling array of meat and seafood dishes. The table was set with fine crystal glasses and silverware fit for kings, with a low-set fireplace serving as the centerpiece. The flames glowed a soft orange and threw off rusty sparks when Manuel would occasionally poke the coal with an ornate poker.

It was a full table with the entire team from across all the states. Seated around the long marble table were the key men from all of the syndicate's territories within the United States – nine of them in all – not counting Bobby Brown himself. Adigun alternated his attention between casual observation of these nine and the mesmerizing effect of the garden outside, visible through the large bay windows, the water from its huge fountain working magic with the light. Beyond the garden, a modest man-made lake shimmered, reflecting the lights of the surrounding estates of the affluent Bethesda area.

"Hey, amigos! Amigos!" Adigun's attention snapped back to the dining table at this cry. The crisp acoustics of the large room were revealed as Bobby Brown hit on his crystal wine glass with a table knife. It sounded like the table was in a concert hall.

"Thank you, my brothers, we have done a great job tonight and we have put to test a great innovation in our distribution system. Before we start to eat, we'll take a few minutes to acknowledge our heavenly father, only on whose mercy we can sit here tonight. I call on my brother from Africa, my partner in upper Marlborough, Maryland, and the only clergyman on this table today.

"Brother Alag...Bah! I've been trying to pronounce this Nigerian name for over twenty years now, but still can't nail it. Ala-Guh-Bah, Alakba... Whatever!!"

There was a mixture of jeering and applause from the guests at the table.

Adigun realized more than half the guests were people he had never seen before, though he remembered some of them having paid visits at one time or another when he worked as a cleaner at the gym. The jeering and side-talk continued until Alagba cleared his throat to speak, and then the room fell silent.

"Thank you so much, my brother, Bobby B, our honorable patron, for honoring my God. I'm so glad to see our partners in Pennsylvania, our leaders in Detroit, and our captains in Baltimore." He closed his eyes and crossed his chest with his hands, going into some sort of mild convulsion, before jerking to his left side. "Jah! Jehovah!" Alagba shook and punctuated his exhortations with drawn-out grunts. "Jah!! Je...hovah! Holy... St. Michael!!" Alagba paused and jerked backward in another, more severe, convulsive jerk. The body of guests, at this point, rolled their eyes and grinned at one another. "We thank you for the successful completion of today's business. We bless your name for this celebration meal. We thank you for all the goods that exchanged hands without any calamity. We give you the glory for this meal. Father, for all the deliberations that would be had here today on the way forward and preparation for the next transactions, may your holy eyes be present."

Adigun opened one eye, scanning the table, and stroking his Mohawk. His gaze fixed again on Douglas Callahan, who simply looked away when his eyes met Adigun's.

The long prayer ended with a very long amen and there was an eruption of movement amongst the seated guests as if, during the stretch of praise, worship, and soul-searching, they had instead found the depths of their appetites. Dishes and cutlery clinked Loudly and there was a swell in the hum of conversation.

"Oh, Mrs. B, your sweet potato pie is from another world."

"Damn! This is like a second Thanksgiving!"

"This fried chicken is made in heaven!"

"I love you, Mrs. B!" Pookie intoned with sober reverence.

"Thanks, Pookie – I'm glad you enjoyed it. The potato salad should be out in a few minutes."

Pookie grabbed a few drumsticks and passed the bowl to the right side of the table. Alagba sat next to Bobby Brown and was whispering in his ear for a long time. They clutched identical drumsticks as they continued their whispered exchange, Bobby nodding continuously, while the others ate. Bobby Brown cleared his throat and there was instant silence on the table. He rose and, to Adigun's mild surprise, Bobby Brown began speaking in Spanish and continued to do so for the next ten minutes. Adigun did not understand a word of Spanish; nor had he ever heard Bobby Brown speak the language so extensively. To his considerably greater surprise, Alagba responded in fluent, crisp Spanish as well. The others around the table nodded their heads as, for about fifteen minutes, the two went back and forth, with animation and obvious mutual regard. The discussion got heated at some point and there came continuous banging on the table and stamping of feet as several of the other guests joined in the conversation. The only person that did not speak was Jerome Englis. Eventually, there was a lull in the hostilities and the participants seemed to pull back, looking pensive. When the silence was greatest, Jerome Englis sprang up in anger and delivered some scathing remarks, also in Spanish, with his fists clenched and speaking through clenched teeth. The lines in his middle-aged face deepened in his emotion and his white tennis shoes squeaked on the polished wood floor as his feet shuffled. Shouting at the top of his voice, he turned sideways to point at Bobby Brown and the gathering heaved a collective gasp as the bulge underneath his jacket swung in sympathy with his sudden movement. When the fluttering flap revealed the polished wood of a pistol butt in its holster, three of the guests leaped up with placatory words and gestures. The tension eased, Englis sat back down, and Bobby Brown began another speech that ended with the word, 'Salut'.

Glasses clinked and they saluted each other.

"Felicidades."

"Felicidades."

"Felicidades."

The Spanish portion of the meeting seemed to be over, and they switched to English. Bobby walked around to Adigun's seat, and, with a nod of his curly-haired head, he placed an affectionate hand on his protégé's shoulder. Looking into Adigun's eyes, he raised his glass, while gesturing for others to do the same, then said loudly, "Viva Adigun; Welcome to the family." The gathered guests echoed, "Viva Adigun!" twice, in an eerily cult-like chant.

"Sorry for the vernacular interlude, Champ; we call ourselves the Edguardo. Our business language is Spanish, and we have been a family for decades. Loyalty and silence are our codes." Bobby Brown's expression was grim as he brought his gaze in from around the table to focus on Adigun.

"You are my only son – I adopted you – and you are one of us now. Soon enough, you will start Spanish lessons. In part, it is simply tradition. On the other hand, it is how you will honor the rich history of this family and its founder and patron.

"We all met on a little farm in Putumayo, Colombia. This is in the south of Colombia, in a corner with Peru on the left – just a few miles to the east – and Brazil on the right, a few miles to the west. We farmed *coca*, working for a common master, Edguardo Ramirez the Third of blessed memory." At the mention of Ramirez, several of the guests made signs of the cross or kissed rosaries, while a mutter of reverence ran through the room. "Third-generation Ramiraldonez. He was a general in the Revolutionary Army." Bobby paused and cleaned tears from his eyes with a white handkerchief. As if this had been a signal, the entire table rose and, with choreographed perfection, bowed in respect for Edguardo. Adigun found himself bowing with them.

"Edguardo taught us the secrets of life. We worked hard, but we learned a lot."

He closed his eyes for a second and made the sign of the cross as another tear streaked down his cheeks. "He paved a way for us to come to America. I was just nineteen years of age when I went to Columbia from Virginia. I had just come out of prison where Edguardo was serving a fifty-year sentence. There had been a change in the Columbian government, and he was able to secure a much-questioned and highly controversial pardon from the President of the United States. Edguardo had protected me in prison and my loyalty made me go with him to Columbia." Bobby paused and looked pointedly at Adigun, continuing, "He took me as a son.

"We all came to Columbia from different parts of the world. Pookie came from an orphanage in Brazil. Alonzo smuggled himself into Putumayo from Peru. Then we had Jerome Englis from Guatemala – his real name was Togonopulous." The table erupted in a gale of laughter. Bobby chuckled as he continued, "I remember when Edguardo sent us to the US, David got sent back at the US entry point." Bobby's eyes took on a distant look and then he turned to one of his guests and asked, "My God, David, do you remember that day?" The man he addressed, David Morales, had long ago come from Columbia to replace Hector Colon in Oregon after he was murdered by the Mexican Cartel.

"Oh no, Bobby... don't do this today..." The man held his head with both hands and giggled, pleading, "... not today!" Laughter seized the assembly once more. Bobby Brown pressed the man, Can I?" David shook his head in disapproval, but his shoulders quaked with uncontrollable laughter. "Oh, David, please let me talk about this today." Pookie was choking with laughter, coughing away from the table.

"The idiot had an imp girlfriend from Brazil – a real dwarf! He packed her in his military rucksack." Each sentence was punctuated by hitching gasps as the laughter threatened to overcome Bobby Brown.

"He was in front of customs when the wild imp started punching him – she had to go to the toilet!" At this point, the guests were in hysterics. "The customs guys noticed something moving in the backpack, then it suddenly began to pour out a golden liquid. It looked like beer until you smelled it… boy, did it stink!"

Now the entire table began to choke with laughter, Pookie was halfway falling off his chair.

"You need to see what happened when the girl was placed on the table."

"She had a dog collar on her neck with a leash attached to it."

They all continued choking with laughter.

"She put out her tongue and went on her knees and arms in some sort of crawl. David told the customs guys she was a pet – a rare, Brazilian dwarf bitch, he said – and the customs officers cracked up! They had never seen anything like it.

"But wait, it gets better! David looked at them and said, "Okay, okay, what are you guys laughing about? What is so funny? Can't bring a Brazilian into America - or is there a size limit?"

Bobby Brown cleaned his eyes with his white handkerchief, still laughing. He managed to get his laughter under control, lost the battle for a moment, then rallied and settled down with a deep, audible breath.

"Then you know our spiritual leader here, originally from Nigeria. Edguardo lived in Lagos when he was wanted dead or alive by the American and Colombian governments and he pushed product around the globe from there. He was later caught in a town outside Lagos – can't remember the name, but it had a South American name like Aperu or Du Peru. . ."

Alagba blurted out "Iperu!! Akesan" and shook his head.

"Aha! I remember they had a young king called Ala Peru or something… Anyway, Edguardo was extradited quietly to Colombia, leaving behind his long-time personal assistant, Alagba. He'd served Edguardo in Nigeria for a long time and took over our supplies from Lagos until Edguardo took him over to Columbia.

"Nigeria is a very integral part of our business." Here, Bobby fixed his gaze on Adigun, "I'll explain more to you soon enough." He returned his attention to the rest of the guests and continued.

"Alagba got to Columbia long before I came in. I'd heard so much about him. This dude used to be Edguardo's *juju* man, now he is a Christian clergyman! I remember we called him Baba Atuma.

"Edguardo was later extradited to America by the DEA and Alagba ran the Colombian operations while he was in Jail in America." "Product was shipped from Putumayo to Lagos, repackaged, and sent to America. Before Edguardo passed on, we were able to create a business triangle with North America as the apex of the triangle. Business boomed in America, but Edguardo could not leave Columbia because of his status; so, he moved *us* to America to handle the supply chain directly.

"Most of us crossed the border on the same day, but we dispersed to different states where we established the culture of diligence and loyalty.

"I will stop here for now. Well done, Adel; you have trained well, and you fought a good fight. Your role as a boxer has brought wealth to the family. I am proud of you, and I will explain things better to you later. You will rest for a few days, then resume training for the next fight, which is in about six weeks. With a major fight every couple of months, you can be the cruiserweight champion of the world in under one year.

"I welcome you to the Edguardo Family."

Someone intoned, "May Patron Edguardo's soul rest in peace!" Shouts arose around the table.

"Long live our Patron, Bobby, The Big Kahuna, Brown!!"

"Viva Edguardo!"

The entire table stood up put their right palm on their hearts and all shouted.

"La vida de Edguardo permanece en todas nosotras para siempre!!"

"I think it is a good time to formally introduce you to the family," Bobby piped up, continuing, "I will let them introduce themselves."

Mrs. Brown moved back and forth between the kitchen and dining areas and intermittently, as she passed by, guests slipped rolls of hundred-dollar bills into her palm. Each time, she would smile and whisper, "Muchas gracias." Her long purple apron swept the polished wood floor as she made her exit at the start of the introductions, which Alagba kick-started. "*Corsin*, you know me already; our own history is already rich in America, but I can tell you it goes even deeper to our roots in the motherland. You think I don't know your father? Even his own father?"

"Get on with it, old man, all right? We don't have all night!" Bobby seemed placid enough, but there was no mistaking the irritation in his voice. "I know you're related to everybody from Nigeria, but there's a lot of people need to talk here, so save the family tree shit for another time, eh?"

Alagba opened his mouth wide, the nostrils on his flat nose flaring as the light from the huge Chandeliers bounced off against his wide shiny forehead. "Well," he said gruffly, "the champ already knows me, so enough said." He collapsed into his seat. The man who was seated next to him went next, introducing himself as Alonzo, from Florida. After Alonzo, dressed in a bright red suit, was Michael Truman. He was originally Brazilian and was in charge of the New York territory. He raised his glass in a toast to Adigun.

"Salute to the champ. I made a lot of money on the betting stand, so thanks for whooping the Jamaican."

Then Pookie introduced himself and Adigun learned that he was married to Bobby Brown's sister. Pookie was in charge of Baltimore but acted more like Bobby Brown's number two man, always close, usually at the gym.

Thereafter the man at the end of the table introduced himself as Jean Sinclair, from Haiti – he was called Haitian Jean – who looked after the affairs of the family on the West coast. Oakland, to be precise. Jerome Englis introduced himself last. "Well done, champ. I know you have been staring at me all night, but you really ought to let old things rest, okay? Including lucky rides from Cleveland to Chicago.

"It is enough that we are properly introduced now, and it is proper that I declare to this assembly that you are a soldier that has passed a harrowing test, showing bravery and resilience and, even more importantly, loyalty!

"I salute you, Senor Adelaide Fernandez, the new Prince George County Champion. I believe, in 18 months, you can become the cruiserweight champion of the world.

"Welcome to the Edguardo Family."

Bobby signaled to Mrs. Brown, and she left the room and climbed up the stairs. When she was gone, Jerome continued, "Please stand up and take a bow."

The lights in the room went off, leaving only the glow from the fire on the table.

Adigun stood up and dipped his shoulders forward, bowing from the waist. As he went down, his arms were seized from behind him, and he found himself pinned to the table by his neck. He instinctively tried to struggle but he was subdued.

"Easy, son, easy." He recognized Bobby Brown's voice, soothing and kind, and the tension went out of his shoulders. "This is the moment we have waited all night for. Membership in this organization is exclusive but, like life, is earned with pain and sacrifice and absolute commitment." Bobby Brown recited some incantations in Latin, then grabbed the wooden handle of a metal rod that had been left in the coals of the fire. From his supine position, Adigun had a panicked moment to realize that it wasn't a poker but a branding iron, before a blinding white pain rose from the base of his neck and blotted out all thought. The smell of burning flesh filled the air as Adigun screamed. He screamed, unaware even after Bobby Brown withdrew the brand from his neck, leaving a livid mark in the shape of a lower case 'e'. Jerome applied a salve to the site of the burn and expertly taped gauze over the area. Adigun rose and looked at his surrogate father with a mix of confusion and reproach – one that asked, "Why have you done this to me, father?" Bobby Brown looked back at him with his own mixture of pride and sadness, then pulled the collar away from his neck to show a mark identical to Adigun's. Around the table, all of the other guests exposed the same area of their necks to reveal their marks and it dawned on Adigun that he was being initiated into an illegitimate group. In his head came the sudden echo of his father's words, *"Ranti omo eniti iwo nse!"* meaning, "Remember whose child you are."

A schism tore open in Adigun's consciousness as he struggled to reconcile the father from whom those words had come, and the values that father upheld – honesty, honor, responsibility – and the man before whom he now placed his loyalty. His mind leaped at the hypocrisy of his biological father, who had betrayed all that he taught Adigun, betrayed Adigun's mother, and Adigun himself. His mind tore apart the fickleness of Dodo's morality and made a nimble transition to the contrast in the morality of his adoptive father; illicit in the eyes of the law, but sincere and genuine with everyone in his family, which Adigun realized he was honored to be a part of. His sense of loyalty had come face-to-face with his desire to honor childhood mores, and a deeply personal core of morality crystalized within him. The phrase *"Ranti omo eniti iwo nse,"* echoed in his mind, but its meaning was transformed as it mingled with the smell of his burning flesh. He did remember who his father – the one he had chosen – was, and he purged himself of all lingering shame. He looked up at Bobby Brown, whose eyes were alight with joy, and felt his emotions settle in serene acceptance. He was happy and honored to be part of the Edguardo family.

The entire group stood up with their right fist in the air and went into a long chant in Spanish. They finished it together with a loud 'Amen'. The lights came back on, and each man took a turn kissing Bobby Brown's hand. Adigun was last and Bobby Brown hugged him.

"Welcome home, my son."

Mrs. Brown came back, and more food appeared from the kitchen. Drinks flowed freely and the celebration soared. Then Bobby Brown tapped his wine glass once more with a table knife to get the group's attention. The hubbub wound down within a few, short seconds. "Gentlemen, I am disturbed at what happened in Philadelphia." The silence was absolute. "I am really worried that we are being infiltrated again. We have been brothers for so long and I know we would never betray one another, but how did the Feds know we were receiving the cargo?

"How did they find out? They had all the information, including the location. I am really worried; do we have a rat in the family?" A low murmur ran around the table. "I've changed the phones again and again. Then we got busted again in Delaware! What is going on? I need answers, and I need them NOW!"

Jerome put up his hand.

"Yes, Jerome?"

"Patron, we are just being paranoid, I don't think we have any rat. But we do have a new person among us - the boxer kid... I mean, it would be unwise not to make the connection, eh? We only started noticing these issues after the boxer kid joined the gym." Adigun was perplexed to hear this from Jerome considering all the praise he had received from the same quarter, not one hour before.

"You will not call my son 'Boxer Kid'," Bobby spat, "His name is Adelaide Fernandez, and he is a bona fide member of the Edguardo Family. You should respect that. This kid has been a blessing to the family! Just look how much money we have made in one freaking night!" At this point, Bobby was shouting.

"Apologies, Patron. Apologies, Brother Fernandez. I am not saying he is a rat at all, just that, maybe, not knowing our ways, he may have spoken carelessly to the wrong people?"

"No!" Bobby banged the table, "My brothers, there is definitely someone telling the feds our schedule. This is no careless talk matter. They have too much detail. I am very worried. Pookie, can you have our guys come and carry out a sweep of the entire premises for bugs?"

"Okay, Patron, I will do that right away."

David piped up, with slurred conviction, "Patron, we will figure that out. Tonight, we celebrate the champ! And our *familia*!

"Charge your glasses and raise your glass to Edguardo!"

"Congratulations to the champ!"

The entire table toasted to Adigun, and they started a long series of Spanish football songs. The drinking and feasting continued for a few more hours until many of the guests were falling-down drunk and some passed out. Only Bobby remained quiet and seemingly sober, squinting and watching the festivities closely.

Book-6

Tuke

Pooli wo kawritan de iida

(Unless birds come together, a flapping sound is not heard – Fulani proverb)

1

On the night of Adigun's initiation into the cartel, as the guests went back to their hotels, a storm blew through the Maryland, DC area. The heavy wind was compressed into a high-pitched whine as it was squeezed through the cracks under the doors. Adigun lay on his bed, face-up, hearing his father telling him to remember whose son he was. Inside him, a storm brewed as strong as the one outside. He remembered the day his father traded him to the Fulanis. He could hear the voice of the Fulani head telling his colleague in Fulfulde that it was a good deal; they lost a daughter, and they gained a slave. The pain was refreshed in his heart, and it mixed in with the roiling tension he felt about the role he had just accepted; about who he was and who he might be becoming. As he seethed over the misdeeds of his birth father, his subconscious turned to memories of a time when he first felt like he was coming into his own - when he first felt like his own man – and he could not mark the point at which he slipped from wakefulness into a deep sleep.

Adigun dreamed.

2

"Welcome to reality. This will be your home for the next five years. There will be no light and there is no potable water here." Again, Adigun dream-recalled his father's disgust as he said, "This is where leaders are created." They navigated the baked red clay road and came to a large football field. The goalposts were made with brown bamboo culms, lashed together with hemp rope. The goal on one end of the pitch leaned drunkenly to the left.

In the tall grass, several students peered at Dodo's 'helicopter', while others hacked away at the grass with cutlasses. The girls were dressed in blue, and the boys were all dressed in khaki. After a thunderous boom from the Beetle's exhaust, all but a handful of the laboring students stood up, the shorter ones on tip-toes to see over the grass, taking in the arrival of the latest "inmate", Adigun thought. As the duo drove slowly towards their destination they noticed a makeshift market, with several women displaying their wares on the ground. These women sold everything needed and approved for the boarding school. Dele Komaiya, Dodo's older brother, was a teacher at the school and had advised Dodo to buy Adigun's boarding house needs at the school, except for the Khaki uniforms and white uniforms for the house wear and class wear respectively. Adigun's mum had made those herself with her old Singer sewing machine.

Thanks to the community largesse at Jobore, Adigun had most of the items he needed already, but Dodo stopped the car and purchased some provisions for him. Adigun was quiet, as he tended to be around his father, watching as the shopping was being done. As his father haggled, Adigun noticed a boy following them from vendor to vendor. He appeared to be trying to catch Dodo's eye but ignored Adigun. The boy was tiny in stature with a prominent, bulging forehead, and Adigun figured he must be the son of one of the traders.

His small body swam in an oversized, brand-new Khaki uniform. 'This can't be a student,' Adigun thought, staring at the boy as he paced around the market, with no apparent aim, except for intermittently trying to catch Dodo's attention. He looked like a 6-year-old but acted with smooth confidence as he stepped up to Adigun's dad and spoke.

"Good day, Sir. Welcome to hell. Is this your son? How old is he?"

Dodo looked at the boy with a bemused silence as if wondering which of the questions to answer. Before he could decide, the boy added another. "Did you buy Kandahar?" Kandahar was the brand name for a very strong black marker; it was waterproof and was used in writing names and identification numbers on everything.

"My name is Bayo. Bayo Badiru," he whispered stretching his neck and squinting his eyes. You can call me Beyustic Beyulica."

Dodo turned away from the boy and bent down to examine a blanket he was about to purchase, tucking the admission letter under his left armpit as he did so. Bayo snatched the letter, opened it up, browsed through it, looked at Adigun, and said, "You are number 504! Everybody has a number. It's right there in your letter." Dodo's expression changed to one of indignant irritation, but still, he said nothing. Bayo flipped the letter to the next page and looked at Dodo. "Oh, he is in my room… room 8." He took the Kandahar from the woman's stall and opened the cap. Looking up at Dodo, he asked, "What is his name?" Dodo surprised himself by answering, "His name is Adigun Komaiya." Bayo quickly scribbled Adigun's full name boldly on the bucket. "Where is his uniform?" Without waiting for a reply, Bayo strode to the Beetle and opened the door. He collapsed the front seat and pulled Adigun's battered suitcase from the back seat. Then he unclasped it and began writing the number 504 on the front pockets of the khaki shirts inside. Adigun and his father were dumbstruck.

"You have to write your number on your chest, it is mandatory!"

Bayo went back into the back seat and pulled out the bucket and utensils there then marched to the concrete slab by the market, where he sat and began etching 504 them. He spontaneously abandoned the tools and reached back into Adigun's suitcase, pulling out one of the white uniform shirts, and writing 504 on the back of the collar. He was pulling out the second white shirt when Adigun pounced on him, pushed him to the ground, and then started raining punches on him. The market women sprang up and approached the fiasco with hesitant steps. Other students ran towards the cloud of dust created by the brawl. Dodo seemed rooted to the spot where he stood. All of a sudden Adigun started shouting *"Eyin, eyin, eyin!"* – Teeth, teeth, teeth! Bayo had seized the meager flesh of Adigun's chest with his teeth and battened down. Dodo broke his paralysis and tried to pull Adigun off, but Bayo was fastened to his chest. One of the students grabbed Bayo around his neck and he released Adigun's chest. Blood-soaked Adigun's shirtfront under his clutching hands.

A dust-covered Bayo peered from beneath the shade of his forehead as Dodo carried dragged Adigun, thrashing and howling, away from the scene. Between deep breaths, he screamed, "Who are you, eh? Who are you? You come from nowhere and just start destroying all my new things?" Adigun seemed on the verge of tears as his rant continued. "Who wants to walk around with a number written all over their shirt?" Dodo dragged his son further away and, this time, the added distance seemed to help. Adigun ceased his kicking and screaming and regarded Bayo through narrowed eyes. Bayo turned away partially, and Adigun noticed that he also had the same calligraphy on the back of his collar. His number was

480. It came home to Adigun that Bayo was actually a student.

Bayo got up, trembling as he brushed the dust off his body, with tears cutting murky tracks down his earth-crusted face. "I am your senior," he wailed, "I got here yesterday. You need to listen to me – to learn about Senior Alayonbere! All these things you have will disappear in 24 hours!"

"What is Alayonbere?" Adigun asked.

"Wall gecko, new boy, wall gecko!! They change into snakes and break into your locker and swallow all your provisions. People believe Senior Alayonbere is the face-less owner of all your provisions, so he comes and takes them when you are gone. There are some kids that came just yesterday; today all they have is their singlet and pant. I'm only helping you." Still attempting the hopeless task of getting the dirt off his uniform, Bayo began a tear-ful song.

"Alayonbere, Alayonbere, mo ri o. Koto dejo mo ti dabere.

Mori e, mori e, Alayonbere mori e, koto dejo moti dabere."

[I see you, I see you, wall gecko. I know you will turn into a snake.

When you turn into a snake, I will change into a sharp needle]

Dodo watched the diminutive boy with sympathy and went over to help dust him off. He whirled about to face Adigun, intending to deliver a scathing rebuke for his violent behavior when Bayo's strident (and surprisingly cheerful) voice arrested him. Dodo turned to see Bayo chatting up another parent who was at the market for the same purpose as he and Adigun were. This man's son was a beefy boy with a sullen aspect and Dodo hoped Bayo was wise enough to avoid upsetting him. "Good day, Sir. My name is Bayo. Welcome to Tuke," Bayo chirped at the bemused man and his staring son. He ignored the Komaiyas like they were never there.

Adigun and Dodo got their personal effects back into the Beetle and drove off towards the hostel. The car's backfires punctuated the silent musings of the gathered students as they marked the progress of The Helicopter with wide eyes. The car stopped at the big, brown building that was the boys' hostel. There were a few students gathered around waiting to see the new arrival, attracted by Dodo and Adigun's vanguard of loud bangs. As Dodo alighted from the car, carrying Adigun's black metal suitcase, Adigun held his wooden hoe in one hand and his grey and blue nylon tweed bag in the other. Adigun's spirits were lifted as he looked around the hostel; a rectangular building with a courtyard, which all the rooms faced. In the courtyard were some students on their knees – eyes closed, hands raised high – with matching, squinty-eyed expressions of agony. Their old khaki uniforms were a faded no-color that contrasted wildly with those of the new arrivals, and Adigun noticed that even the

Khandahar numbers on their collars had faded to ghosts. From one of the middle rooms on the ground floor came the sound of several boys chanting. "*Eeekpo, epkpo,*" they cried.

"We are looking for Room 8." Adigun turned at the sound of his father's voice to find him addressing a tall, coal-black boy, wearing a large towel, knotted over his chest. When the boy replied, it was with a single word, delivered in a surprisingly effeminate voice. "There," the boy said pointing to a room on the left and walking away toward the room with the chants. Adigun stared at the receding figure, contemplating its wriggling waist, and wondering if they had just spoken to a girl in the boys' hostel.

3

Room 8 was to the left of the main entrance. An old man welcomed them and showed them to Adigun's bed. The boys in the room called the man Delicate Millionaire, hailing him as he walked between the bunks, dressed in a green kaftan, lightly stroking the bed frames as he passed them. He had some sort of skin disorder and his hands looked like they had been splashed with custard. Many of the beds had students lying on them, most in their under-wear, most with a sheen of perspiration on their bare skin. The room was dim, mainly because the leaves and branches of a large umbrella tree prevented sunlight from making it through the windows. Still, there was enough light to see the crudely drawn graffiti on the walls, de-picting nude women, phalluses, and assorted profanities. In equal measure were personal proclamations that seemed to cry out for individual recognition in this regi-mented khaki world; *Koko was 'ere* or *King Jaja forever*. The bunk beds had towels hanging over their foot-frames and, visible under the mattresses of the top bunks, were carefully laid out white uniforms. Not all of the students had pressing irons and, for those that did, electric power was a rarity, so this sub-mattress practice was the only way the boys had to give their uniforms a good press and gators after sleeping on them overnight. On the ceiling was a fan with only one blade hanging on its thin wire. The room smelled vaguely of sweat, dampness, and camphor, though it wasn't stuffy (especially since most of the windows had lost their louvers).

"Good afternoon, Sir," the boys greeted Dodo from all the corners of the room, many of them under tented, mostly dirty, mosquito nets. Adigun was right in the middle, peering at one of the upper bunks, on the frame of which his name was printed in white. The bunks were arranged on opposite sides of the long room, barrack-style, and separated by wooden lockers. Against the wall, by the bunk bearing his name, Adigun saw two lockers stacked one on top of the other. Adigun's name was on the top locker. It had a latch meant for a padlock. Dodo placed all the provisions into the locker, padlocked it, and handed over the keys to Adigun. The boys in the room took an avid interest in this process, as they did their inventory of what the new kid had brought with him. Adigun pushed his silver bucket under the lower bunk and changed into his khaki shorts and shirt. Dodo and Delicate Millionaire had a short discussion and Dodo began making his way back to the Beetle. As he exited the room, Adigun pulled his shirt.

"I guess this is it. I will never see you and my mother again."

"What are you talking about son?"

"The Fulanis – I belong to them now, right? You swapped me for aunty Hadezah. Well, dad, I just need you to tell mama I will be okay with the Fulanis. It was nice knowing you... *father*."

Adigun's crude and bitter sarcasm did not escape Dodo. "Nooo, that is not what happened, my son. No, Adigun, no, I will always be your father."

There was silence. Father and son stared at each other, and a scattered number of students stared at them. Then, head down, rubbing his head with his large left palm, Dodo turned and walked out to the car. As if in deference to the solemnity of the moment, The Helicopter started up and pulled away without any of its usual noise. Adigun stood on top of the concrete road demarcation watching the loud brown Volkswagen till it disappeared behind the cloud of smoke and red dust it had stirred up. When the car was out of sight and earshot, Adigun ran. He ran across the clay path with his hands spread wide like an eagle, all the way to the field, past the kids with the cutlasses, through the tall grass in a wide, roughly circular path. As he ran, Adigun roared.

"Who is that boy?!"

Adigun stopped. The shout had been so loud, that it seemed that God himself asked the question. Looking around him, Adigun realized he had run through the football field and his progress through it was clear in the upturned manure and freshly planted grass. Unknown to him, there was an important soccer match coming up and the students had spent weeks planting fresh grass and spreading manure from the school poultry. It was forbidden to run across the field. Adigun scanned his surroundings for the source of that arresting shout and fixed upon a man standing on a podium in front of another big building – the dining hall. He was dressed in old khaki shorts, knee-length, and had on a long pair of white socks; socks that almost reached his knee. The legs beneath the shorts and socks seemed to have been carved from granite, as did his hands, which cupped a huge brass bell.

"Bring that goat! *Ewu pia fukpa isi!*" In his Igbo language, he was expressing his hopes that a goat would destroy Adigun's head. Four boys immediately ran towards Adigun who, by reflex, ran away from them, shouting "*Oogun o, oogun, o,*" meaning 'war' in his own Yoruba language. The boys chased Adigun until they caught up with him by the chemistry laboratory building. They lifted him high and carried him spread-eagled back to the fuming figure at the podium. Adigun had barely spent an hour in his new school and was already in trouble.

When he was set down before his new tormentor, Adigun was shocked to discover, by the evidence of his outfit, that the man was a student too; Senior Paulinus Igwe, to be precise. Though not against the rules, it was odd for seniors to wear shorts, but Paulinus Igwe had his preferences. He had a thick mustache and a tangled mass of bushy hair. It was rumored that he had fought during the civil war – on the Biafran side, of course. He was light in complexion and wore glasses with a thick black frame.

343

"How dare you???!!!!" He grabbed Adigun's head with his large hands, pulling Adigun towards his bushy face.

"Lie flat!

"Lie down, stupid goat!"

Adigun looked at him with a frown, still trying to figure out who he was.

"I say lie down!!"

Before Adigun could comply, he was struck by an open fist that flung him to the ground with a high-pitched whine in his left ear. He immediately stretched out on the ground with his face touching the soil. He trembled as he struggled to control his breathing to avoid inhaling the red earth. He could now hear the sound of bells and wasn't sure if they were real or part of the after-effects of the slap he'd received. As he recovered, he realized that the continuous ringing was indeed real, and he could make out the sound of footsteps running toward him. That ringing was the emergency bell. The students of Tuke knew to leave anything that they may be doing and run towards the bell anytime it sounded. The ringing went on as a hushed chatter grew around Adigun, who dared not look up.

He could hear others running towards the scene but could not see as they filed into lines according to their classes. Many of the new students had come in the night before and had been instructed on the bell, an important feature at Tuke. Ignoring an emergency bell might earn you a suspension from school or, at best, a session at 'Siberia', the school farm where students dug deep compost pits to manufacture manure for the crops.

Senior Paulinus, still sounding like a celestial parade commander, bellowed, "Fellow students, this is Government College Tuke-Ajose. We are all very privileged to belong to this model government school.

"We have facilities not known to any other school in the nation, but the government can only do so much. The campus does not have water! We must eat! We have survived by fetching water from the stream about 3 miles from the campus!" Here, he paused to regard the gathered students, homing in on the new ones and sneering, "I know our new rats will not know where the stream is. Rats, can you hear me?"

The new students all shouted, military-style, "Sir, yes-sir!!!!"

Adigun remained prone, with his face in the dirt, petrified, as Senior Paulinus resumed his exhortation. "By the count of three, you will get back to your rooms, grab your buckets, and follow the red hat. If you lose him, you will be lost rats in the jungle, waiting to be eaten by lions!

"Each one of you rats will fetch four buckets of water. You deliver three into the tank at the kitchen, where you shall register your name with the food prefect.

"None will eat if his or her name is not on the list. The fourth bucket you will deliver to the tank at the principal's house.

"This message is for the rats; the rest of the school, report to the field opposite the classroom with their cutlasses." He glared at the assembly, then he shouted, "Move, you little rats!"

The new kids raced to the hostel, boys and girls running to their respective dormitories at opposite ends of this section of the campus. The figure with the red hat walked in the direction of a huge Iroko tree where he squatted and waited. The area in front of the dining hall emptied in seconds. Adigun was beginning to enjoy some perverse enjoyment of his punishment when he found himself being addressed directly by the terrifying Senior Paulinus.

"Who are you? What is your name? Why were you running over the newly planted carpet grass? It took us weeks to plant the entire field!" His voice was picking up speed and volume as he fired off his questions and, at this point, he was screaming. "Who are you? How dare you? You will die today! When did you come on campus?" Here he paused as if the answer to this last question was one that he actually wanted a response to.

"Today, sir," Adigun whispered, "I'm sorry, sir."

"Meet me at Room 14 after night prep'. And woe betide you if you don't bring your three buckets to the kitchen! Get up and run to get your bucket!

"Rabid rat," he called after the scrambling Adigun.

Adigun jumped up and ran against the students who had already grabbed their buckets and were assembling around the fellow with the red hat, the guide to the stream. Adigun climbed the stairs at the hostel entrance and sped to Room 8, where he came to an abrupt halt, gaping with wide eyes and an open mouth at the place where his bed was. His locker was wide open, and it was empty. His padlock was left dangling with a compass sticking out of the keyhole. The stragglers in the room went about their business with complete indifference. Nobody said anything to Adigun as he reached under his bed to get his bucket – this too was gone. His metal suit-case was open, and all his uniforms were gone. He heard snatches of a song that the students in the room were now singing, clearly a version of the wall gecko song Bayo had sung at the school market. He would later learn of the campus mythology, which held that the song had a spiritual effect, protecting your belongings from being stolen by the notorious wall gecko.

"Alayonbere Alayonbere, mo ri e

Bami gbe eru mi o, Alayonbere

Alayonbere mo ri e o, bami gbe eru mi

347

Mo ri e o, Alayonbere, mo ri e o

Koto dejo mo ti di abere."

4

Adigun stood in the middle of the room with tears running down his muddy face. The wall gecko Bayo warned Adigun warned about had struck within less than two hours of his arrival at the school. His entire belongings, purchased by his father, were gone. The metal suitcase was empty. Rage and anguish rose from his belly and emerged from his mouth as a miserable wailing. "*Ole ooooh! Ole oh! Ole,*" he cried, using the Yoruba word for 'thief'. "There has been a robbery. A robberrryyyyy!" He saw Bayo, running out of room 8 with a bucket and caught him by the arm. "I've been robbed," Adigun beseeched him. Bayo barely paused as he replied, "What should *I* do about it? If you don't find another bucket and let's run, you will also be robbed of both tonight's dinner and breakfast in the morning."

"They took my bucket too," Adigun whimpered, then added with numb realization, "It had my number written on its side." Bayo pulled him and they raced to the bathrooms where some magically unperturbed students were bathing. In one of the open shower stalls, a boy lathered himself with soap, foam forming a white afro and beard on his head and face. As he reached blindly down for a scoop of water with the top half of his sponge case, Bayo pulled the bucket out of the stall, splashed the contents over the soapy boy, and ran. He handed over the bucket to Adigun as they ran off, both looking over their shoulders a few times to make sure they were not being pursued. The boy whose bucket they had hijacked was strangely silent.

They could see the heads of the students in the distance and increased speed to catch up with them. The duo ran through the bushes, down a steep slope, and through a narrow path into the bamboo forest. Then they got to a mangrove swamp where they caught up with the larger body of new students who looked about them for the stream. "This is the stream," said the boy with the red hat, stepping out from behind a mass of mangrove roots. He was clearly a fellow student, but the old khaki and long pants of his uniform marked him as a senior. His name was Debo Omotade he was in the fourth form. He was diminutive in stature and looked younger than many of the new kids. 'Senior Debo', as some kids called him, was one of the 'returnees' – the term used to refer to students who came to Tuke after stints abroad. He spoke with a fine English accent and kept taking off his red hat to comb his hair with a brown afro comb.

"Is this the stream," Adigun asked, "This dirty water?" The water in the mangrove swamp was murky, almost black, and teeming with larvae and insects. The tall bamboo culms provided shade from the sun and their fallen leaves formed a springy carpet on the boggy swamp floor. Several of the students had already begun scooping water into their buckets, even as Adigun expressed his disgust. Bayo looked at Adigun. "Come on," he hissed, "We have four trips to make. It's a long way from school and it will be dark soon." Adigun joined Bayo and began scooping dirty black water into his stolen bucket. Soon, those with full buckets placed them on their heads and began to navigate the narrow bush path back to the school campus.

Debo Omotade, still combing his hair, walked majestically through the mangrove bushes like a slave master on a cotton plantation. When enough of the students had their buckets filled and, on their heads, he replaced his red hat and eased back the way they had come. Adigun and Bayo filled their buckets and followed. At the steep slope, the red earth was slick with spilled water and Adigun almost lost his footing, slopping water onto the already sodden slope. As he struggled to regain his balance, he saw palm prints in the clay; clearly, somebody had fallen. At length, they tramped out of the bush and into the campus, filing past the blue bungalow on their right, with flowers planted near it. "This is the principal's house," said Bayo, "My dad brought me here yesterday before I was dropped off at the hostel. I can't remember his name, but he was my father's friend in high school, just like you and I." Adigun's heart melted at Bayo's purity and his exceptional spirit of forgiveness. Barely three hours ago, he was raining punches on his head and now he calls him his friend. Then a movement in the bushes caught his attention, making Adigun look closer, and then freezing him.

Bayo tapped him on his shoulder with his free hand, while holding the bucket with the other.

"Are you okay? Are you okay, Adigun? What are you stopping for?"

Adigun was staring at a herd of cows emerging from the bush. Then he bolted, initially holding his bucket in both hands as he ran, but eventually abandoning this effort altogether and letting the bucket fall to the ground with a thud and a splash of water. Bayo stood in shock. "They are cows," he shouted, "just cows." The Fulani herdsman, unaware of what was going, on walked behind his cows.

Adigun stood frozen in fear, across the road from the principal's house, for the next two hours, as Bayo rushed to the stream and back again multiple times. Each time, he would glance at Adigun, seemingly catatonic as he stared at the grazing herd, then Bayo simply returned to the task at hand. Bayo went back and forth between the stream and the kitchen six times, then two more times between the stream and the principal's house before he was done. Bayo had fetched double his portion so he could write Adigun's name and he was exhausted, but both their names were on the list. At some point during his last three trips, Bayo noticed that Adigun had disappeared. He walked into the hostel and turned into their room. Adigun was on his bed, with his hands on his head, crying.

"Why did you behave like that Adigun? You are scared of cows? They were not even anywhere close. What is this? Cows, Adigun, cows!"

"I got back into my locker there is nothing left from all the goods my father bought for me. They broke my portmanteau… they broke my locker. Took everything!"

"You have not answered my question; why did you run away to leave me to fetch water alone?"

"Bayo, all my provisions – my school uniforms – all gone."

"Are you surprised? Did I not tell you? We will sort that out; we may get it back if we quickly report to Uncle Kan in Hostel B. They told me he is the only one that can fight for justice here. We will deal with that one later. What happened out there by the principal's house, Adigun?"

"Bayo, it is a long story. I thought… thought they came to get me… ahead of time."

"Who?"

"The Fulanis."

The boys in the room overheard the conversation and burst out laughing. They stopped abruptly when a light-skinned senior walked up to where Adigun and Bayo were. He looked furious as he looked over the bed beneath Adigun's, then turned his hostile gaze onto Adigun himself.

His name was Maxman. From the Midwest, he was born to a Portuguese merchant and a Nigerian mother, which accounted for his near-white skin, freckles, and aquiline nose. He tended to blink rapidly and squint, such that only his dark, curly hair saved him from being mistaken for an albino. His blinking struck Adigun as similar to Aunt Hadezah's and he was peering back at the senior boy when Maxman barked at him. "Rat," he bellowed.

"Sir!" Adigun sat bolt-upright on his bed.

"Don't call me 'sir'. My name is Peter Maxman!" He glared at Adigun, who was still trying to figure out if he should repeat the senior's name. The other juniors in the room drifted towards the brewing conflagration as if it were drawn in by gravity. Maxman ignored the loose circle forming around them and asked Adigun, "What is your name?" The full effect of his glare was diluted by his flapping eyelids and was almost comical. Adigun felt treacherous laughter rising from his belly and he struggled to suppress it, knowing it would only make a bad situation much worse. Stress and panic made him blurt out the first thing that popped into his head at Maxman's question.

"Booka," Adigun said, unable to stop himself from going on, "Booka Sooka Dimka." That insane laughter was threatening again, and he looked down at his feet.

"You climbed on my bed."

"No, Senior Maxman."

A sigh ran through the circle of spectators and Adigun knew he was in trouble.

"So how did you get on your bed?"

Adigun realized the trap he was in with bright, painful clarity. No one had briefed him in his short time at Tuke, but it was evidently an abomination to make any sort of contact with a senior's bed. Once more, without any kind of internal debate at all, Adigun's hair-trigger dishonesty took over.

"I flew, Sir."

"You bloody, lying rat! So why are there marks on my bed? Get this into your thick rodent head; I don't want to know how you get on your bed but if your feet ever touch my part of the bed, I will have you fed to the bush babies." Bush babies were small primates that made childlike, wailing calls in the forests, usually at night. The mythology amongst the students, particularly the younger ones, was that they had this mat, which was of immense value to them, and the key to wealth for anyone who could dispossess them of it. The lore held that, upon losing its mat, the bush baby would cry until the mat was returned, or it died. Such mourning bush babies were said to be hostile and aggressive and would eat humans alive on sight.

Adigun sat on his bed helpless, wondering how he could be experiencing such an ordeal in the space of hours. His feet were sore, his neck was stiff, and his muscles were aching from the non-stop tension in this place. His immediate challenge was how to get off his bed without stepping on Maxman's. He could jump, he supposed, but was reluctant to land on his feet in the state they were in. The decision was made for him by the loud clanging of the school bell, followed by a thunderous drum of feet as students rushed to the dining hall.

He saw others in his room gathering their stainless-steel spoons, forks, and knives and realized what the metallic clattering sound was that accompanied the rushing feet. He also realized, with considerable relief, that the bell meant it was time for supper. He had thought they had to go to the river again.

The room was poorly lit by the small lantern on the other side of the room. Adigun jumped off his bed and landed with a hollow thud on the terrazzo floor. He began searching for his footwear, then remembered that everything was gone. All he had in his possession was the khaki uniform he was wearing. And a stolen bucket. Adigun ran barefoot toward the sound of the bell and joined the throng. A few students had created an ensemble, making a rough percussive rhythm with their forks and spoons – suppertime was one part of the day's routine that was eagerly anticipated. It occurred to Adigun that he didn't have any cutlery of his own but, as the crowd broke into rough queues at the three main entrance doors to the dining, hall, Adigun went with the flow.

There were seniors at the doors asking students for their dormitories and classes and directing them to long, 12-seater tables, laid end-to-end in sets of two, with long wooden benches on either side. On each table was a stack of dented aluminium plates, which each student picked one from and waited their turn to be served. From two large metal pots, two designated servers dished food into each supplicant's plate. One provided a mound of *eba*, cassava dough the size of two little fists, and the other would scoop a piece of fish and some stew and pour it on the plate with the *eba*.

Adigun walked towards his assigned table and did as the others did. As he sat down, there was Bayo, who had already finished his food. "There you are again, Digs, my newfound friend," Bayo chirped. "Poor you; look at the size of your food. You always have to get here early. Early birds get the best portion. You should have seen the size of my fish. And the large portions of *eba* are always served first. I'm always in the front of the line. Nobody beats me to it. This is my second day here trust me." He paused and leaned back to better see under the table. "Why are you here with bare feet?" he asked. Adigun stared at Bayo, incredulous.

"Have you forgotten what happened to me today?"

"Oh, yes – Alayonbere," Bayo said simply, picking his teeth. "Eat up, Digs, I want to show you something."

"Thanks, Bayo, for fetching my portion of the water, I owe you, my friend. Thank you."

"What are friends for? Now, clean your mouth and do as I do."

Adigun followed Bayo out of the dining hall, did an about-face, and joined the line shuffling into it. They were assigned another table, which they strolled to, sat down, and got served again. "That's how to stay alive here," Bayo whispered with smug satisfaction. "It's called DR."

"DR?"

"Yes, DR. I learned it yesterday – Double Ration!"

"Is it allowed, though?"

"The food portions are very small. You will die of hunger if you don't do this."

"This is wrong! What if we get caught?" Adigun asked, sinking his fingers into the hot cassava paste.

"Naa, nobody will catch you, it is too dark to identify anyone here," Bayo replied as he swallowed the balls of *eba* he had rolled on his plate. He had a peculiar way he rolled his *eba*, swiping a large portion into his fist, squeezing out a small ball, and deftly cutting it off with his index finger before dipping it into the stew. "After we leave finished here, we will go back to the hostel. We will be allocated to our classes tomorrow. I hope we can be in the same class."

"But what will I do about uniform?"

"Never mind, my best friend, Digs. I will sort you out in the morning."

"Oh, no! I'm not going to steal again," Adigun erupted.

"Don't worry, I will sort you out".

The bell rang again, and the students filed out. Adigun went with Bayo to all the other rooms and Bayo introduced him to other students. After barely 48 hours in the school, Bayo seemed to know everyone. As they walked around in the dormitory, there was a throaty roar from afar; the school generator coming on for the routine two-hour period that would usually be night prep. Bayo introduced Adigun as "Digs Komaiya from room 8." In one of the rooms, some boys recognized Adigun from Jobore – his mates from primary school that had left him behind a year before – and they ran out of the room, shouting his nickname from back home. "Adigun Oloogun," they cried as they fled, remembering the rumor that he had murdered a teacher through magical means. The news of Adigun's arrival spread like wildfire. The name Adigun Oloogun was whispered from ear to ear.

Bayo was also shocked. "They all know you, Adigun. Why are they terrified? Why did they call you Oloogun?" Before Adigun could respond, he heard the name, Booka, being called and echoed by students in the usual Tuke tradition.

Adigun knew he was the one being called, and he knew it was Senior Maxman calling. Junior boys leaned over the railings of the dormitory balcony relaying the name, Booka Sooka Dimka. Adigun ran towards Maxman's room, wondering what trouble he had gotten into this time. Maxman had returned from the classroom block to find that someone had left muddy footprints on his bed, giving the impression that Adigun had stepped on it to get

359

to the top bunk. "Booka," he called again. Adigun arrived at the room trembling with fear. The room was quiet as he made his way to his corner, except for the muffled giggles that came from within some of the ratty mosquito nets draped over the beds. "Did you step on my bed again, Booka Sooka Dimka?" Maxman's voice was sinister in its quietness.

"No, sir. God is my witness, sir, I swear!" Adigun touched his tongue and raised his hand to the sky."

"God?" Maxman shouted, "Catch the bus now, you devil!"

Adigun stared blankly at Maxman who was blinking some sort of rapid-fire Morse code. "Which bus, sir?" Adigun asked.

"One boy!" Maxman shouted, and all the boys from the first to third years leaped off their beds and ran toward Maxman. Even some hapless passers-by, walking along the corridor outside the room ran in in response to the call. You didn't want to be caught trying to elude that call. When the thunder of running feet subsided, the boys were lined up in the order of their arrival. The last to reach the senior would usually have to perform whatever task the senior wanted. Maxman pointed at the last boy to arrive and shouted, "Show this new rat how to catch the bus!" The boy leaped at the foot of the double bunk, placing his left foot on the thin metal cross-bar at the bottom and holding onto the top cross-bar with his left hand. His right arm and foot he held outward, suspended in the air.

Within seconds, the cross-bars began digging into his bare foot and fingers, and the boy groaned in pain. Adigun stared in fear, recognizing the similarity of the position to that assumed by bus conductors and passengers, hanging out of the open doorway when a bus was full.

"Take over, Booka," Maxman ordered.

"My name is not Booka, Sir."

"God will punish you! I say, catch the bus!"

Adigun hastened to take over from the relieved boy and caught the stagnant bus. In minutes he was pouring with sweat. Maxman paid him no attention as he groaned, and he soon began to cry. "I swear, sir, I did not step on your bed. I swear, sir. I was not even in the room."

Adigun rode the bus for almost two hours. Maxman had dozed off by the time the generator was turned off and the bell went for lights out. When Adigun realized Maxman was asleep, he began to groan louder, hoping to wake him up. At length, Maxman, without opening his eyes, told Adigun to go to bed. His legs were sore, and his left thigh was in spasms. He was stiff at the waist and could barely place any weight on his left foot. He collapsed onto the floor and lay there in the dark, wondering how he could possibly get on his bed without touching Maxman's. The mosquitoes were feeding fat on Adigun's blood and taunting him with their whines. Adigun stayed quietly on the cold floor, unmoving, unsure whether Maxman was fast asleep, and he might chance the herculean task of getting onto his bed. He decided to wait for a while, just to be sure. Minutes later, he was asleep. He woke up in the middle of the night and he looked at his bed from the floor. It might as well have been on the moon, even though – judging from the snores that came from just above him – Maxman was almost certainly asleep. Adigun stared at his bed from the cold floor until he fell asleep again. It seemed to him like he had barely closed his eyes when the morning bell rang.

5

The day had broken. This time, the bell was followed by a whistle. The entire hostel woke up and there were loud footsteps again, it was the morning drill. It was mandatory for every student to participate in the early morning exercise. The students of room 8 all jumped up and wore their blue PE shorts and white vests. Adigun had only his khaki shirt and shorts on. "It's morning drill," a loud voice announced. The whistle went off again, followed by the bell.

It was Paulinus again; he was in charge of the morning drill.

"Everybody, oh! Everybody, oh," the students shouted, "Jump up!" It sounded like a military battalion. Adigun took off his khaki shirt and ran out with bare feet, joining the group that was running towards the girls' hostel. When they got there, the commanding senior shouted, "All girls, wake up!" And it was immediately repeated by the students. It was very loud. Then there was another group coming toward them from the girl's hostel. The two groups jogged into the large field. Visibility was poor as the morning light was smothered by the thick harmattan fog. Eventually, both groups met at the big field in front of the administrative block. It was a collage of blue and white. Both the girls and boys were dressed in their official physical education attire. Blue shorts and white t-shirts. Most wore white canvas shoes. The exercise went on for about an hour and the students all raced back to their hostels.

Bayo came into the room and ran towards Adigun's corner.

"That was fun," said Bayo, stretching his short hands towards the ceiling.

"Not fun when you only had one hour's sleep," murmured Adigun, recounting his ordeal with Maxman.

"Where is your bath water?" Bayo asked.

"I have none."

"Oh! You will have to dry-clean then."

"Dry-clean?"

"Yes, dry-clean – the art of taking a bath with a cup of water. Just concentrate on your armpits, groin, and your face, then you're clean, and you are good to go. I learned that just yesterday." Bayo went to his corner and Adigun watched with fascination as he squatted by the bed, while fishing for something in his right pocket. He pulled out a key and reached under the lower bunk to unlock the padlock that held together a chain, which was looped tightly around the handle of a metal bucket of water. Bayo dragged the bucket out, scooped some water into a bowl, and handed it to Adigun. "This is your bath water, Digs. You always have to organize your bath water the night before. This is all you get, so get with it and get ready for school." Adigun took the bowl of water and headed for the bathroom. It was dry-cleaning indeed and, when he was done wiping himself down, there was barely enough water to brush his teeth, but he did his best.

Back in the dorm room, Bayo gave him a white shirt and a pair of white shorts. "You can wear this; it's mine. I hope it fits." His shorts were like bikini bottoms on Adigun and his shirt was so small the lower buttons on the shirt would not fasten. In the absence of his sandals, Adigun had only his pair of rubber flip-flops to wear; he used a pair of brown shoelaces and laced them up, fastening the laces into a bow at each of his ankles. Bayo looked at his feet, shook his head, rolled his eyes, and said, "Brown sandal it is." By the time Adigun and Bayo got out of the hostel the students had finished breakfast and were heading to the assembly hall. "We have missed breakfast, Adigun," Bayo intoned with mournful soberness. "We have missed breakfast." They followed the students through the red clay road.

The school campus was enormous and green, with several football fields, all surrounded by a lush tropical forest. The students marched towards the massive assembly hall, like a white river flowing past colorful banks of beautiful flowers that lined both sides of the road to the administration section. On the left was a neat, long bungalow that housed another hostel, before the classroom blocks. Adigun and Bayo walked fast as they approached the generator house, racing to merge with the white river ahead of them. Rounding the curve in the road, and passing the generator house, they had a clear view of the assembly hall.

A loud mechanical cough drew Adigun's eyes to the school gate, where an orange Volkswagen Igala was passing into the campus. The eruptions from the busted exhaust pipe were familiar to him. He was wondering if he could match and compare the sounds of this car with those of The Helicopter when the thunder of running feet snapped his attention back to the mass of students approaching the assembly hall. They were running. Scrambling seemed like a better word to Adigun, some of them appearing to try climbing over those ahead of them. From the frantic glances many of them cast in the direction of the farting orange Igala, it was clear to Adigun that they wanted to be in the assembly hall before the vehicle – or its occupant – reached it. The car came to a sudden, dusty stop about 50 meters after the gate and its driver-side door flew open. Out of this door shot a short, portly man, running towards the students. He was dressed in a beige Yoruba outfit, with a short dashiki made of cotton material. On his large, round head sat a red traditional cap, winged to cover both ears – Yorubas called it '*abeti aja*'.

Bayo and Adigun gawked as they walked, occasionally stumbling as they were shoved and bumped by students running past them. Their own pace was that brisk walk people assume when they see others running for unknown reasons, as they try to make up their minds about whether they should also run. Ahead of them, the short, fat man stood waving a long cane. There was red dust hanging in the air now but, as they moved closer, they got a better view of the man. His beige dashiki had thick brown embroidery on the two pockets flanking his big belly. The same embroidery was on the neck portion of the garment. He wore a red turtle-neck sweater inside his dashiki, which hovered over his slim pants. The drawstring of the pants, a startling black, stood out as they hung against his beige-clad thighs. Some of the students ran past Adigun whispering, "Bami Komaiya! Run!"

Mr. Komaiya, his jowly face swiveling, button eyes squinting in the thick flesh of his face, had his arms wide as students swerved to avoid him. As he pirouetted, and with lightning speed, he swung the long branch he held, connecting with the backs of the students that ran close enough. The sound of the lashes was so loud, that it galvanized Adigun and Bayo out of their puzzled, musing state – they broke into a sprint – each trying to cut as wide a swathe as they could through the panicking stragglers, hemmed in as they were by the hedges on each side of the road. "That's Big Daddy," Adigun gasped, with a look of terror. His sandals flapped as he ran behind Bayo, deeper into the dust cloud and closer to the specter of Bami Komaiya. "He's my uncle," he wheezed. "Oh, Lord, Bayo, it's my first day."

Adigun and Bayo, heads down, increased speed but they could not make it past Dele Komaiya. The herd had thinned, and it was harder for them to race anonymously past him. Now, he was able to arrest them with his recognition alone. "Kasali, stop there!" and "Patrick Okochi, kneel down, now!" As Adigun approached him, Dele Komaiya's eyes widened in recognition – to the extent that his piggy little eyes could widen, anyway – and his nostrils flared as he took in Adigun's school uniform and makeshift sandals. He pointed at the ground, issuing Adigun the silent instruction to kneel. Adigun went to his knees, panting. Mr. Komaiya, also panting from his exertions, bellowed at his captives, "If Dele Komaiya can get to school before eight a.m. from Irede – by seven forty-five dead – all students should be at the assembly hall, well dressed! *Awon omo oshi.*" Useless kids. He turned to Adigun and murmured in Yoruba, staring closely at Adigun's face, "*Maa na mamu ona Ibadan si iwo yi lara. Iwo, omo adojutini yi.*" He meant he was going to beat the living daylight into his brother's disgraceful son. Inside the assembly hall, students crowded at the windows, most missing their louvers, to watch the scene. Bayo got his strokes and ran into the hall. Adigun was kept on his knees, so Mr. Komaiya could flog him intermittently, between delivering strokes to others whom he subsequently released. Adigun twisted and turned in pain as the dry wooden cane seared his body.

Bami Komaiya was a terror; the worst nightmare of any student. He was notorious from his time as a teacher in Irede, a town under a different school administrative district. When Komaiya reached retirement age in Irede, he left to start a fresh teaching career at Tuke. Falsifying one's age was not especially difficult to do though, obviously, he was long past the retirement age. The mouth underneath his Hitler-style mustache was crumpled; he had none of his lower front teeth and few of the upper ones. 'Bami', as the students called him, was in his late seventies but was strong. If not for his missing teeth he could pass for sixty-five. He was a great supporter of corporal punishment and was quick to flog any student till they bled. His justice did not discriminate; he flogged both boys and girls, usually on the buttocks, murmuring in his Ijebu dialect as he flogged the girls, "*Ken gbe idi?*" or "What is there in the buttocks?" He would hold the girls' dresses tight with one hand and deliver the strokes with the other. Sometimes he would ask two boys to lift the female student and would savagely tear up her buttocks with a strong cane.

Mr. Dele Komaiya was more powerful – or at least feared – than the principal himself, and was the self-imposed disciplinarian at the school assembly sessions. Flogging at the school assembly was a daily occurrence. There was a disciplinary list compiled every morning and 'Bami' Komaiya always administered the flogging on the school stage. As he crossed the stage with his pronounced limp, students would whisper the phrase, "T*alalantolo*; a bargain is a bargain," to the rhythmic up-and-down gait of the terror. Bami had an ill-fitting prosthetic leg; he had lost his limb to a student's attack during a riot in his former school. The principal was a well-read and respectful gentleman, a man of few words but a strong proponent of discipline and responsible living. He always dressed very smartly and loved his bow ties. There was a silent competition for power or perhaps a clash of egos between 'Old Komaiya' and the actual school principal, Mr. Cosmos Ashaye. Bami had taken over the school and was not apologetic at all. The principal was younger than Komaiya in age and it was apparent he also was bullied by Komaiya, who unceremoniously became the de-facto principal, and went so far as to address himself as "Ceremonial Principal", ignoring the presence of other teachers that had been in the school longer than him.

Mr. Komaiya drove from Irede; a two-hour drive on a narrow road. The students were terrified of him, and even his car – the dirty, orange, smokey, loud Volkswagen Igala – became a symbol of terror to the kids. On sighting Mr. Komaiya's car, students would run for their lives. On this day, after the last student was flogged, Bami turned to Adigun, who was still on his knees with both hands raised to the sky and his eyes closed.

"*Adigun oro, omo alapa kija mole joyin joyin,*" he eulogized in Yoruba, referring to Adigun's warrior ancestors. "What is this? Why are you dressed like this? Rubber slippers to class? Did you not just arrive a few days ago?"

"Big Daddy, I was robbed. The Alayonbere took all my things!"

"The what?"

"The Alayonbere, Sir! Senior Alayonbere!"

"Senior Alayonbere," repeated Bami, with his nose wrinkled in a sneer so severe that his upper lip was almost touching his nostrils.

"They are the robbers in the hostel, they broke the lock on my suitcase and stole everything, Sir. My friend, Bayo, gave me all I'm wearing."

"Meet me in the staff room during the break." Bami rained another series of strokes on Adigun, prompting a series of howls. Students peered through the glass louvers of the assembly hall windows, wondering why Adigun got so much more than other students. The cane had left rusty stripes on Adigun's white uniform, which disappeared as he squirmed and rolled in the dirt, turning his shirt almost entirely rust-colored. Adigun then leaped up and grabbed hold of Bami Komaiya's dashiki, pleading and hopping from one foot to the other. Bami grabbed Adigun by his shorts and gave him another three strokes, shouting, "Say, 'Thank you, daddy!'"

"Thank you, Daddy!" Adigun screamed, racing into the assembly hall.

6

As Adigun entered the assembly hall, the students were singing the second verse of the national anthem.

"Oh God of creation,

"Direct our noble thoughts,

"Guide our leaders right,

"Help our youths the truth to know…"

The students were organized according to their classes, and Adigun scanned the faces of the junior students until he spotted a few faces he knew to be new students. He immediately joined their line. There was a short announcement by the principal, crisp in his powder-blue French suit and red bow tie, instructing the new students to wait in the hall after the assembly. Then the assembly was over, and each class trooped out of the hall in a single file. The seniors were so big and strong, that they made the juniors look like baby locusts amidst eagles as they left them behind in the hall.

An older student addressed the locusts, introducing himself as James Ibanofor, the senior prefect. His white shirt gleamed as he read his remarks from the foolscap sheets he held. "We take this opportunity to welcome our new students to Government College, Tuke. Your parents made a good choice by choosing this school. This is one of the five model schools in this school district, established by the government to create the leaders of tomorrow. There are students from very diverse family backgrounds," James droned, adjusting his thick glasses and taking a quick look into the crowd. "Some of you have also come from abroad to benefit from the unique education this country offers. You will follow the lady with the yellow flag to the front of the classrooms where you would all be allocated your classes. There are desks in the classrooms; some of them have lock-up spaces, but some don't. Don't worry, each student will be entitled to a wall locker.

"At Tuke, we do not tolerate rowdy behavior and indiscipline of any sort. I implore you to be very organized and well-behaved during this process."

The students marched to the lawn in front of the classrooms, where a female senior read names from a hardcover notebook and allocated classes to the students. Adigun was in class 1C. There was a mad scramble for the lockers with built-in locks with their dangling keys, and the rumble of stampeding feet blended with the screeching of metal table legs being dragged across the floor; it was an awful din. Within minutes, the chaos in 1C began to subside as every student acquired a desk and a locker, and as they settled into their chosen – or unavoidable – positions. Before they could catch their breaths though, in strode another senior. Tall, wiry, and hairy, he could easily have been one of the teachers. "Come here," he snarled, grabbing the hapless juniors at random and asking them for their names. When he had the attention of the entire class, he announced, "I am Saheed Agboola, the labor prefect. You will love to hate me; I ration the work in this school.

"What kind of sitting arrangement is this?"

The children looked around, heads swiveling to take in whatever problem the labor prefect might be referring to. The sharper ones soon recognized that all the boys were on one side, and all the girls on the other. Except for one girl who stood like an island of femininity in a sea of testosterone. "Why are you standing?" the senior asked her. "This boy would not let me sit next to him," she replied, gesturing to a petulant fellow straddling two desks to her right. The boy, Banjo Adelodun, was a scowling, talkative, argumentative fellow who had no intention whatsoever of sitting next to a girl. His philosophy was evident in his silent hostility. Senior Saheed, unsympathetic to Banjo's preferences, then barked the class into a new sitting arrangement, making sure each boy sat next to a girl. The boys were displeased. Some drew lines on the wooden benches designed to seat two, giving themselves the larger portion, such that girls were forced to sit on just one butt cheek.

Not all of the boys were unhappy, though they all made a great public show of their disdain for girls. Adigun sat next to a girl from Ghana, named Adjua Prempe. Her dark skin was the richest, gleaming deep chocolate and her eyes were large and slightly sleepy. Slim in her well-starched and ironed uniform, she had turned to Adigun, without any shyness at all, and introduced herself.

Adigun stared into her eyes as she told him her name, trying not to fall into them. He was smitten. This was the first time he was experiencing this sort of reaction to a girl, and he was confused. Adjua Prempe looked at the gawking Adigun with languid amusement and shifted closer to him, squishing him against the wall. She smiled as she offered Adigun a small pouch, saying, "Close your eyes and take one." Adigun closed his eyes and reached into the pouch. His fingers registered the contents, se-lected, and withdrew. "It's a Koko Mala," he said as he admired the little black lollypop on its white stick. "Thank you. I haven't had one in a while." Adigun was surprised that his voice sounded steady and reasonable, and inwardly rejoiced as he unwrapped the black candy and stuck it in his mouth while letting the orange wrapper fall to the floor. He sucked on the candy, twirling its white stick as he did so, enjoying the strong, minty sweetness.

Adjua told him about a town in Ghana called Kuforidua, and she told him about herself. Adigun found the conver-sation easy to maintain and the white lollypop stick bobbed up and down as he spoke with the hard candy stuck in his cheek. They continued their conversation un-til the math teacher, Mr. Olofin, walked in. His egg-bald head sat atop his towering frame, which was barely diminished by his slight slouch. The new students rose to their feet and greeted Mr. Olofin, who cast his placid gaze upon them like an indulgent deity.

"Good morning class. This is the math period. If you don't know mathematics, you are in trouble. I expect you should all have basic algebra and also basic numeric skills. To do well in my mathematics class, your body must be hot! Your blood must flow. If I come into the class and find anyone talking, I will make your blood hot by unleashing Mr. Black on you. This is Mr. Black," he declared, brandishing a long switch with one hand and twisting his straggly mustache with the other. "I come with Mr. Black when I need to give you *Foka*." '*Foka*' was a Yoruba phrase meaning to destroy the fingers, which Mr. Olofin simulated by rapping the cane across his knuckles. With his point made, he turned to the board and began teaching algebra. Throughout the lesson, Adigun and Adjua continued getting to know each other by passing notes. By the end of the period, they each possessed significant fistfuls of paper scraps, through which they had established a solid bond. They were basking in their newfound kinship, as Mr. Olofin exited the class, when Banjo Adelodun slapped the paper scraps out of Adjua's hand and gathered them up. Adjua and Adigun watched in utter horror as Banjo sauntered up to the front of the class and began reading out the contents.

"You have eyes like my mother."

"Your nose is like my sister's."

"Can we get on?"

At this last, the entire class went into a laughing frenzy. Banjo didn't stop; he just read louder.

"Will you sit with me at the dining hall today?"

"I wish you and I can be in the Garden of Eden."

"You be Eve and I Adam."

By now, the entire class was jeering and shouting.

"Have you ever kissed?" Here, Banjo strained to be heard over cries of, "*Iyama*!" and, "That is disgusting."

Adjua buried her face in her hands. Adigun went face down on the wooden locker table, resting his forehead on its edge and staring down between his mismatched bathroom slippers." The noise had attracted children from neighboring classes, who peeped in through the windows. Then the bell went off. "It is break time," somebody shouted and, mercifully, the mob scattered.

The hallway was packed with students walking toward the kiosk. Everybody was talking about Adigun's romantic advances to Adjua. Adigun walked to the kiosk with Adjua, both seemingly swept up in the current flowing in that direction. They didn't speak. The rope on Adigun's rubber slippers had come off. His too-small shirt strained at every seam, and Bayo's registration number screamed from the breast pocket. At the kiosk, he watched as Adjua purchased a Caprisone orange and a pack of biscuits.

"You are not buying anything?" Adjua asked.

"No, I don't have any money. Somebody broke into my locker at the hostel. All my belongings were stolen yesterday – my pocket money was also stolen." The pair walked around to the back of the classroom block, refusing to acknowledge the snide remarks that followed them. "Love in Tokyo," someone said, and "Love *wan tin tin*," said another. Apparently, it was strange for boys to fraternize with girls in the junior classes.

Since the majority of students appeared to have gathered at the back of the classroom block, Adigun and Adjua kept walking until they arrived at the tree in front of the block. As they approached, one of the students sitting on a massive broken branch looked up and spotted Adigun. His eyes widened in terror as he leaped up, yelling, "Adigun Oloogun!" He picked up his bag and ran, starting a mini-stampede amongst others sitting around the tree. Adigun sighed as he made his way to the shade of the tree, then realized that Adjua wasn't keeping pace with him. He turned to find her a few feet behind, rooted to the spot, and gaping at him. "Why are they running from you? Who are you? What is that other name that boy just called you? I'm getting scared." Then she turned and walked away from Adigun.

Back in the class, Adigun noticed that the distance between his desk and all of those around it had increased, such that he seemed to be a little island within the class. The boys from Jobore had spread the word about Adigun's indelible reputation. Though most of his new classmates now avoided any kind of eye contact, Adigun caught one of them staring every time he looked in his direction. He was about Adigun's height but heavy-set and muscular, with a huge Adam's apple; It was so large, that it looked like he had an oversized golf ball stuck in his throat. Adigun had heard some students call him 'Gege' but found out later that his name was Segun Obasanya. His bow legs had been a source of private amusement for Adigun earlier, but he now found himself perplexed and concerned by the veiny, slab-like muscles that adorned them. Gege wore a fleece napkin wrapped around his neck that did nothing to detract from the aggressive, predatory aura he projected. Adigun looked away every time their eyes met.

Adjua, meanwhile, was increasingly hostile, sitting as far from him as possible on their shared bench. There was no note-passing in the classes that followed. Eventually, during a free period, Adigun took a deep breath, leaned slightly in her direction, and spoke to her in a soft voice. "You see, Adjua, I went to a village school, way out in Jobore. I am a normal child born to very normal parents. A teacher punished our entire class for noise-making, and I was only joking when I told my friends the teacher would die.

"The teacher fell from an uncompleted building broke his neck and died. I had nothing to do with the teacher's death, but my schoolmates thought I did. "Then, another time, when the headmaster caned me, I told my classmates the headmaster's hands would swell up. It was only a joke... but by some coincidence, I don't know, the headmaster came to school the next day with a bandage.

"I had nothing to do with it. The students started calling me 'Adigun Oloogun'. They became scared of me, and nobody wanted to play with me. I am not evil, Adjua. I am not! If I was evil, would I be allowed to serve communion in church?

"Everybody is running from me. You are the only true friend I have. We have formed such a good friendship and I truly don't know why you would join them to become hostile to me."

"Leave me alone," Adjua shouted. Gege launched out of his seat like he had been awaiting this signal.

Approaching Adigun, he began to murmur some incantations, while licking his palm and raising it to the ceiling. When he reached Adigun, Gege pounded his chest with his palm and said, "I am Obasanya, the last son of the *Jagbo Jagbo* of Ilishan. Adigun Oloogun, or whatever they call you, I will squeeze you! In fact, I will cage you! Why have you been harassing the poor girl? We have heard about you. You hit her with a *juju* amulet to make her fall in love with you? Well, it has now failed, so leave her alone. She cannot fall for your *juju* anymore, Adigun Oloogun!" Adigun hardly heard Obasanya – Adjua's cry to be left alone still rang in his ears – and did not say a word in reply.

On the way to the dining hall after school, he walked alone. When he got to the dining room, he walked around looking for Bayo, whom he found sitting with some second-year boys. One of them was from Jobore and, as Adigun approached, they hastened to another table. The news had spread of Adigun's evil, supernatural powers, and he was disheartened to see that Bayo had also turned away from him. Just like with the boat at the harbor, Adigun was alone again. He could barely finish the pieces of boiled yam on his plate, leaving the hall mid-meal to return to the dormitory.

His first term in boarding school and Adigun was the most feared among the junior students. The rumors were so pervasive and compelling, that even seniors steered clear of Adigun. In the weeks that followed, when the school recited the Lord's Prayer at assembly and said,

"…deliver us from evil," the entire class would turn around and take a look at Adigun. Adigun began spending his free time at the school library, reading works of fiction about the Italian Mafia and how they ruled New York. He read about stories of American law enforcement and how they prevailed against the crime families in New York. He dived deeper into these imaginary worlds and pulled further away from the one he was forced to live in. Adigun grew to hate Government College, Tuke.

8

The school campus was located in a fishing settlement on a peninsula; the Atlantic was just about five miles through the lush tropical forest at its rear, and the air was salty. Some of the students said that if one's food was bland, one should just suck the air into one's mouth and the flavor would change. In any case, the constant breeze that passed through the village was considered a blessing by all. Joda, the neighboring town, had a busy harbor and was a bustling commercial center. Tuke was a small community with big superstitions, many of which filtered into the student body at the school. Tuke's fishermen wouldn't fish on Mondays because mermaids came to shore on Mondays. They wouldn't whistle in the village because some sleeping spirit would be offended, awakening to hit the whistler's mouth so hard that the individual may never be able to talk again. Adigun assumed that this very spirit must have struck his biology teacher, whose lower face looked like a train wreck (it would only occur to him decades later that the poor man had some sort of cancer of the mouth), and who sputtered words out from the left side of his mouth. He stammered a great deal, and the children made a sport of mocking him behind his back. Adigun, ever empathetic, could not restrain his sympathetic stammering till after his teacher was gone. He didn't know what had befallen him one day when, in response to the teacher's question, Adigun found his mouth forming a leftward sneer, and heard his voice coming out of that left corner in choppy, staccato bursts. "B-b-b-b-b-b-iology i-i-i-s t-t-t-t-the st-t-t-ud-d-d-y of-f-f-f-f…" Adigun's eyes were squeezed shut as he spoke, and he never saw the biology teacher's blow coming. He came to in the principal's office to find himself being held down by the same two students who had carried him there for a good ass-whooping.

The first stroke hurt so much that Adigun, struggling to plead and explain himself at the same time, began to stammer for real. This only served to signal his non-repentance and the flogging intensified. Episodes of this sort plagued Adigun's early years at Tuke. He was constantly on the punishment list and his name was routinely called at the school assembly for one act of mischief or the other. At Tuke, it was survival of the fittest. The school had no age limits, and some classes looked like a combination of kindergarten and night school. The city boys were generally much younger than the rural kids, who seemed unsure of whether they wanted to fish or get an education. Adigun spent much of his time in the fields, cutting grass with his cutlass, serving one punishment after the other.

Towards the end of his first term, Adigun was in Siberia serving punishment for fighting at the assembly hall. He labored under the blistering sun, digging large holes for the school farm's compost. Tired and thirsty, he sat down to take a break and was soon lost in thought. He was startled out of his reverie by the unmistakable crunch of a footfall on a dry anthill and, when he turned, was surprised to see Adjua. She carried a small cloth bundle with some fruits and cold water. Adigun drank the water, whispering, "Thank you," as he devoured the delicious mango. Adjua held his hands and apologized for joining the other kids to judge him. He forgave her immediately. No lingering disappointment, no angst, no malice. Just a simple instant kindling of joy and the stirring of that strange feeling he had never had for a girl before. Adjua returned to the seat next to Adigun and they were inseparable from that moment until the first term ended and everyone left for the holidays. Adigun was happy to get a break from school but sad to be away from Adjua. He was even sadder to be going back to Jobore, where the Fulanis lay in wait to claim him. He made sure he went nowhere near the Fulani camp at Sabo and kept to himself at home.

9

Adigun had taken Adjua's address in Irede and visiting her was the only thing he looked forward to in the entire holiday period. He set out early to head to Irede because he had no money for transportation, but he knew if he walked at a steady clip, it would take about 4 hours. He navigated the narrow bush path, whistling old church songs, and helping himself to low-hanging cashews along the way. He also stopped at the agbalumo plantation. Agbalumo was the Yoruba name for the African Star Apple, a deep orange, tangy-sweet fleshy fruit that thrived in the area. Adigun plucked a number and tied them in a piece of Ankara cloth he carried with him. He would present them to Adjua, he thought, and show that he was a man that provided.

He stopped from time to time to rest in the deep shade of the trees or tall grass, enjoying the interplay of the green with the spotty red of the *Obi Edun* – or Monkey Kola Nuts – the wild red fruits that monkeys were reputed to prize. After walking miles uphill, he was drenched and was deeply relieved when he passed the giant termite hill at the top of the rise and beheld the beautiful aerial view of the village of Irede. The small town glowed with the warmth of its earthy tones, rust-red roofs capping dust-brown earth houses, seeming to beckon to Adigun. Even stronger was the tug of Adjua and Adigun down the hill into the town, seeking the central mosque – Adjua had told him her home was right next to the central mosque. Her family migrated to Irede from Ghana when she was two years old. Shortly after, her father died, so she now lived with her grandmother while her mother attended nursing school at Kuforidua in Ghana.

True to her description, Adigun located the address Adjua had given him right beside the small mosque. There were other similar houses on the street but this one stood out with its new roof and the bamboo stake with the Ghanaian flag on it; the black star fluttering in the breeze. There was a small metal gate that led into the yard and as Adigun approached the house, he noticed a tomb to his right. He could not make out the inscription on the tomb because there were clothes spread on the memorial stone. It doubled as a drying patch for laundry, he thought. He saw Adjua a few yards away and, with joy, he beamed, lifting his Ankara bundle of *agbalumo* in unconscious offering. Adjua saw him and immediately ran off into the house. Adigun stopped, surprised and confused, then drew closer to the house. As he approached the house, he saw an obese lady, around seventy, sitting on a cane chair. The chair's legs were splayed under her weight. Under her green head tie, wiry grey hair poked and straggled. She had on green and orange wrapper, made from the traditional Ghanaian *Kente* material tied around her rotund bosom and Adigun marveled at the coal-black flesh that spilled over and around its knotted top.

"Young man, good evening. How can I help you?" Her voice brought Adigun's attention to her face, where her beady eyes peered at him from under her hooded, fleshy eyelids.

"Good evening, ma. I am here to see Adjua Prempe."

The woman frowned.

"From where?"

"From Jobore, ma," Adigun answered with confidence.

"You came all the way from Jobore to see Adjua? What is your relationship with her?" She pronounced this last word, 'heh'.

"She is my girlfriend, ma."

"Your girlfriend?"

"Yes, ma."

"How old are you? Where are your parents? Who gave you this address? How did you get here?"

Adigun gulped, not knowing which of the questions to answer first. The old lady's aspect had grown increasingly hostile with each question she asked or, perhaps, with each response he gave.

"Your girlfriend." She repeated with dripping sarcasm.

"Yes, ma, my girlfriend. We even sit on the same chair in school – she is the only friend I have." Adigun paused as the import of his last statement seemed to weigh on him, then he brightened, saying, "I also brought these fruits for her." Adigun handed the cloth-wrapped *agbalumo* to the lady. She collected the bundle, sniffed at it, and handed it back to Adigun. "Wait here," she ordered, then heaved herself off the chair and lumbered into the house.

Adigun sat on the bench, waiting for Adjua's arrival. He spent the next twenty minutes slapping at the sandflies that zoomed around his shaggy head and dive-bombed his bare arms and shins. He could hear the sounds of children somewhere in the compound and other thrashing sounds he couldn't quite place. The old woman came out and told him Adjua was on her way. Adigun had put the *agbalumo* on the floor and the lady stooped to pick the bundle up and handed it to him. Adigun wondered why she did that.

"Are you Adjua's grandma?" Adigun asked. She sucked air loudly through her pursed lips and rolled her eyes. "Very soon, you will meet her grandfather in heaven." Then she murmured some phrases in her native *Twi* dialect. Adigun sensed the anger in this woman and his instinct for self-preservation stirred. The thrashing sound he had noticed earlier and the sounds of children in the yard seemed less like benign background noise and more like portents of grave danger. Adigun had barely registered this impression when the thrashing stopped and the sounds of the children crystallized into a war-like chant as a small mob of them came around the side of the house, carrying long, pale green switches.

Adigun had a moment to grasp that the thrashing sounds had been made as these children – about ten of them between the ages of five and twelve – were stripping a tree of its supple branches. Then they were on him. To Adigun, it felt like he was under attack by a hundred angry wasps. One of the switches caught Adigun on his right ear and he dropped to the ground, rolling in pain. He screamed as the kids rained strokes of fire on his back and began calling out to the absent Adjua; "Adjua, ooooh! Adjua, oooh! *Oriya mi oh*, Adjua, oooooh!". The thin switches sliced his skin as he cried under the swarming children. One of the kids (no more than four years old) climbed onto Adigun and began to bite him through his shorts. He bit so hard that Adigun could feel his little teeth sink through his shorts. This little boy's jaws were as strong as those of a shark. These kids were evidently trained for war.

Adigun leaped up and began running, leaving a swatch of his shirt in the fist of one of his assailants. The kids chased after him, flogging him as he ran with their 4-foot switches. Adigun flew past the black entrance gate and accelerated down the road in front of the mosque. He ran back up the incline and past the giant termite hill, slowing down to a fast walk when he realized his pursuers hadn't followed him beyond the mosque. Night was falling and Adigun walked fast through the bush path, running intermittently and wondering what would become of him when Dodo found the flog marks all over his body. He could think of no excuse that would serve. He couldn't think at all. In Jobore, one only got lashed this way if one was caught stealing; there was no other commonly known reason for a flogging. Today, Adigun had learned of another reason for flogging, certainly, but not one he could present to his parents. The shame and the pain were too deep.

Adigun ran through the motor park, through the church cemetery, hopping from one grave to the other until he got to the locked church gate. Adigun climbed the gate and jumped into the vicarage. There was a little hole on the south fence of the vicarage that opened into the Adigun's residence backyard. As he poked his head through the hole, there was his father in the backyard about to take his evening snuff. As Adigun's eyes met his father's, he froze with half his body still in the vicar's compound. Dodo, shouted, "Obiageli, *biko*, come here straight away! Your snake just crawled through the hole." Adigun's mother strode into the yard, holding a wooden spoon and advancing in an ominous, wide-legged gait as she adjusted the wrapper of her red George outfit.

She was about to rain blows of the wooden spoon when she saw the blood all over her son's body. "*Chimoooo,* who did this to you? Who beat my son like this?" She spun Adigun around and saw the back part of Adigun's shirt was torn off, crying out when the bite marks and bleeding lacerations were revealed. "What is in the bag.?" She looked into the bag and saw the agbalumo fruits. "Chineke! Chineke! Where did you get these? You stole it? Is that why you were beaten; you stole?" Now she dropped the wooden spoon and wrung the cloth around her waist in anguish, wailing, "Adigun has killed me! Adigun has killed me!"

The neighbors on the left and right sides of the fence had gathered to watch the spectacle her loud voice created. She noticed her neighbors and glared at them in turn. "What are you people looking at?" Then she whirled about to face her husband. "Dim! Dim," she howled at her husband, cocking her head to peer at him slantwise through slitted eyes, while he sat where he was, wooden. "He is your son – yes – he is your son! I have been telling you this boy will go rotten someday! He is your son!" Adigun's father tapped the lid of the little snuffbox, adjusting his brown George wrapper, saying nothing. Obiageli grabbed hold of Adigun's shirt and shook him violently.

"Where did you steal these fruits?

"Who did this to you?

"Adigun who beat you like this?

"His body is bleeding, Dim.

"He is bleeding!

Adigun said nothing. In the moment, he decided he didn't much care what his parents thought of him, considering whatever they may have thought before had not stopped them from trading him off to the Fulanis. In his exhausted state, he could not appreciate the irony and the contradiction in the fact that he would rather that they saw him as a thief than discover he had gone to see a girl. "See your life? See your life, Adigun?" His mother had not let up. Adigun kept quiet. His mother shook him and dragged him around, leaving scuff marks in the red earth as she tried to extract more information. Adigun said nothing. His father stood up and walked into the house. Adigun's mother followed, shouting, "Dim, our son has started stealing, and you have not said anything."

"Woman, please leave me alone," Dodo growled, "I have no thief as a son. You should tell me where you found that boy and then take him back where he belongs." Adigun limped through the hallway and went into his room, where he continued hearing his parents' raised voices, but not much of their words. Within seconds, he was asleep.

Adigun's deep sleep was broken the next morning by the crowing of the red rooster right outside his wooden window. He jumped off his bed feeling famished and sore. He stretched with his hands raised and his back arched, then walked out into the backyard where he saw the white polythene bag that contained his *agbalumo*. He picked it up, selected one of the fruits, and began to suck on it, spitting out the shiny black seeds. He nearly choked on one of those seeds when he was shoved on his back onto the ground. He looked up and there was his mum again, fuming. She snatched the white bag from him and began hurling the fruits at him, spattering his face and upper body with the sticky juice and ebony seeds. He was grudgingly impressed by the accuracy of her aim.

"*Onyeoshi! Onyeoshi!*" She shouted at Adigun. "If you do not tell me what happened, I will take you out of this world. I brought you into the world, and I will take you out with my bare hands!" Adigun did not say anything until his mother gave up and rushed back into the house. She emerged carrying the blue plastic basin containing the water she washed Scotch-Bonnet peppers with, white pepper seeds flying about as the water in the basin sloshed. She poured the water all over Adigun, producing instant agony as the liquid pepper ignited in his open sores. He screamed, bringing the women from the vicarage running into the yard through the wooden side gate.

"You will not kill me," Obiageli snarled, thrashing as the women crowded her, "I didn't kill my mother." She tried to break loose from them, straining towards Adigun, and the boy took a half-turn, trying to flee. But he was too weak and hungry to run. Obiageli broke free of the women and caught hold of Adigun, flinging him against the clay fence.

"Where did you get the bag of *agbalumo*?" She asked again. The women from the vicarage pulled her back, pleading with her. "Look at his body," Obiageli shrieked. "We spent the whole day worrying where he had gone, looking for this goat! He comes back looking like an escaped criminal!" Adigun still in pain, realized, in a distant, disconnected way, that his mother had been worried about him and that her fury was probably more about that than anything else and he nearly softened. He almost told her that she didn't have to worry about him stealing, that his injuries were not due to any crime on his part, that he was simply betrayed by someone he had fallen for and trusted, and who had thrown him to the wolves. Then Adigun's resolve hardened. This was what they did, these females; they lulled you to sleep with their soft bodies and sweet smiles. They made you want to do anything to make them happy. Then when you were all helpless and stretched out, they attacked! Here his own mother was, doing the same thing – making him think she had been worried, afraid for him, making him want to soothe and reassure her – just so she could squeeze out information to use against him. He remained silent.

The rest of the break from school was dreadfully long. The air was thick with tension and Adigun spent most of his time in the backyard. He avoided providing grounds for any more parental interaction than necessary; he performed his chores on time and with diligence. His wounds healed, but his heart was scarred and, though he knew he would never forgive Adjua, he couldn't wait to get away from his home and back to school.

10

Another long, silent ride in his father's smoky, loud car, and Adigun was back in school for another term. His stomach knotted as the car negotiated the last bend into the school, he felt the ghost of the pains from his beating at Adjua's house, but he was oddly glad to be back. His father had given him a terse warning not to be tardy in settling his fees, so, as soon as he had placed his things in the hostel (secured by bribing a roommate to watch over them), Adigun headed directly for the accounts department. On his way, he ran into Bayo, who had already paid and was on his way back to the hostel. Bayo seemed to have shaken the fear and revulsion he had contracted from the Jobore crowd, and he approached Adigun with high praise and enthusiasm. He called him *Adigun Oloogun* often, but like a title now, rather than a badge of horror. "O*mokomo wole iye re bu ekun* (The rascally child that gets home and makes his mother cry)," Bayo cheered with delight. Adigun and Bayo walked through the football field by the three-story building that housed the classrooms. They were in the company of other students that needed to hand in their payments before the hands of the outlaws got to them. Theft was a regular thing at Tuke, especially when the students had just resumed after a holiday. As they walked, Adigun narrated his ordeal at home to Bayo, and how Adjua ran and made her grandmother set the kids on him.

He removed his shirt to reveal his scars to Bayo.

"Oh my God, she did this to you?

"You know one thing, Digs? Forgiveness is the best weapon of revenge. You leave her, stay away from her because you don't want to get into more trouble. If you get mad and attack her, you would be expelled. You are already on the probation list as it is; one little infraction would get you out of this school, and your life is ruined forever!"

Bayo and Adigun walked by the hall and saw the long line of students waiting to pay their fees at the bursar's office. Bayo looked at Adigun and told him, "You should not join this line, it's too long. Follow me." He took Adigun past the line and through the car park where, smoking a cigarette under a tree, they found Chukwudalu, the school bursar. The kids called him 'Shukwutey'. He was a dark, stocky young man with a long, hooked nose and ever-bloodshot eyes. Shukwutey used to be the boys' hostel house master but was sacked for starting up an illegal shop in the hostel, selling fried fish and other provisions after lights went out. For some reason, he reappeared in the school accounts department as a Bursar. As he dragged on his cigarette, Bayo called his attention and collected the envelope of fees from Adigun, which he handed to Shukwutey. He counted the money fast. He wrote the amount on the receipt and took the money. He had a bag full of money from other boys that brought their money directly to the bursar, whilst other kids lined up to pay at the office.

"Thank you so much, sir," Adigun said, then flinched as Shukwutey whipped his bloodshot gaze in his direction. "Am I going to eat 'Thank you'?" Shukwutey drawled with derision, continuing, "My friend, do something!" Bayo whispered to Adigun, "Just dash him small out of your pocket money. That's the deal." Adigun did as he was advised, and he and Bayo walked away from the bursar.

"You see, you have to know these things," Bayo quipped. "Why stay in line when you can use the hookup."

"Thank you, Bayo." Adigun was pleased, feeling like a man of the world.

"Let's head to Hostel B, Adigun, I have some friends there."

11

Hostel B was a spillover from the main boys' hostel, further from the teacher's quarters, and subject to less supervision. The hostel was like a banana republic. They had a ruler and officers. They did not observe the lights-out rules, did not attend afternoon or night prep classes unless they felt like it, and they even had a kitchen in the woods behind the hostel where they cooked all manner of meals. Hostel B was like a rebel stronghold within an occupied territory. The students there were generally bigger than the average boy, many of them closer to adulthood than adolescence.

There were characters like Ginger Baker, a 6' 4", 250-pound giant reputed to have killed a lion with his bare hands; and Dillinger, the fair-skinned, afro-sporting, merry-making rockstar, that was the love of the ladies. But most distinguished amongst the Hostel B cast was Kayode Bajulaiye, also known as Uncle Kan. Uncle Kan was the resident judge and arbiter, holding court in Hostel B. Cases came to him from all over the school, and he was a guru in dispute resolution; he spent a lot of time at the library studying philosophy, jurisprudence, including contracts. Hostel B became a courthouse, with the bush behind it, called Land of Settlement, being the measure of last resort. Here, when Uncle Kan's judgment didn't work for the parties, they were allowed to go into the bush to settle it with their fists, under the able supervision of Ginger Baker.

Uncle Kan was so respected, that he even treated cases on appeal from the girls' hostel. He was most loved by the junior students as he was totally against bullying, his stern visage and deep voice brought to bear on whatever acts of unfairness he came across. He always had his shirt buttons undone, hippy style, and walked like a proud stallion. Junior students wanted to be him, senior students wanted to associate with him, and even teachers accorded him a restrained reverence, sometimes referring cases to the Kan court in Hostel B themselves. He was the face of justice at Tuke, and the main reason everyone wanted to be at Hostel B. Bayo and Adigun walked briskly to Hostel B, Bayo chatting steadily. "You have to know how to survive here, Adigun. I come here to earn some extra cash. The seniors at hostel B are rich – they have so much money – they pay me for washing their clothes. Not like our hostel; that is just slavery! You watch; by the time we leave, here we will get some money from Dillinger."

"Who is Dillinger?" Adigun was intrigued.

"Dillinger is a *Gbogan*."

"What is a *Gbogan*?"

"*Gbogan* is a senior *ra-rey*. When you are a *Gbogan*, *Gboyens* will respect you."

"What are *Gboyens*?"

"*Gboyens* are chicks – heavy chicks! Dillinger is teaching me how to become a Gbogan. I've only just started training with Dillinger and I have two *Gboyens* already. You see Adigun, if you were a *Gbogan*, you won't have gone all that way to Adjua's house; you keep it local, keep it local, that's what Dillinger says. You don't travel for any *Gboyen* – they should be the ones traveling to see you! Look at all your body with marks, because of one Ghana girl that is not even a *Gboyen*.

"*Chai*! if it was me," Bayo raised his already pronounced lower lip and frowned. "Me, Bay, no girl will treat Bay like that! Not me, Beyustic Bayulica, the only *ra-rey* in Ipetumodu."

"Can I be a Gbogan too?" Adigun asked. Bayo drew air through his teeth, making a derisive sound. "You have to be a *ra-rey* first," he replied, "then you can think of being a *Gbogan*. Just follow me and do as I do. I will teach you how to become a *ra-rey*, Adigun. Look at you; you can't even fly your collar. See how I'm walking like uncle Kan? You have to be able to walk like that." Bayo had adjusted his collar, 'flying' it high, and he was almost limping with his right shoulder dipped lower than (and slightly ahead of) the left. Adigun followed suit and they both went into Hostel B.

Dillinger was nowhere to be found but, to Adigun's surprise, everyone knew Bayo. The junior boys all went into a hailing frenzy, shouting his nickname.

401

"Bayustic Beyulica," they chanted. In no time, Bayo had brokered a washing gig and Adigun washed clothes whilst Bayo watched and played around with the seniors that owned them. At the end of the session, Adigun's hands were sore and the pain in them seemed to flare when Bayo handed him twenty Kobo for his troubles – he knew Bayo had collected more – and protested.

"Bayo! Twenty Kobo? That's all I get? Twenty Kobo? Look at my hands bleeding!"

"Adigun, I'm a businessman. I really didn't want to bring you into my business, but I decided to help you. You didn't have a penny, now you have twenty Kobo. Why are you moaning? It is just your first day and you are complaining; you think this is how to become a *Gbogan*?"

"Okay, I'm sorry, Bayo, I won't complain again."

And Adigun didn't utter another word of complaint. He went directly to the main hostel and offered a few boys ten Kobo to wash for seniors. By nighttime, Adigun had recruited an entire laundry squad, after which he flew his collar and had a meeting with Senior Dillinger. He struck a deal for two Naira per bucket and paid his crew ten Kobo each for an unspecified number of buckets, ensuring that, even on a per-bucket basis, he was making twenty times the earnings of those who actually washed the clothes. By dinner time, Bayo was shocked to see Adigun, Senior Dillinger, Ginger baker, and Uncle Kan at the same table laughing and enjoying dinner together.

He watched from afar as it was an abomination for junior students to approach the dining tables on the east side, occupied by seniors.

The next morning Adigun saw Adjua and walked away from her, collar flying and walking with the Uncle Kan gait of course. Bayo, of course, had told everyone that needed to hear about Adigun's trip to Adjua's house and the treatment he got. That news too had spread all over the school. Boys came to Adigun asking to see his marks from the beating. Adigun knew Bayo had done it again – keeping secrets was not Bayo's strength – but he maintained the mystery of his scars, subtly turning them into positive reputation points. The foundation of this reputation-building demanded that he was openly and fiercely cold towards Adjua, an attitude he maintained for the years that followed, even after he could barely remember why he was upset with her. Even when he felt the treacherous yearning for her company, her smile. Years later, when Adigun would have his trouble with the bursar and have to leave school, Adjua tried reaching him with notes sent through his friends. Adigun never replied. He did not like or trust the feelings thoughts of her sparked. He did not trust her – like he could not trust his mother – and decided that he didn't trust the female tribe at all.

12

Adigun snapped awake and found Phoebe seated on his bed. He jerked his head, wincing and shielding his eyes from the sun's rays.

"How did you get in? Who let you in?"

"It's 10 a.m., Diggs. Mrs. Brown was in the garden when I came in. Look at you, you're wasted!

"I could hear the singing and jeering from my apartment last night. What were you guys drinking?

"Oh, I laughed so hard when they talked about the short midget smuggled in a bag pack."

Adigun started and, in shock, asked her, "How did you know about that? You were not here; no matter how loud we were, you can't have heard the actual words from your apartment!"

Phoebe stuttered, realizing she had goofed. "No, I had highlights from Mrs. Brown."

"Oh, hm, okay."

"What are we doing today?"

"The fight is over, and I have to rest for a week then start training for the California fight against Drake Paqua. It is a big fight."

"So how much did you get paid for winning?"

"A lot."

"What is a lot, Diggy boo? I can't know how much you get paid, as your woman?"

"Y'know, Fibi, I just would like to keep that to myself for a while. You know I have come from far away, a poor African kid from Jobore."

"Yeah, right! That is played out now; you are more American than apple pie now. You only chose to be African when it suits you. So, when are we going shopping?"

"To buy what?"

"Some Jewellery – like boxers do for their girlfriends." As she spoke, Phoebe's beeper went off and then cut out. Then it went off a second time and a third. Adigun looked at her reflectively asking, "Who is the person beeping you continuously?"

"It's the restaurant."

"Then use my phone and call them." Adigun pointed to the black phone with its transparent rotatory dial. Phoebe shook her head, replying, "I don't want to. They may want me to come in tonight. Anyway, I have to go now. I hope you are spending the night at mines. At least you are not training anymore. Your girl needs some sugar and spice in her life. It's been a while."

"*Nkan ta rie si niyen?*"

"What is that? Now you are speaking African? Are you going to come over or not?"

Adigun walked into the bathroom and grabbed his blue terry-cloth housecoat. "I have told you there is nothing like speaking African."

"Whatever, man! It's very rude when people speak a language that the other party can't speak. See you later, boo." Phoebe went into the bathroom and grabbed Adigun from behind. Adigun turned around and grabbed her, kissing her until she spun around and walked out of the room. Her beeper went off again. Adigun hollered from the bathroom, "Your boyfriend is beeping you! again; you better call him, lover girl!"

"Oh, piss off, Diggy!"

Phoebe went out through the kitchen door, into the backyard, and walked past the swimming pool to access the alley door at the side of the house. As she crossed the road her beeper went off again. When she got to her apartment, she dialed a number and was hissing into it almost before it was picked up. "Hey, easy with the pages; you trying to blow my cover?" The man on the other end of the call ignored her question, replying, "Can you believe what we got last night? What it means? The entire crew, first time, all together in the same city?

406

Maybe you don't need to worry too much about your cover, Phoebe; we may be on the verge of breaking this case wide open."

13

Adigun's phone rang repeatedly. He heard it from the shower and was just considering throwing a towel around his waist to answer it when it stopped. Almost immediately, he heard Mrs. Brown shouting his name. "Hey, Adel? Adel!! Telephone!" Adigun's room was right above the kitchen so he could hear her quite clearly. "I'm in the shower," he yelled back. "Please take the person's number and I'll call him back." He rinsed off and emerged wet from the bathroom, shrouding the area around the bathroom door in steam as he stepped out. He was still drying himself when the phone rang again, and he snapped it up. It was Bobby Brown.

"Champ, I've been calling you. I have good news; I just spoke with Jonathan Erlbaum."

"Yes, I remember him. The promoter from New York."

"You are fighting Donny Chez in Atlanta, then you fight Rocky Sanchez in New York – Madison Square Garden – you're big time now, son! Last night's fight is all over the news; front page of the Washington Post."

Adigun stood in momentary silence as water from his body dotted the floor.

"Thanks, so much, Dad," he replied gravely. "I am so grateful."

"I've sent the Limo back to the house. Join me at the Gym as soon as you can; there's a rack of fans and press waiting outside the gym for you."

Adigun finished drying himself off and threw on his new Adidas hoodie with matching lycra pants. Once his white Adidas tennis shoes were on, he slipped his favorite blue coat over the entire outfit and then rushed down the stairs. The TV was on in the living room and Mrs. Brown was in front of it listening to the news on Adigun's victory.

"Good morning, ma."

"Good morning, Sweetness, I'm so proud of you."

"The news has gone gaga about your fight."

"Oh, wow!"

"There's some oatmeal and toast. Should I get you some?"

"Oh no, ma, no hard carbs just yet."

Adigun grabbed the newspaper off the dining table, and he smiled as he saw the picture of his knockout punch all frozen on the page to which it was opened.

"Mum, please, can I speak to you for a second? Phoebe was here early this morning; Did you tell her anything about the discussions at the dinner table last night?"

"Oh, no! I was in the garden, and she just came up. We never got the chance to speak."

"What time did she come in?"

"It was about eight a.m. Your father was out of the door at seven on the dot and she came in about an hour later, just as the news came on."

"Oh, okay. So, she came in at eight?"

"Certainly."

"Hm."

"Is anything the matter?"

"Oh, no, mum, nothing at all."

Adigun grabbed his gym bag and walked through the large foyer toward the entrance door. "Bye, mum," he called. "See you later." "Okay, love, see you at dinner," Mrs. Brown smiled. Adigun stepped out, signaled to the driver of the limousine, and ran across the road toward Phoebe's apartment. He pressed the buzzer and waited a few seconds until Phoebe buzzed him in. He rode the elevator to the 10th floor and strode to Phoebe's apartment, finding the door was already open.

"Hey, Diggy boo, you are all over the news! Damn, I didn't know you hit the Jamaican boy that hard. He is still in the hospital."

"That's not why I came; I asked Mrs. Brown and she said she never said anything to you about any midget. As a matter of fact, she never had any conversation with you at all! You woke me up at ten, right?"

"Yes?"

"But you entered the house at eight! What were you doing between eight and ten?"

"Oh, Diggy Boo, I gave myself a tour of the beautiful house. I was dying to see you, but it was so quiet when I got there, and I figured you were still tired and sleeping. I figured I could let you have a couple more hours and see the rest of the house while you did. Where's all this coming from?"

"You can't come into people's private space and just give yourself a tour; that's not right."

"Oh, okay, Saint Diggy, but didn't you give yourself a tour of my apartment? How did you find the guns?"

"That is not my house, Phoebe. It belongs to Bobby Brown. So, who told you about our discussion last night?"

"Mrs. Brown, goddammit! The woman has bloody dementia and doesn't remember her own name. She is old."

Adigun recalled the rather maniacal pleasantness with which Mrs. Brown treated him and decided to let the matter drop. "Anyway, stop giving yourself tours of people's houses," he grumbled.

Phoebe matched his mood and stepped it up a notch, asking, "So, what's the patch on your neck about?" Adigun's hand strayed up to the dressing over his brand and his eyes dropped as he replied. "I got a new tattoo."

"Oh, you got a tattoo overnight?"

"It was there before the fight; you just didn't notice."

"I massaged you before the fight, Diggy Boo, you did not have a tattoo. Maybe you have Dementia too, huh?"

"Can we just drop this?"

"You started it!"

"I have to go into DC. You coming?"

"No, I'm working on my new recipe book, but I can drop you off if you want."

"Oh no, I have the limo. Bobby Brown sent it to pick me up."

"Okay, boo, see you later. I hope you can keep to your promise. Bobby Brown said we can celebrate today, so, I can have you to myself today."

Book-7

Her Majesty's Probate Service

Duroowo paabi, kam anndi layooru

(The shepherd of frogs recognizes the limping ones (a layman thinks they are all limping) – Fulani Proverb)

1

Oxford, 1984

At the age of fifteen, Adigun had been commissioned to assassinate Chike by his greedy uncles. Chike had escaped with the help of his would-be assassin. He never disclosed to his father – or anyone else – his knowledge that his uncles were the perpetrators. Chike was moved out to England from the NsonsoSoronsonso, his father's country mansion. Both he and his father decided not to disclose to anybody that he was alive.

Chike was taken to his father's Belgravia mansion and home-tutored. After the attempt on his son's life, Dr. Obidike wasn't taking any chances. Chike's mother spent practically the entire year in Belgravia, watching tutor after tutor oversee her son's preparation for the entrance exams into the top schools in England. The year of home-schooling gave both parents a chance to build some assurance that there was no lingering threat to their son's life. Chike did so well at the exams, that he was spoiled for choice, narrowing it down to either Eton college or the equally prestigious Harrow school for boys. He settled on Harrow, a high-priced private boarding school,

414

and began his time there with discreet private security and under his mother's maiden name, Onyeodikara.

Chike's schedule at Harrow was packed, as he was active in sports and popular with the students. Unlike the reticent bookworm he had been at Jobore, Chike had grown to be an energetic, physically – if not so much socially - active boy. By his second year, he had become the captain of the school rugby team and, by his final year, he had traveled all over Europe playing against other elite secondary schools in Europe. Chike Oyiodikara, as he was called, was something of an icon in the rugby scene and was already being approached by scouts to join professional clubs. Dr. Obidike kicked against this vehemently but conceded that Chike's rugby resume' came in very handy when they began to search for a university during his A levels at Harrow. His grades were exceptional, but competition for spots was fierce and rugby tipped the scales in his favor.

At his interview for Oxford, Chike was surprised to be interviewed by the rugby coach who had been a referee in a few of his matches. They spent the entire interview time speaking about the last season. Chike knew he was going to take the Oxford offer, having already become certain that Oxford would offer him a place. They had an amazing rugby team and their facilities were second to none in the UK. Chike was offered a full rugby scholarship to study economics, but Dr. Obidike turned it down, instead making the University commit to offering the scholarship to another child, of African descent, from a poor family. The university was familiar with Dr. Obidike's wealth – he was known for his philanthropy and support for universities and the arts – so they weren't inclined to argue.

Dr. Obidike's empire was extensive, by any standards. He was sitting on a multi-billion-dollar estate with only a sole heir, and he was painfully aware that he was getting old and had a heart condition. When, years ago, Dr. Obidike had a pacemaker installed in his body – at the William Beckwell clinic – on the famous Harley Street in West London, he had to depend on his brothers to manage his businesses. He had discovered their dangerous greed but never knew they might have any plans to hurt his only child. Nevertheless, it was clear to him that the only way to protect his hard-earned wealth was to quickly immerse his son in his business affairs.

2

Now in Oxford, Chike lived in near-penury in England. Dr. Obidike paid for Chike's very expensive tuition and boarding, but little else. Chike lived in the dormitories – Saint Christopher's Hall, to be precise – a stone's throw from the Oxford train station. The railway tracks passed right by Chike's window and, when the trains went by, it felt like they were running through the building. He lived with a cocky British Aristocrat, one African-American student on the Marcus Garvey scholarship, Tyrone Chuck, and three Chinese boys. Chike was always at loggerheads with the British boy, Arthur Forbes the Third, who was a blue-blooded, conceited boy from Windsor. His grandfather, by some evil coincidence, had led the British Army into Arochukwu during the Anglo-Aro war in 1901. Chike and Arthur hated each other as much as their warring ancestors must have, and they had a cold war between them that was little more than an inherited feud. Chike got along well enough with his other roommates; even Young Duck, a poor fellow from Shanghai, in Oxford on a Chinese government scholarship. He was one of the brightest brains in China and was already on all the merit award schemes in his department after only two years. He was studying Nuclear Physics and maintained a 4.0 GPA. A committed communist, he had converted the flat Kitchen into a mini-laboratory and his friends half-teased him he would someday invent a nuclear bomb from that kitchen, run back to China, and remotely detonate it.

Young Duck was not a cheery fellow and he always complained about people eating up his food, despite always cooking huge quantities and offering anyone that strayed near. "Again and again, you guys keep eating up my noodles. I swear, some of you liberal rats will eat poisoned noodles and die someday. This is not right," Young Duck would whine, stamping on the wooden floor. "I'm just a poor Chinese student. My father didn't bring me to Oxford on a private Jet and we don't own a Rolls Royce, but I'm the one supposed to feed everyone in this house? This is not the United Nations refugee camp."

"Chicken Licken," he would shout his nickname for Chike, "When did noodles become African food? When you cook your African juju storm, no one can eat it; it stinks like the ass of a pig." Chike would snipe back from his bed in the corner by the old radiator, "Fried Rice! I know you are talking about me. Why can't you be man enough to speak to me directly? You are always losing your noodles. You know, like everyone else, everything in the kitchen is for all-comers. You don't want it to be eaten, leave it in your freaking locker." Lee, the mildest of the three Chinese occupants would usually rise in defense of his countryman; "*Brackuh* African Chyke, stop calling him Fried Rice."

"Zip it, Lee! Oh, yes! the dorm cat is nowhere to be found since you got here. We have looked everywhere for it. We don't know if she left after you scooped up all the rats, or you made a pot of 'roast meow' with it."

"That is *dispickabuh anduh racist*! I swear to God, I will report you guys to the school authorities." Lee's accent got progressively thicker as he grew more excited. Rat eater," Chike would crew with maniacal glee. "Oh, my! You guys are disgusting. I hope we don't all get infected with some strange disease from your weird culinary practices."

There was an abrupt silence when Chike stopped speaking, followed by a burst out of laughter and bodies thudding on the floor as they slid off the bunk beds.

Chike fell last rolling on the floor with laughter almost choking. The three Chinese students smiled indulgent, plastic smiles. Lee hissed through gritted teeth, his strong Chinese accent more choked than usual, "With all the *upper-crass-uh* training and *booording* finishing schools you claim to have attended, I would expect you learned how to treat foreigners that have come so many miles across the seas to study in your country, *Diu Lei*," he ended, using a most insulting swear word in Cantonese. All three Chinese boys chuckled in their beds.

"Why can't you speak in English?" Chike retorted. "Point of correction, Chopsticks, I'm a Nigerian prince from Arochukwu. I am not from England, so, I'm not your host here. I'm just a foreign student, like you."

419

Arthur interjected, "A slave in a Burberry suit, reliving the life of his colonial masters."

Chike jumped up, pointing his finger at Arthur. "I think I've about had it, Mr. Forbes; this has nothing to do with you! This conversation was not about you, you spawn of a savage British soldier who maimed and raped humans for a living! It's about time I told you who your grandfather was. Sir Arthur Forbes Montenaro led the British army into Arochuckwu and he and his 87-man troupe got a good ass-whooping by the great warriors of Arochukwu."

"Haha! what a joke, Chike, your juju tribe had only spears and knives and some clubs"

"Li-l-l-listen, li-li-li-listen, stupid," Chike had stammered – Chike had battled with this speech impediment as a child and had been successfully treated, but it would rear its head whenever he was aggravated or angry – and the room hushed, knowing a storm was imminent. The last time he'd begun stuttering during an argument, it had ended in a physical brawl. "Listen," shouted Chike.

"No, *you* listen, Chike Onyeodikara!! Your depraved people had been terrorizing your countryside for the longest time, using their long Juju or whatever, luring fellow blacks in, only to capture them as slaves." Arthur spoke in crisp Queen's English, enunciating each word carefully. "Your people are the reason Tyrone Chuck is in America. The British government came into Arochukwu to stop the slave trade."

"Slave trade? Slave trade?" blurted Chike. "May the powers of *Ibin Okpabi* strike you down!"

"Come now, Chike, I don't believe in that nonsense! All I know is my grandfather, Arthur Forbes Montenaro Smith came to your juju shrine, and you all had a right walloping."

"How dare you, Forbes? How dare you? I am from the lineage of *Okoro Toti*, the General of the *Aro* army! I will educate you on things your coward grandfather hid from you! The Aro's had been dominating our region since the 1800s; your people started sneaking in to raid and kidnap. The Aro's put that in check. When we could not stand it anymore, the *Arochukwu* army launched the first offensive attack, and they chased the British Army back into their silly boats. They then came back in 1901 and got the final licking."Young Duck and their fellow roommates always enjoyed these sessions but, at this time, they'd sit right on the edges of their beds, ready to restrain the combatants should it turn into another physical assault.

"The *Arochukwu* warrior came against 1,550 soldiers and 2,100 carriers in four axes of advance to Arochukwu. They came from *Oguta, Akwete, Unwana,* and *Itu* on a counter-insurgency campaign. *Okoro Toti,* my great-grandfather (may his soul rest in peace), resisted fiercely. It was a four-day battle, the *Aro*s were winning. We were chasing them back to the sea until their cannon blew up the *Ibini Ukpabi* shrine; that was when the *Aros* receded. They did not surrender, it was a religious decision and, I swear by the power of *Ibini Ukpabi*, if you say one more word, the *Arochukwu* war will end here today." Arthur had gone red, and his eyes were bloodshot. He was looking around for a weapon and Chike was about to launch at him when Tyrone Buck jumped in and held Chike while Young Duck held Arthur against the wooden wardrobe by his bed.

"You son of a savage cannibal," Arthur shouted. Chike tried to break from Tyrone, shouting in Igbo, "*Onyeoshi! Onyeoshi*," meaning 'thief'. "Have you heard about the *Nri* conflict? Did your grandfather tell you what happened at the *Ekumeku* war? Go and ask your coward grandfather about the Igbo women's war in 1929?" By this time Chike was weeping with rage and it took all of Tyrone's strength to hold him. Chike had a hard enough time dealing with his financial constraints amid snotty sons of privilege like Arthur, but to have them assert privilege in the realm of culture – and history – was trying to the extreme. Chike was usually an easy-going economics student, but that history topic brought out a different side of him and Arthur always pushed that particular button. In the years that followed at Oxford, Arthur, and others like him, came to be the single most important aspect of Chike's development as a man, teaching him to reign in his emotions; teaching him to vent his frustrations through measured, deliberate, productive action. Even if the only tangible outcome was the punishment of his enemies, that was 'productive' enough for him. Chike was a serious scholar – he had won several prizes for academic excellence in his department – and a serious athlete, known as the Nigerian Nightmare for his formidable presence on the rugby field.

However, those close enough to him knew him to be one who managed near-sinister victories over all who crossed him and, soon enough, they learned to avoid crossing him at all – Arthur included.

1

London, 1990

Chike had maintained a phenomenal GPA throughout his time at Oxford, and it was no surprise that he had several job offers even before he graduated with a first-class degree. As a result, he had had lots of time to consider his next steps and immediately took up the offer of a job, in central London, as a caseworker at the Her Majesty's Probate Office. He had far more lucrative offers with several top-notch private firms, but he was not driven by the salary prospects. He loved the idea of the civil service and wanted to avoid the high-powered private firms that gave young entrants high expectations and practically stole their lives. Chike's other option, an unwelcome one, was to return to Nigeria to work in his father's conglomerate, which he refused despite his father's entreaties. The Probate Office was situated in the high-traffic section of Holborn, and Chike had found a modest converted box-room in a quiet suburb, thirty minutes, by train, from the heart of London. One morning, as he prepared to resume his first day at work, the phone in his tiny abode rang.

Chike was not entirely surprised to discover that it was his father on the phone; Dr. Obidike was resourceful, and London was his backyard.

"Yes sir?

"No sir, I really can't do that right now sir.

"No sir. I should not take the job with Probate? Sir? Sorry?

"Can you hear me? Sir? Sir?"

"The connection seems to be bad, Sir. Did you say something about returning to Nigeria?

"I can't hear you, Sir, the connection is awful."

With a neutral expression, Chike broke the connection and replaced the receiver. He stopped taking calls for the next couple of weeks until he could change his number, and then he moved house. Over the next year, when his father kept successfully finding out his new addresses and phone numbers, Chike got rid of his home phone altogether. He kept away from Nigerians in London. He coordinated things at work so that only work-related calls came in and, after a while, he stopped hearing from his father. Within another year, Chike had changed offices a few times and, faster than usual, got a promotion into the Directorate of Records of the Probate Office in Westminster. The department had never seen such a rapid rise in the ranks – and Chike was still under thirty. His work was exceptional; he was so good at solving cases, that within these two years, he became considered a subject matter expert in probate administration, speaking at conferences and seminars.

Chike's efforts to cut off communications with specific people – mostly his father and those linked to him – resulted in him cutting off just about everyone else. Without a phone and near-zero social activity, he became something of a recluse. His time at Oxford produced a deep-seated disdain for the silver-spoon crowd and he scorned their dependence on their parents. He developed an obsession with writing his own destiny, for forging his own path, independently of his father's wealth. His mother was able to keep sending him letters through his office mail, but Chike never replied. He changed residences until found a quiet place in Luton, an airport town about an hour away from London. It was here, when he seemed to have thrown his father off his scent, that Chike allowed himself a home phone once more.

At work, Chike was not a team player. He buried himself alone in the file room, combing through files, digging up difficult, old, 'cold' cases. He tracked down files of people that died intestate, with no clear way to locate their next of kin. Chike demonstrated a particular knack for finding relatives and liaising with the banks and other custodians of un-administered estates. Chike connected these bereaved, often astonished, family members with the wealth the deceased left behind. He lived in the file room, murmuring to himself until he got a breakthrough, when he would usually shout out a name. "Yes! Yes!

Duran Kennedy!" Then he would rush to his desk and grab the phone. By this time, phone calls of this sort were something of a legend in the office.

"Hello?"

"Hello."

"Can I speak to Duran? Duran Kennedy.

"Oh, my! When did he pass on?

"Really?

"Can I have *his* number? I'm from the Probate Office in Westminster.

"My name is Chike Onyeodikara; I've been working on this case for years.

"Absolutely!

"Yes.

"Absolutely. I will call him right away."

Then Chike would take the files and run out, dart into the staircase, and up the three flights to the 9th floor. When he'd burst into Director General's office, the office grapevine would already be buzzing.

"It's another one," they would say, or "Another discovery," or "This guy is a genius. Bless him."

Chike would usually emerge from the DG's office beaming. The entire body of staff in the open office would stop

427

what they were doing to gawk at Chike with admiration. He, in turn, would gaze imperiously at them like Superman after a heroic rescue. He would sniff and nod his head, intoning, "It's a big fish, this one," which usually meant some unwitting bum on the streets of London had just become a millionaire. More people than might be expected in England die without any wills or instructions regarding their wealth. Chike dug out the files, some over fifty years old, and would trace the family lineage to the next legal relative, which would qualify for the inheritance, sometimes running into millions of pounds. Often, these estates would have been under administration for decades, accruing considerable interest. Chike's efforts served not only the identified beneficiaries, but the government as well, as it could now peel off a portion for itself. On this day, it was the estate of an old goldsmith that had died in the early sixties. His money was saved in Midland Bank, which was bought over by National Westminster Bank, where the money had been lying without a claimant for ages.

Chike walked proudly to his desk and put his feet on his desk. "Get your stinking African feet away from me, you silly sausage," John Loughborough growled and Chike replied, in broken English, "Bad *belle*," which simply meant envy. In short order, the DG of the Probate Office came down and rang the bell at the entrance by the stairwell. "O, ye, o, ye! The Probate Department, 357 Westminster, London has done it once more! We have successfully solved another major probate 'nut-up'." Muffled laughter and cheery muttering greeted his announcement.

428

"Thanks so much to our special bloodhound, Chike. He keeps doing it. This week alone he has solved seven cases! He broke the department's record last month." The cheers became more animated. "We thank you so much, Chike." It was payday for Chike as well. As was the tradition of the department, there were bonuses and cash incentives associated with each successful solution to an abandoned case.

Chike was so good at what he did that, within six years, he rose to the position of Deputy Director-General. He earned a handsome salary but remained in his old, dark, rented one-bedroom in Luton. He had converted the living room into a bedsit, which he rented out to Kabiru Salaam, a Nigerian history student at the University of Luton. Proximity did not breed warmth between the cohabitants, and their contact was limited to perfunctory grunts when their paths crossed at the entrance to the flat or in the living room. Chike lived like a pauper, owning little material property and having even less by way of social life. He was always working, even at home. There was a Park in front of Chike's apartment where he would sometimes sit on a bench with a little red book, muttering to himself. Kabiru would watch Chike from the little window in his room, trying to figure out if his landlord had some mental issues. When Chike was in his room, he never seemed to make any social calls; everything seemed to be work-related.

Kabiru heard Chike introducing himself several times, over the phone, as the Director-General of the Probate

429

Department, and over the years, Kabiru figured out Chike was often speaking with banks and financial institutions. These calls were countless, always on the same subject matter, and usually followed one of his park bench soliloquies. Kabiru had never been into Chike's room and Chike took steps to grant him as little visual ingress as possible. On several occasions, Kabiru tried to snatch a quick look under the pretext of handing Chike his mail but had to make do with slipping the papers through a crack in the doorway that opened onto darkness behind its occupant. Kabiru gave up and just minded his business.

It was the beginning of summer in 1990, and right in the middle of Kabiru's final exams that Kabiru got a glimpse into the secret life of his landlord. He was still asleep when Chike went out but was roused soon after by the loud ringing of the alarm in Chike's room. He decided to do some studying but was barely fifteen minutes in when the alarm went off again, strident and piercing, for another five minutes. It would do so every twenty minutes for the next several hours., becoming a source of mounting frustration for Kabiru. He tried to ignore the clamoring bell and focus on his books, but soon it became like a splinter in his palm that he just had to get out. Kabiru didn't have Chike's work number and couldn't call him, but he was glad of this inconvenience because he subconsciously relished the excuse to find a way into Chike's room.

Kabiru walked out through the back door into the garden and, looking up, was pleased to see that Chike's window was open. He saw the neighbor's ladder leaning against the fence and slid it over before carrying it to the building and setting it against the wall underneath Chike's window. Without giving himself any room to chicken out, he climbed up the ladder into Chike's bedroom. The sight of it shocked him to his core. The room was festooned with files and banded documents, and the air in it was dizzy with the smell of damp paper and stale food. There were several pizza boxes on the heap of rubbish in a black trashcan. Limp clothes hung off the edge narrow cot and others seemed to be crawling along the floor, making their way to a coatrack that stood beside the oak wardrobe in the corner. It looked like a suicide queue of garments, each waiting its turn to hang itself on the coatrack. Beside his bed, on the floor, were several files. There was barely any space to move around.

Two large corkboards covered most of two walls – both covered with thumbtacked notes and Post-Its – looking like a movie-type investigation room. The yellow Post-It notes had names and figures written on them, ranging in value from piddling sums to amounts over millions of pounds. Each had a red tick on it, applied with what appeared to be a red marker. The alarm was still clanging as Kabiru grabbed one of the brown files and opened it. It contained some personal details and documents of a deceased individual. There was a death certificate, dated, 30th of July 1953, and sheaves of bank correspondence. Kabiru opened other files with similar contents. In some places, the folders were stacked waist-high. Taking one last look around the room, Kabiru turned off the alarm and climbed out. He returned the ladder and went to his study desk.

Chike returned and went up to his room in silence, which was typical; he truly never said much. But after the clandestine visit to his room, Kabiru began listening more carefully to Chike's phone conversations and, soon enough, could piece together a rough picture of what was afoot. He had heard him talk to several banks about transferring money into the account of the person he felt sure Chike impersonated. Kabiru was in utter shock but chose to seek further confirmation of his suspicions. He had always had a vague curiosity about the assortment of directed mail, under unfamiliar names, that came to the residence. These took on a fresh significance with his recent discoveries and he could not wait for the next mail to come.

On the next mail-drop day, Kabiru made sure he was at home and thanked the stars that Chike wasn't. As soon as he heard the rattle of the mail slot and the muffled thuds of the packages landing on the hallway carpet, he rushed to the door; most were directed from assorted European countries. Kabiru grabbed a bulky envelope and opened it. It was a statement of account for one Damian Rivers. The account had a balance of one million Euros (and change) and indicated transfers into several accounts in batches of ninety thousand Euros. Kabiru sifted through the details and searched for the recipients of the transfers, finding them all issued to the same individual: Alfred Evans. Digging further, Kabiru saw the transfers recorded and the moneys withdrawn from several post offices in Belgium, and the entire process became clear to Kabiru.

He marveled at how Chike could have so much money – albeit from illegal transactions – but still live like a poor introvert. No friends, no social life, no apparent family ties, no romance. Nobody came to visit Chike at home. He sat alone in his room, playing rock music and, apparently, defrauding Her Majesty's government and subjects. Kabiru elected not to act on his discovery. He went on to graduate and begin working, also in Luton. He remained Chike's tenant, despite his worries about his landlord's operations. The rent was good, and he had his privacy. He remained there for another two years and four months.

4

On a cold Friday morning, Chike came in with a bunch of balloons and a bag-load of gifts. He also had a cake (actually half a cake), which he squashed against the radiator that led to his room – he was quite tipsy. Kabiru's room was to the right of the entrance, and the kitchen door was opposite the entrance. Kabiru heard the racket and opened his door to see what was up.

"Hey Kabs," Chike chirped, "I'm retired. I resigned from my job and today was the 'leaving do'. I will drop the cake in the kitchen; I brought it for you. There's also some wine." "Oh, congratulations," Kabiru said, peeping out of his room.

"Thanks, Kabs, it was an amazing party. The Mayor of Westminster sent a representative and the Westminster MP also attended. I'm so proud of myself! Chikereuba broke all the records in performance in the department. I'm going to miss it but I just got tired and want to see the world. I want to travel around Europe and then, after that, hit the Americas." Chike threw this last over his shoulder as he ambled into the kitchen.

Kabiru stood by the door in his velvet housecoat, bemused. Chike had spoken more words to him in this hallway encounter than in all the years they had lived together. When the silence stretched from seconds to a minute, he went into the kitchen himself. Chike was asleep on the armchair in the kitchen. Kabiru tapped him on the arm, saying, "Why don't you head to your room, Chike." Chike got up and staggered up the stairs to his room. They would not have any such chatty exchanges again.

In just three months after Chike retired from the Probate office, he traveled to Europe over a dozen times, flitting in and out of continental Europe like he was going to the corner shop by his house. Chike had amassed millions of pounds within England alone and banked tens of millions in Brussels and Lithuania. He'd opened these accounts all over Europe with identification made by his criminal facilitator, and the closest thing to a friend he had, Samantha. She was a co-worker at the probate office who had preceded him in the fraud. Chike discovered it easily enough but, rather than turning her in, carefully studied Samantha's operations. He then perfected the scheme and raised it to a level she couldn't have conceived. Samantha had studied graphic design at the South London Polytechnic and was an expert in forgery. She had a lucrative sideline making fake British passports, which had passed muster at airports all over the world. Nun-like in her modest outfits, she showed no outward hints of any criminal propensity, except her excitement when she had a new commission for false documents – then her eyes would gleam. Chike had prompted that gleam several times in his years at the probate office.

Kabiru had now come to terms with Chike's lifestyle but never discussed it with anyone. He would visit, via the window, Chike's room now and again and marvel at the passports and driver's licenses from different countries. All had Chike's photographs on them, but an assortment of names. It was clear what Chike was up to, why he'd resigned from his job, and his mission. Kabiru would read random correspondence and find bank accounts with huge sums of money in them. Chike gave numerous instructions, directing the banks to pay out huge sums of money to fictitious next-of-kin designees. What amazed Kabiru the most was Chike's lifestyle of penury amidst so much wealth – Chike would not lend Kabiru just three pounds to renew his travel card – including the extent of self-deprivation to which he subjected himself.

At length, the combination of lifestyle and exertion appeared to take its toll on Chike. He looked fatigued, after traveling almost non-stop for close to six months. Next came the bonfires at the back of the house, always in the middle of the night. There was the strong smell of burning paper in the house every morning for several days. Chike's rock music became increasingly loud and more frequent as he was now home more often. Neighbors had complained and even called the police to intervene a few times. The presence of police at the door was traumatic for Kabiru each of those times, causing him to worry that an arrest was imminent and that he might be roped in. But each time, Chike had quiet words with the officers, and they left him with little more than a mild rebuke.

The bonfires marked a drastic reduction – almost a complete stop - in Chike's trips and Kabiru was very interested in knowing why. From his intermittent snooping, he knew Chike's funds were intact, so what was happening now? He often kept his television volume down so he could eavesdrop on Chike's phone conversations. Eventually, he hit paydirt. On this day, Chike was unusually ebullient, speaking expansively, and his side of the conversation was easy to hear.

"Please can I speak to Samantha?

"Sammy Dudu! How are you?

"Sammy Doo, chillax, I have your money but it's in Europe.

"Sammy, I will pay you… soon as things cool down a bit.

"Come now, Sammy, you know how hard it's been…

"In and out of Europe, in and out of banks, money in bags, money in train station lockers; it's been tough!

"I feel watched – black man, in all these very white cities – hard not to attract attention. I need to lay low for a while.

"Then where do I put the money? All that cash?

"Safety deposit boxes need records, Sammy, but I have figured something out.

"Yeah, I get it, thanks. Talk soon."

Chike began going into Peckham and buying large brass sculptures, into which he stuffed his cash. He stopped flying into the European countries where his money was banked, choosing to go by road instead. He smuggled the cash back into the UK and systematically concealed it in the hollow brass sculptures he was acquiring. Many of the initial sculptures he bought were African-style art, but he was motivated more by the size and internal volume of the pieces than anything else. In no time, Chike's corridor and backyard were filled with an assortment of statues and vases.

Chike began exploring ways to secure expensive art. He walked into a Japanese Merchant bank in Shoreditch and asked to deposit some of his sculptures. The manager was baffled; he had never heard such a request in his entire banking career. "Sir we are a bank, we bank money. While I appreciate your love of African art, and the desire to put them in a secure location, we only keep cash in our vaults. We may take in jewelry sometimes, but we only provide small safe deposit boxes." Chike realized that he would have to get his money out of the UK and into Nigeria, where he could secure his wealth from unwanted scrutiny.

Chike registered a non-governmental organization for the repatriation of ancient African art. Within a few months, he had written essays on the need to find African art and return them to Africa. He had gathered a movement of Pro-African activists, and they began to have hyperintellectual discussions on the repatriation of lost African art taken by slave masters and colonial masters.

In a short time, Chike was known as a subject matter expert in African art and had begun giving talks on art and the need to repatriate them to their original country. While the artwork had started out having only functional utility in Chike's grand scheme, with time, he developed an active interest in the field of bronze sculpture. He took a class in bronze sculpture with a famous sculptor in Northampton, traveling from London to Northampton daily to learn the art of welding and shaping brass. He took to the craft quickly, having had the benefit of his childhood apprenticeship with the blacksmith in Jobore. Chike's back garden became a studio, soon filled with life-sized statues, each stuffed and sealed with currency. The noise from the hammering, cutting, and welding became unbearable to the neighbors and it wasn't long before they complained.

One morning, there was a loud knock on the door. Chike looked through the peephole and spied police officers; two of them.

"Hello, officer. How can I help you?"

"Do you mind if we have a quick chat in your back garden?"

"Do you have a warrant, sir?"

"Sir, we have not come here to harass you in any way, but there is an old lady with a serious medical condition next door –"

"Yes, the old cow that has been spying through the curtains for the last few years."

"– who has made some complaints about public nuisance activities in your backyard." The tall officer, clad in his dark uniform, had his hand on the walkie-talkie at his shoulder while he spoke to Chike.

Chike realized there was a third officer who had now joined the ones by the door. The two who stood slightly apart wore white short-sleeved shirts and black pants. They were also having what seemed to be multiple conversations over their walkie-talkies. The neighbors had all come out of their houses waiting to see who'd get arrested. The old lady next door stood next to the large green garbage can outside her house, dressed in a pink housecoat and fluffy bedroom slippers. She topped her old-lady outfit with a blue hair net. Kabiru sat quietly in his room as this conversation went on.

"I would love to see your back garden, sir, to make an assessment of the old lady's complaint." The officer spoke calmly, unfazed by the squawking interruptions from the radio gadget on his shoulder. Chike had his bristles up, snapping, "Look here, mister, if you got a report from the old lady, then you should go to the old lady's house and look from there. I'm just an art lover, practicing my art. It's African. Please, leave my house. Is it a crime to make sculptures? This is the third time you lot have come here to ask the same questions in the last couple of months! Don't you people have better things to do? I am definitely going to have a chat with our councilor about this; this is pure racial harassment!"

The officer bore Chike's tirade with placid resignation then, with a curt nod and 'Good day, Sir,' turned around and shooed his colleagues away towards the fuming old lady. Chike never had any more visits from the police after that day.

The old woman, whose name was Eunice, was an inquisitive widow who lived alone. She was often up at all hours watching the neighborhood, marking every strange face and incident, recording everything in her remarkable memory. Eunice was loved by the police, having often provided vital information and descriptions in local crime investigations. She lurked behind the curtains, watching, even at night, and Chike had noticed this behavior soon after he moved in. Every time he trotted up his porch steps, the woman was up by her window spying. She had called the police many times with frivolous reports, including one in which she reported that Chike was burying some things – probably dead bodies – in his garden. Another favorite of hers was to call the police to rescue one of her many cats that was '… stuck in that dodgy neighbor's tree.'

Eunice seemed to be in her early 80s and lived with roughly a dozen cats. While her memory and faculties of observation were as sharp as ever, she exhibited clear signs of lapses in her reasoning, if not outright senility. Chike was told she was a retired policewoman, with a reputation as one of the officers on the case of 'Hatchet Harry', a notorious serial killer in the East End of London in the 60s. Eunice was sure she was fated to spy on Chike and had a network of similar-aged women with whom she met once or twice a week to compare notes. Very little happened around the district that they didn't know about. Chike was painfully aware of these ladies and was always extra careful because he was being watched by these witches. He ensured the stuffing of the sculptures took place in his room and had even gone to the length of installing a hoist system so he could get the heavy sculptures in and out of his room through the window. He also stepped up his drive to establish a formal organization for the recovery of traditional African art, thus cloaking his illegal pursuits in the garb of legal and moral nobility.

Chike's African Treasure Repatriation Organization became popular amidst the growing outcry surrounding the colonial pillaging of African art. He acquired a huge warehouse/office at the Barbican Centre in central London and engaged African history students as interns. Soon, a movement developed and organized protests became routine in front of various museums in England. The Nigerian High Commission offered considerable support to Chike's cause, which he cultivated with great care – a degree of diplomatic cover couldn't hurt his enterprise at all. He built a vault in the Barbican office to store his cash-stuffed artwork, each piece identified by an engraved plate, the last six digits of which recorded its cash content. These pieces shared storage space with historical relics and art pieces that had either been donated to Chike's organization or that it had raised funds to purchase for shipment back to Africa.

It was an elaborate, time-consuming procedure, which Chike had to complete alone. Now that he had begun to produce his own brass statues, Chike quickly mastered the art and began to sculpt pieces that outstripped those he bought in terms of quality and aesthetics. Based on photos he shared with some of his dealers in Peckham, he began to receive offers for his art but, of course, they were not for sale. He only offered for long-term exhibition, on the premise that you could have the statue on lease on your premises for a renewable term. His most sought-after piece was a colossal statue of David, with sword drawn, and the head of Goliath by his feet. It was a fierce and dramatic piece, given a degree of controversy by the full head of dreadlocks Chike had fashioned on David's head. This controversy bloomed in the artistic and theological communities and sparked a trickling pilgrimage to the Barbican Museum to see this controversial work by the Nigerian sculpture artist. None knew it was filled with cash, belonging to people that had died intestate.

Chike's growing notoriety as an artist made it much harder to circulate within Europe discretely to withdraw these monies. People had begun to ask for his autograph even in the dark nooks of Sweden and other Scandinavian cities where Chike had banked large sums, and he knew he had to speed up the extraction of his funds. He doubled the frequency of his trips to Europe (under the loose pretext of understudying European brass art) and he was returning to his room with three times the amount of cash he used to bring into London. His room now had more cash than files and he was almost running out of space. He increased his work hours to manufacture more statues, often working through the night, smelting brass and molding amazing statues.

Each statue could conceal about two million Pounds in fifty-Pound notes and Chike now had to do the cash-stuffing in sections, as the new statues were too large – and much too heavy – to hoist up through his window in one piece. Chike began to place more of his art in galleries and office buildings on loan across England. He signed contracts that allowed them to keep the artwork until he was ready to take possession of them. He even had one of his larger works placed in the forecourt of Scotland Yard, the police headquarters located on the London embankment. And, to complete his poke in the collective eye of the English justice and law enforcement system, Chike made a statue of 'Justice' that was loaned to Old Bailey, the highest criminal court in England. These statues weighed tons and were loaded with cash.

Chike settled into his newfound role as a sculptor and his work made it into the Museum of African art in Piccadilly. He had articles in several journals about African art and his art pressure group on African art repatriation had become notorious in the United Kingdom. He was invited to give a talk in the House of Parliament on the repatriation of stolen African art in museums across the United Kingdom. It was inevitable that all of the attention would put Chike in the news, though he refused to grant interviews and had somehow managed to keep his picture from ending up in the public eye. Nevertheless, a magazine article on Chike's Black David ultimately provided enough information for his mother to track him down and she was able to reach him through the South Bank Art Gallery, an old art gallery on the London embankment. Dr. Obidike immediately boarded his private jet and headed to London to find his lost son, while his mother worked the phones. She persisted until she was able to speak with Chike at a seminar in Aberdeen, Scotland. She then informed Dr. Obidike, who had searched London fruitlessly for two weeks, where their son was, and he immediately arranged for his private jet to take him to Scotland. The silver Global express aircraft took off and Dr. Obidike stayed on the phone, speaking to his wife. His rose gold, diamond-encrusted oyster perpetual Rolex lashed and created subtle light patterns on the beige leather seats. In just forty minutes, the jet touched down at the Wigglesworth Execujet airport in Aberdeen, where a black S-class Mercedes waited on the tarmac.

Dr. Obidike had on the traditional, black velvet Igbo garb, with the lion heads boldly printed in gold on the fabric. He stepped out of the aircraft into a strong wind that forced him to clutch at his red cap with the feather at its side. "No luggage, please," he instructed the captain standing behind him in the narrow doorway of the aircraft. Dr. Obidike climbed down the stairs and entered the Mercedes S-Class, shutting out the aggressive wind with the thud of the heavy door. The driver already knew where to go, and the black Mercedes raced through the windy old Scottish town of Aberdeen. The seminar was still in session when they arrived at the old opera house at the Aberdeen harbor, and Dr. Obidike walked into the full hall where his son stood at the podium, addressing the huge crowd on African art and its intrinsic value to the future economy of the African continent.

The room was well-lit and quiet, save for Chike's amplified voice so, when his father walked in, Chike noticed him immediately. He stopped for a few seconds, dabbed at the corners of his eyes with a white handkerchief, sipped some water, and continued his lecture. At the end of his presentation, Chike ran to his father like a child seeing his parent after being lost in the mall. Dr. Obidike stood by a green pillar at the side of the large hall. The two men hugged each other wordlessly, both their faces streaked with tears. Dr. Obidike held Chike's hands and said, "I'm sorry, son. I am so sorry. I was wrong, so wrong to disrespect your right to make your own choices in life. We have searched everywhere for you. Your mother has been a recluse all these years and I have been an object of blame. I am so sorry, Chike."

Without letting go of Chike's hands, Dr. Obidike swiped at his eyes with his wrists before continuing. "Everything I have done, all my life, I have done it all for you. I went

446

about it the wrong way and I'm so sorry, son. Look at what you have made of yourself; I am so proud of you... WE! We are so proud of you."

They embraced once again as the seminar's attendees looked curiously. "Dad, you taught me a long time ago, to be hardworking and, remember, you told me about the rat that fell into a bowl of milk, then swam so fast, for so long, that he whipped the milk into butter? I just had to get out alive, so I made my own butter." Dr. Obidike replied, "Chike, I am old and frail; your life is yours, but I need you now son. If you have room for your father, I need you."

The duo made their way out of the hall, often pausing as many of the seminar participants came up to Chike to thank him or ask for pictures or his autograph. They walked through the foyer and out to the waiting car with a group of people trailing Chike. They drove through the ancient city of Aberdeen to the Wigglesworth airport. Once they boarded. Chike called his hotel to arrange for his things to be sent to him. Then, Dr. Obidike called his wife, spoke briefly with her, and handed the phone to his son.

"Yes, mum.

"I totally understand.

"No, mum... I really don't want to discuss that.

"No! You guys listen to *me* for a change!

447

"No, mum, listen to me. Please, listen to me."

Dr. Obidike could figure out what the conversation was about and was dismayed by what he could hear on his son's side of it. Chike was upset. "That I should come and take over the business; what about *my* business? Who will run that? You guys are having a laugh, right? Do you have any idea how much work I've put into building my business?"

There was a long silence, the phone still in Chike's clenched hand. Dr. Obidike held his head and looked at the floor in utter dismay. Gained ground lost, the conversation ended and silence prevailed for the next twenty minutes when it was interrupted by the landing announcement of the captain.

5

Dr. Obidike leaned forward on the beige leather seat, seeming to contemplate his son's question. He took Chike's free hand and tearfully whispered, "You are all I have – my only child. Everything I own belongs to you."

Chike dropped the phone on the table and the tinny voice of his protesting mother could be heard. He took his father's hairy hand in both of his and squeezed it. "Enough of the lies, dad. Enough!

"I am not your only child! I know our culture and these things you call mine all the time do not belong to me!

"Enough of the lies, dad!"

Dr. Obidike's eyes widened.

"Dad, I knew this from when I was a boy.

"I am not your only child – certainly not your only son. And, more to the point, I AM NOT YOUR FIRST SON.

"I thank you for the amazing education and all that you have done for me. I am a man now and can stand on my own; I have my own business and I want nothing of your wealth. I mean, nothing!

"It does not belong to me!

"What father abandons their child in the village?

"My life is more than your wealth, so, please, father, let me be."

Dr. Obidike had a patina of sweat on his face and he stammered as he tried to respond to his son. "Eerm, emm, mmmm, m-my son, Chikereuba!"

"Dad, I know everything! Mum told me everything!"

"Chikereuba, it is not like that. I can explain."

"Explain what, dad? Explain that you left these people to suffer all these decades?"

"Chikereuba, I am human. I am not infallible. This was a long time ago."

"Does that make it right, dad?"

"My son, I have given you the best education money can buy and given yourself and your mother a good life."

The cabin rocked as the light turbulence they had been flying through became worse. The seatbelt lights flashed on, and the pilot's voice came over the PA system. "Please fasten your seatbelts. We are encountering some turbulence."

Dr. Obidike and Chike fastened their seatbelts and Dr. Obidike continued.

"Chikereuba, you will not disrespect your father; you will listen to me.

"*O bia mgbe Alio Ene gburu atu, ya biakwa ma atu zogbuo Alio Ene* – He who calls whenever Elder Ene kills a deer, let him call if the deer kicks the living daylight out of Elder Ene.

"I made a mistake, and you will listen to me, and you will forgive me."

"You don't need my forgiveness; I was not the one that was abandoned in the village."

"Chikereuba, it is true I met this lady, in a distant village. We had planned to get married when my father learned, thanks to my brothers, she was an *Osu*.

"They lied! My Elder brother was also in love with the same girl and wanted her to himself. He was incensed that she chose me.

"You know there was a caste system in our culture - *Osu*. Certain groups were outcasts, and it was an abomination to interact with them. They were families dedicated to the deities and they pretty much lived in their own secluded communities.

"My brothers came with the news that she was *osu*. At this point, I did not know she was with child, and the marriage was canceled. Because her village was very far from ours, when she returned there, I never heard from her. Therefore, I never learned the truth; that she was not

451

osu at all but could not defend herself against the accusations from my brothers."

"Why couldn't she just speak up for herself?" Chike, despite his anger, was drawn in by the tale.

"Because of shame, fear, and to protect me," Dr. Obidike answered with a soberness that further penetrated Chike's rage. "She was pregnant, yes, but wasn't sure who the father of the child was – me, or your uncle. He had forced himself on her in a drunken frenzy many months before and she never told me. She wanted to protect me from the shame of it and prevent me from seeking revenge against my older brother."

"So, the boy might be Diokpa's son?" Chike was aghast.

"No, Chike, eventually we could conclude that he was mine. You see, Diokpa cannot have children. Over time, we learned that he is sterile. I have always suspected that this is the major reason for his hatefulness and anger. And envy towards me."

"I cannot deny that, since the mother was not an *osu*, the boy is my legitimate first son. However, I have never set my eyes on him, as your mother forbade me from going anywhere near that family.

"My brothers have been the ones managing that relationship ever since.

"They have come incessantly to make financial demands of me for the upkeep of these two, and I have always given money for their welfare. I did not abandon them." Dr. Obidike paused as the pilot announced that they had commenced their descent for landing, then continued, "I planned to discuss this with you at some point, but it really has been a very painful topic when brought up around your mother.

"I am sorry, my son, I am sorry."

Dr. Obidike lowered his head and, in the silence that followed, Chike's attention was caught by his mother's voice, which was still screeching from the phone. Chike picked up the phone and his mum was still ranting. "I will call you back, mother," he said, hanging up. He zoned out and visualized the incident at *Nsosoronsoso*, the assassination attempt. It flashed back through his head like a movie and Chike blurted, "Now it all makes sense!"

"What Chike?"

"Hmm, now I see."

The aircraft touched down softly on the private runway of the air force base in North London. Chike was exalted. "Dad, I thank you for a good life. I love you and I respect you. I will come to Nigeria, but I need some time to round up things here."

"When can you come? I can send the jet to pick you up."

"No dad, I won't be needing a jet, I will come at my own time with my own means.

"I will return to Nigeria, Dad. I will return."

"Chike my son, I have thought of this day and this season, and I have made plans with my lawyers to ensure you and your mother are all right when I'm gone.

"I also assure you that Ngozi and her son will be well looked after."

Chike hugged his father, who wept as Chike turned and walked through the aisle to disembark from the front of the aircraft. He looked back and waved one more time.

6

Dr. Obidike's company had grown to become one of the largest and most successful on the continent of Africa, but Chike was more concerned with how to move all of his money into his African brass statues and where to store them. The cash-filled art pieces were becoming a right menace at Chike's house and he still had a trip to The Netherlands planned; he still had a great deal of his loot there. Chike had opened several accounts in Amsterdam under various identities and he was not about to lose the funds in them. He drove across the continent into the Netherlands, to the outskirts of Amsterdam in a little town called Keukenhof, a village known for its beautiful tulip fields. Chike spent the night at Keukenhof, walked the gardens in the morning, and resumed his two-hour journey to Amsterdam. On arriving, Chike parked at the old train station in Amsterdam and began his usual chore of cash withdrawals from banks and post offices.

He had collected a small locker near the bicycle stand by the quiet ticket machine. It was the perfect location as it was usually deserted and dark, making him more comfortable when returning from his trips to the banks with cash to deposit in his locker. Nevertheless, the sheer frequency of his returns to the locker caught the attention of the station security, who ultimately alerted the Netherlands Inland Police. Cursory surveillance as Chike filled the locker made it obvious that he was retrieving cash and stuffing the box. The law enforcement officers were certain the cash must be the proceeds of drug transactions and put a tail on Chike. They followed him into several banks and watched him make withdrawals at the counter. The police officers interviewed the bank staff who asserted that Chike's transactions had no red flags and he was just collecting money he had saved. However, as they followed Chike into other banks, the officers soon found that he was transacting in different banks with different names and multiple identities. Yet, in each bank, his accounts and transactions all seemed kosher. The icing on the cake for the investigating officers was that they could estimate, from the banks they had trailed Chike to, that he had drawn cash in the millions of Euros.

Meanwhile, Chike was tired and hungry. When he saw a sign that pointed to the red-light district – and curious about all he had heard about the Dutch red-light district – and decided to take a quick tour. The plain-clothes policemen followed. The Netherlands was fast becoming a leader both in legal and illegal trends, and Amsterdam was truly the world headquarters of sex. The city was littered with thousands of shops with sex-related merchandise. Some of the shops didn't have mannequins; they had naked women on display, like mannequins waiting to be dressed. The streets were paved with red concrete and bustling. Chike noticed many mad-looking people, some of whom sprawled on the floor, sleeping or begging for money. They were of diverse origins and seemed to buttress the legend that junkies who go to Amsterdam usually buy a one-way ticket. To them, it was the promised land, the Mecca, because Amsterdam was also the unofficial world headquarters for drugs in all forms and shapes. Chike was quite aware of this fact, though he never used any drugs himself.

Though walking around the district and being entertained by the window girls was fascinating, Chike was intent on finding some food so, when his eyes fell upon a neon sign declaring, "Cafe De Paris," he didn't hesitate. In his experience, 'café' meant food and nothing in the sign or appearance of the establishment led him to think otherwise. The tall Nigerian man carried his skinny, ghostly frame into the café, where he advanced to the service counter without as much as a glance around. "What kind of food do you have?" Chike asked in his English accent. The café attendant, looking closely at Chike, replied in Dutch.

"Do you speak English, sir?"

"Oh yes, certainly I speak English. We don't serve food here. Does this look like a restaurant?"

The hum of conversation in the café dwindled as the patrons now turned their attention to the conversation between Chike and the attendant. The voice of the attendant had been raised on his last interrogative with ill-concealed irritation. On the counter, in front of Chike, was a transparent bread bin with all kinds of delicious-looking cakes, and he completely ignored the stroppy attendant's bad attitude as he took a closer look at them. Colorfully iced and adorned, the cakes fascinated Chike and he felt his stomach churn. He asked,

"What kind of cakes are those?" in an exaggerated version of his already thick, aristocratic Queen's English. He had noticed the attendant's reaction to it earlier and decided not to be cowed by the reverse snobbery. The cafe attendant, routinely frustrated by ill-bred tourists, and particularly displeased by this lanky fellow's questions, answered, "Space cakes."

Unknown to Chike, these cakes were a cocktail of different species of cannabis baked into brownies and cupcakes – some cafés had the dubious reputation of going beyond marijuana plants in the dusting and accessorizing of their wares.

Sweet-toothed junkies ate space cakes. "Space cakes," Chike echoed the attendant as he pulled on his little goatee. Perhaps a reference to how light and fluffy they were, he mused, before dismissing further consideration and ordering two of the cakes. The security had taken up station in the sidewalk crowds and watched as Chike devoured the hard drugs; they knew this café as one of the more dubious sorts. Also in the crowd were the Teddy Boys, recruiters for a major producer of Dutch pornographic films. They combed the streets of the red-light district for willing and unwitting talent, whichever they could find. Willing wanna-be porn stars or innocent drunks and overdosed tourists were all the same to the

458

Teddy Boys. They would often add their own special hallucinogen to the assortment of substances in their victims' systems, effectively rendering them submissive and pliable – slaves, in essence, taken to a private location where the filming would take place. Many 'performers' would not return to wherever they had come from, before being immortalized in snuff and hardcore porn films. These characters too were observing the clueless Chike's ingestion of the potent 'space cakes.'

Chike devoured the first cake in front of everyone and the whole bar stood up and gave him a standing ovation. Even for space cake veterans, each cake was an hours-long project; a respectfully careful process to get just the right high and maintain it without having a bad trip. The patrons were amazed by Chike's three-bite demolition of his first cake, demonstrating either phenomenal African strength or, more likely, woeful ignorance and stupidity. Underscoring the likelihood that he fell into the latter category, Chike waved to the crowd and took a bow, having no idea what potent forces he had just messed with. He paid for his order and walked out eating the other cake.

I wish I had known this cake was so sweet; I would have bought more, he thought to himself. Time was running out and Chike remembered he still had a long drive back to England, so he walked briskly to the train station where he had his money and his car. By the time he reached the train station, Chike was surprised to find himself feeling famished. "What kind of sudden hunger is this?" he soliloquized. The quiet train station was almost deserted and there were no food vendors around, except for a fruit basket by the payment counter. Chike helped himself to an apple and paid for it. "This is a city of surprises," he commented to the storekeeper as he made the payment. "These are gigantic apples." As the drugs began to course through his bloodstream and hit his brain, the world took on a different quality to Chike; bigger, bloated, stretched out. "First the café only sold cakes and then they grow apples as big as coconuts. O, What a country. Dutch Engineering." Soon, the apple was so big, that he had to hold it with both hands. It was not long before Chike started regretting eating the apple; it moved around in his stomach in bubbles, racing up and down his digestive tract like something was chasing after it. In a moment Chike found out that this mysterious apple could be controlled. He would chase the apple around in his chest with both hands until he finally caught it, holding it thrumming in place. If he let go, the apple would begin its race again.

At length, the spectacle of the black man, with the shell-shocked expression, scrabbling over his abdomen and chest with both hands, then intermittently freezing in place, while drool dripped in a steady stream of his chin, drew the station security to Chike. At this point, he was stock-still in the fetal position, content to have conquered the apple. He had to remain still to have full control of this piece of matter threatening to run amok in him if he let go. The police had watched from a distance as Chike rolled on the floor, chasing the apple in his body. Chike had attracted a small crowd, many asking him if he was okay in Dutch.

"Gaat het?"

"Gaat het?" They all asked.

Chike began to scream loud repeating the phrase.

"Gaat het? Gaat het?" He began injecting a few Igbo words with, 'Gaat het?'

"Gaat het iberi ibe!" He screamed loud.

"Gaat het, ooooh! Gat het I beri ibe!!!"

"Gaat het Iberi ibe," he kept shouting.

The security agents in front of him radioed for backup. Chike took his hands off his chest where he held the apple and it began to race around his chest again. "Oh, man, do you see what you have done? Do you know how long it took me to catch this apple?" Chike got up and began running in widening circles until he ran out of the station onto the street and the police thought it was a plot to escape. They ran after him. Chike broke out onto the four-lane highway that led to the station and there was the piercing wail of screeching tyres as cars swerved to avoid him. The police ran after him and, when he turned around and saw them, Chike increased his speed, screaming, *"Gaat het Iberi ibe!"*

Chike jumped onto the grass by the highway and slowed noticeably. He had removed his shoes while he was on the floor at the train station and the feel of the soft grass under his bare feet arrested his attention. As his mind swiveled to this new sensation, he forgot about running

461

and decelerated. The police finally caught up with him and tackled him to the ground, where he started to foam at the mouth shouting at the top of his voice. "I can't cross the river! I can't cross the river!!" He was gone. He had crossed the Sanity River. A crew of paramedics caught up with the police and, with practiced ease, bent to attend to their struggling patient. Chike's widened into red ovals as the paramedics injected him with something and his tongue seemed to thicken as his speech slowed, making him sound like a vinyl record being played at a slow speed.

The ambulance came to the side of the road and Chike was bundled into the vehicle and whisked to the hospital. The police cars followed. Hours later, Chike woke up and realized he was handcuffed to the hospital bed.

"Let me go.

"Let me go!

"You guys sell mysterious apples to tourists.

"Please, I just want to go back home." His words shot out of his mouth in staccato bursts. The doctor was a tall brunette in pink scrubs. "Sorry, sir, you can't go home just yet; the police need to have a short chat with you," she said. She asked him what he had eaten. He told her about the apple and, on being asked what else he had eaten, Chike innocently told the doctor about a cake he had eaten at the Cafe De Paris. The doctor chuckled, and asked, "Space Cakes? Oh my God, not another one!"

That was when Chike learned about the cake, its potency, and the fact that he could have sustained permanent brain damage. He had regained his coherence, but he could not do anything at normal speed. His movements were twitches and jerks and, when given a cup of tea, Chike poured the tea all over himself.

The doctor came back after a few hours and informed Chike that he would have to spend the night at the clinic. There was nothing they could do for him; since the matter had been ingested, he had to wait to let it work its way out of his system. The police maintained an ominous, re-strained presence outside the door and Chike understood what carrion must feel like under the patient gaze of vul-tures. At length, he slept.

"I can hear voices! I heard voices! I heard voices! Help! I'm hearing voices!"

Chike woke up in the middle of the night sweating pro-fusely. A nurse came in to soothe him and Chike recog-nized her from prior visits to his room. She asked him several questions and, like with all of her other checks, she emptied a syringe into Chike's IV line. Chike went into another deep sleep.

7

On the third day, Chike had stabilized, and the Dutch police came into his room.

They read him his Miranda rights in Dutch and English, then prepared to escort him to the waiting van outside the hospital. The doctor came in and informed them that Chike could not leave the hospital because, from his tests, it appeared that he must have endured significant organ damage and would require further observation and care. The police officers grumbled, but they deferred to the doctor's wishes and Chike was left in his bed. In the lull that followed, Chike was able to appreciate the hospital facility for the first time since his arrival. It was more like a five-star hotel than a hospital if one could ignore the beeping machines and the tubes that connected Chike to them, and Chike was able to subdue his worries long enough to be impressed by the quality of his accommodations and the service.

Worn out and thirsty, Chike called for the nurse to ask for water. It turned out to be the same nurse from his first night in the hospital and she quietly left and returned with a glass and a pitcher of water. As he thanked her, Chike was struck by the strength of his reaction to her presence.

He figured it may be partly because his drug-addled mind may have romanticized her a bit when she attended to his fevered night-sweats days before, but there was no denying her beauty. He began to feel drowsy again and wondered if she had dosed his IV line again. No matter, he thought groggily, she could dose him any time. A stunner indeed. She could pass for Egyptian or Somalian but was almost certainly of Arab descent.

After She had cleared the tray, the nurse came back and cleaned the table with a white cloth. Chike watched her, catching the flashes of her caramel thigh in her short uniform skirt, unable to look away from the front of her shirt when she leaned forward, mesmerized by the ridiculously long lashes that adorned her dark smoky eyes. Her head was covered but you could see some of her jet-black, curly hair. It was hard to tell her precise age, but Chike guessed she was somewhere in her early to mid-twenties and was almost positive she was Nigerian – he had heard her speaking to another nurse (who was clearly Nigerian) in the distinct Nigerian Pidgin English – and wondered in a distracted way how his current troubles may have some sort of silver lining. Chike began to turn, stopped short, and realized his hands were still handcuffed to the hospital bed. "Where are my things, miss?" he asked.

"Shhh! Try not to talk too much. There are some people outside the door just waiting to get you talking."

"Are you Nigerian?"

"Yes, Fulani."

She smiled as she adjusted her navy-blue headwrap. She had a freshly made henna tattoo on her right hand. "Both my parents are Fulani."

"What is your name?"

"Talatu. You are obviously Igbo. *Kedu*?" Meaning 'hello' in Igbo. Chike saw how beautiful her small lips were. She had a black dot on the right side of her face just between her nose and her mouth.

"*Odinma*," Chike replied, staring lustfully at the beautiful nurse. "Pardon me, but I have never seen any human as beautiful as you. You are… spectacular."

"Thank you," Talatu blushed. "Sorry, I can't speak Igbo. Only some Yoruba."

"No need, we are doing quite well with English. I was born and raised in the south-west, but I also speak some Fulfulde."

"I don't know your name; the record just shows 'Suspect'."

"Don't worry about my name; it is irrelevant at this time."

Chike spoke to her in the Fulfude tongue, and she responded, giggling at his accent, and he was smitten. Smiling amplified her beauty in an impossible way, showing her remarkable white teeth as her large eyes narrowed into dark slits.

It has been four days now and Chike was still cuffed to the bed. From the occasions when the privacy curtain was pulled back, he knew there was a very sick man in the bed next to his. The man, who seemed advanced in years, was hooked up to a ventilator and could not speak, which was just as well for Chike, who had begun to feel restless. He knew he was in great trouble but also that law enforcement couldn't ascertain his real name. They must have contacted the banks, but they had nothing that connected to Chike Onyeodikara. He guessed he should also be worried about whatever medical emergency was keeping him in the hospital, but he felt fine. The doctors seemed puzzled because Chike seemed fine to them too, but some of his test results were alarming.

The bright morning sun streamed through the window and bounced off the stainless-steel wrist cuff that tethered Chike to the bed. He had just called for a nurse to bring him the bedpan, which he was forced to use to avoid repeated un-shackling, chaperoned toilet trips, and re-shackling. He drowsed while he waited for her. He opened his eyes to find himself surrounded by a group of medical students and two doctors. One of the students was Indian, while everyone else was Dutch. They all had writing pads and stethoscopes hanging from their necks. The apparent supervising physician, an old Dutchman with a chest-length white beard, asked, "What are your comments on these cases?"

The students all took turns speaking elaborately about the reports on Chike's datasheet. The Indian boy raised his hand and inquired, "Dr. Van Beest, I'm sorry, I noticed the blood tests of both patients are remarkably similar, showing very low antibodies and very low sugar."

"… Okay"

"The urine samples also produced similar results, with dangerously low glucose, but only the one on the left seems to be exhibiting the symptoms."

"Uhm," the doctor stroked his beard, "That is unusual, but possible too, considering they have similar causative factors, in this case, narcotic use, but are of different ages and in drastically different states of health. In any case, great observation; let's watch this closely." Chike turned his head to his right to look at his roommate. He had been unconscious and without movement since Chike arrived. The sound of rapid footsteps drew Chike's attention to the nurses' station where a young gentleman marched up and had a terse exchange with the supervising nurse. It was in Dutch, but Chike could tell he was the subject of the conversation by the glances both the man and the nurse darted in his direction.

8

Talatu walked in to take routine blood and urine samples, eventually stopping at Chike's bed. This time she spoke only in Fulfude. She explained that the young man was a detective and was applying intense pressure to have Chike released for interrogation. The nurse was relaying the hospital's position that, regardless of outward appearances, the patient was too sick to be interviewed and practically on the verge of a diabetic coma. Seeing Chike's befuddlement, Talatu explained, in hushed tones, that she had been submitting the blood and urine samples of Chike's sick neighbor as Chike's.

"Talatu, you are a savior! I'm so grateful."

"Honey, I don't know what you have done but I think you are in deep trouble."

"Yes, I know.'

"That's one of two reasons I have been trying to keep you here."

Chike's eyebrows rose. "What's the other reason?"

"I like you," Talatu mumbled, high color in her cheeks, continuing, "You make me laugh. I always look forward to coming to work because you are here."

"Talatu, I'm so glad to hear you say that because I feel the same way. It's crazy but, even with all the problems I'm facing, I spend most of my time thinking of you.

"What's really crazy is that I am falling for someone who is in trouble with the law, and whose only hope is to escape the country. Falling for someone who will either end up in prison or far away. I don't want you to go to prison, so we have to get you out of the country. The border is . . ."

Chike looked into her eyes and saw tears.

"… I haven't dated anyone in a long time; I haven't *felt* like this in my life!" Talatu held his hand, registering the cold cuff bracelet. She took a deep breath, then began speaking rapidly, still in muted tones. "The ferry port is just about ten minutes' walk from the hospital. If you are willing, I will help you." She took a deep breath, seeming to steel herself. "Your neighbor is due for surgery tonight; the consultants are preparing. I am the person liaising with the police and I will ensure I make a mistake that gets you to the theatre instead. When the mistake is discovered, you will make your way out through the emergency exit. When you get out, you will find my car parked right in front of the exit, it is a Renault, dark blue."

Talatu fussed with Chike's IV line, visibly concerned that this hushed conversation might already be too long. "You should catch the 11:45 p.m. ferry to Harwich. Leave the car at the ferry port. I don't know your real name and I don't know if I will ever see you again. But if I don't, I just want you to know I feel something deep for you and I hope I do. Even if this costs me my job, it feels right to me." Her eyes were brimming as she slipped a piece of paper into Chike's cuffed hand. "This is my number. I suggest you don't call me – IF you ever do – from a traceable phone, as I may be the subject of investigation and my incoming calls might be tracked."

"My name is Chike Obidike. Thanks, so much Talatu. I know we will meet again."

"I hope so.'

Talatu had come around to the other side of his bed, and she slipped something else into his free hand. It was a roll of money. "Take this; you will need it for food and to move on from the ferry station on the other side. Oh! There is also a change of clothes for you in a duffel bag in the car's back seat; can't have you running around in a hospital gown." She giggled softly then leaning over Chike and arranging his covers, whispered, "Till we meet again, *ko*?" She was gone.

Chike was asleep when he felt his cuff being removed. "Good luck with your surgery," the cop seethed. "I hope you make it back here because you have a ton of questions to answer." The cop then leaned over, much like

Talatu had done, but his tone was very different when he whispered, "And if you die, I hope you go to hell, you black African crook." Shortly after the orderlies came with the gurney to move him.

The anesthetist came in and promptly stuck a hypodermic in Chike's shoulder.

Talatu, too late, tried to stop him. "No, don't do that now! Dr. Beehgan instructed that this be done in the theatre."

"Too late, Talatu, already gave him."

"Fine, I will take over from here."

The men expressed grumpy bewilderment over why the nurse would want to roll the gurney on her own but were cowed into submission when Talatu turned on them, hissing, "If you brutes would pay attention to clinical procedure, you would respect the approach to preparing a patient for anesthesia; you don't just stick him in his arm. His psychological preparation for its effects and for surgery is vital. Now, you have forced my hand by limiting the time I have to prepare him. So, get out of my way and let me do my job, *while* taking him to the theatre, thanks to you!"

Talatu rolled Chike past the orderlies through the first swivel door and then the second one. Then she helped him up and they ran to the stairway, where he found the bag of clothes hanging on the railing. Chike put on the loose-fitting denim pants, and she helped him into the shirt. They held each other and kissed deeply – no

472

hesitation, no awkward contemplation, just a natural coming together. Then she whispered, "Run, Chike. You have no time to lose. Drive very fast."

"I promise you, you will see me again." Chike ran down the stairs. Talatu heard the car start up and a brief squeal of tyres, then she counted to forty and screamed. The staff nurses who ran to her aid found her on the floor in an apparent faint. Someone held smelling salts under Talatu's nose and gasped and sat up. "He choked me," she coughed hoarsely, repeating more loudly, "He choked me!"

"Who choked you?"

"He freaking choked me!" She was gasping, still buying time for Chike. "The patient."

They raced to the police at the door and there was a serious panic at the hospital as the cops scrambled to call for backup. They had no idea where Chike might be and had not yet ascertained that he had taken Talatu's car.

Chike arrived at the ferry, within minutes, without encountering any problems at all. This was fortunate because his vision was blurring, and he was beginning to feel disoriented. It was 11:40 p.m. Chike saw the signs to the port and drove right to the entrance. The ferry was about to leave. He boarded the ferry without incident and went straight to the bottom deck, found a bathroom stall, and locked himself in it. Then, as the sedative took over him, he slumped by the wash hand basin and passed out.

9

About seven hours later, the ferry arrived at Harwich and the few passengers on it disembarked. Chike awoke in the toilet, stiff and cold from the sea breeze coming in through the open window. The ferry was empty as he emerged and walked through the vessel hall and out of the open door on the second floor. Some cleaners were working to get the boat ready for the next voyage.

Chike caught a bus to the train station where he was lucky to catch the train that would take him to Luton. It was a long trip and Chike was wide awake and very hungry. He felt for the roll of money Talatu had handed him and found a rolled-up, type-written note in it:

If you are reading this, then you made it to the ferry on time. There is much I would love to say, but I cannot. I will take comfort in the thought that you know my heart already.

Do what you can to free yourself then, if you can find me. I am waiting for you.

Love,

The Milk Maid.

Chike smiled and forgot about his hunger until he got back to Luton and back home. He knew the time was ripe to pack it up and head back to Africa. He had only four more cash-stuffed statues left, and he had already negotiated lease agreements for them. He was only waiting for the clients to collect. Kabiru was in the living room watching a movie with his girlfriend Sonia, who usually spent weekends with him.

"Welcome, Chike."

"Hey, buddy. Hi, Sonia."

Chike didn't linger but continued up the stairs to his room. He immediately began to pack his valuables. He knew he had to leave London as soon as possible. He wasn't sure how they would be able to trace him from the Dutch bank, but he knew he wasn't going to take any chances. He had bought two very large suitcases and had been planning for this time. Chike packed exactly enough to fill these two suitcases.

By the time he woke up the next morning, he was all packed and ready to go.

He called Kabiru and informed him he had to sell the house as he had to return to Nigeria. Kabiru was terrified and knew something had gone wrong. He packed his bags and all his belongings and moved in with Sonia in Bedfordshire. By the day after Chike had called the estate agent and there was a 'For Sale' sign on the fence.

Chike and his father spoke every day discussing his travel plans. His mother was very happy that her son was coming home.

Book-8

Trouble in
Paradise

Si neddo fiyii howru banndum fuu, nyoofa howru mum

*(He who hits his neighbor's knee, curls up his own legs –
Fulani proverb)*

1

"That was awesome, Diggy Boo."

Phoebe stayed buried under the white duvet and reached out for her pack of cigarettes. She grabbed the lighter next to it and lit up her cigarette. She blew out a long trail of smoke and brushed her hair backward with her hands.

Adigun was on the other side of the large presidential bed, lying flat on his back. His large feet stuck out of the covers.

"Whoa, what happened to you? We haven't had it like this in a long time. I think it's the fight."

"I think it's the seafood; heard Oysters make you twice a man."

"That wasn't twice a man, that was a whole village! Jeez, I feel destroyed!"

Phoebe rushed into the bathroom and Adigun drowsed to the sound of water running for a while. She came out with a white face towel, emerging from a cloud of steam, then she knelt by the bed and dabbed Adigun with the steaming towel.

"Whoa, that's hot!"

"It's only hot water and a towel."

"But it's too hot!"

"Need to clean my king."

"You're going to melt your king with this hot towel of yours."

"Oh no, my king is not made of wax."

Adigun chuckled. Phoebe went into the bathroom again and this time the towel was not as hot.

"You know, this is the part I like."

"Cleaning me up after? I'd like it too if the towel wasn't this hot."

"You are such a spoiled brat, African man, you should be the one cleaning me up."

"After doing all the work?"

Adigun wrapped himself up with the white linen sheets and got out of the large oval-shaped bed. He held the sheets together with one hand and brushed his mouth and jaw with the other.

"Damn, I have your hair all over my face, and in my mouth. If I lost this much hair, I would be bald.

"Why do you shed so much hair and still have a rack of hair on your head?"

"Quit complaining and get your beautiful black ass back here; we are not done!"

"Not done? I fight next week! I'm not meant to be doing this."

"You have no idea Phoebe is the reason you win your fights? Every time we do this, you win!"

"So, I should stop training and just stay in bed with you and win all my fights?"

"Exactly. Stay in bed where I can see your beautiful chocolate body all the time."

Phoebe dragged Adigun back under the duvet, but he rolled off the bed from the other side and headed into the bathroom.

The blast of the shower running with full force came from the bathroom.

"Black man, you are taking your shower already?" Phoebe called over the noise. "I can't hear you, babes, I can't hear you!" Phoebe settled back into bed and didn't bother responding. He never spent very long bathing anyway, typical man. Within ten minutes, Adigun came out of the bathroom wearing a white towel around his narrow waist. His chest was broad and muscular, ripped from his training. His neck was thick and his arms were ropey and heavily veined.

"You are getting bulkier, Diggy Boo."

"Yes, I'm trying to get into that heavyweight category. Just a few more pounds to go."

"People are not going to come to your fights anymore; you end them too quick."

"It's not a soap opera, Fibi, I can't take chances. I knock them out as soon as I can. With the first punch, if possible. I've put a lot of work into building up that hook."

"But some people were still trying to get into the arena when the last fight ended."

"You don't understand, Fibi, I don't have time."

Phoebe sat up and lifted the sheet over her breasts. She grabbed the remote control the TV flicked on. It was already on the local sports channel and one of Adigun's previous fights was being discussed.

"That's my boo, again – you're the talk of the town."

"Oh, wow! It's my first time seeing this! That's the fight in Dallas! Turn up the volume!"

Adigun stood in front of the TV and listened to the analysis of the fight, preening and scoffing according to the comments made by the presenters.

Phoebe encircled Adigun gently from behind and squeezed his muscular frame.

"I don't like this profession, Diggy Boo. Will I still have you in one piece when we are old, or will you just be staring at me all messed up?

481

"I had to close my eyes after his nose began bleeding – after just a few blows – so much blood!

"I can't stand the thought of you being hit like that. Do you understand what that could mean for your old age?"

"I don't plan on getting hit like that."

"What about at the sparing sessions? Those are pretty intense too!"

"Cause I let them hit me. Besides, we use protective gear."

"You don't like Bobby Brown's business; you don't like my boxing…"

"But you like to go shopping and buy diamonds, right? You sure you can handle me getting a job at the post office? Make up your mind, sweetie."

"But your head, Boo, your brain! Are you even aware that the head is not designed to take blows continuously? I get really worried, Boo. It spooks me out! "But, yeah, I love the diamonds."

"*Ole! Onyeoshi!*"

"Don't you talk Nigerian to me, rude muthafucka! Unless you're smacking me with your magic wand!" Phoebe held Adigun tighter and pushed her face into his back. The doorbell rang.

"Room service!"

"Please give us some time.

"It's 1 p.m. Fibi, we need to get back to DC."

"Oh, yes! The pilot has been calling; we've had him stationed for four days now."

"*Mo gbe*! The charges!"

"I love you when you say *mobe*," Phoebe chuckled.

"It's not *mobe*, there's a 'GB' in there. I told you when there is a 'GB' it is pronounced 'gbuh' not 'buh'."

"I'm getting there, Boo, I'm getting there."

"On a serious note, we need to leave, it costs too much to have an aircraft waiting at the airport."

"You know Bobby Brown will cover that."

"But it comes out of my purse."

"Can we stop at the Mandalay Bay on our way to the airport?"

"What for?"

"To pick up that tennis bracelet you promised me."

"Here we go again! Don't you get tired of shopping? How many bracelets do you need?"

"There're never too many diamonds for a lady. For God's sake, my man just won a million dollars knocking a Mexican out; I can't have a diamond bracelet?

"You know I deserve it, Diggy Boo; I fought with you at ringside."

"Here we go again. Listen, Fibi, I have a whole village to feed. We don't have social security or free emergency room treatments; the entire village is waiting on me! Your bracelet can feed twenty villages for an entire year!"

"Come on, Diggy Boo, Aka Adelaide Fernandez, you have never sent a dime to any village in Africa since I've known you.

"You have selective citizenship; you never talk about Nigeria, and don't even hang with Nigerians in DC."

"Oh, yeah? What of Kunle?"

"Kunle is not Nigerian, he's from the Republic of Benin."

"Same *tin*. The Yoruba Kingdom extended to the Benin Republic geographically during pre-colonial times. That's why he is 'Kunle' – a Yoruba name."

"That's why he can't speak one word in Yoruba and speaks French all the time? "Are we getting the bracelet or not?

"It's an investment; diamonds are forever.

"I don't know what you want to do with all the money in the bank; you should spend some on your boo."

"I spend *time* with you."

"Whatever!"

"We keep eating expensive food."

"No, we don't – we eat a lot of Nigerian food."

"Yes, we do."

"I've put on so much weight from being with you! Remember when we first met, all you wanted to eat was Nigerian food?"

"I'm Nigerian. Besides, Phoebe, you love *fufu*, and you love you some Adigun."

"You're right about that!"

Phoebe reached out and pulled Adigun closer.

"Oh no! Not again! *Haba*! *Won fi se e ni*? Don't you get tired?"

"Whatever!"

"We have to leave."

"Diggy Boo, I need to tell you something very serious; I don't want you to go to the harbor in Philadelphia tonight."

"How do you know about the harbor? Who told you?"

"I have my connections, Diggs. You will not go!"

"Bobby Brown will kill me if I don't show up for that pickup; it's the most important one."

"You are a boxer Adigun, you are a boxer, and a role model to a lot of young people. Leave that trade to Bobby Brown and his Columbian cronies.

"Leave the trade to them! I don't like it!

"You have made so much from boxing, you don't need drug money, Diggy Boo; you don't!"

"I have explained this to you over and over again; my biological parents sold me into slavery!"

"No, they didn't!

"From what you told me, I think they made a deal with the Fulanis to buy time."

"Who makes that kind of deal?" Adigun roared and he pointed at Phoebe.

"Woman, get this right once and for all! My father betrayed his friend by putting his only daughter in a family way.

"Part of his restitution was to hand over his own child, me, to his friend's people!"

"Even when he cut that deal, he bought five years. But you couldn't wait, you had to go and kill somebody!"

"Phoebe, now you are out of line - I didn't kill anybody."

"Oh, no? So, why did you run to America? Nope, darling, it's high time somebody told you the truth!

"You get to America and you are a successful boxer, but you cannot share your success with your family!"

"Phoebe! Stop! I say, stop! I have one family; that is the family that saved me from starving to death or freezing to death in the dead of winter. The family that has kept me employed all these years!

"Bobby Brown is my father!

"Some have priests as fathers, some have doctors; my father is a drug dealer! I am obliged to do as he says."

"Even if you end up in jail?"

"We don't choose our fathers. If I have to lose my life, I don't care. I owe it to Bobby Brown.

"This conversation is coming up too often; can we just let sleeping dogs lie?"

"This is not a sleeping dog; this is a foolish dog about to be incarcerated. You know if you continue this life you will go to jail, Dig? For a very long time!

"I hope you know I will not come to visit you and I will not be around when you get back."

Adigun froze in front of the large mirror.

Phoebe came in front of him and stretched her arms around his neck.

"I'm sorry if I offended you.

"I appreciate you sharing your life's stories with me, and I will never judge you." Adigun stiffened at her touch.

"I'm sorry, my darling. Please forgive me. I'm just uneasy, that's all. There is something big going down tonight at Baltimore harbor.

"I know it is very big, and I don't want you to go. Please, Dig, I smell a lot of trouble."

"I didn't tell you about this one, so how did you know?"

Phoebe went silent, unable to come up with a plausible response. Then she said, "I overheard Bobby Brown talking about it."

"He doesn't talk about his transactions," Adigun took her shoulders and pushed her back, so he could see her eyes.

"How did you hear about tonight's transaction?"

"Diggs, you are hurting me. My shoulders hurt."

Adigun let go of Phoebe's shoulders.

"I truly heard Bobby Brown speaking to someone on the phone about a big shipment today in Baltimore.

"Diggy Boo, I don't want you anywhere around Baltimore today. Let's stay here in Vegas for another day."

"Fibi, I cannot disobey my father. He specifically wanted everyone to be present in Baltimore.

"Come on, let's head to the airport. Call the concierge to come for the luggage.

"It is about five hours to Washington, and we need to get moving. I have a big assignment tonight."

The limousine drove through the quiet Las Vegas strip – Vegas doesn't really wake up till the darkness comes. The wait on the runway was almost an hour before the pilot's voice came over the speakers.

"We have clearance now, Champ. Permission to put the wheels up?"

"Wheels up, Captain Jackden.

"I'd like to take a nap. Are you joining me, Fibi?"

"I'm just fine here, my dear," Phoebe replied coolly. "You know I'm not laying down with you. I don't want you to go to the Baltimore harbor tonight.

"My spirit is uneasy."

"Since when does your spirit dictate where I go?" Adigun growled combatively, his shoulders hunched as if the confrontation was on the verge of becoming physical. He stalked over to the bed at the rear of the jet, pristinely made up by Ruby, their tall, skinny air hostess. Ruby had worked with Bobby Brown from the time he acquired the Bombardier Jet two years before. Twenty-Two years old and hailing from Saint Lucia, she had spent almost all her life in England as was apparent from her accent.

"Would you be needing your pyjamas, Sir?"

"No, I'm not going to be sleeping for long."

"Will you be having dinner, Sir?"

"Nothing for me; ask Phoebe."

Adigun tucked himself under the warm linen duvet and grabbed the soft white pillow.

Five hours later, they were taxiing to the executive jet hangar. It took them forty minutes to get to Phoebe's home in Bethesda. Adigun got on the phone with Bobby Brown for a call that lasted almost an hour. Phoebe heard him confirming the meeting time at the Baltimore harbor.

"Some fresh lemonade, Diggy Boo?" She sounded placatory as she approached with the clinking, ice-filled glass, and Adigun's demeanor brightened.

"You know I can never say no to your lemonade; you make the best lemonade on earth!"

Phoebe changed into her grey lycra jogging suit and slipped into her running shoes. "Will you be here when I get back? I need to run a few miles."

"Oh no, my dear, I have to head to Baltimore; it's almost seven o'clock."

Phoebe stepped out and sprinted to the bank of payphones a block away, where she picked up the last one and dialed. The voice at the other end didn't bother with pleasantries.

"I've been waiting for your call. All units standing by. Were you able to confirm the operation with Bravo Bravo?"

"Yes, Sir, Bravo Bravo en route." Phoebe hung up, looking grim, and left the phone booth running. Phoebe ran for a half-hour then she went back to her flat. Adigun was on his back on the bed, fully clothed, jacket and all, unconscious. Phoebe glanced at him, thoughtful, then turned on the TV and went to take a shower.

Adigun woke up around seven in the morning, disoriented and woolly-mouthed. He was still trying to figure out why it seemed so bright outside when the contents of the news on TV seeped into his consciousness. Breaking news about a drug bust at the Baltimore Harbour. The picture cut to a handcuffed Bobby Brown being escorted into a police car, then successively to other heads of the Edguardo cartel being arrested at different locations.

Adigun shouted, "Noooooooooooo," leaping for the remote control to increase the volume.

"… shootout left four policemen dead and the DEA were able to recover the shipload of heroin with a street value totaling about three hundred million dollars. This DEA drug bust is the largest of its kind in the State of Maryland."

"Phoebe! What did you do?"

"Why are you griping, Dig? You just avoided jail."

"But I'm better off in jail than dead! I'm dead, Phoebe. Dead!

"What do I tell the family? How do I convince them I didn't snitch?

"I cannot remain here; I will be assassinated within a day." Adigun began pacing. "We have to leave right away; my killers are on the way.

"You are not safe, either. I even saw Alagba on TV – He has been arrested as well. Pookie, Alonzo, and David Englis. And Mrs. Brown, they were all paraded on the news. We were to have a national meeting in Baltimore last night... I have to leave! I cannot even go to Bobby Brown's house!"

"Oh no, you can't."

Phoebe lit a cigarette and took drag after drag, combing her hair back with her fingers. "Can't go there; it's infested with the feds as well."

"I have my passport here, and I know where to get a chunk of money. Maybe I should head to Mexico."

"That's the easiest place to find you, Diggy Boo. A black man in cartel-owned Mexico. You will be dead five minutes after you cross that border.

"I'm not going to leave, Adigun, I'm staying right here. I'm not scared of anyone. I am not in the drug trade.

"You can use my car. Here is the address of my friend Digger; he lives on a quiet farm in Marlborough, Maryland and you will find some cover there. Head there right away!

"I will call him to expect you."

"Thanks, Phoebe."

Adigun reached for his pager on the table, but Phoebe snatched it up before he could reach it.

"Oh no, you can't use this anymore – leave it with me."

"Oh, my! What have I just gotten myself into?"

"Come on, Diggy Boo, off you go."

Adigun pulled her towards him, and tears rolled down his cheeks as his lips touched hers. He realized he was the only one crying.

"You seem to be taking this very well, Fibs."

"My father taught me to be calm during adversity. I am certain that everything will be fine. Keep your head low for a while, Digs.

"Here, take this address. If you have any trouble, there is a map in the car that should help you find Digger's horse farm."

2

Adigun rushed out of the apartment block and looked across the road to Bobby Brown's property. He only could see the woods and the long driveway after the huge brass gate. There was an empty police vehicle parked outside. He got into Phoebe's car and switched on the radio. The news was on rotation. It was the largest drug raid in the history of the world, blah blah blah – 'disaster' in so many words. The raids took place simultaneously in twenty-seven states. There were commentaries on every station, the achievement being celebrated in every precinct and police station. Adigun drove slowly and his heart beat fast, skipping every time he saw a cop car.

It was all a freeway ride and one quick turn into the horse farm. It was larger than Adigun had expected. He parked right in front of the paddocks and looked about him. About ten horses were grazing in the field adjoining the freeway. The house was an old Victorian structure to the right of the paddocks. A tall black man with cornrows walked out of it, wearing a blue terrycloth bathrobe over a red-and-green lumberjack shirt and raw denim. On his feet, he wore blue leather Scholl exercise sandals. "Welcome to Gershom Ranch, my brother. Watch your step." As Adigun approached the man, he caught a flash of movement from the corner of his eye and turned to see three huge Cani Corso dogs charging at him. "Down," the man commanded, and the three dogs came to a halt at the same time and went down on their chests.

"Sorry about that. Phoebe called me. You will be okay here. *Mi casa es su casa* and all that. Please feel at home. My name is Didi Gershom," he said extending his right hand. "Please call me Digger." He grabbed Adigun with his extra-large palm and squeezed hard.

Digger must have been about six feet seven inches and barely made it through the doorway of the large, seven-bedroom home. It had all kinds of basketball paraphernalia, and Adigun saw, on the foyer wall, a Utah Jazz jersey with 'Gershom' printed on it. He also saw a large, framed action picture of a younger, but just as large, Digger in flight. Digger looked at the large picture and back at his guest.

"Yes, that's me in my younger days; power forward for the Jazz.

"You like basketball?"

"Yes, I do."

Digger looked closer at Adigun. "Gaddemmit, you look like the kid Adelaide Fernandez!"

Adigun paused, not knowing what to say.

"Yes, it is you! I was at your match in Idaho, where you whooped the Haitian kid's ass in two minutes.

"Phoebe got us tickets.

"I'm a big fan.

"Welcome to my home Shango!!"

Digger looked to the top of the spiral staircase and yelled.

"Tishan! Tyrone! Wake up! Guess who is here?"

Two mixed-race boys in their early teens ran down the stairs, got halfway, and stopped with their mouths open. They were identical twins.

"Hey, bro, these are my boys, Tishan and Tyrone. Good luck telling them apart. Ten years and I still get them mixed up."

"Good evening, Sir," they chorused. Adigun gave each boy a handshake.

"Oh, my, I've seen you fight twice; with my dad in Idaho and also your first fight in DC, when you beat the Jamaican fighter."

"I'm quite honored to be here, Mr. Digger."

"Oh, champ, call me Digger.

"What should I offer you – some scotch? I only do single malt, twenty-one years."

"Did you shoot that?" Adigun pointed to the large head of a deer on the wall. It looked alive.

"Yes, I did, right here in the woods on the east side of the property.

"We are on three hundred hectares here. We have about six polo fields.

"We just did a real estate joint venture with a developer to build a nine-hole golf course and twenty townhouses, so we are down about twenty hectares, but we still have enough space for over two hundred horses."

"Awesome!"

"This is my life now; I'm retired, and all I plan to do is breed thoroughbreds for polo and play golf.

"I will show you the herd of mustangs tomorrow. They have been on the property for generations – originally in the wild.

"Strictly regulated by the Department of Wildlife but we have a permit to capture and train them.

"We crossed them with Argentine polo horses, producing the most magnificent breed of polo horses! Sought after all over the world!

"The Japanese police just purchased some from us.

"We are the largest breeder of Argentine polo horses in the United States… hmmm, I take that back; there is a breeder in Florida that might be the largest.

"I'm sure we are number two, though.

"My boys love polo, Tyrone is an 8-goaler and Tishan is a 6-goal – and they're just twelve! They already made the cover of the Southern Equestrian magazine, you know? Polo season takes a big chunk of their lives, so their mum home-schools them.

"Oh! My wife teaches show-jumping and dressage at an equestrian farm in Virginia. She is away right now, so you're in luck, 'cos I'm making dinner.

"Please sit down. I hope you eat pork."

Digger kept talking while he poured two glasses of whisky, and Adigun absorbed the conversational barrage in attentive silence.

"Do you want some ice?"

"No, I prefer it neat, and, oh yes, I love pork."

"I never liked pork until I met my wife. Nothing to do with religion, I just couldn't stand the fat, as an athlete. Then came Diane with a new way of cooking pork – roast it first to get out the fat, then we cook it, then roast it again, after marinating it.

"Diane comes from the deep south – she's a farm girl – but I come from Brooklyn. There ain't no pigs in Brooklyn! Only rats!"

The twins burst into laughter, both yelling, "Daad!"

"Yes, Tyrone, we grew up on a mouse farm!" Digger was laughing as well.

Then there was a sharp honk from outside.

"Oh, talk of the devil!"

"Oh, your wife is here?" Adigun felt a small flutter of nerves. Digger seemed content to prattle on and not ask questions. Women were always much more inquisitive.

"Oh, yes, she is. Tishan, go up and check your room. I'll fix the living room." So saying, Digger set straightening out all the pillows and cushions on the couch.

"She likes everything straight. Sit straight!

"Just messing with you. She's cool. She's cool."

He ran towards the large TV and picked up the video game joystick and hid it behind the picture on the floor. Diane came in, yelling as she opened the door, "Whose car is that, baby? It's blocked the paddock gate."

"It's Shango. You remember the boxer, Shango? Adelaide Fernandez?"

"Oh, yes! From the two-minute, waste-of-money boxing match in Idaho? He owes us our ticket money.

"*And* our airfare!"

She was now in the living room and sized Adigun up with cool, appraising eyes. "We paid for entertainment, not a one-minute knockout. We got to the arena, sat down, and the match was over! I didn't even see the punch!

"Good even, Sir."

"Ma'am it's a pleasure being in your home," Adigun replied, staring hard at her. "You have a beautiful family." He was finally able to tear his eyes away from Diane's face and turned to Digger, saying, "I'm sorry, she looks like Phoebe so much!" Digger almost choked on his scotch.

"God forbid I look like that witch! I should dye my hair!" Diane looked combat-ready, and Digger stepped in quickly with a placatory gesture.

"Oops! That name is banned in this house, Shango. Anyways, welcome to our home, where Phoebe the witch ain't allowed anywhere near!"

"Some people can't keep their hands off people's property," Diane muttered. Then she seemed to shove the issue out of her mind and her face cleared. "Oh, la la, the traffic was out of this world. Three hours! The beltway was a parking lot! Do I smell something roasting?"

"Yes, we are roasting pork."

"That's great. Is there some salad in the fridge?"

"Yes, dear."

"So, Shango here is Phoebe's friend? Same Utah-bred, tomboy, trigger-happy, gun-loving Phoebe?"

Digger looked bashful, "Yes, dear, gun-loving-Phoebe's boyfriend."

"Oh, Lordy Dordy," Diane crowed, "I remember she loved her some Digger too! I bet she still does!

"You bring Phoebe's boyfriend into my home? How long is he here for?"

"Come on, Diane," Digger soothed, "Not now; dinner is served.

"Tyrone! Tishan! Dinner is ready! Please bring up a bottle of red from the cellar – oh, Shango, I didn't tell you I make my own wine. I get grapes shipped to me from Napa. Know what? Come on, let's go and choose one together."

Adigun and Digger walked down the stairs that led to the basement, which housed a full-fledged winery, with bottles of wine and barrels laying on their sides.

"These bottles look familiar," Adigun murmured, peering at one of the racks.

"Yes, we supply all the major grocery chains across the state. You can also get our wine at some specialty wine shops.

"What's your taste like?" Digger pulled out what appeared to be a test tube, which he filled from a spigot attached to one of the barrels. He handed it to Adigun and said, "Taste it, Shango. Smell it."

Adigun tasted it.

"That is the Cabernet Sauvignon, but it is a bit heavy, and you can taste the barrel. Full-bodied, isn't it?"

Within ten minutes Adigun had tasted from several barrels.

"Which one should we have for dinner?"

"Can a drunk man choose? I'm wasted already."

"Come on, Shango."

"I heard white wine is good for white meat. We should do the white one that tastes like oranges."

"Oh, good choice! That is the Pinot Grigio. Though, technically, pork is still red meat, but I think it will work out nicely.

"Okay, grab that bottle… yes, that's the one."

"Guys! I knew your food would get cold when you went down there," Diane called from the dining room.

"We need to head back up."

The men clambered up the stairs like toddlers in trouble.

Dinner was a pleasant affair, at the end of which Digger raised his glass in a toast. "Cheers to Shango! Cheers to a better boxing career!"

The phone rang as everyone sipped and Digger rose to answer it. It was Phoebe.

"Yes, Phe.

"Sure, Phe.

"We love him, and you're not getting him back.

"Anytime, Phe. My pleasure. Hold on for him."

Adigun got up and took the receiver from Digger's outstretched hand, looking grim.

"Fibi?" The rest of his side of the conversation was mumbled, except for the tail end, when his words were easier to discern.

"Thanks so much for doing this.

"Don't worry, I will lay low here. Love you too." He replaced the receiver in the wall mount and returned to the table.

"Does anyone want more cornbread?" Diane asked. "'Cos if not, I'm giving it to Union." She caught Adigun's blank stare and said, "Union loves cornbread," with a mischievous grin. Digger, also catching Adigun's confusion, explained, "Oh, Union is her favorite horse. That animal just loves human food so much, she eats from our pantry!

"If Diane had her way, she would have Union sit here with us for meals. We adopted her from Argentina, and she has birthed a lot of fine stallions.

"Her son won the Kentucky Derby about two years ago. Do you like horses, Shango?"

"Oh, yes, I do! I spent a lot of time around them growing up." Adigun tried to keep his face neutral as he recalled his time with the Fulani community in Jobore – they had had many horses. He realized that he may not have been too successful as Digger was looking at him closely after his response. Then Digger said, "Memory Lane, huh?" Then he smiled broadly and got up. "Let me show you your room. You can retire, or you can join me on the back porch. I love sitting there, just tuning into nature."

Digger walked up the stairs with Adigun, through a tasteful, rustic-style hallway, and stopped by a dark-hued door on the left, which he opened with a flourish. "This is your room."

"Oh, my! I love the skylight." Adigun walked into the room, looking around.

"Oh, you should see it when it snows."

"The shower is impressive, man!"

"Grohe baby! Hundred percent Grohe!"

"All this marble; must have cost a lot."

"Yes, the entire floor up here is marble. Huge slabs imported from the middle east – Mecca, to be precise – same marble as the Kaaba.

"Holy stone, baby. Are you Muslim?"

"No, Digger, I'm Anglican."

"Never mind me; I'm Muslim on Fridays, Sundays I'm Christian, and I may decide to be Jewish on Saturday If I need a reason to lay around and do nothing.

"It's the Sabbath, Gaddemmit!"

The duo laughed loudly and Diane Hollered from downstairs, "Is everything okay up there? Sometimes, Digger, you just become a child again."

Adigun looked at his watch and started violently. "Oh my God," he exclaimed. "I have something I need to do in Bowie – I have one hour to get there!"

"Bowie, Maryland?" Digger asked. When Adigun nodded, he continued, saying,

"Oh, I'm the king of the forest route. I can get you to Bowie through the old forest road in exactly fifteen minutes. But not in your little Volkswagen Polo; We need a four-wheel-drive and I have the perfect one for the trip."

They headed out of the room and back down the stairs. Digger kept talking.

"My vet is in Bowie and I've had to drive sick horses there several times. Always made it in fifteen minutes."

"You want to bet on that?"

"Put your money on it!"

"Fifty Dollars."

"Hundred."

"Deal"

They stepped into the living area. "Sweetie, we need to go to Bowie for a minute. I'm taking the truck."

"Is there a sick animal?"

"No, baby. Shango needs to have a meeting there in an hour."

"No drinking, boys! Not after all that wine. And I don't fancy you driving in the woods in the dark; be careful."

The two men raced down the freeway and, in about five minutes, exited into the woodlands. It was dark and bumpy, but they made good time.

"These are the old colonial roads built by slave labor. They were built for carriages and horses.

"It's federal property and they decided to keep them. The government kept the land to the left and right of the carriageways as a 'green area' and no one can build on it.

"It is the best-kept secret.

"In a few minutes, we will cross the marshlands-

"Oh, I think I spoke too soon; we are already there! I have to change to auxiliary four-wheel-drive.

"Yeah, you can't do this with just any old car. This is the Dodge truck – one of the best off-road vehicles ever made."

Adigun looked out the window as Digger spoke, feeling anxious that there was no way this lonely route would get him where he needed to be on time. Digger, seeming to pick up on his mood, fell silent. Minutes passed, then Digger said, "You see that windmill in front of the giant oak tree? That is the Bowie post office!"

"You are kidding me!" Adigun was incredulous. How could they be in Bowie already?

"Yes, Shango! Please start counting my dollars.

"The post office is right beside the cemetery; I'm going into the cemetery."

"The cemetery? For a meeting? You are joking, right?

"Okay, now, *that's* spooky!"

3

Digger drove slowly through the dark cemetery towards the steel gate, which swung open as they approached. A sentry stuck his head out of the gatehouse window and peered into the truck. "Buenos Noches, Senor Fernandez," the middle-aged Hispanic guard greeted Adigun. Digger thought it odd that anyone would be so recognizable at a cemetery but kept his thoughts to himself and kept driving. They passed through an automatic barrier and Digger marveled at the level of the security – for a cemetery. The duo drove into the parking area in front of an array of imposing Royal Palm trees. There was a white Mercedes S-class parked there with a personalized number plate, '1945'." There was no one in it. "Stop here. Yes, right here." There was an edge to his voice that brooked no dissent and Digger turned to look at him. His jaw was set in a look of determination and his eyes were little more than slits.

Adigun was bent on continuing all his routine transactions and ensuring all monies were paid. It was the only way he could prove his innocence. He feared that the family by now would have put out a national shoot-on-sight on him. His face felt slick and hot, and his heart raced.

"I will be right back."

Adigun walked into the cemetery, under Digger's perplexed gaze, pulling what seemed like a pistol from his waistband under his shirt. Digger was sure he heard the ratcheting sound of a round being chambered and felt a cold sweat break out on his skin. Adigun walked towards a Caucasian man standing under one of the street lamps at the far end of the parking lot. He was tall and lean, in his seventies, with white hair slicked back like a rockstar. Adigun hugged him and kissed him on each cheek, using the opportunity to check the man for any concealed weapon. Then they walked into the cemetery together, the man clutching a black briefcase in his right hand.

"Awful thing, what happened to the family," the man said. "I'm shocked you came; I was not expecting anyone to be here." "Come on," Adigun replied. "We meet third Friday of every month. Have I ever missed it?" Adigun still eyed the man, checking for tell-tale signs of weapons or aggression. The man caught his look and the tension in his frame. He sighed.

"Come on, if I had any weapons, they would have been found at the gate. Though the word on the street is that you snitched on the family."

"I know. But I swear to God I did not!"

"Time will tell. It's not my business, as long as I get my supplies."

"Don't worry. The Edguardo operations remain unaffected."

They walked deeper into the poorly lit cemetery until they reached the family vaults. "Wait here," Adigun said softly.

"Oh yes, I know the drill."

Adigun walked further and turned right into the high vaults. He stopped by a tombstone covered in dry leaves from the branches above it. Adigun cleared the leaves and revealed a small panel with a spring catch. He opened it and punched in a combination on the keypad beneath. There was a click and a soft hum, then the tomb slid open like something out of a sci-fi movie. There was a muted grating sound as the tomb slid aside to reveal a concrete receptacle in the ground. Adigun reached in and picked up two black briefcases, then pressed another button and the tomb slab slid back into its original position. He walked back to the man and handed him the two briefcases. The man opened one and pulled out a gleaming letter opener that sat in it, alongside two bulky, cellophane-wrapped cakes of powder. He stuck the letter opener into one of the parcels and used its tip to scoop out the brownish-white substance. He licked at the tip of the letter opener and nodded in approval.

"Dude! Why do you always do this?" Adigun could not mask his irritation. "You always do this. Have we ever supplied substandard stuff?" The old man was dressed like a runway model, in pure white linen and a very expensive-looking pair of white loafers. He said nothing in reply to Adigun's complaint but handed Adigun the briefcase he had come in with. Adigun held the briefcase and just stared at the man. Then he sneered and asked, "Now how would you feel if I started counting this right here out of distrust?" The old man said nothing.

"Thanks. You can leave now."

Adigun stood in the same spot until he saw the Mercedes drive away.

"What a nerd," he muttered, then walked into the small chapel at the back of the cemetery.

There was a man behind the altar in a priest's garb, standing so that the marble podium concealed his lower right side – particularly his lower right arm, which was completely obscured. In a thick Hispanic accent, he said, "Welcome to the house of God." He kept his right hand out of sight as he peered at Adigun, then asked, "Offering complete?" Adigun lifted his hands, palms outwards, and the man visibly relaxed and stepped from behind the altar.

"Offering complete, Sir. You have nothing to fear," Adigun stepped forward as he spoke. "I'm not the rat; I was unconscious on the night of the transaction. I think I may have been drugged." At this last, Adigun paused to consider a thought he hadn't given space until now –Phoebe did this – and his arms fell back to his sides.

"If I ratted out the family, would I be here to deliver money?" Adigun's face became hard. "Operations will continue without interruption!" The priest was taken aback. "But, senor," he blurted, "With all the manpower we've lost…"

"Without interruption," Adigun bellowed. "Even if I have to do it all myself! Do you understand?!" Adigun had to drive home his continued authority.

"Yes, Senor. Of course. Have you been able to speak to Patron?"

"No, I haven't spoken to him."

Adigun moved closer to him, faces inches apart, the priest's strong garlic breath hanging between them.

"Our operations will continue," said Adigun. "Everything! As normal."

"Absolutely, Sir."

Adigun walked back down the concrete path between the tombstones, towards the truck, where Digger sat dumbfounded. Digger was jittery.

"No, no, no, no! What the hell was that all about?" Adigun fixed him with a cold gaze, replying, "I will have to explain some other time; better you don't know what's going on…"

"Dude this is spooky! You should have told me!" Digger was sweating. "I don't know what just went down – I don't want to know – but can we get out of here? You can keep the bet money.

"Gaddemmit, I ain't going through that dark shortcut; I'm going through the freeway, where there's light. If it takes us all night to get to my house, so be it."

Digger was silent for the rest of the ride back, except for one outburst, when he blurted, "I can't have this around my family."

They got home and he slammed the door of the car, stalking angrily into the house and leaving the door open.

Adigun got in and quietly walked upstairs into his bedroom, where he turned on the TV and fell asleep to the sound of the local news. The story about the Edguardo raid was on rotation all night. In the morning, he woke up to a full documentary on the same story. He was surprised at how much information the authorities had on the cartel, but it was clear that the one thing they did not understand was the distribution mechanism, despite knowing all the players. Adigun recalled his very first trip to the cemetery with Bobby Brown, who told him that he delegated everything except the distribution, which he had run directly for almost thirty years. The Patron told him how they initially purchased derelict cemeteries from the county, as well as most of the major funeral homes. At that time, the crematoriums were a big attraction – disposal of their enemies was just that much easier and more effective – though, even then, the places of death provided excellent venues for clandestine exchanges. Pookie took care of the operations, carefully coordinating legitimate interments with illicit body disposals.

The family also bought the electronic safe manufacturing factory in Delaware, and installed vaults dressed up as tombs and mausoleums. Every tomb in their cemeteries was fully hydraulic and had security access codes. They had spent a lot on research and development, and Chicano Safes became a lucrative side-line for the family, being worth many millions of dollars. The cartel kept the equity structure strictly private, turning down many investment offers. The sophisticated setup incorporated the funeral homes, staffed by loyal Edguardo members, whose duty was to escort hearses to the cemeteries. They were rotated around the cemeteries to ensure none ever became too familiar with each one's schedules and systems. The cemetery network became the largest heroin and cocaine storage facility in the history of crime. Every cemetery had a mini solar power plant that provided power for the electronic tombs of the chapel. Each chapel had a resident priest who was the cartel's accountant; he banked the cash in special briefcases that fit in the main vault in the basement of the chapel. The cartel owned the company that manufactured the briefcases too, which were specially designed to secret muriatic acid by remote activation, dissolving the contents. This technology had thwarted police investigations and jeopardized several detectives' careers, due to questions about disappearing evidence. It didn't help that the chemical release mechanism would self-destruct, leaving no trace of the technology, except for the sludge left behind by the dissolved dollars.

Adigun laid on his back for hours thinking. His pulse racing, he began to speak to himself.

"Can I be certain that I am the only one that has the knowledge of the distribution?

"It is quite worrisome.

"The accounting operation was totally decentralized; Bobby made it that way on purpose.

"The only way I can prove I'm not the rat is to keep the business running.

"Keep the business running."

For a moment everything came out of Adigun's mind in a soft echo. He could not tell if he was asleep or awake. His vision was blurry. His reverie was shattered when his door flew open and Tishan and Tyrone crashed in. They jumped on his bed and began a pillow fight. As they dueled, that old ability to turn his mind away from troubling thoughts kicked in and Adigun grabbed a pillow. For the next minute and a half, the three had a spirited battle, the twins giggling non-stop.

"Boys, enough!!!" It was Digger. "Head to your bedroom now!!"

Digger shut the door and walked towards Adigun.

"I will let you stay here and hide but I need you to stay away from my family.

"I mean, especially from my boys.

"I will not have it!!

"If I ever see you with my kids again, I will kill you!"

Adigun crashed back into his reality with a jolt. He stared as Digger stormed out but said nothing. He stayed in his room for the rest of the day, feeling trapped. Caged within his hiding place.

"The business must go on," he said to himself.

"The business must go on."

Book-9

This is Lagos

Lobbe rimata lobbal

(A good cow bears a good calf – Fulani proverb)

1

The morning of Chike's departure eventually came; the minicab was exactly on time. He had to prepare his first speech to the board of his father's company. His father had informed him he was coming home to resume as the Managing Director, while his dad remained the Chairman of the Board. The Managing Director position had never been formally occupied. Chike arrived at Heathrow airport, and it was packed full of Nigerians trying to get on the flight to Lagos – British Airways, the most popular choice of Nigerians. Chike was approached by an elderly gentleman for help with checking one suitcase as he had exhausted his baggage allowance. He explained that his wife had died in car accident in Nigeria and that he was heading back for the funeral. Chike was sympathetic and he obliged the old man, adding the suitcase to his luggage. The man introduced himself as Chief Afilaka.

The Chief was in a wheelchair, and he had on a full, blazing white Yoruba *agbada* outfit. He had a black large wallet, the size of a lady's purse, in his lap. His full head of hair was made even more striking by the streak of white in the front. "Thank you, my son, I am very grateful," he said to Chike as the airport porter placed his suitcase on the scale to be weighed along with Chike's. "No problem,

Sir. I don't know if our seats are close but, no matter what, we will see when we land." After boarding, Chike settled into his window seat and clasped his seat belt immediately. He was aiming for a long nap. He slept for four of the six-hour flight time but was awake when the descent to the Lagos Murtala Mohammed Airport began.

"Ladies and gentlemen, thank you for flying British Caledonian Airways…" Chike tuned out the rest of the announcement and looked around the cabin to see if he might spot the chief. The aircraft landed with a boom and a squeal and taxied to the gangway. The cabin brightened and there was the chorus of clicks that attended a planeload of people impatiently freeing themselves from their seatbelts. At this point Chief Afilaka showed up, gushing, "Thank you, my son, for checking my luggage in. I will have to run out of the airport to meet with my brother who is travelling at another terminal. I am certain I should be back by the time the luggage comes out, but please just wait for me with my case at the bar . . . if I am a bit late returning." Chike raised his thumb and bowed his head in respect. "Okay, Sir, see you at the carousel."

Chike's arrival in Nigeria was a very spiritual thing for him; the land of his birth, the motherland. Chike had left Nigeria after the assassination attempt that was foiled by Adigun over a decade ago. No one but Adigun, Chike, and his wicked uncles knew the true culprits behind the assassination attempt. Chike's father thought it was planned by his Lebanese business partners and had quickly whisked his son out of Nigeria. He had also done everything necessary to uphold the fiction that Chike was missing and presumed dead. This was done at a limited cultural cost to Chief Obidike, as it was the widely held view in his clan that he had a son somewhere in the village. But the personal cost was huge indeed.

While in the UK, Chike had searched for Adigun for many years in America but could not find him. He even hired a private investigator at some point, but Adigun Komaiya had just disappeared from the face of the earth. As he came out of the plane, that heat blasted him in the face. The humidity was at its fiercest and his sweat glands kicked into high gear. Somehow, the airport's stale smell made the heat more excruciating. The passengers that had cleared immigration waited impatiently by the noisy conveyor belt for their luggage. Chike was still waiting for his suitcases, but he had located Chief Afilaka's and pulled it off the carousel. He looked around but could not find Chief Afilaka, so he fixed his gaze on the large opening that the luggage came through, until

he was approached by some men he guessed were customs officials.

"Where is *ya* passport," one asked with the muzzle of his AK 47 pointing at Chike. He immediately surrendered his passport. "We are from the Nigerian Drug Enforcement Agency."

"Okay, good evening, Sirs. I see you are dressed in army uniforms. I don't see anything identifying you as a DEA agent. I'm sorry, but I am uncomfortable releasing my passport to you."

"Are you questioning my authority?"

"Sir, can we do this after I find my luggage?"

"Oh, you are giving me instructions? Do you know who I am?"

"Sir, If you are in doubt of whom you are or looking for someone to tell you who you are, this is the wrong time. I have been traveling for a long time and need to find my suitcases.

"You have no right to hold my passport or ask me any questions!" Chike's voice had risen in righteous indignation. "You are not a customs officer, you are a soldier," he said in his clipped, Queen's English accent.

One of the men grabbed Chike's arms and pulled him towards a table at the side of the hall on which a bunch of customs officers sat. A black German Shepherd was circling Chief Afilaka's case. "Hello, puppy," Chike muttered, stretching his hand out toward the dog. It continued bounding around Afilaka's suitcase in a frenzy. Then came about ten or more security agents, customs police and a, few military men. They all walked toward the table, and the customs officers sitting on it all got up. One of them gave Chike a hard, sweeping kick at his feet and Chike landed in a heap on the shiny floor. Another placidly opened Chief Afilaka's suitcase and pulled out a clear plastic bag of a white, powdery substance. He dug deeper and extracted several bags. A third officer, one of the men who initially approached Chike, used a penknife and cut through the handle of the black suitcase, discharging more of the powdery substance. He sliced the external skin of the suitcase, and even more was concealed there.

The man rose and rained a few blows on Chike's face. A crowd of spectators formed a ragged ring around Chike and the officers. Chike, in shock, heard someone screaming, "Chief Afilaka! Chief Afilaka," and realized distantly that the screamer was himself. Stars erupted in his field of vision as hard slaps struck his face. A soldier pulled at Chike's red sweater and lifted him to his feet. He pulled him away, slapping the back of Chike's neck as Chike had both hands up trying to shield his face. While being led away, Chike looked around for Chief Afilaka. The airport was filled with people who stared at him, and he combed the crowd between slaps, but could not spot the chief. He touched his swollen eyes and they felt like water-filled balloons. Chike's vision was blurry, and he saw a spectrum of rainbow colors seeping through his eyelashes.

"Who sent you?"

"Who do you work for?"

"How many of you were on the plane from Jakarta?"

"Why did you go through London?"

"Where is your final destination?"

Chike gasped as each question was punctuated by a punch to his ribs. The people around looked at him with disdain and no sympathy at all. He was dragged through a small door at the side of the hall and hustled through a poorly lit corridor into a large office with many tables and piles of luggage. A large window gave what might have, under different circumstances, been a pleasant view of aircraft on the tarmac. The officers dug deeper into Afilaka's suitcase and found more of the substance. The entire bag was stuffed with drugs.

"This is ridiculous!"

"Absolute nonsense!"

"This is not my bag," Chike pleaded. "I only did this chief a favor!

"He is in Nigeria to bury his wife!

"Can I have my phone call? Can I speak to a lawyer?

"The suitcase is not mine! It belongs to Chief Afilaka!"

Thick ropes of blood spurted out between Chike's swollen lips as he tried to speak. They landed on the grimy tile floor and spattered some of his captors' boots, earning him further abuse.

A team of men in white lab coats and latex gloves arrived and Chike was stripped naked. A vicious gut punch doubled him over, retching and clutching his abdomen.

"Open your mouth, you monkey!" Chike's chin was slapped up as his head sagged on his neck. The violence was delivered with rehearsed efficiency. A bright torch was shone into Chike's gaping mouth, and he gasped, then wailed as merciless fingers were buried in his rectum. Chike screamed and tried to resist but was overpowered. Chike surrendered to the onslaught. Then it all stopped. Chike looked up through the slits his eyes had become and squinted at the bright light directed at his face. This was someone else, different from all the others who had accosted him. Chike couldn't see more than his outline, but he clearly heard the man's deep baritone and thick Hausa accent.

"*Shege!*" The voice sounded amused. "*Na who send you with dis tin?*" Chike refused to say a word. After a barrage of blows and slaps, he looked up and asked again for a lawyer, sending the assembled men into a frenzy of laughter.

"Where do you think you are? *Engilandi, ko?*" asked the Baritone voice.

Chike, knowing they could kill him in that room, and no one would ever find him, started shouting. "Somebody help me! Heeeellllp!"

A tall, light-skinned lady, in civilian clothing, walked into the room. Chike, feeling a glimmer of hope, stretched his hand to the lady and shouted.

"See? See? See? Is this legal?

"Call somebody! These people will kill me! Help me!"

The woman went about her business and ignored Chike. She was one of them.

"I don't know anything about the bag! The bag belongs to Chief Afilaka!

"And can I have my phone call and a lawyer?" he shouted. Another slap landed on his face, which was now swollen beyond recognition.

Meanwhile, in the Arrivals area, Chike's father's driver waited with a simple sign that read, 'Bronze Maestro', a pre-arranged subterfuge. After hours spent scanning the crowd emerging from the luggage section, and then simply waiting, he returned to the office. His father felt Chike may have got cold feet and decided not to return after all. Maybe he had simply gone back into hiding. But after a few calls, his consternation turned to outright anxiety. The flight manifest showed that Chike had been on the flight from Heathrow so he could only have disappeared after landing in Lagos. Chief wondered if his enemies had got wind of his plans. If another plot had been hatched. If they had finally succeeded in killing his son.

2

The room was dim, and the weak lightbulb cast ugly shadows through the network of cobwebs hanging from the ceiling. The slowly rotating ceiling fan provided no relief from the stifling heat as Chike languished on the water-stained carpet, in one of several threadbare patches that revealed the concrete floor. Several other men sat on the floor with their arms handcuffed and their feet bound. They appeared to have been subjected to the same violence that Chike had, with bruises and sores in various degrees of freshness. Many had the faded, dusty look that suggested they had been in that position for days. Chike was too weak to cry. He lay on the floor like a cow awaiting slaughter, half-dead, with heavy-lidded eyes.

After an indeterminate number of hours, he was picked up and led into the office of a legal officer of sorts, or perhaps a magistrate. Chike was told he would be remanded in custody pending the next trial date to be communicated. He began to cry when he realized he was going to prison. He was hustled through a dark corridor and out into the holding area of the aircraft. As he got into the big black van, he caught glimpses of some other people sitting on the floor, but he could not identify them in the dark interior. There was some light coming from small holes by the door. He heard the men in front speaking, and he tried to listen to the conversation.

The van started moving and the roar of its diesel engine impaired his hearing. The conversation was not audible anymore. They took a sharp bend and Chike was thrown against one of the men in the van who immediately shoved him away with a violent thrust of his shoulder. He landed on his side, and he could not breathe for a moment. He felt like his ribs were fractured as he curled in the dark. His eyes were sore from the slaps and punches at the airport, and he realized that every time he closed them, it took a longer time to regain his vision. He decided to just leave them shut. He could feel the truck, popularly known as "Black Maria" weaving through the streets, alternately at high speeds and at a crawl. From the sounds outside the van, and with his recollection of Lagos traffic, it was evident that they were usually being forced to slow down at major bust stops. The drivers of *molues* and *danfos* had no regard for traffic rules and they created havoc everywhere they stopped to discharge and pick up passengers. The Black Maria would slow down, and he would hear people shouting, in crude auction style, such that the destinations they called out roughly mapped the path they were following.

"*Palmgroove, Onipan!*" Chike found his mind clutching at the mispronunciation of 'Palm Grove', an old peeve of his, then relented as he remembered that he had bigger problems than the local bus conductor lingo.

"Palmgroove, Onipan!!" A different voice, from a different bus. A sudden blast of loud music, then just the sounds of traffic again. A while later, the destination announcements would change and so it went until Chike heard,

"KiriKiri, Mile Two!" He felt a tightening in his chest at the mention of the most dreaded prison in the country. His eyes were still swollen, and he could feel the quickening of his pulse thumping in them. He squeezed them tighter and found some temporary relief from the pain.

"Mile Two!"

"Kirikiri!"

'How can this be happening?' Chike thought, writhing in pain. The answer flashed in his mind, and he blurted it out in a hoarse shout, "AFILAKA!"

He didn't realize it, but this was about the twentieth time he had uttered that name since boarding the Black Maria. A voice came from one of the occupants on the dark floor.

"Afilaka, or whatever your name is, *abeg* let us rest!

"Afilaka, Afilaka, since morning.

"Abeg, park well make we hear word. Afilaka ko, Afileke ni!

"Na we send you go carry drug?

"If I hear that Afilaka again, I go come strangle you, end your life inside this moto!"

528

Chike got the message and was quiet for the rest of the journey.

At length, the Black Maria came to a stop and the large rear doors of the van were thrown open. Chike squinted through one eye and saw the huge gate of the prison yard as he was led onto the lobby. A loud voice proclaimed, "Welcome to Jungle City, *Kirikiri* Maximum Prison!" They were led into a small room. "Spread your legs, empty your pockets and do as I say," said the gigantic, dark-skinned prison guard – better known as 'warder'. The five men did as instructed, and each was subjected to a cavity search.

"Easy!

"Easy!

"Easy, man!"

Chike groaned as his rectum was probed for the second time that day. He felt the abrasion from the latex glove and bit down on his swollen lip to avoid crying out. No one else was crying and his instincts told him he didn't want to get singled out for special treatment in this place. He was allowed to dress up – minus belt, tie, and shoe-laces – and escorted to his cell.

They walked along a grimy concrete row of cages with steel bars of indeterminate color. The prisoners gripping the bars and peering out blended into the dark brown mold that covered the once-green cell walls, often seem-ing like amorphous masses of fists and eyes, with occasional flashes of teeth. At one of the dimly lit cells, they stopped, the steel gate was opened, and Chike and two of the men were pushed in. There was a black double bunk bed and a metal toilet in front of it. The gate slammed closed behind them and the heavy lock clicked into position as the warder twisted the key. Several men were sitting on the floor in the crowded room, and they all seemed to peer balefully at the new arrivals. Nobody said anything and Chike squirmed in the uncomfortable silence. "Good evening, sirs," he mumbled through his mashed lips, noticing that the other two men who had come in with him had not succumbed to this pressing need to greet their fellow inmates. The room reeked of stale cigarette smoke and spent mosquito coils.

Nobody responded. Instead, the majority of the inmates seemed to lose interest in the new arrivals and a subdued hum rose as pockets of conversation began around the room. Those that still focused on Chike stared at him as a lion would patiently stare at its prey before pouncing on it. Some instinct told Chike that he would need to dial down his English accent in this place; being identified as foreign would be bad in this place. He was approached by a man so short that Chike was certain he had to be a midget. The man wore only a pair of trousers – they looked like they had once been white – folded over at the waist and rolled up from the cuffs so that his shins were exposed. Small as his frame was, he was heavily muscled and he walked the way bodybuilders tend to, with their arms held away from their bodies – like their wide backs won't let the arms fall to their sides. "*Hey, you! Governor say make I bring you come. Wetin be your name?*" One of the men that came in with Chike replied, "*Him name na Afilaka,*" and the other one chuckled. The midget chuckled with him, saying, "Welcome, Afilaka Fileke. *Governor dey call you!*"

The little man clasped Chike's shoulder, pulling him down and simultaneously stretching onto his toes to whisper to Chike. "*Governor say make I bring you come. You bring any money*? If you have any money, *bring am now so I go keep am for you.*" "Who is the governor?" Chike, still hunched over, whispered into the ears of the imp. He could smell the sweat baking off the man's skin and mingling with a more general smell of ammonia in the room.

"*The governor na president of this cell.*

"*All di cells get governor – di strongest person for di cell na governor.*

"Just obey and be loyal and everything will be okay.

"Fine boy, you hear me?"

Chike, battered as he was, had no interest in the governorship or the imp, but was compelled to listen as his new acquaintance talked him through the basics of Kirikiri life – diet, eating protocols, and sleep schedules. Chike was looking around the cell wondering how sleeping worked when the cell held no beds, then his attention was dragged back to the imp by his next utterance.

"*Now, you na fresh meat.*"

"Fresh meat?"

"*Yes, naa! Na you go dey fan governor as him dey sleep.*

"*We dey call dat one, HAIRKONDISHON.*

"*Also, na you be governor new wife.*"

"Wife?"

"*Yes, naa! Governor go tempere you naa!*

"*You see any woman here?*"

Chike shivered. "What is your name?" Chike asked.

"Tebolor, *but dem dey call me* Teyhanger!

"*Or you fit call me Tey Boxer. Na me be Chief of Staff for this cell… four years running!*

"Afilaka Fileke! *You bring igbo?*"

"My name is not Afilaka. I'm Chike. Chike Obidike." Chike didn't even notice that he was using his actual surname for the first time in many years.

"Harrow School alumnus.

"Oxford alumnus.

"I'm not a criminal. I shouldn't be here.

"I'm innocent, I received a bag-"

"Shut up," Tebolor interjected. *"Bros one advice wey I wan give you, no talk too much here; governor no like too much talk.*

"Governor dey wait you oh; make you follow me."

Chike followed the short man to the darker part of the cell through the door arches. The governor was on the floor with his feet on top of two men and he was resting on another man who had crouched by the wall to make himself into a human pillow for the governor. There were two men with large, cut-off pieces of cardboard cartons fanning the governor slowly. The process circulated the hot smelly air, making Chike sick so that he almost threw up.

The governor turned his head and looked up at Chike. He was a middle-aged man, with coal-black skin and a bulbous, hairy nose. His hair was a bushy mass of locks. Two large incisors protruded from his mouth – one of them brown and misshapen – and there was a wide gap between them.

"What brings you to Jungle City?" the governor asked as he sucked his teeth bending his head to the left. Chike, not knowing how to begin his account, simply flapped his arms and hands about, looking as if he was a deaf-mute and could only speak in sign language. At a silent signal from the governor, one of the inmates went to the other side of the cell to wake Shehu, who was a teacher at the school for the deaf and dumb. He had been arrested for selling bags of food, donated by the trustees, to feed students. To Chike's surprise, he miraculously appeared to be communicating with Shehu, who watched him avidly and seemed to derive coherent messaging from his gestures. When Shehu interpreted, however, Chike's flappings were senseless.

"I like the ceiling to have each and every one of you for dinner."

The eyes of the governor lit with anger and Chike found his tongue, blurting, "No, mate! NO, MATE! I am not dumb, mate." The assembled inmates marveled at his posh accent. They gathered in a circle as the governor made Chike tell them stories about London and, by the next day, Chike had begun to enjoy the company of his fellow inmates. He had told them of his predicament at the hands of Chief Afilaka and they made ambiguous offers to help him. There was only so much help they could give. They were all locked up. The governor was well-versed in the criminal law and procedures of Nigeria, and explained to Chike that he was looking at a very long jail term.

Weeks went by and Chike gave up all hopes of getting a lawyer or reaching his family. Then the warder called Chike to his office and informed him that he would be going to court the next day. Chike informed all his cellmates and they celebrated with him, offering wistful prayers and hopes that he would not return. On the morning of the trial Chike hugged all the inmates and bid them farewell. He was able to see the city on the ride to the courthouse, as he sat with the prison staff at the front of the Black Maria. At the court, Chike was led up a short flight of stairs and then down another flight of stairs into a dark room. The room was crowded with black-robed lawyers and their clients, huddled in preparation for their respective cases. A young gentleman approached the warders that had escorted Chike. They exchanged documents and the man looked at Chike. "Good morning, my name is Rimi Muhammed. I am the court registrar.

"You have applied for a government defense lawyer. I'm sorry to let you know she is not around yet. Her name is Tundun Olaiya.

"She is new at the bar but very astute.

"One of the best young lawyers we have today."

"He had barely finished the sentence when a young lady pushed through the crowd, holding heavy-looking volumes in her left hand and some files in her right.

"Mr. Rimi! Mr. Rimi," she called. "I'm so sorry I'm running late – I was stuck at the magistrate court across the road."

She dropped her cargo of books and files on the rusty metal table before them and stretched out her hands to Chike. "You must be Chike Obidike." Chike shook her soft hands, squeezing a bit harder than he intended.

"My name is Tundun Olaiya."

"Please get me out of here. I am not a criminal. It wasn't my bag!

"Chief Afilaka gave me the bag to carry. He had excess luggage, and he could not afford the fee…

"Believe me, Tundun, it is not my bag!

"I am not a drug dealer, I… am an artist.

"I am a graduate of Oxford and I deal in art – sculptures, to be precise.

"I'm the founder of the Back to Africa Foundation in London!

"I CANNOT return to that prison!

"I will die there." Chike seemed to lose all his air with that last statement and his entire aspect drooped.

"Calm down, Mr. Obidike."

"Call me Chike; Chike is okay."

"Mr. Obidike-"

"Chike!"

"I have read through your case file, and I am afraid we have a tough one here."

"What do you mean we have a tough one? What do you mean?"

Chike grabbed her gown and pulled the slight young barrister closer to him.

"I am not spending one more night in there!

"Which part of, "It is not my bag" don't you understand?"

The warders saw the scuffle and rushed to Chike, yanking his hands off the lawyer's black gown. Her white bib was rumpled and askew from the short scuffle. Chike was immediately pinned to the ground, face down, and handcuffed.

"Let him go," Tundun implored. "Please let him go. I say uncuff him!

"Get up, Sir.

"I am your lawyer.

"We have to fight this, but we will fight this together.

"You are being charged with possession of narcotics with intent to distribute.

"The drugs were in your possession and suitcase clearly labelled by the airline with your name."

"He gave it to me at the airport and checked it in my name... Chief Afilaka.

"He owns a car shop in Victoria Island. If you take me there, I can find him and hand him over."

"Calm down, Chike, calm down. It doesn't work quite that way.

"We have no real chance of picking up flaws in the prosecution's handling of the case and we have no procedural issues to attack.

"We don't have any substantive defense as the suitcase is yours.

"You were asked certain questions by the airline agent as to packing the suitcase yourself, and awareness of its contents, and you answered in the affirmative."

"Talking of the airline, can you bring me my suitcases from the airport? I have valuables in them. Money as well."

"I'm afraid, Mr. Chike, that won't be possible. All the valuables in the bag will be converted by the state as belongings purchased from the proceeds of crime.

"Let's forget about that and focus on your case.

"Without procedural lapses, and with the evidence so strongly against you, we cannot create the reasonable doubt needed to acquit you."

Chike scratched himself continually, rubbing the itchy mosquito bites on his arms. Tundun's next words froze him in mid-scratch.

"Are you related to Chief Obidike, the owner of Obidike holdings?"

"Yes! That's my dad! He must have come to the airport to receive me!

"Please can you reach him?"

"Certainly, I know his lawyers. I think he had a hearing today, actually – Court 16 – a controversial real estate case.

"I will certainly send the message through his lawyers; I'm in court with one of them later today."

Chike had resumed scratching until his lawyer's next utterance stopped him again, bites forgotten.

"I think you should plead guilty.

"First offender, it is obvious you were misled, you could be out in two years."

"Two years?" Chike was aghast.

"Yes."

Chike sagged against the steel table, muttering, "I can't survive one more day there."

The wait at the courthouse was lengthy and he spent that time speaking to Tundun. She painstakingly broke down her legal arguments and Chike's mind fractured under the weight of his fatigue, distress pain, and the utter hopelessness of the scenario she painted. This must be some sort of karmic retribution for my grift in the probate office, he thought. Perhaps two years is not so bad after all, he mused, despite inwardly cringing at the thought of prison life. So, when Tundun suggested the possibility that his sentence might even be suspended, that finally persuaded Chike to plead guilty.

Then they went and sat in the courtroom for another interminable stretch of time until, finally, Chike's case was called. Tundun made a wordy – and to Chike, confusing – submission enumerating the reason her client would opt for a guilty plea. He heard words that indicated his repentance and called for leniency and, even in his fractured state, something deep in him squirmed with discomfort. I did not do this thing, his soul cried. The judge took copious notes and summed up the case, reading out portions of Tundun's submissions, then, Bang! The gavel went down and the judge said, "Guilty!" Chike was sentenced to seven years imprisonment without parole. He shrieked and jumped out of the witness box, pursued around the courtroom by the security officers. He managed to hobble out of the courtroom into the lobby. With his hands and legs in chains, Chike leapt over the railings, missed a concrete slab and landed on the hood of a grey Mercedes, making a huge ugly dent. The owner jumped as the impact occurred and, as Chike got up to flee, the man grabbed his shackles and held him.

"I'm not a criminal! I'm not a criminal," Chike shouted, then fell silent as the man holding him seemed to slump against his chest. The pursuing security agents thought Chike had assaulted the man until he seemed to regain himself and threw his hands around Chike's shoulders.

"Chike! Chike! Chike! What are you doing here?"

"Dad?"

Dr. Obidike, Chike's father, was speechless. Chike jumped on him and started shouting, "Daddy, don't let them put me in jail!" He wept as the prison wardens dragged him away from his father.

Dr Obidike looked up at the crowd of people on the balcony above. A mass of white wigs, black gowns, and avid faces. The trial judge had also come out to witness the drama Chike created, his white wig hanging askew on the left side of his head. The Black Maria pulled up behind Dr. Obidike's Mercedes Benz and Chike was carried into the black truck, frantically kicking and gripping any object that would keep him from being forced in. Dr. Obidike, with tears rolling down his cheeks, shouted as the Black Maria rolled out of the courthouse.

Chike was absolutely silent on the ride back to Kirikiri, save for a few hitching sobs. Exhausted, he fell into a deep sleep, vaguely grateful for the chance to sleep without the roach-sized mosquitoes that plagued the prison inmates. The roaches themselves were tolerable; they never bothered anybody, but they asserted equal tenancy rights with the inmates. They could often be found doing languid laps in the single cell toilet and the inmates were careful not to give in to the impulse to flush them – flushing the toilet could yield varying results and was not something the inmates would do casually. It could overflow and fill up the cell with sewage water, so a degree of preparation was necessary before each flush. Several of the inmates were involved in cleaning up one of such spills when Chike was returned to his cell. His cellmates were disappointed to see him come back. They had all gotten to like Chike and they held out some vicarious hope that he would escape the horror of Kirikiri. He seemed more likely to manage that than most of them, and his return felt like a nail in their collective coffin. Tebolor was particularly distressed and expressed his disappointment with high emotion.

"How many years?" Asked the governor.

"Seven."

"Take heart. Take heart," said Taju, who had been in prison for eight years out of a twenty-year sentence for armed robbery.

"Time flies," said Toks.

"We, English people, are known for waiting; it's only seven years," Chike sighed with wry humour. Toks claimed to have been born in London and wrongfully deported at the age of three with his mum. He never stopped talking about going back home. He always told his story of being friends with the Queen of England. "To God who made me, I had her number," he would declare. "She used to call me on Sundays at our house in Shoreditch. I called her Liz just to prevent people from knowing who I was talking to."

"*Abeg, make we rest,*" Tebolor would interject, usually ending with, "You too lie!"

"You will need this," said Taju pointing at a small bag containing charcoal. The charcoal was used to draw marks on the wall, indicating how far one's prison term has gone. Each stroke represented one month, and the walls were covered with clusters of strokes. They went around the room like crude, two-dimensional dominoes waiting to fall. The inmates were not allowed to keep calendars. They were not allowed any form of paper, not after an inmate burnt down the north wing.

The warders were not known for their ability to keep secrets – somebody once compared a warder's mouth to a chicken's butthole – and, within a couple of days, the whole jailhouse had found out who Chike was. They knew of Dr. Obidike's wealth, and they gave Chike all sorts of preferential treatment. They offered to move Chike into a private cell, but he declined, opting instead to spend his term with his friends; he accumulated friends the way open wounds accumulate germs. Chike's ration of food tripled, and he got the best seats at the monthly half-hour of TV viewing the inmates received. They would eagerly wait for the Joy soap advert, with its catchy jingle and gorgeous 'Joy Girl', the model used for the ad. Whenever the commercial was aired, the inmates would roar, their faces avid with wistful longing. This was a special moment for the tenants of Kirikiri. This was their monthly virtual sexual experience, with a tangible object of desire – not subject to their faulty imaginations - a beautiful, chocolate-skinned lady with dimpled cheeks, long hair, and a white spaghetti top revealing a good quantum of cleavage.

"I have to wash my clothes today," Tebolor would say. "I have a date with Joy Girl tomorrow.

"She stood me up last month, but I'm just going to keep on trying."

Chike could not believe how seriously these inmates treated this soap advertisement. It's early days yet, he mused; I may be just as enthusiastic after another few months here. How on earth will I survive seven years?

3

Chike's father was relentless in his efforts to get his son out of Kirikiri. He had come to the prison personally and paid huge sums to the warders to ensure his only son was treated well. They even allowed his mum to bring food each day, and there was a feast once daily in his cell. They even brought in boxes of Perrier water and a fridge to store his dessert. Chike's cellmates were looking robust and fresh in only a matter of days, after all the good food, and the governor began to sell their leftovers to inmates in other cells. Dr. Obidike had bribed everybody, from the judge to the commissioner of police. Huge sums. Yet, every time he went back, there was always somebody else that needed to be taken care of. "Everything is fine with me," the judge soothed. "I would release your son in a heartbeat if it was in my power to do so." Rolling his eyes up to the ceiling, he continued, "But, you see, the Chief of Staff just found out about the case and wouldn't let the file move further unless you put some grease under it to allow for smoother movement." Money was the grease. Nothing moved in Nigeria without grease. The whole system was a mechanical plant needing lots of lubrication. Nevertheless, Dr. Obidike soon determined that trying to secure his son's release through the courts was a protracted, and possibly futile process. After a few weeks, he decided to call in some real favours. As a major donor to the ruling party, he held considerable influence with the chairman and, after a short series of closed-door meetings, the governor of the state granted an immediate pardon to Chike. This was not very good news to the warders and Chike's cellmates. It meant the end of a very beautiful era. Nevertheless, they were happy for Chike and the entire prison community held a prison send forth party for him.

Now that his son's freedom had been secured, Dr Obidike turned his considerable resources to finding the elusive Chief Afilaka. His offer of a huge reward for information yielded a flood of phone calls, letters, and even occasional deliveries of trussed and bound would-be chiefs. Some of them did indeed bear the name, Afilaka, but they all turned out to be dead ends. The flight manifest did not yield any leads, but Dr. Obidike had enough money to shake the city, and he did. The reward money was enough to change lives but there was nothing concrete to help find the man who had put his son in prison.

When the documentation for Chike's release was complete, Dr. Obidike went personally to collect his son from the dangerous Lagos penitentiary. Late that Friday morning, his convoy wove through the Lagos traffic with the help of the police-manned private escort car. At Kirikiri, with the least possible fuss, Chike was released and assisted into his father's burgundy Maserati. The convoy then reversed course for the Obidike estate. As they turned into estate grounds, Chike marvelled at the beauty of his father's house. He knew his father had moved into some castle in Nigeria but he had no idea it was as big as Buckingham Palace. It was twice the size of their country home Nsosoronsonso. The colossal white edifice was in situated at a huge roundabout in Ikoyi, in the center of which stood grand sculpted crest of an Eagle, two swords crossing, and a palm leaf tied into a beautiful loop. The same crest adorned the 20-foot-tall white gate.

"That is the 'Omu Aro', a great symbol and crest of the Aro Kingdom," Dr. Obidike pointed. "It was designed by the great TK Utche, the best friend to my father, Eze Nri." Dr. Obidike shook his head, cleared his throat and murmured.

"I have been having arguments with those old men about it for a long time now; I hope they don't go into the topic again today."

"Which old men, dad?"

"Your uncles are here; I'm going to surprise them.

"They don't know you're alive.

"They will be so happy to see you, Chike.

"I am so glad you took much interest in the culture and history of Arochukwu. Now you are back, you have to begin to live the culture. The rich culture of Arochukwu."

The cathedral-like mansion could be seen from the road, with its gargantuan columns and stained-glass windows.

547

The wide driveway leading up to the house was red-hued, like a vein cutting through the lush lawns on either side of it. Three thorough-bred horses grazed near a paddock to the left of the paddock. On the lawn on the opposite side, three giant Harlequin Great Danes were being walked by three handlers. They were so large that Chike initially mistook them for horses as well. The handlers had the same crest on the breast pockets of their immaculate white uniform. As the convoy rolled past, they looked up from the dappled shade of the trees that lined the driveway, then they fell behind and Chike's view was filled with the tennis courts and the 50-meter oval swimming pool as they approached the mansion.

Closer to the mansion entrance, they drove past the bank of carports, where five men with brown dusters were polishing the noses of that stuck out and glinted in the sun; three Mercedes Benz G-Wagon trucks, and three white Rolls Royces, one of which was a vintage Cornish 1971 convertible. Directly opposite was another bank of carports housing two red Ferraris and a yellow Lamborghini. Parked parallel to the carport on the right was a white 1962 Cadillac limousine. Chike opened his mouth wide as the convoy pulled up at the mansion entrance. Dr. Obidike caught him looking and smiled. "Son, I still love my cars. The roads are not particularly good, but I have the cars trucked to the North where I flog them.

"The roads in the North are amazing."

Now, close to the mansion. Chike could see, on the massive pillars, Igbo poetry all etched into the white marble. He turned to survey the path they had followed from the gate and beheld a majestic scene, with the double row of tall palm trees that swayed and bowed as though paying homage to a king.

"This is all ours," his father said with pride in his voice. "You stay in London wallowing in poverty whilst your own so much here.

"You are my son, Chike; who do I leave all these to? Who?"

Hung above the gleaming oak entrance door, Chike saw a banner with his name on it. He couldn't figure out the rest of the text on it because it was written in the native Igbo language. Beneath the banner was a group of people waving their hands. "These are my domestic staff," Dr. Obidike muttered with what Chike interpreted as rueful resignation; he knew his father would have preferred to have an assembly of siblings, nieces and nephews welcoming his son home. The only family members around were Chike's uncles and they were sequestered in another part of the mansion, oblivious to Chike's return. The sheen on Dr. Obidike's heavy beard sparkled. With his full head of hair, still mostly black, and the new spring in his step, he was the very image of manliness. He scratched his beard with his ivory tusk, a chieftaincy symbol.

"What are they saying, dad?" Chike asked.

"They are welcoming you. They shall be serving you."

"Wow!"

"Later, we will visit our businesses and you will understand the full breadth of your inheritance. For now, enjoy your welcome."

The huge door was adorned with a brass Arochukwu crest; they stepped through it and into a huge blast of percussive instruments with the sound of a melodic flute in the background.

"Chike, those are the *Ogene* boys," Chike's father remarked, gesturing to the performers in the enormous foyer. "I brought them from *Ojoto*.

"They are the best the East has to offer. I took them with me to the Okuzo's wedding a few weeks ago. I wish you didn't have that situation at the airport; you could have been there with me.

They reside here permanently and welcome me when I come in every day. There is nothing more important to an Igbo man than the welcome he gets when he reaches his home.

"The *Ogene* sound is the sound of our forefathers – I have to be welcomed by the sound of our forefathers."

The percussion band boys were dressed in bright, colourful clothing, with ostrich feathers of different colours tucked into their red woolen hats. Their music was pure Igbo culture and its melodies evoked the proud history to which every Aro man clung. The constant, sweet 'tonk' of the big gong pierced through Chike's goose-pimpled skin. Dr. Obidike's chest moved in and out as though his heart was pulsing right beneath his black velvet traditional attire with the lion prints on it. He spun around, bent his knees, and began using his hands to paddle the air to the left and right of his waist, following the beats of the drums. Chike mirrored his father's movements. He had learnt the traditional steps from childhood and could still remember. He was very happy.

The 'Ogene' boys had several instruments; they had the small metal gong, the medium-sized gong, drums, and several calabash shakers. One of them blew a special local wooden flute, it was different from that of the little boys. He palmed the instrument expertly, making the high-pitched note that was its signature. The *Ogene* boys sang praise songs:

Okosisi, welcome again o', welcome.

Obodo Oyibo don come to stay o', welcome.

Okosisi, welcome again o', welcome.

The roaring lion, welcome again o', welcome.

The cat with nine lives.

We have come to bear witness to the victory of another day.

Okosisi, Okosisi, let your son come in.

The son of a lion is a lion.

Let him come in – into the treasure the Lord has bequeathed to you."

A troupe of female dancers appeared, wearing matching green *Ankara* wrappers and white lace blouses. Bent at the waist, they wiggled their hips to the rhythm of the Ogene percussion, dancing towards Dr. Obidike as he also danced alongside his son. He briefly mimicked the ladies' dance moves, then pulled out a wad Naira notes and 'sprayed' them with it. The shower of bank notes seemed to signal an increase in the volume and intensity of the music, which went up another notch as Dr. Obidike ripped the band off another bundle and sent the currency flying. Chike danced in the wake of his father, who turned, beaming, and roared over the music, "Welcome to the Omu Castle; custodian of the great culture of the Arochukwu kingdom."

One of the servants came towards Chike, took his black polythene bag from him, and offered to show him to his room. Chike took off his cheap rubber slippers and padded bare-footed across the polished marble floor – he had made a gift of his shoes to one of his friends at Kirikiri. Chike was escorted from the foyer to the elevator that took him to the second floor. His room was right in front of the elevator. The servant's walkie-talkie squawked, "Kitchen housekeeping. Kitchen to housekeeping. Come in."

"Housekeeping, over."

"This is Chef Duke. Is that you, Obiageli?"

"Yes, Sir."

"Please inform Mr. Chike that dinner will be served in exactly thirty-eight minutes. Over and out."

Obiageli relayed the message to Chike. She told him dinner would be served in thirty minutes and retreated to the elevator. Chike pinched himself. "This seems like one of those dreams," he said, then continued after a pause, "Lord, why art thou messing with my mind?" He looked outside the gold-framed window at the sky, muttering to himself. As he looked to the sky soliloquizing, a little German Shepherd – the same breed and color as the sniffer dog at the airport – came trotting along the corridor. The movement caught Chike's attention and he shrieked, ran, and jumped on the oak sideboard, screaming, "It isn't my bag! It belongs to chief Afi-" He collapsed on the floor and a maid, emerging at that moment from Chike's room, came running. "Master! Master! Master!" she shouted. Chike had hit his head on the hard edge of the sideboard and fainted. Her voice was faint and had a far-away quality. Chike opened his eyes and beheld the vision of loveliness before him. He felt the feather-light touch of the world's softest fingertips on his chest and smelled the sweet aroma of coconut oil as she bent close to examine him. Her skin seemed to be glowing and Chike wondered if he might have suffered a concussion. With half-closed eyes, Chike fantasized about mouth-to-mouth, with the angel hovering over him becoming a merging of itself and Talatu from Amsterdam. Deliriously, he whispered, "Kiss me, oh kiss me, Talatu."

The maid brushed his forehead with a damp towel and soothed him. "That was Lucy," she said softly. "Sorry that she scared you. You have travelled far. You should rest. I am Ada, from Ojoto. I came to Lagos with the *Ogene* boys when Chief carry the band come." Ada had been barely literate when she arrived but could now count to a hundred and her spoken English had improved, although she sometimes got her tenses mixed up. English was the business language at the 'Obidike Castle'. Chike stepped into his room and made straight for the bathroom. He took off his trousers and peeled his dirty white boxers off his skin. In the pristine bathroom, his smell seemed to intensify and fill the space. He had worn the same boxers from the day he left England [which was a little over six weeks ago,] and his armpits reeked. Removing his shirt in front of the mirror, he saw the raw sores left by the mosquito bites he was constantly scratching. On the marble slab was a new toothbrush and a tube of Euthymol toothpaste right next to it. He pressed the toothpaste on the brush and began to brush his teeth, using his free hand to turn on the gold faucets of the colossal white bathtub. The pressure from the tap could sweep a toddler off its limbs and Chike briefly considered showering but, as the steam rose from the rapidly filling tub, he decided that he would prefer to soak. He sprinkled exotic bath salts in the bath water and the bathroom filled with the strong, sweet smell of ginger and lime. He rinsed off his toothbrush and

554

slid into the large tub and laid still in the hot water. The dirt from his body sloughed off and formed a black, foamy scum on the sides of the bath. Almost totally submerged, Chike looked around, admiring the beauty of his new home. Chike was not a stranger to the lavish tastes of his father, but this new piece of real estate was striking even to him. He was drifting into sleep when he heard a loud knock on the bedroom door. It was Ada again, calling out, "Chief said I should tell you they have been waiting for you in the dining room, Sir."

Chike got up and put on the white terrycloth robe that was draped by the door. He opened the bedroom door and won a brief internal struggle to compose himself at the sight of Ada – she really was quite stunning. "I have nothing to wear," he said.

"Chief said I should take you to pick some clothes from his room."

Chike and Ada hurried up a flight of stairs, and she led him into Dr. Obidike's room. Chike's mother, all dressed for dinner, was about to step out of the room as they were walking in. She gasped and grabbed a hold of Chike and hugged him, crying.

"Look at my son, look at my son! Who did this to my son?" she wailed.

"Dr. Obidike had not told her Chike was coming home from prison that day, but she wasn't upset. She knew her husband, and he wasn't one to release information until it was a historical fact or an absolute certainty. She also knew he would have wanted to clean Chike up before letting her see him. She made hasty adjustments to her makeup and left Chike to change into his father's clothes.

Downstairs, in the dining room, she walked in on a routine argument whenever the Obidike brothers got together, arguments about the history of the Igbos. "What are you talking about? Let me educate you people! Let me educate you!"

"There is nowhere in this country where you don't find the Aros."

"The Aros are special people. They are indeed royalty. You just refuse to accept how our people came to be!"

"Do you know?" Another voice shouted. "You want to tell me about the Aros? You want to tell me about the Aros now?

"When where you born? Ehn? When where you born?"

"Dede, I know I'm a small boy, but I can educate you."

"For you to say that Chibike had a right to behave like that is wrong."

"We are brothers."

"We are brothers."

"Nri and Aro are brothers."

"We cannot totally alienate ourselves."

"This was how it happened.

"Nri and Aro were brothers. Aro was the older of the brothers. When the father was dying, he sent for the brothers and crossed his hands to bless the brothers thereby blessing the younger more.

"Aro was very mad at this gesture and left the land.

"He walked until he got to the sea. That is why Arochukwu is the closest Igbo village to the Atlantic Ocean.

"You see, when the white man came, he came in search of slaves and offered spices and other precious ornaments in return.

"The Aros became the official middle man in the trade.

"I shouldn't have to tell you that the Aros fought the white man and actually won the war!

"Dede, please pour me some of that wine."

"Doctor you cannot drink the last drop of this bottle, we have to pour it for Diokpa."

"This is true," Dr. Obidike replied, then his tone dropped as he continued, saying, "You know I said I had a surprise for you?" His brothers nodded as he raised his head and called loudly, "Ada! Ada! Where is he now?!"

Chike knew his father was calling for him, but he stood behind the door. He had dressed himself in a beautiful white linen kaftan and was looking almost princely. Hearing the good-natured argument his father had been having with his brothers had shaken him. He was the only one here who knew his uncles had tried to assassinate him. Chike took a deep breath and walked into the large dining room. The reaction from his uncles was extreme and almost synchronised. They leapt from their chairs in shock, both sloshing wine from their glasses and wearing identical expressions of horror and confusion. They had been sure Chike was dead. Adigun, the young man they had recruited, had told them it was done. Their driver had confirmed it. They had seen the blood. Doctor himself had confirmed it. This was impossible!

Chike began the long walk into the dining room and toward the red oak table – it was large enough to seat thirty guests easily. Chike felt a cold disconnection from the tension and high emotion of his uncles, finding himself struck instead by the beauty of the room and its décor. The chandelier was colossal, yet dignified as it presided over the dining table, its gold-plated petals creating a magical spectrum of reflected light. The red-stained oak table and matching chairs gave the room an ivy league college aspect and, on the walls, bronze masks from the 17th-century Benin Empire cast their placid gaze upon the room's occupants. The silverware was engraved with gold inscriptions. *'Ogiil'*, they read, meaning 'endless ocean', a testament to the reputed boundlessness of Dr. Obidike's wealth. He loved modern art and decor but was an unapologetic traditionalist that celebrated black culture in every manner he could. He loved the land of his roots, Arochukwu, and could hold endless conversations about the history of the place.

Chike approached the dinner table amid a flurry of activity by the white-clad servants. They had just begun to serve the *abacha*, a local salad made from very shredded vegetables and red oil and the distraction gave his uncles a chance to compose themselves. Chike stood behind one of the seats, looked at them one after the other, and, in an icy tone, said, "It's me, Chikereuba Obidike. I'm alive and well." His father frowned in disapproval, asking, "Is this how you would greet your family elders, Chike?" Chike assumed an apologetic demeanour and gave his uncles a proper traditional greeting. His father then signalled to him to use the chair at the head of the table. It was the biggest chair. Dr. Obidike rose and pulled out the distinct seat for his son and Chike sat. His brothers looked at each other and the electric tension in the dining room changed to cold hostility. It was into this atmosphere that the last dinner guest, Barrister Chidi, arrived. He was the Obidike Holdings legal adviser and a close friend of Dr Obidike. He walked in with Mrs. Obidike on his arm, engaged in deep conversation. He looked up briefly with his sharp, piercing eyes widening slightly when he spotted Chike in the 'special' chair, but his face betrayed no emotion as he returned his attention to his client's wife.

Parallel to the table was a large picture window overlooking the back garden, which sprawled at the bottom of a pavilion-sized flight of flagstone steps. The kitchen was east of the table and its giant swivel door flapped as Ada swept quickly through with a tray. Chike didn't notice her; he was a seething bundle of nerves, uncomfortable with his dangerous uncles' presence. These men had tried to end his life when he was still a child. Dr. Obidike introduced him to his legal advisor as everyone tucked into their starters and, after noting the frosty discontent emanating from his brothers' end of the table, whispered into Chike's ears.

Dr. Obidike was the youngest of three brothers, the only one with an education and, without question, the wealthiest. As a matter of fact, the older brothers lived off the doctor. Everything they own belonged to Dr. Obidike but, under the auspices of cultural norms, they asserted their seniority in age and acted with a sense of entitlement. Dr. Obidike whispered to his son, preparing him for the inevitable hostility, while assuring him of his inheritance. The older Obidikes knew Chike's homecoming was like the coronation of a new king. That their youngest sibling had placed his son in the seat of honour at this table was a clear message that they would not wield power in the way they expected. During the main course, unable to contain himself further, Diokpa blurted, "But he is dead!"

"No, brothers, my son is not dead."

"We thought he died from the hands of your Lebanese business rivals."

"Chike did not die, brother. The Lebanese attempted to take his life but God saved him and I hid him in Europe all these years." Chike noticed the way his uncles searched his father's face as he said this, looking to see if he meant what he was saying, or if he knew the truth and was laying a trap for them.

"We give God the glory for his life," Diokpa offered with forced good cheer.

"This is the happiest day of my life; our family is complete again."

After his father's whispered words, and following this exchange, Chike began casually asking questions about his father's empire, his uncle's roles in it, and what the extents of his coming empire were. His uncles were disgusted at his onslaught, hating the fact that this upstart would compromise their slice of the pie, but presenting their umbrage as irritation at Chike's disregard for traditional forms of address towards elders. "You guys are rather quiet," Chike quipped, with pointed good humour, after it seemed that he was talking to himself. "Eeeeh?" Diokpa's jaw dropped as he yelled his indignation. He had just bitten off the entire head of a fish and was deftly reassembling the bones within his mouth and ejecting them when Chike made his observation. "You guys?" He echoed Chike's words while giving him a look that spoke volumes.

Mrs. Obidike noticed this and stroked the back of her son's head protectively, as though to communicate to the family elders that Chike was only a kid.

Dr. Obidike's brothers bolted to their feet – Diokpa first – having found a suitable pretext for their rage. As they washed their hands, Diokpa spoke through clenched teeth.

"You have fed us good food and good wine; do we have to eat insults and disrespect for dessert?

"We have had enough of your son.

"He has gone all night breaking the rules of our people, calling us by our first names and asking stupid questions.

"If you cannot train your son yourself and you let the white man train him, why don't you leave him with the white man? Who is he calling 'you guys'?

"Enough is enough!" The two men stormed out of the room with Dr Obidike on their heels, imploring them, "*Gini? Ogini? Gini*, brother? *Oghinemegi*?!"

There was silence for a while, then the heads of everyone at the table lifted slightly when they heard the squeal of tyres – the older Obidikes making a dramatic exit, no doubt. Dr. Obidike returned looking perplexed, though no one in the room was blind to the mild amusement that danced in his eyes. He asked Chike and Barrister Chidi to enjoy the rest of their meal and Mrs. Obidike escorted him to their room. Chike began to question whether coming home was really a smart Idea then he remembered his troubles in Europe and thought he would just have to make it work.

The weekend that followed his welcome home dinner was a restful one for Chike. Each morning was nostalgic as he arose to the sound of the cock's crow and he made it a point to sit out on his balcony each morning watching as the roosters flapped their wings and stretched their necks, crowing to usher in the new day. His father seemed to understand the need for a period of decompression, and they did not speak of the events of Friday night. His mother was a pure traditionalist and would never dream of discussing her husband's business, even with her son, without his express permission. So, Chike was left to his own thoughts about how to navigate the situation with his uncles.

Monday was Chike's first day at work. He had barely slept and couldn't help pondering the fact that he'd been in a prison cell two days before. The smell of freshly brewed coffee made its way into Chike's room. The cocks crowed and the birds sang such beautiful songs as well; luxuries Chike had missed in London. Living next to a railway track, he was used to the early morning commuter train noise. Just as he was thanking God for such a lovely morning, Ada came into his room. Their eyes met just as she crossed the threshold onto Chike's soft bedroom carpet, which put an engaging spring in her step. She smiled and, with a strong accent, whispered, "Morning coffee, Sir?" as she held the tray, Chike couldn't help noticing her hands; the way her fingernails looked so clean. He imagined that they had never been tarnished any nail polish nor any form of chemical. Her dimpled cheeks, combined with the gap in her front teeth to make her smile even more angelic. As she leaned over to set the tray down, he caught a glimpse of her cleavage and noticed the nubs of her taut nipples straining against her shirt. The mix of sexuality and innocence was heady, and Chike was glad he was mostly under the covers, though he was sure he looked like a puppy soliciting attention. Chike retained his awestruck expression even after Ada quietly left the room. "Good gracious, Lord," he whispered to himself. "This is love." At that moment, his mother walked in, overhearing his muttered comment. "Good morning, sweetie," she chirped. "Who is the girl you are mooning over now? Is there someone in your life?

"You look smitten! Not two months away from your London girls and you are already pining.

"It's high time you picked out one of them; I want to start babysitting my grandchildren!"

"No, mommay," Chike chuckled, still thinking about Ada.

Faintly, he could hear his father speaking on the phone from downstairs. He got out of bed and headed for the door, still listening.

"I don't believe this.

"Why did they do that?

"What else did they say?

"And the safe too?"

Chike walked down the spiral stairs a little slower, trying to figure out who his father was talking to in such a loud voice. His father was on the back porch, which faced the lake. The ducks in the lake were arrayed on the opposite bank, seeming to scowl at Dr. Obidike's loudness.

"Good morning, daddy," Chike greeted.

Dr. Obidike had a frown on his face as he looked Chike up and down.

"First day of work and you're not dressed? All your time in Harrow and Oxford and you haven't learned anything about timeliness?

"Do you realize you're about to head one of the largest pharmaceutical companies in sub-Saharan Africa?"

Chike took his father's stern rebuke with a jovial casualness. He could tell when his father was pulling his leg and, besides, he'd done and been through too much to be so easily intimidated… even by the Great Doctor Obidike himself!

"My wardrobe's empty, daddy," he said mildly. "Not a stitch to wear to work."

"Everything is in the suitcase with the Drug Enforcement guys".

"The rest I have shipped to arrive sometime next month."

Dr. Obidike favored him with a small smile – he was proud that his son was no pushover – and yelled, "Jonathan!" Three men came running out to the porch at such a pace that the last one actually skidded in the doorway. They were dressed in identical white khaki shorts and round-necked shirts. "I called Jonathan, not the three of you." Dr. Obidike grumbled, though he looked amused. Jonathan stretched to his full height and the other two looked a bit disappointed. The workers in Dr. Obidike's palace were unerringly efficient and responsive, inspired very much by what they called 'fringe benefits'. It was a known habit of Dr. Obidike to randomly dish out bails of money to his workers as he pleased. They fought over every opportunity to serve him, knowing that, if the mood took him, huge tips were always a possibility.

"Jonathan, bring me the suits the drycleaners delivered last week." In less than three minutes, Jonathan returned, wheeling in a hanger laden with what must have been twenty suits, most of them grey with a few blacks and navy blues. Chike's eyebrows rose as Jonathan wheeled the hanger to a halt by their wicker seats.

"This is what I'm talking about son. Forget about your suitcase; I trust your taste and I know you have a lot of good corporate wear but, for now, we need to fix you up."

Dr. Obidike told Chike he had ten minutes to meet him in the car. Chike hurriedly grabbed the suits and ran up the spiral stairs into his room, selecting a plain white shirt from the wardrobe and dressing quickly. In eleven minutes, he joined his father who was standing beside a 1979 Rolls Royce Silver Spur, the engine of the car so silent, only the white mist from the exhaust indicated that it was on. The driver snapped the rag as he polished the car. When Dr. Obidike saw his son, his face lit up. "That's what I'm talking about, my boy," he said, smiling as his gaze fell on Chike's shoes. "I knew you would pick those ones; I got them hand-made for me at Crocket and Jones. I have them in brown as well.

"You look great Chikereuba. You look good! It's amazing how we wear the same size."

"God is good, dad – just so I can clean out your wardrobe."

Both men chuckled as the heavy doors of the Rolls Royce thudded shut and the silver car pulled out of the huge driveway.

It was a long drive to work, and Chike looked out of the window trying to catch a glimpse of every fascinating scene he saw. At length, the Rolls Royce pulled into the car park of an impressive, multi-storey complex. This was the headquarters of Obidike Holdings. Dr. Obidike dashed out, hastening his son along. "Hurry! Hurry! We should not be late for the meeting." They rushed through the double doors and along a well-appointed series of corridors and hallways, to a mounting chorus of "Good morning, Doctor." the workers sure had huge respect for his dad. A swift elevator ride and they walked into the conference room where ten people sat around a massive, oval conference table of gleaming oak. These people seemed less pleased with his father than those they encountered on their way up and there was a pregnant silence in the room. Dr. Obidike looked at Chike and said to him, "Would you mind waiting outside the door for a few minutes, Chike?"

The moment the door closed, there was an eruption of sound from behind it. Though difficult to discern the words or the speakers, it was easy to determine that there was an unhappy bunch in there. Chike waited outside the door for about thirty minutes, occasionally startled by the thumps of fists upon the oak table, until there was relative quiet for an unbroken stretch of about three minutes. Then Diokpa Obidike came out and beckoned Chike into the room, obviously still aggrieved from the dinner last week. Chike felt that silence was wisest and did not make a sound. He stood in front of a huge oak chest of drawers, hands behind his back and head bowed, focusing on the red carpet at his feet. He only looked up when his eldest uncle, Dike, rose and cleared his throat, adjusted the lapel of his huge coat, and started to speak.

4

"We, the board of Directors of Obidike Holdings Limited, welcome our son, Chike, to the group." Neither his tone nor his eyes bore any hint of welcome as he ended, saying, "I will pass this responsibility to Dr. Obidike to finish." Dr. Obidike stood up, looking like a wolf at risk of being cast out of his pack.

"Chike, my dear son," he said, "Members of the Board of Directors of Obidike Holdings welcome you.

"They have decided to bestow upon you the responsibility of Chief Executive and Managing Director, a position that has been unoccupied for over a decade.

 "We all pray that our children do better than us and grow to step into our shoes.

"Chike, this is your heritage.

"This is your father's company, and this is how far we have come.

"The baton is yours.

"May God give you the strength to take this group to greater heights."

There was some bogus throat clearing from around the table at this point, making it clear to Chike that the members of the board were not willing parties to the decision that was just announced. From the looks on their faces, and the tense silence greeting the announcement, Chike knew he was not in for a smooth term.

The meeting broke up shortly after, as the older Obidike brothers made their excuses and left the conference room, nodding curtly to Chike and his father. Dr. Obidike calmly enumerated the benefits that accompanied the position - free company car, free membership at the yacht club and such – and thoroughly detailed the responsibilities of the role. The two board members who remained walked over to Chike and congratulated him, then quietly left the room. Chike was escorted into his office, a huge room with wooden panels, formally occupied by Chief Dike, whose portrait still hung on the wall. As Dr. Obidike stretched to remove Chief Dike's picture, Chike blurted out, "I don't like this! I don't like this! This is not what I came here for."

"You did not come here; you were brought here." Dr. Obidike's voice was a low growl.

"But, dad-"

Before he could continue, Dr. Obidike raged at him.

"Shut up!

"Shut up, you weakling!

"Are you an Obidike?

"Are you an Obidike?"

"But, dad-"

"Shut up!" Dr Obidike shouted slamming his hands on the oak table.

"I built this company with every drop of my sweat!

"When I was spending sleepless nights in my backyard mixing chemicals and grinding tree barks, these men joined the world in calling me a mad man.

"When I had just a room a table and a chair in this same building my brothers were not around.

"I did this all for you, Chike.

"This is all for you, and I intend to make it clear it is yours before I leave this earth."

Chike opened his mouth to speak, but Dr. Obidike broke in again.

"What else can I do? What else?

"I educated all the children of these ungrateful touts.

"I have given them wonderful lives in the past eighteen years.

"It is time these people know who really owns all this.

"My Lebanese partners tried to assassinate my son and I quietly took him out of the country.

"None of these idiots showed any concern – they remained friends with the Lebanese bastards.

"Now I have brought him back to take his rightful position they are having a fit?

"Do you guys know what this boy had been through, trying to survive in Europe while you charlatans feed off his fathers' wealth?" Dr. Obidike raged as if the subjects of his rant were in the room with him.

"I will not take it anymore!

"*Agwo emeghi nke o jiri buru agwo, umuaka achiri ya hie nku.*

"*Iwuatago*!

"Chikereuba, if a snake fails to show its venom, little kids will use it in tying firewood.

"I shall not take this anymore!"

Dr. Obidike was overcome by a coughing fit so intense and long that he sank into the velvet couch in a state of near-delirium. "Dad!!!" Chike was concerned about the way his father looked; he seemed to have aged twenty years in the space of minutes. "These men won't kill me," his father muttered.

"They won't kill me."

"Dad? Are you okay?"

"Your mother always warned me about my brothers, Chike," Dr. Obidike seemed to be in a trance of sorts. "She always reminded me that my brothers and I are not of the same mother; that they don't have my best interests at heart…"

"The woman was right after all.

"I told you how Diokpa, raped my wife to be.

"Lied the girl was an *Osu* and convinced my father she was not fit to be my bride, only because he wanted her to himself.

"Why do they want everything I find or anything I build? Why?!"

`Dr. Obidike managed to walk Chike to the different departments of the business, and he introduced him as the new Managing Director. They did not spend much time at the office as his discomfort intensified. They drove back home and called in the family doctor. As time passed, Dr. Obidike's health worsened, though the doctors were unable to identify the source of his malaise. Despite his father's incapacitation, Chike went to the office every day, working diligently and learning the business operations, in spite of the open hostility from his disgruntled, dangerous uncles.

5

Over the next four months, Chike settled well into his new position, making sweeping, company-wide improvements. He kept the Obidike brothers away from the head office where he had his office and relocated them to the new building the company had acquired on Lagos Island. Politics aside, his competence was soon evident to all stakeholders, and he was able to achieve an uneasy peace with the board. One Wednesday, Chike left work early to go home and tend to his father whose health had rapidly deteriorated over the months. He usually went directly into his father's bedroom but, on this night, he walked made a detour through the kitchen. Ada was there preparing the dinner pastries.

Ada, glowed as she looked at him, smiling.

"I knew you would come home early," she said, giving him a knowing look.

"Well," Chike leered, "Wednesdays are off days for the kitchen staff."

"I knew you would come as usual."

"I missed you all day, sweetness. Couldn't concentrate at work. How is dad doing today?"

"It's one of those bad days," said Ada. "He can't hold down food. The coughing has reduced but he is losing a lot of weight."

"I will go up in a moment," Chike said, then continued with his brow arched, "Am I getting the usual?"

"Not today, Chiks. Not today, I'm very worried. It still has not come."

"How late is it?"

"I don't know, Chike; I just know something is not normal."

"Are you feeling sick?"

"No, I'm okay. I'm just worried. What will I do with my life? Mama will kill me. I told you I didn't want this, Chike, I told you!"

Chike opened the fridge and took out a bottle of milk.

"Let me help you with that," Ada offered.

"Never mind, Ada. I always tell you I can do things myself. Let's get back to your issue."

"My issue? Chike, *my* issue?" It's *my* issue now, eh?"

"I don't mean it that way."

Chike pulled her to himself, kissing her deeply. She stood on her toes with her long hair dangling as she reached for Chike's neck and pulled him closer. He reached behind her and fiddled with her zipper but she pushed him away.

"I told you, not here. Not anymore." Her tone was indignant.

"No, no, no! Not on the kitchen floor; I'm not a whore!"

"Not anymore, Chike." Ada was weeping. "What am I going to do, Chike?"

"Calm down, Ada, calm down," Chike soothed. "This is exactly the reason it hasn't come; you worry too much. Don't you know the worry alone can cause you to skip a few months?"

"You have now become medical doctor?" Ada sucked air through her teeth derisively. "Doctor of Injection, please let me go. I need to take this sandwich to Chairman. He hasn't eaten anything all day." She picked up the tray and Chike tried to swat her butt but missed. She walked away, wriggling her waist seductively, while looking at Chike over her shoulder and batting her eyelashes.

Chike allowed a half hour before going up to his father's room. The curtains were drawn, and the room was dimly lit. Chike walked to the drapes and drew them apart, letting in the bright sunlight and causing his father to squint and cover his face with his hands. Gently, Chike told his father, "You need sunlight, dad. You need some sun!

"Look how frail you are – you have lost too much weight."

Chike made him a cup of hot tea with plenty of milk.

"I'm going to vomit it," his father croaked.

"Oh no, you won't. I'm here to spank you like you did me when I was a kid," Chike joked. Then his expression turned grave once more. "You need to get well, dad.

"I spoke to the doctor from the office. All your tests have come back but they can't find anything wrong with you."

"They almost took all of my blood for those tests."

"Nothing, dad, nothing! They found nothing! You need to get yourself together and shake this off, dad! There is nothing the matter with you."

Dr. Obidike waved Chike's encouragements aside dismissively. "Chike, I'm dying," he said in a matter-of-fact tone of voice. "I know I'm dying."

"Stop speaking like this, dad. All your tests have come back okay, can you die if you are not sick?"

"Chike, I am not good inside. I can feel it."

"Call the captain to get the jet ready for tonight, I may have to head to my doctors in the Netherlands for further tests."

"I want you to come with me, also, call Dr. Benson; he will have to accompany me to my doctor in Rotterdam."

"There is a lot I need to discuss on the plane."

Chike walked towards the balcony on the side of the room and made all the necessary phone calls.

Shortly after he got back from the calls, Dr. Obidike's phone rang, and he grunted as he picked up the receiver.

"Hello? Yes?"

"Really?"

"I told you I wasn't feeling right…"

"Oh my God! Arsenic?"

"How?"

"We fumigate…"

"Arsenic?"

"No, I have not bought any of that nonsense in traffic!"

"It is impossible. You say it is a miracle I'm alive? Ambulance?"

"That serious, eh? Okay."

Dr. Obidike held the receiver to his chest and activated the speaker. The frantic voice on the other end blared out, "… you, no, you cannot travel! Based on the toxicology test, we have to examine you closer to ensure your organs are intact. And you are sure you did not come in contact with arsenic in the company laboratories?"

"I hardly go into the pharmaceutical factory." Dr. Obidike looked up and saw his wife standing stock-still in the doorway into the bedroom. He was about to ask how much she had heard when she rushed to his side, asking, "What is this about arsenic? Is that not poison? Eh? *Ghini*?"

She took off her headgear and flung it to the other side of the room, then she grabbed Chike, wailing, "Poison? Who ate poison?"

"Mum, calm down. The doctor is on the phone, the ambulance is on the way. The toxicology test results showed high traces of arsenic poison in dad."

Mrs. Obidike sat on the floor abruptly, with her hands on her head, and began to howl.

"*Awalame, Awalame, ooooooo!*

"Aaaahhh, poison! Poison ooooooooooh! Poison!

"They finally got me!

"Jesus! Jeeezus! Blood of Jeeezus!

"Ahhhh, they cornered me!

"I told this man to let his brothers be, eh?

"Daaddeee, you have finally finished me!

"Daaadddymmoo, you have killed me!

"Where do I start?

"I told you they were snakes! I told you they will kill you!

"'My brothers, my brothers, my brothers,' you insisted!

"Daddy, *Idon ku*!

"*Idonku! Nku doogi*!

"*Hapun Nku*!

"*Hapun Nku, ooh*!"

"You are walking on the road, you pull firewood, fire-wood pulls you back; do you know what is pulling the firewood on the other side of the bush?

"*Hapun Nku*!

"*Hapun Nku, ooh*!

The ambulance arrived and the paramedics raced up to Dr. Obidike's bedroom. They placed him on their gurney and stuck an IV in his arm and an oxygen mask on his face. Then they wheeled him off, Chike keeping pace with the gurney. His mom pursued them, still loudly bemoaning her fate, while struggling not to trip over her loose *Ankara* wrapper.

"Call Barrister Chidi right away," Dr. Obidike's urgent voice seized Chike's attention even before his father grabbed him by his shirt front with his free hand. The other was holding the oxygen mask away from his face. His eyes were piercing in the intensity of their stare. The stretcher came to a halt by the ambulance. "Call Barrister

Chidi to meet me at the Cardiac Centre right away. Tell him I said, 'Emergency Procedures.'"

He was taken away in the ambulance, while Chike and his mother followed in the white Jaguar. The entire staff of the residence stood outside watching the ambulance leave. The Ogene boys were outside too. They were not playing any music. Everyone wore mournful expressions.

Chike and his mother waited in the lobby of the hospital, Chike seated in one of the lounge chairs, his mother pacing, praying, and intermittently shouting in a random mixture of Igbo and English. Barrister Chidi arrived, carrying several files, and walked up to Chike. "I've spoken to the doctor, and he asked me to come into the ward." That said, he walked away toward the wards. Shortly after, two ladies that Chike recognized from Zenith Bank walked past, almost at a trot. They also followed the same path as Barrister Chidi. Fifteen minutes passed and one of the ladies from the bank returned and beckoned Chike, saying, "He would like to speak with you."

Mrs. Obidike, who had eventually taken a seat, jumped up. "Thank you, Jesus, thank you Jesus, he is speaking!

"Chike we are going together, oh! He will speak to me too!

"He will speak to me!

"My husband will live!

"My husband will not die!"

She followed them through the hallway, wrapper trailing behind her and her pale pink underskirt partially exposed. She had left her scarf behind in the lobby and her hair was a wild mess. Chike walked into the private room and saw a shadow resembling his father laid up with all sorts of tubes going in and coming out of him. Barrister Chidi was standing by his side and holding his hand, but when Dr. Obidike saw Chike, he let go of Barrister Chidi's hand and waved Chike closer. Once Chike was close enough, his father pulled him close and whispered to him for a long time, occasionally pointing to the lawyer and banker respectively. Mrs. Obidike respected her husband too much to interrupt – and she held her peace close to the door of the room – but she looked like a coiled spring with all her barely suppressed anxiety.

Dr. Obidike turned to the banker and said with a frail voice, "I have signed all the papers; execute my instructions right away. I mean right now." He pulled Chike to him again and whispered a few more sentences.

"What is he saying? What are you people saying so quietly?" Mrs. Obidike could no longer contain herself. "My husband will not die," she declared in defiance. "Daddy, you will not die. You will not leave me, you hear, daddy?"

She moved to her husband and Chike stepped out of her way, allowing her to take hold of Dr. Obidike's face and kiss him while shaking him and imploring him not to leave her. The medical staff moved in then.

"Easy, ma, easy. Ma, we need to move him into surgery right away." As the doctor spoke, nurses and two male orderlies transferred Dr. Obidike from the bed to a gurney, and then wheeled him out of the room. Chike noticed that one of the gurney's wheels had a pronounced squeak and something in the rhythm of the squeaking wheel made him was certain this was the end.

The banker and lawyer crowded Chike with their encouragements and consolations. "It is well Chike, it is well. Let's thank God he had this moment to tidy up everything."

"It is well."

The squeak of the receding gurney wheel mocked them. Nothing is well, the squeaking wheel pronounced; this is the end for this passenger I bear. They all walked back into the lobby and Mrs. Obidike continued her prayers.

They were there for about an hour. The bankers and Barrister Chidi had left within minutes of Dr. Obidike's removal to the theater. "Chike what was your dad telling you?" Mrs. Obidike felt she had piled up enough prayers to take time to satisfy her curiosity.

"Man talk, mum, man talk."

"If I slap your head off your shoulders... what was he telling you?"

"Muummm! No more violence! Enough of all the throwing of slippers and slaps. I'm a man now; no violence. It doesn't even hurt anymore! You are growing old."

"You said this the same way when you were about five years old."

"Ma, if you paid me a dollar for every time you told me you would slap my head off my body, I would be a billionaire now."

Mrs. Obidike flared her nostrils and raised her right hand, almost like she was about to take an oath, and snarled, "A headless billionaire. Now what did he tell you?"

"Nothing that is important right now, mum. Trust me."

"*Sebi* he will get well and come and explain everything to me?" Mrs. Obidike muttered to herself and wandered off.

The doctor came out and signalled to Chike. "We administered an anti-poison intravenously before he went into surgery. He appears to have developed some radical allergic reactions to the anti-poison and we immediately went into transfusion. We have to wait for the transfusion to be complete and stabilize him before we can attempt any surgery.

"We remain very hopeful the surgery will be fine, but I must confess, you have to prepare for the worst."

"Doctor, save him. Whatever it costs, save him!

"The jet is standing by at the airport. If you can't handle this, just let me know on time. We have a Challenger 650. In exactly five hours, we can be in Amsterdam."

"Chike, your dad's condition is bad. His liver will pack up in another few minutes, but we are going to open him up – we found a liver that matches – but what do we know has happened to the other organs? Long-term exposure to the effects of arsenic poison can be devastating to the organs, Chike. Make no mistake, his condition didn't just begin recently. The damage is extensive!

"Chike, get your mother together - your father may not make it back from the surgery, if he makes it past the transfusion in the first place."

"The prognosis is not good, so please follow me and come and say your farewells."

6

By the time they got to the prep room, Dr. Obidike's sheet was pulled over his head. Mrs. Obidike gave a long, loud wail that was heard all through the large hospital. The doctor gave a sign to the nurses, and they immediately gave her an injection that sedated her. She woke up in her bed at their mansion and found two nurses standing at her side and Chike sitting beside her.

"It is over, Chikereuba. Over! Nothing to live for, Chike.

"That was my best friend, that was my life. My life is gone, son, all gone…" Chike said nothing as his mother dissolved in tears. He merely held her hands as she wept. He remained silent even when his mother began to rant.

"But can't we go there to pray? Jesus woke the dead! He said we will do the same things he did!

"We should go back and wake him up!

"We are Christians! Jesus said we have the power to do everything he did on earth!

"Chike, prayer of agreement! Prayer of agreement! Let us not give up!

"We have the power to wake him!"

Mrs. Obidike wrung the bedcovers and began to speak in tongues.

"Rabashaka logo reke robo! Chike, come closer. Pray, pray, pray!" She fell back on the bed and then bolted into a sitting position again, still praying.

"He's not dead, Chikereuba; he is not dead!"

One of the nurses approached her and Mrs. Obidike turned on her with fierce eyes, shrieking, "If you come any closer, I will wipe your face with this table lamp! You people want to make me a widow? I reject it! I reject it in Jesus' name! God forbid!

"Chike, get these evil nurses away from me, and let me show them my God is able."

Chike nodded to the second nurse, and she pulled out a hypodermic syringe and began to draw up liquid from a small, clear bottle.

"They want to give me injection and run me mad? Chikereuba, stop them! Get them out of here at once, I say!"

Chike said nothing and sat still as Nurse 1 expertly secured his mother's arm and Nurse 2 jabbed her with the needle. She opened her mouth, perhaps to scream, but was unconscious before it could open fully. The nurses eased her back into a lying position and turned to Chike.

Nurse 2 said, "We will stay here with her while you go back in to complete all the necessary paperwork." Chike left to do the paperwork… he was good at paperwork.

7

When Chike got back from the hospital, Mrs. Obidike was still fast asleep. He sat by her side until she awoke. In a hoarse voice, she asked, "Where is my husband?" Chike just looked back at her with a heartbroken expression.

"Nnamdi where are you?"

Mrs. Obidike was still very weak from the sedative and failed when she tried to get up. She slumped back on the king-sized bed.

"Mum, you need to calm down. Dad is in a better place and… you need to be strong. Dad and I spoke before he passed, and he was able to do the needful."

Mrs. Obidike struggled to sit up, gasping, "Chike, we need to act fast! Your uncles killed your father! They are deadly and they will come after you next." Then she seemed to give up her struggles to rise and her eyelids fluttered. Chike stroked her clammy brow and said, "Mum, lie down. I have everything under control. Rest for a while and we will discuss next steps properly when you are strong again." Chike shut the heavy white door as he walked out of his parents' room. He looked down from the mezzanine into the large living room and he saw all the domestic staff seated on the floor, wearing almost comically identical expressions of sadness. They looked up and saw Chike and there was another long bout of wailing and crying.

8

In his room that evening, Chike knelt by his bed, covered his head with a pillow and he cried out loud. His jaw itched with the untended crop of thick black hair that covered it – he had not shaved in weeks – and he had become the spitting image of his father. In the days that followed, sadness descended on the Obidike compound, and the staff despaired, not knowing what would become of them. Some had left immediately, while others lingered, waiting to learn their fate after Dr. Obidike's demise. The week was longer than usual as many dignitaries far and wide came to the Obidike mansion to commiserate with the family. Many of these visitors paused to consider the life-sized portrait of the late chief, standing in the entrance foyer, before bending to sign the large, leather-bound condolence register beside it. Some people came just to sign the register and leave, others simply didn't leave at all. It was customary for family to come from the village to mourn their relative, but it was hard to contend with the horde of strangers that arrived under this guise and took up residency in the mansion's rooms. They did this as a matter of course, without seeking permission. The chef worked round the clock to prepare meal after meal for these uninvited guests. The pantry had to be restocked twice in a week. Within a few days, all twenty-two bedrooms at the Obidike mansion were filled with 'family' from Mbano and Arochukwu.

In theory, all these people were here to make preparations for the final rites of their illustrious son, and the elders guided the meetings on the burial arrangements. The estate gate was left open for a never-ending stream of cars and pedestrians, some bearing personal belongings, which included goats and chickens. The mansion soon developed a foul smell to accompany the tense atmosphere. Aggravating as it was for Chike and his mother, according to the traditional rules, the house now belonged to the family – the deceased *man's* family, apparently, not the wife and family that had lived with him up till his death.

Duke, the head chef complained to Mrs. Obidike about the eating habits of their guests and asked that she make provision to replenish the pantry. She erupted. "Over my dead body! Over my dead body! Who are these people?

"Who are they?"

"Where were they when we were at Jobore with nothing?!"

"Where were they when I had to sell my blood in Liverpool to pay my husband's school fees?"

"Who does this? Shows up in a dead man's house and declares a festival!?"

"Duke! Shut the Kitchen! Stop the cooking! Enough is enough!"

"I will not drop one kobo for their feeding. *Sebi* they have said I'm a witch; but they can come into the house of a witch and eat up all her food!"

"Duke, stop the cooking! Enough is enough!"

By this time, Mrs. Obidike was shrieking, and her sentiments were clearly heard all over the mansion.

Yet, more 'relatives' arrived. Some had started camping out on the lawn in front of the swimming pool. The entire estate was littered with people from Dr. Obidike's village.

A week and four days passed and many of the guests had started cooking their own food with firewood on the lawn of the premises; there was smoke everywhere, but not enough to obscure the piles of trash and dirty pots and pans that littered the grounds. Firewood smoke accompanied the non-stop flute-and-percussion sounds of the *Okenga* musicians, who had an unspoken pact with the *Ogene* boys, ensuring that they never occupied the same part of the estate while playing. Both groups performed mourning songs for Dr. Obidike. The once quiet neighborhood became a noisy village festival. Elder after elder arrived from the village to make preparations for the funeral of their son and, with each arrival, the heated arguments that accompanied their deliberations intensified.

They argued about traditional rites, ceremonial details, roles of the titled elders, and the logistical 'support' that should be made available to the key players. On this day, the bone of contention was on which parcel of their ancestral lands Dr Obidike's body should be buried, and the yelling could be heard at the opposite end of the street. This was when Mrs. Obidike, who had been left out of all of the planning up till that point, sauntered into the midst of the shouting men, banging a rolling pin against a silver tray until they fell quiet and glared at her. "Since nobody has asked me," she declared casually, "I have no choice but to come and tell you; I and my family want my husband to be buried in Lagos."

The elders, to a man, leapt to their feet, enraged. "Abomination! Abomination," Mazi Obidike shouted. "Over my dead body!

"Lagos? Lagos! Woman, you insult us once again!

"You insulted us all through the life of our brother and sat on his head with your witchcraft. Now, you want a Red-Cap chief to be buried in Lagos?"

"*Tufiakwa*! Over my dead body!"

"Our brother was a very wealthy man – we all know – and obviously you are now trying to secure your piece of the pie, eh?" Here, he turned away from Mrs. Obidike and panned his gaze around the gathering of men. Mazi Obidike had a vicious parody of a smile on his face. "*Igbo kwenu*," he roared, and the room shook as the gathering roared back. He turned back to Mrs. Obidike and his voice dropped to a bemused hiss.

"So, because our brother treated you like a little queen, you now feel like a ruler of men, eh? Telling us where we will bury our blood?"

"Mazi, I am not interested in ruling any men, please! I am his wife and mother to his only son; have I no voice in the matter of his burial? All these people invade my home, destroy my things, decide my fate, and I should just keep quiet? Have you no regard for me at all?"

Mazi Obidike turned to the elders again, this time with genuine amusement, then rounded on Mrs. Obidike once more. "Wife? Mother to his only son? Your home? Your things? Woman, you would do well to be quiet. In fact, SHUT UP!" Mazi's visage was livid as he howled at her. "You own exactly NOTHING of my brother's."

"Or you don't know my brother had a family in the village?"

"Oh, he didn't tell you?"

"Oh, you think all this is for *your* only son?"

"Your husband did not tell you your son is not the Diokpa?"

"Let me enlighten you; my brother had a family in the village that you have always been at pains to keep him from. A woman who bore him his *first* son. Whom he would have married, but for your seductions and witchcraft. Now the rightful heirs will claim what is theirs and you –"

"Which family," Mrs. Obidike shrieked. "Which family, I ask you? A bastard child that YOU fathered?" Mazi Obidike froze and his eyes darted about the room. He noticed that several other people, men and women, had filled the room, and many of them seemed to be Mrs. Obidike's relatives.

"You think I don't know that you slept with your brother's fiancé? Why not claim your son so he can inherit your rags when you die?"

"Woman, *mechieonu*! Your viper's tongue will not work here today. Your charms cannot work on us! Your lies and your disrespect expose you for who you are! You were just after his money, otherwise you would never seek to have him buried in Lagos. Lagos! A descendant of Okoro Torti! *Ngwanu*, go and bury him now, and see if the god of thunder, Amadioha, will not strike you dead!"

The younger Obidike brother slammed his fist against the wall, adding, "Carry him and bury him and see if Amadioha, the only god of thunder will not destroy you and your bastard son!"

"Whose son are you calling a bastard?" a voice shouted from the crowd by the room's entrance. Mazi Obidike realised that Mrs. Obidike's people did not come in here simply to spectate and, as he turned to the source of the voice, a bottle sailed across the room and shattered against the wall, dowsing the two of the elders in fermented palm wine. The living room erupted.

The men and women of Mrs. Obidike's family had come prepared for war. When one of the elders from Aro-chukwu slipped in the spilt palm wine, he grabbed blindly at Mrs. Obidike's wrapper to stop himself from going down. Mrs. Obidike keened at the affront and the hapless elder found himself being clubbed by two portly women bearing pestles. In the bedlam that ensued, the Obidike brothers slipped out of the room with the practised ease of men who know how to foment trouble and how to avoid its fallout. The luxurious living room was ripped to pieces as the brawl went on for several minutes. The large glass centre table was smashed, a bead of blood hanging suspended from one of the shards left sticking out of its gilt frame. The pale marble bust of Ceasar, once adorning the grand piano, laid on its side, surrounded by broken glass from the sliding door it had been thrown through, casting its serene gaze on the combatants. The domestic staff joined in the brawl to protect their late master's wife and kin. Duke came out of the kitchen with a large wooden mortar, his chef's hat flopping about impossibly, and joined the fight.

The Onyeadora side was badly outnumbered by the Obi-dike contingent, however, Mrs. Obidike soon found her-self being rough-handled by a group of irate Aro women, some of whom brandished knives and pans they had gone to get from the kitchen. The gardener, Chukwumereije, seeing his mistress in such peril, stepped out through the broken sliding door, over the prone bust of Ceasar, and returned with the high-pressure hose from the garden out-side. With barely a pause to aim, he pointed the nozzle in the direction of his mistress and unleashed a jet of water. The mob scattered as the water was sprayed everywhere. There was bedlam as the warring parties fled – and Chukwumereije caused about as much damage with the hose as the fighting itself had caused – but the hostilities within the house ended.

The Obidike brothers were joined outside by their towns-people, who chanted war songs and hurled gravel from the driveway at the building. Mazi Obidike told his people to stop destroying their own property and ushered them off the grounds, as they gathered their tattered clothes about their bodies and favored their wounds. Mrs. Obidike stood at the main entrance in triumph as they left, but Mazi Obidike was to have the last word. "Jezebel," he cried, "I will not allow you to deliberately destroy my brother's things just because you know you cannot have them.

"He is gone now and, according to tradition, I AM DI-OKPA! How his wealth will be apportioned is MY decision! So, first of all, I will leave instead of giving you and your riff-raff an excuse to spoil what is mine."

"But when we return, you and your ill-bred spawn, Chike, will be driven out! Mark my words, woman, DRIVEN OUT... WITH NOTHING!"

9

Mrs. Obidike stood on the balcony overlooking the swimming pool. She was dressed in the black boubou that had become her uniform over the past month, with a black silk scarf that dangled over the stainless-steel railings she was leaning on. She looked drawn and emaciated, with noticeably darker skin. "Chike," she called, "Come and see what your father's people have done to my Bonsai tree! *Chai!* See what they have done to my garden, oooohhhh!"

As she surveyed the wreckage of what was once a lush garden, an old lady drifted toward the Bonsai tree, followed closely by a group of four other seniors from the village. The lawn had grown wild and the compound was littered with empty water bottles and trash.

Following the dust-up in the living room, there had been a temporary exodus of the Aro invaders from the late chief's mansion. *Mazi* Obidike was not going to allow the enemy hold what he now claimed as his own territory, but he was practical enough to want to avoid the all-out war that would ensue if he sent the titled elders back to continue planning his late brother's last rites. So, in a cunning master stroke, he simply sent in the oldest available relatives he could find, along with a few small children – essentially daring Mrs. Obidike and her horde to mistreat them or deny them shelter. The deliberations over the funeral were now conducted at one of his unoccupied houses, where he had sequestered the relevant group of titled elders. Meanwhile, the feeble old and vulnerable young infiltrated Dr. Obidike's mansion within two days of the living room brawl and acted as a reminder to Mrs. Obidike that the war was far from over.

"Mama, please leave my Bonsai tree, ah beg you," Mrs. Obidike barked down at the little old lady who had finally shuffled her way to the ragged tree. The old lady ignored her and ripped off a branch, breaking off several small twigs and handing them to the small group of two other geriatric women, one shriveled old man, and a 3-year-old girl. They all promptly stripped their twigs of their barks and stuck them in their respective mouths, chewing and cleaning their teeth. They wandered away from the tree, much like a flock of birds in formation, and perched by the edge of the swimming pool, into which they began spitting their chewed-up mulch.

"No, you can't do this! Not in my pool!" Mrs. Obidike's hoarse protests were feeble at best – more reflex than anything else – as she was resigned to the carnage that had befallen her home.

"Chike, see what your uncles are doing to us; see, see, see?

"That old man had just washed his clothes and poured the soapy water into the swimming pool."

Chike, who had come up behind his mother, gently stroked the stubbly growth on her scalp where her long, dark hair had been.

"Chike, why? Why? Why are you not doing anything to stop these people?"

"Mum, calm down. I'm working on something. Sorting everything out. You just need to trust me."

"Trust you, Chike? Trust you? The Mbano elders say they are coming on Friday to throw us out of this house! Already the whole place is littered with their stinking old bushmen. Look what they have done to my house. They have to be stopped! Dealt with!"

"I have told you to leave these people alone," Chike soothed. "These are mercenaries from the village, sent by my father's brothers to make your life miserable. Don't let them succeed!" Chike paused, taken aback by his mother's intense glare. "Mum, what is it? Why are you looking at me like that?"

"Chike, I went to the morgue; your father's corpse has been moved!

"How can they just move my husband's body?

"Why won't they let me bury my husband?

"What did I do to *Mazi* to deserve this?

"Chike what are we going to do?" Mrs. Obidike was crying quietly.

"What will we do, Chike? What will we do? They won't let me bury my husband so the man can rest in peace." She leaned on Chike and her shoulders rose and fell as she sobbed.

"Calm down, mother, I told you I have everything under control. It shall be well, trust me."

"When I raised the alarm, the Mbano people told me they too went to the mortuary yesterday – to arrange to move your father's body to the village – and the body was not there! See the games they are playing, Chike? They stole the body and now are acting like they don't know anything.

"How can anyone move a corpse from the state morgue without a death certificate?

"Chike the death certificate is with you, right? They must have forged i-

"Look at that one, Chike, look at that one!" Her voice cleared for a moment and went up an octave as she took in the scene unfolding before them in the garden below. "Stop! Stop! You can't urinate there, you animal! I mean, who pees in a swimming pool?

"Chike, please call the police. I cannot take this any longer."

"Let's go in mother. Forget all about this mess, take your meds and get some rest."

"Rest? They have stolen my husband's body from the mortuary; how can I rest?"

"A few more days, mum; everything will become clear soon. Soon you will see the full picture and you will be at ease. Please just be patient."

Chike walked his mother through the sliding door, pushing the heavy velvet curtain aside to allow her through. She sat on the bed, looking wistfully down at the rumpled sheets. "This is my darling's side," she sighed. "This is where he sleeps. He would tap me on the back and say, 'Winnie, this is my side of the bed for a reason; it is closer to the door! I have to protect you from any intruder – *that* is why I sleep on this side." She burst into tears and fell on her side with her face in her hands. Chike looked down at his mother, feeling helpless at the sight of her shaven head – a requirement according to the Igbo tradition – and marvelling at how small it was. Finally, he said, "This is war, mother. You need to brace yourself and be strong. We have already won, but our enemies don't know it yet."

Days swallowed days and several delegations came to Mrs. Obidike to threaten her over her late husband's missing body. They accused her of hiding it to force her agenda of burying him in Lagos and she accused them of stealing the remains to torment her. She was convinced Dr. Obidike's brothers were in possession of the body and were toying with her. The date fixed for the funeral came and passed and there still was no body to bury. Nobody knew who hid Dr. Obidike's body. One afternoon, two weeks into the debacle, Chike came into his mother's room with Barrister Chidi and they went to the adjoining study to talk. They sat around the coffee table and Barrister Chidi, resplendent in his black pinstriped pants and a white tunic shirt, opened his black pilot case and brought out a blue manila file, looking questioningly at Chike.

"Should I?"

Chike nodded.

Barrister Chidi cleared his throat and began to speak.

"I won't speak for too long. My client, your husband, had anticipated a lot of what is happening now and spent the last few years preparing for it.

"He gave me specific instructions to commence filing emigration papers to the United States.

"He had been negotiating the purchase of a large hospital group with its headquarters in Chicago, and I made several trips to negotiate the purchase.

"He had paid several large tranches of money and the final payment was due a few days before he passed on. Your husband was very meticulous. He ensured he transferred these funds without breaching any money laundering legislation. His taxes were duly filed too.

"Simultaneously he had begun the immigrant business residency program, which gives automatic residence to

604

the family of an investor – of a certain quantum – in the United States.

"Chief exceeded this quantum, and the government of the United States was very pleased about this capital injection, which was fully approved before he passed on and I am in possession of the papers.

"Doctor had bought a piece of land, roughly the same size as this property, in the suburbs of Chicago and commissioned the same architect, to precisely duplicate your home in that city. As a matter of fact, we went to Italy together to meet with Fabrizio, the Italian interior decorator that did this mansion. Your husband was a man of remarkable taste." He looked up at Mrs. Obidike, who stared at him with shocked incredulity, then looked down at his papers and continued.

"We successfully acquired immigration papers for the key domestic staff and some of their immediate families, so your domestic operations can also be transferred with minimal disruption.

"Your husband's instructions were that you should not have to take a single item with you from here, as it had been carefully replicated in Chicago, in every detail, including the cars.

"Dr. Obidike was able to consolidate all his cash into one account and gave Chike sole power of attorney over that account. This would be effective upon signing this document." Barrister Chidi turned a sheaf of papers such that

Chike could read them and spread them out before taking a deep breath and continuing. "The entire cash balance came to about eight billion US dollars."

Mrs. Obidike gasped but could not speak.

"I have included audited accounts in my report. We have completed all the fiscal compliance processes for moving this capital to the United States and we have paid all the inheritance tax expectations of the United States government.

"Dr. Obidike owned two Bombardier aircraft, the larger of which will transport the staff. The smaller one would be for yourself and Chike.

"His will has been deposited in the probate department and we will make certified copies available before you head out of Nigeria.

"For your safety, I will suggest you not discuss any of these details with anyone. I promised your husband I would get you out of here safely and the pilots are on standby at the airport. It is vital that you make swift arrangements to depart as you are no longer safe here, madam."

"God forbid," Mrs. Obidike finally spoke up with a tone of aggressive obstinacy. "God forbid that I should leave my husband's body and go to America! You and Chike can take your billions and go if you like, but I might as well die here too, if I cannot bury my husband!"

"Madam, provision has been made for your husband's corpse," Barrister Chidi replied.

"What?"

"I moved daddy's body, mum," Chike said softly.

"*Chai*, Chike!" Mrs. Obidike was aghast. Barrister Chidi placed a gentle hand on her shoulder. "Your husband's remains will be on that flight with you to Chicago. The undertakers are preparing to receive him, and a befitting resting place has been prepared for him there."

Mrs. Obidike looked at Chike with tears in her eyes and hugged him.

The following week, Dr. Obidike's last will and testament was opened and read at the probate department of the Igbosere High Court. After the reading, the family walked out in silence, Mrs. Obidike leading. She was dressed in a black gown and had on a pair of large, dark Channel sunglasses. Chike held his mother's hands and walked by her side, while Barrister Chidi walked behind them. Bringing up the rear was the head chef, Duke, the longest serving staffer of the Obidikes and the informal chairman of the equally informal Obidike Domestic Staff Union.

"Say nothing, mum," Chike reminded his mother quietly as some commotion broke out behind their small party. The Obidike brothers were behind their group, cursing and taunting them in the Igbo language. "Barrister! Barrister! You did not say anything about the whereabouts of my brother's body.

"You people have stolen my brother's corpse!

"Whooooooooooooo," *Mazi* cried derisively. "You people have stolen my brother's corpse!

"You came here thinking my brother left property for you – *onyeoshi*!

"Husband snatcher!

"You will sell *akara* in this Lagos! You and your bastard *Oyibo* son!

"*Onyeoshi*!

"Did I not tell you your son is not *Diokpa*?

"You people will move out of that property by tomorrow morning!

"The real *Diokpa* is moving in!

"I trust my brother; he will not disappoint his REAL family.

"*Chineke*, everything in the bank belongs to me, the *Diokpa* of the Obidike family! *Shishi* you people will not get!

"Nsonsosoronsonso belongs to Amadi, his first son, *biko*.

"All the cars belong to me.

"*Ashawo*, what did you get? *Deadi-Bodi*! *Deadi-bodi*, oooohhhhhh!" He flapped his open palm against his mouth as he keened, making an ululating sound of mockery.

Mrs. Obidike looked back but didn't say a word. Chike held one of her hands and grabbed her opposite shoulder to help her down the large stairs of the High court. The sky was thick with dark clouds and a light drizzle warned of heavier rains to come. There was very heavy foot traffic outside the court gate, as people hastened to find shelter before the imminent downpour. The black Rolls Royce pulled up and Chike grabbed the silver door handle, pulled it open, and eased his mother in. He looked up one final time at *Mazi* Obidike and his brothers and gave them the middle finger. Then he headed around toward the other side of the car. Mazi Obidike, started shouting again.

"*Oyeoshi*! Thief! Thief! Armed robber!

"You people will suffer in this Lagos. *Una tiff deadibodi!*"

"*See weda dead body no go fight una!*

"*Make una chop am! Onyeoshi!*"

His brothers held him as he shouted louder, almost falling down the beige concrete stairs. As Chike reached the back door on the other side of the car, he was blocked by his cousin - the son of the youngest of the Obidike brothers – Emeka.

"Chike, let me speak to you for a minute."

"I have nothing to speak to you about, cousin. The will has been read and we are not contesting it."

"Chike, you guys are finished! You got nothing! I think you should join us, and we will be merciful to you. Your wicked father gave you nothing... Nothing!"

"Please, can you move out of the way, so I can get into my car?"

"Chike, you people will suffer, don't you get it? In a few days, you'll be thrown out of the Obidike mansion! Join us, Chike, join us! So, you can get a small something to take care of you and your PROSTITUTE MOTHER! Hahahahahaha!"

Chike slammed the heavy door, shutting out the scornful laughter, and the Silver Spur glided out of the court premises, the driver making an elegant right turn in front of the Tafawa Balewa Square. Chike grabbed his mother's hands and squeezed them. "God bless dad, mum, God bless dad. He tidied up well."

"Oh, Chike, your father always planned well . . . but this is almost funny, though. His will said his brothers can take possession, 'within the law', of the Ikoyi mansion, but they did not understand the language. The land belongs to the Catholic church and the lease expires next month!"

"Hmmmmm. Now I see. I always wondered why our house looked like a church."

"It was designed like a cathedral, Chike, so the church could take possession whenever we vacated it. It had been a 5-yearly lease agreement but now there is no one to renew it. They are in for a rude awakening."

"Your father gave the house in the village to his first son and the mother, which truly is the fair thing to do, along

611

with a stipend that sorts them out for a very long time."
She paused, musing, then chuckled. "All the money left
in the Zenith Bank account... bequeathed to Mazi Obidike!" At this point, Mrs. Obidike was laughing hysteri-
cally. "Oh, my God!"

"Did you see Mazi's eyes when that part was read, mum?
He has no clue! There is only about a thousand dollars
left there and, in the Naira account, maybe twenty k!

"That was what dad was doing at the hospital when the
bank lady came with Barrister Chidi. Even in death, he's
a comedian."

"But, Chike, you kept all these from your mother?"

"Mum, dad specifically told me not to mention anything
to anyone."

"Oh, I'm anyone now?"

"Muuummm."

"Eight billion dollars and you kept mute?"

"I had to respect the wishes of the dead. My father's dying wish."

"Do you know I didn't know your father had this much?"

"Yes, dad made a killing from the last vaccine. He also
sold the shipping line to the Chinese for twenty times
more than than he paid for it."

"But I am baffled by the mansion thing, though. Building a mansion like that on leased land... Who does that?"

"Your father was a major supporter of the Catholic church. He built the house like a cathedral. If you knock off the high internal walls what you would get is the most beautiful cathedral. It was designed by Fabrizio, who built the mini basilica in Prague – we met him on one of our European cruises – and he has designed our home in Chicago the same way."

"Well, I hope that one doesn't belong to the Catholic church too."

"No way! Come on, Chike!"

"This is the joke of the year. It won't take long for his brothers to realize they just inherited a cathedral that will belong to the Catholic mission in a matter of weeks.

"He who owns the land, owns the building on it."

Book-10

War

Si mawdo wi'ii modan jammbere ni nannganaa dum legal

(If a man says he will swallow an axe, hold the handle for him – Fulani proverb)

1

Adigun sat alone on his cot, flipping through the Maryland Herald newspaper. He was reading through a write-up by Bridget Cambridge, who laid out Adelaide's boxing career and the speculations surrounding his disappearance from the scene. There was talk in the boxing federation about him relinquishing his regional title if he didn't stage a defence within about a month. Might as well mail you guys the belt right now, Adigun thought numbly, mourning his now-dead boxing dream. There was no way he could pursue it without Bobby Brown, his trainer and handler, even if he didn't have bigger problems with elements on both sides of the law. He ran his fingers through his thick afro – he hadn't had a haircut since arriving at the ranch – and contemplated the course of his life.

Adigun had spent five hostile months at the ranch. He had seen Phoebe only once. at the train station, when she brought him some food. The relationship between himself and Digger was strained after the episode at the cemetery, and it became impossible for him to remain in the main house. He moved into the shed next to the stables and spent a pretty penny refurbishing the warm cabin, turning it into a comfortable bedsit. He put in air conditioning and a top-of-the-range Bang & Olufsen home entertainment system and often played host to the horse grooms and ranch hands that he had befriended. Notwithstanding his inability to fight professionally, Adigun created a mini-gym next to the paddocks, re-purposing disused car axles, flywheels and other scrap metals from around the farm. He was as fit as a bull. Despite his discord with Digger, he helped groom the horses and, over the course of the five months, he had become a horseman of beyond average competence, including the ability to break and train wild horses.

Through the classifieds, he found and discreetly arranged the delivery of an almost new Land Rover Defender to allow him to make the weekly trips to all the distribution cemeteries around Maryland without recourse to taxi services, which he considered too risky, or having to rely on Digger, his reluctant host. He learned that Phoebe was not allowed on the Gershoms' property because of the heavy feud between her and Diane from long ago. Phoebe was not willing to talk about it but she made it clear to Adigun that if Digger tried to evict him from the ranch, he would be in jail after a single phone call from her.

She had once covered up a very serious crime for Digger and she had him by his balls. Her exact words. She didn't elaborate, but Adigun believed her assertion and was less anxious about the possible consequences of Digger's antagonism. He relaxed enough to enjoy his new, secluded lifestyle and was sure that, as long as the business kept running, he would remain alive.

Adigun stayed away from the main house but continued to run the business of the Edguardo cartel. Impossible as it seemed at the beginning, he had bought himself some time by sending a message to the Colombian Boss of Bosses through the Bowie accountant. The message was simple; *If I was the snitch, then I would be running or in witness protection, not a fugitive from the cartel and the feds alike. The books are still in order and the business is still afloat. I know there is nowhere to hide and I'm not trying to hide. Give me the room to operate and let me honour my father. If I do not prove myself, you can do with me as you will.*

He kept up the cash deliveries to the accountants in all the cemeteries and kept ongoing transactions in play. The shipment lost to the raid had been substantial, but the immediate distribution activities had not yet been affected. The part he felt worst about was having to drag Phoebe into the operation. She put up a hell of a fight but, in the end, was persuaded that Adigun's only chance of survival was to keep the business running and try to make good with the cartel. Now, reluctantly, she was helping him with the product distribution until they could figure out some other solution.

Adigun heard the unmistakable sound of tyres crunching on the gravel outside and looked out of his small window. Several cars had pulled up and were offloading a colourful bunch of children dressed up in cowboy and Indian outfits. Adigun recalled that it was Tishan and Tyrone's twelfth birthday and they were hosting a costume party. The twins, decked out as Apaches, complete with bows and arrows, met their guests outside and the grooms started prepping the children to mount the already-saddled horses. Other children arrived and were soon mounted on horses of various sizes. It was clear that the grooms were carefully instructed in the specifics of which child should be given which mount, according to their levels of horsemanship, and Adigun was certain that this was Diana's doing. She was organized like that. Neurotic too.

The children were all good enough to participate in the equestrian games and they had a rollicking time. Adigun sat on his double bed, watching them in an absent-minded way until his attention was drawn further out to the training section, where Diego, one of the grooms, was helping one of the children mount a horse, and having some trouble by the look of things. Adigun knew the horse – it was Cadaver – and knew it had a habit of bolting off to the stables. The way the animal was bucking, Adigun was certain it would be bolting any second and his body was moving before he was aware of it. He lost sight of the horse as he turned away from his window, but he heard the gasps and cries that could only mean Cadaver had bolted and was charging towards its stable, with a terrified child in its saddle. As he emerged from his doorway, and with no thought at all, Adigun threw his arms in the air, yelling, "Hya! Hya!" causing Cadaver to veer away from him and rear up on its hind legs momentarily. This gave Adigun the chance he needed to grab the reins and bring the horse under control. He clucked in Cadaver's ear, soothing the animal, as he stroked its snout gently.

Carlos reached Cadaver first and immediately busied himself with dismounting the trembling child, a small

Japanese boy who was already reaching for his parents as they rushed to the scene. "Good grip, kid," Adigun called out to him before he was smothered by his parents, who kept casting grateful glances in Adigun's direction. The other children and parents gaped from a distance, not having had enough time to ascertain that it was now safe to gather around the near-victim of a potentially fatal event. The father stood, taking a backward look to ensure his son was secure with his mother, then approached Adigun and bowed deeply. "Thank you for saving my son," he said as the other parents broke their paralysis and came closer. Soon there was a chorus of thanks and remarks about his heroism. One of the parents looked closer at Adigun.

"You look very familiar. You look like the cruiserweight championship contender that disappeared from the scene."

"Oh, wow! I get that all the time," Adigun replied with forced cheeriness.

"Oh, wow he does look like the African kid, Fernandez or what's his name?"

"Oh, no, no. I am much better-looking than he is."

Digger emerged from the house and trotted toward the group surrounding Adigun and the grateful family.

"I'm so glad Kazoo didn't get hurt," he said to the shaking boy's father, then turned to Adigun and continued, saying, "Thanks so much, Michael. I'm very grateful.

"Mrs. Kobayashi, can we proceed into the house? I think it's time to stop the riding and turn the horses out."

Adigun walked quickly back into his cabin.

The party continued in the Gershom's living room and on their porch.

Adigun left the ranch and drove to the Pimlico cemetery in New Hampshire, where he took delivery of a routine deposit. It was a long drive back to Maryland, and he had arranged to meet with Phoebe at the Grand Hyatt in Mateus Vineyard. He checked in with his real name, Adigun Komaiya, and went up to his suite. He immediately picked up the phone and called the concierge.

"I asked for the Presidential suite – there seems to have been some sort of mistake…"

"I have stayed in so many Presidential suites, including the one your Las Vegas property; the presidential suite always has a separate dining area…"

"Well, if you say so, but this hardly seems *presidential*."

"Yes, I have seen the roses in the pool, they've been broken down to the petals! I gave no such instruction; I wanted them whole."

"Anyway, let's move on. Please have a butler and chef sent up right away…"

"I know you are fully sold out because of Valentine's but I want what I want, and I want you to make it happen!"

"That will NOT be accepta-"

"Hello? Hello?

"Did that twat hang up on me?"

When the phone rang, Adigun was on the balcony bemoaning the rose petals in the pool. He raced back, stockinged feet skittering on the white marble floor.

"Hello?

"Thanks so much.

"Please, can you make it quick? My guest will be here anytime now."

Adigun was flipping through the TV channels when the doorbell rang, and he opened the door to admit a tall, gaunt man in a tailcoat and a top hat.

"Good evening, Sir. I am Robert, your butler." Robert leaned forward in a tiny bow, inclining his head slightly.

"The kitchen awaits your instructions regarding dinner, Sir. I have with me a menu, but that is merely a guide; you have unlimited access to just about any cuisine from anywhere in the world."

"Oh really? Let's start with Nigeria then," Adigun cast a challenging glance in Robert's direction. The butler's unflappable demeanour wasn't at all ruffled. "You might find, Sir," he sniffed, "that we are more knowledgeable about dishes from that part of the world than you might expect. Some of our most prized guests are high networth Nigerians, and it might amaze you what our chefs can do with, say, potash, for example. We keep a ready supply of *pomo* for just this reason."

"*Pomo*? It's, '*kpomo*"; there is a 'K' at the beginning. You want to cook it and you can't pronounce it?"

"Pardon me, Sir, *k-pomo*," Robert sniffed. "In any case," he continued, "You will find that our chef's culinary skills far outstrip my linguistic abilities, Sir."

"Ah, Robert, *carry go, carry go*, but please let my guest come before we start; I don't want her to miss out on this."

"Don't worry, Sir, we have a food delivery chute directly from the kitchen. All dishes will arrive in a jiffy, nice and fresh."

Robert handed Adigun a wine list. "Sir, will you be having cocktails, spirits, or wine? We have a global vineyards tour, in which you get to taste from all the top Vineyards in the world including the famous Chateau Thieuley in Bordeaux, and Prosecco from Antica Cascina dei Conti di Roero."

Robert was French, as was apparent from his accent, in his mid-fifties, with a long, aquiline nose and arched brows that gave him the appearance of a snob. Adigun was still pondering his choices when the doorbell rang again. Robert glided to the door and returned, quietly announcing the arrival of *M'mselle* Phoebe in French.

Phoebe stalked into the room looking dishevelled. She was wearing a grey jogging suit and her hair was in an untidy ponytail. She dumped her bag at her feet and aimed a pointed look at Robert.

"Can you leave, please?"

The man looked at Phoebe, then, with some hesitation, at Adigun.

"I said get out," Phoebe snapped. "I need some privacy with my man!"

Robert glided silently out of the hotel room.

"What do you take me for, black man?" Phoebe's voice was rising, and Adigun was bewildered. "What do you take me for?"

"Calm down, Phoebe. What's th-"

"Shut the heck up! I will destroy you!!!"

Tears poured from her red-rimmed eyes. Adigun stood frozen, backing the glass door that revealed the blue Atlantic and the sunset over Mateus Vineyard, which cast a fiery glow across the rose petals in the pool.

"Adigun Komaiya, I will mess you up!" Phoebe snatched her bag off the floor and pulled out a sheaf of glossy prints and thrust them in Adigun's face. He reflexively slipped the gesture, just as he would any jab, and stepped back to try to focus on the images as Phoebe shook the pictures at him.

"What is this?" She screamed, "What is this? I save you from prison, get a place for you to hide and you go sleeping with the wife of your host?

"How shameful! After all I have done for you? All I am still doing?

"You have me making deliveries of drugs for you – drugs, motherfucker, drugs!" She flung the pictures to the ground in disgust.

"Twice a week I make drop-offs for you in several locations. Do you even ask me how I do it?

"This is how you repay me?

"Adigun why? Not with Diane! You are sleeping with Diane? I will deal with you, Adigun. I will personally send you to jail!"

She crumbled to her knees by the bed, weeping, while Adigun flipped through the pictures strewn across the floor. He had a moment of disorientation as he saw the images captured in the photographs – Diane pressed up against him, his hands on her shoulders, part of his face visible, the rest obscured by her head as she leaned into him in an apparent kiss. The situation coalesced in his mind around his crisp memory of the day these pictures must have been taken.

It had been a bizarre incident. Not long after he had moved into the shed, one morning, Diane came knocking and, when he opened the door, simply pushed her way in and lunged at him, planting a clumsy kiss on his stubbly chin and pressing herself against his body. He recalled that she had left the door open, and it was clear that the pictures had been taken by someone staked out in the shadows of the building opposite his entrance. At the time, he didn't even notice the door, focused as he was on untangling himself from Diane. As gently as he could, he had pushed her away from him, softly insisting that whatever she was thinking could never happen and that she wouldn't want to mess her life with Digger up over a silly indiscretion. She hadn't replied, although now that he thought about it, she hadn't had the look you'd expect from a woman who had just been rejected. He hadn't been able to interpret her expression that day, but he could now; it had been malice... and triumph. The pictures also cleared up something else that had puzzled him at the time, and he did not doubt who had taken them. Carlos, the Argentinian head groom, had come to him the next day and apologized to him. When he asked what for, Carlos – with whom Adigun enjoyed a pleasant relationship – just shook his head and walked off.

Adigun reached for the back of Phoebe's neck as he tried to tell her about what had happened. She flinched violently and whirled around, hissing, "If you ever put your hands on me again, I will kill you."

"You are nothing but an ungrateful dog! User! Treacherous pig!"

She buried her head deep in the white soft bedclothes and sobbed deeply.

"Why? Why?" Her cries were now muffled.

Adigun stood over her and said softly, "It isn't what you think, Phoebe. You should give me a chance to prove my innocence."

"Innocence? You slept with her, Adigun; she told me everything. To spite me. It was her revenge and you just handed it to her on a silver platter."

"I once dated Digger, but she took him from me.

"We were engaged to be married before this bitch came from Mississippi.

"That was my man!

"So, yes, we had an affair, but we called it off and promised it would never happen again. But of course, she has to sleep with my man, right? Balance the equation!"

"I didn't sleep with her, Phoebe."

Phoebe went on as if Adigun hadn't spoken.

"Then you prepare a Valentine's dinner? All this? With your drug money?

"You are going to jail, Diggy Boo. I promise you that.

"The parcel I delivered to your Silver Spring contact last night was the last one. Oh! I don't know how you got me into this mess. All to show that I love you.

"If any of your drug agents call my number again, I will hand them over to the police, you ungrateful bastard.

"I will cage you, Adigun! You will regret you ever got on that plane to America."

Phoebe snatched up her bag and sprang up, sprinting for the door, which she slammed behind her. Adigun stood in the silence she left behind for a full three minutes, then he settled his bill and left the Grand Hyatt.

2

By the time Adigun screeched to a halt at the Gershom ranch, his rage had built a full head of steam. He headed straight for the paddock, where Carlos was mounted on a white horse, scaled the fence and dragged the head groom roughly to the ground. As the horse galloped away, Adigun delivered a cocktail of hard slaps to the face of the stunned Carlos. Even in his volcanic rage, somewhere in the back of his mind, Adigun realised that, if he were to really hit this man, he would have a corpse on his hands. Still, by the time he stopped, Carlos was half conscious.

"You found out?" he sputtered weakly."

"You have ruined my life," Adigun growled. "Did you take the pictures when Diane came into my room to harass me?"

Carlos nodded in the affirmative, wincing at the pain. "I'm sorry. I didn't know what she was going to do; she just told me to start taking pictures once you opened the door or else. These people, Diane, have done a lot for me, my friend. I owe them everything." Blood was pouring out of his nose and mouth, so Adigun pulled him into a sitting position to prevent him from choking. He braced Carlos's back against the paddock fence. Without another word, Adigun rose and walked briskly toward the Gershom mansion.

The door was open and, as soon as the twins saw Adigun, they rushed towards him shouting "It's Shaaaaaaaangoooo!"

Adigun couldn't help the smile that rose on his face at this, until Didi and Diane came into view. "Diane, Didi Gershom, I will not have this conversation in front of your children – please can we talk outside?" The twins caught something in his voice and they nervously retreated into the mansion.

"I have been waiting for you as well," Didi snarled, "I need you to leave my property right now or I will call the cops. This is getting too messy.

"I will give you five minutes to leave this property, or I will call the police!"

"Oh my God, I am so sorry for you Adigun, I am sorry for you - you are in deep shit, and I want no part of it."

"Plus, you have no idea who you are dealing with; Pheobe?! Hmmmmm, you will find out yourself!"

Adigun's eyes slitted as he looked straight into Didi's face.

"You are threatening to call the cops?"

"Please ask them to bring two vans as I will kill you if I have to share a van with you."

"First of all, dude, the last time I checked, the offence of harboring a criminal and obstruction of justice carries the same jail term as the substantive offence; when they come for me, you will be also culpable.

"We are both criminals, and we will both be going to jail.

"I don't know who Phoebe is? Yes, I know Phoebe has some dirt on you, dude, and she will not watch you bring her man down!"

Didi Gershom paused for a second and shook his head. It occurred to him that he had stirred up calm waters and the whole situation could go south.

"No, no, no, let's talk this over like real men," he said demurely. "No need for all this talk of jail – not jail, not jail. I don't want to go to jail."

Adigun replied to him with a soft voice, almost whispering, "Okay, Mr. and Mrs. Stupid, I shall remain here in peace, and I will mind my business."

"Everyone will be at peace, but one thing has to be done; you, Diane, will look for Phoebe and you will let her know how you set me up."

"I don't care how you do it, but just get it done!"

"I have not come to harm anyone here, but if anyone lets slip anything about my being here to anyone, we are all going down." Adigun spread his arms wide and affected a sunny grin. "Now, let's all live like one happy family… like before. I'm only here for a short while, okay? I'll respect whatever you say about me interacting with the twins, but please let them hang with me. I would never do anything to harm any child."

Digger shook Adigun's hands and hugged him.

"I'm sorry, dude. I saw what you did to save that boy out there and I think I know where your heart is at. Besides which, you saved me a hell of a liability lawsuit risk when you caught that horse!"

"I'm sorry. Diane, please, can you give us a minute?"

Diane walked back silently into the house, shutting the large mahogany door behind her.

"Hey, buddy, I need to level with you; I have been paying attention to your moves over the last few weeks, and it's clear you are into some big-money shit. The way you kitted out your pad in the stable shed, that's liquid cash, man!" Digger's eyes fell and a look of shame came across his face, then he looked up at Adigun and said, "Man, with things like they have been, we still have the ranch and the business and all, but Diane and I are well over-extended. I got creditors on my ass and we aren't liquid at all." Another downward glance and when Digger looked back up at Adigun, his eyes were ablaze. "How can I be down? I'm willing to keep my mouth shut," he pleaded, "But how can a brother get a piece of the action? I know you can use a trusted hand."

Adigun realised he was gaping at Digger as if his jaw had a broken hinge. This one-eighty was a complete shock to him. He could barely respond. He remembered the near smugness with which Didi had shown him around the mansion, bragging about his expensive décor and exotic horses. Then he remembered his father telling him, many times, 'Don't believe everything you see, Adigun. Before you covet what you see, look at what is behind it.' Now, he looked at Didi and said, "it's more complicated than you think. There is a process, and I am not in full control of that process.

"I will need some time to think about this, okay? And if we do take this forward, I will first have to confirm your trustworthiness and loyalty before you can be in. You get me?"

Adigun shook his head as he looked at his shoes and muttered, "*Chai!!! Baba oloshi ni bobo yi, sha,*" as he started walking back to the shed.

"What was that? Was that African you just spoke to me?" Digger called after him. "Dude, what did you just say?"

Adigun saw Carlos, still down in the same spot where he left him, and helped him up.

"I'm sorry, buddy. Sorry I hurt you." Adigun went into his cabin and stayed there for the rest of the evening. It was already dark when his ringing phone woke him up. He looked at it and figured it must be Phoebe. He didn't pick it up.

Come morning, Adigun checked his messages. A dozen or so from Phoebe, pleading with him to pick up and one from Diane, curtly asking him to call her back. The latter worried him - Diane never called him. He jumped into a change of clothes and headed out toward the mansion.

Carlos was in the paddocks, lining up the first set of students for the day's lessons. Adigun reached the mansion and banged on the front door. "Is everything okay?" He blurted as Digger opened the door, then froze in place as he saw Phoebe sitting on the stairs with a cup of coffee.

"One big happy family again, right?" Digger smirked as Phoebe ran to Adigun and hugged him hard.

"I'm sorry, Diggy Boo. I'm so sorry.

"I love you, babes. I will never do anything to hurt you.

"I'm going to kneel the Nigerian way you taught me."

Still holding fistfuls of Adigun's sweatshirt, Phoebe dropped to her knees, whilst Digger and Diane watched. Adigun looked down at her calmly.

"Damn, Phoebe! You wasted a great night – that suite at the Grand Hyatt cost a lot of money!"

"Come on," he softened, "Get up and let's just go out for a walk in the fields."

As Adigun and Phoebe walked towards the door, Tyrone shouted out, "Can we come, Shango?" Digger replied immediately, "Not today – not right now."

They walked through the horse trail on the east side of the estate and watched the horses grazing at the bottom of the hill, all different shades of brown and several Palominos. Several Buckskins were grazing on the other side with a large herd of chestnuts.

"Oh, wow look at that!"

Adigun followed Phoebe's gaze to a beautiful cream horse galloping away into the meadow. "Oh, that's my favourite horse; it's a Cremello," he said. "it's such a calm horse, with a very soft mouth."

"What is a soft mouth, Boo?"

"Different horses have different degrees of responsiveness to the bits."

"The more responsive the horse is, the softer the mouth. You see the bit is the communication tool between the rider and the horse. If you have to yank the horse hard to communicate your intentions to the horse then that horse has a hard mouth."

"Oh, my! You have learnt a lot in such a short time."

"You can say that again, but I focussed more on the caring aspect than horsemanship, although Carlos told me I am a natural polo player and riding has been very therapeutic for me.

"But back to the reason why we came for this walk –"

Adigun stopped and looked into Phoebe's eyes.

"Don't you ever, I mean, *ever*, threaten me again. I have been through a lot to get where I am today. I didn't plan it or choose my path and I'm going to take every day as I find it, Phoebe."

"Adigun, your life is in danger. Bobby Brown is in jail with the rest of the Edguardo crime family and they are bound to blame you for it since you are the only one that didn't get pinched!"

"Phoebe, don't worry, I think I have bought us some room to operate; what kind of snitch gets you arrested and continues running the same business you were arrested for, huh?"

"I have kept the business going, I have remitted all the monies to the accountant, I have kept the secrets of the family safe. I am the only one outside of jail that has all the access codes to all the vaults – the entire network!"

"Everything continues like they were never arrested! But if he kills me, the business will stop, and nobody will know where the goods are or where the money is."

"Adigun, I'm sorry, but when does this end? I'm out, Boo! I'm out!"

"Shut up!" Adigun grabbed Phoebe's shoulders and shook her. "No, you're not, Phoebe; you are in too deep!

"There is something I need you to know; I paid the shops in all the drop-off areas you worked in for all their CCTV footage. It gets delivered to a mailbox I set up just for that purpose – my fancy home entertainment system isn't for cartoons, you see – I just need you to know I have footage of you distributing.

"Clear footage, from multiple angles. What I don't understand is the vehicle you used was a Lincoln that I have never seen before - it looks like one of those undercover cop cars."

"Oh, yes, I'm a cop," Phoebe sneered, "and I also working part-time as a chef! Hello? I rented the car from

Jiffy's rentals. Oh, you expect me to use a car registered to me to distribute narcotics?"

"You have footage on me? Dude, are you blackmailing me?"

"Not really. I love you Phoebe, but I have to build my own insurance scheme against this kind of foolishness you just pulled off. Read my lips; If you ever try to mess with me in that way again, remember we are in this together, we all go down!"

"Now that's what I call love!" Phoebe dripped sarcasm.

"You can't stop, Phoebe. If you stop, Bobby Brown will have me killed. As long as the operations are going on, I will be alive and, maybe with time, I can clear my name with the family." Adigun stopped and looked back the way they had come. The Gershom mansion looked minute from where they stood.

"We should head back; we have walked far.

"Why are you silent, Phoebe?"

"I want out, Adigun. I can't continue this. I want to know when this is ending! "There should be enough money to go around four generations! I understand you have to continue the business, but you also need to figure out how to clean the money - the cash is useless in the vaults!"

"I will think about it and find a strategy to clean up the money. I love you, Phoebe."

"Yeah? Do you love me? And you have me on a blackmail leash? Oh, yeah. I love you too, boy."

Adigun pulled Phoebe and they sank into the soft grass, kissing. Before they could come up for air, Adigun was nudged in the back and looked up to see a young colt staring at them.

"Hi, Mimah," he said warmly.

"Meet Jemimah, the most adorable animal on the face of the earth.

"She has become so attached to me. I helped deliver her and her mother died birthing her."

"I guess she sees you as her dad or something. Poor thing."

Phoebe stroked the young horse continually as they walked back to the stables. It was a long walk and Jemimah came all the way back with them.

3

Taking over the business was a source of great conflict for Adigun – his involvement in the drug trade had always been grudging – but it was also dangerous. He was now front and center for the affairs of the Edguardo cartel and that painted a huge bullseye on his back for every enemy of the organisation that saw its recent troubles as an opportunity to move in on their territory. He had to take serious precautions, which included a security team, especially after his car was shot at by unknown men at a traffic light in Baltimore. His arrangements were discreet though, as he wanted to keep a low profile and avoid the attention of law enforcement. As Patron, however, Adigun was crisp and efficient. The business operations ran like a well-oiled machine. He brought in Digger to handle the airport runs, picking up couriers and settling them into a converted extension of the cabin by the stables. Adigun gave Digger an assessment framework for the couriers that determined whether they could stay at the ranch or not. It worked something like this: if the courier looked and dressed like Chloe, stick them in a motel. Diane coordinated logistics and paid attention to the safest windows within which to move product and money. With her natural organization and attention to detail, she excelled at the role. Phoebe had mastered street distribution and she was able to distribute safely. Adigun still marveled at how Phoebe was able to get the products on the street seamlessly, but neither Digger nor Diane made him aware that she was with the FBI; let the lovebirds work that out between themselves, they agreed.

This increased efficiency soon had a negative effect, as the vaults in the cemetery chapels ran out of space. Cash was stacked to the ceilings, and you could barely close the doors. Until they could find other ways to expand their storage, Digger's farm was the safest location. Cash was being moved from all the cemeteries to the farmhouse and the Hershoms made some extra money for the additional service. On off days at the ranch, Diane, Digger, Adigun and a couple of guys from his protection team would move cash into a section of the stables, under hay. To keep this activity hidden from the stable hands, they sealed off that entire section, citing a form of quarantine to deal with a potential contagion among some of the horses. Only Didi, Diane, Adigun and visiting 'vets' were allowed in those areas. If any of the stable hands noticed that the 'vets' looked and moved more like mercenaries than doctors, they said nothing about it.

Soon, however, even the ranch began to run out of space. Adigun knew he needed to confer with Bobby Brown as soon as possible to make crucial decisions about the cleaning of the money. He had tried all he could to reach Bobby Brown without success. The Feds kept moving BB around to prevent him from establishing a system to operate his business from behind bars. Adigun's success with managing the cartel's operations had caused some consternation in law enforcement circles. They had all the big fish caught, but somehow couldn't see the signs of the crumbling empire they expected. Twenty-five people were arrested and detained in the Edguardo Cartel sting, mostly scattered around different facilities, but BB had managed to keep his key men with him. Eventually, the cost and hassle of the constant movement became more than the Feds could sustain and Bobby Brown and his crew were left in the Baltimore Maximum Security prison.

Bobby Brown was quiet in prison, minding his business and flying under the radar. When it looked like he would be in Baltimore for a stretch, he created a book club, made up entirely of Edguardo men. To deflect suspicion, he would occasionally allow outsiders into the club, but they would usually leave soon after or were never present when serious meetings took place. They met in the library twice a month and their mode of communication was a form of broken Spanish. They soon crafted a secret code language that incorporated the symbolic use of objects and phrases, as well as a complex system of signs. Unless you were schooled in the code, it was impossible to break. But secure communications were not the main concern of the Edguardo family. They were respected by all the rival gangs and none of them would openly move against Bobby Brown, but there were clandestine moves to undermine their dominance. More openly, the members of the Arian Nation were at war with them and both sides were sustaining casualties. News reached Adigun that Alagba and his Nigerian associates were murdered in prison, found hanging in their cells. Alonzo Ramirez was poisoned and found in the kitchen, sparking a major scandal in the facility. The authorities had to evacuate the pantry and test for poison, forcing the entire prison population to feed on cold-packed food for almost a fortnight before the Kitchens opened up again.

The only people that had any communication with Bobby Brown from the outside were the resident accountants at the Chapel cemetery. Under the cover of religion, their priestly garb got them in and out of visitation without undue hardships. Adigun tried sending messages to Bobby through the accountants, but it was a strictly one-way affair; he never got any replies to his messages, nor even confirmation that the messages were delivered. On the sheer faith that the messages were getting through though, Adigun sent BB blow-by-blow reports of developments within their business. He informed him of the involvement of Digger and Diane. He made him aware Phoebe was in charge of the street distribution and also informed him in these letters when he had to move cash to the Gershom ranch. He crosschecked the accounting from the resident accountants, and all was intact, to the penny.

During his last stop at the Laurel cemetery, Adigun was making a deposit when the priest, Ronaldo Sanchez asked him to wait. Sanchez had come from Colombia with Bobby Brown at the same time and had been with the family for too long to remember. Ronaldo spoke very poor English, but he managed to piece it together in a way people understood.

"*El Patron te hablara,* speak, you, Patron, in five minutes."

"Oh, really?" Adigun's face was a careful mask, concealing his shocked excitement at the news.

"Wait. I get *telefono*. Me soon come."

Adigun sat in the front pew and waited with a barely controlled impatience. Ronaldo brought out a large satellite phone with a long antenna. He detached the handset, connected to the all-black contraption with a spiral cord, and handed it to Adigun.

"Daddy! Daddy, how are you, sir?"

"I cannot talk for long." Bobby Brown's voice was curt and delivered with a terseness that made Adigun involuntarily straighten up in his seat. "You will apply for a visit at the Baltimore penitentiary – you can do that by phone - the meeting will be in exactly two weeks.

"Ahead of that meeting, you will come to the public payphone in front of the Bowie cemetery at 2 p.m. every day and wait one hour. Every day, mind you, until the phone rings.

"When it rings, a gentleman by the name of Peter Flaherty will arrange to meet with you to study the book of codes..." Bobby brown paused for several seconds. When he came back on, his voice was slightly cracked. "I wish you had continued your Spanish classes. Make sure you study this book properly and destroy it immediately after.

"There are two things you must pay attention to: how to communicate and how to have a conference. We have designed communication protocols so we can communicate with each other in one room, but it will make no sense to an outsider.

"Suspend everything else and study these protocols . . ." This time the pause was longer, more pregnant.

"I am very impressed by all you have done. You have saved the family and I thank you, my son. I thank you."

"Daddy, I thought you were trying to kill me! Why are they trying to kill Phoebe? Twice they came to assassinate me!"

"There has been a lot of confusion, my son, and mistakes have been made, but you would be a fool to think all attempts on your lives have been at my direction. And you should know better than to speak on such matters over the phone, even if it is secure.

"Just be certain that you have enemies, but Bobby Brown is not one of them. You have my protection. You are a good man, a true Edguardo."

"How is mummy doing?"

"Oh, she is well. She was moved to California because of her health. We speak very often.

"Again, I'm very grateful for all your efforts, and you will be duly compensated. For now, I have to go."

"Miss you, Bobby B."

"Miss you too, my son."

Adigun was so elated, he practically skipped through the Laurel suburban cemetery. As soon as he got into his car, he called Phoebe to leave her a message. He seemed to be on a roll as Phoebe picked up her phone on the second ring.

"Hello, Fibs."

"Hello. You're sounding merry; what's up?"

"I have good news."

"Tell me we are running away from this life to Australia."

"Hahaha. No, I got to speak to Dad."

"Dad? In Africa? Thought you said you had no contact with your father."

"Not him, Bobby Brown. He's very happy with me; I can come home now."

"Oh, that's awesome! How is he doing? Did you speak to Pookie too?"

"No somebody will be calling me, and I would be going to meet with them in the pen. Oh, this is such a happy day."

"But what if it's a set-up... to get you out of hiding?"

"No, Phoebe, it can't be. He told me how happy he is we are continuing the operations. I have to report to the Bowie cemetery payphone at 2 p.m. every day. But that is another matter. Listen, Fib, I will call you back and we can talk some more."

Adigun hung up the phone with a look of worry on his face. He had driven through the Gershom Ranch gate and saw a couple of strange cars in the driveway. His instincts told him they weren't cop cars, but he was concerned. He parked his Land Rover and took a look through one of the living room windows. There were about three visitors in the house, and he saw the twins sitting on the floor. They looked distressed and, as he strained to hear better, it seemed they were being questioned about how they came to have a hundred-thousand-dollar bundle of money at school. Adigun made the mental connection immediately – the twins had discovered the cash hidden in the hay-stacks and taken a bundle to school! Adigun rushed to the front door and bustled in, just as Tishan blurted, "I didn't steal it, I found it!"

"Yes, he found it in his school bag," Adigun interjected, "I put it there. *I* put it there. I'm so sorry. It was for the sale of the two stallions." Here he looked pointedly at Digger. "I brought it to give it to you, but I was called by Carlos on an emergency at the stables. I didn't want to go back saddled with the cash, so I just stuck it in Tishan's bag – somewhere easy to remember – and rushed out." He hugged Tishan, gushing, "Oh, sweetie, I'm so sorry I put you through this. Please forgive me." Tishan's face was buried in Adigun's shirt and none of the visitors could see the expression of confusion on it.

"Instead, there was a sigh of relief amongst the teachers and a flurry of comments about how relieved they were to find that he was the same student they all knew him to be. One of them admonished Adigun to be more careful about where he put things, and he just nodded as he ushered Tishan and Tyrone out of the room, rubbing Tishan's head and still apologizing. The teachers finished their cups of tea, and it was all good. After the teachers drove off, Adigun returned.

"What the heck, Tishan! What were you doing with a hundred thousand dollars in school?"

"I wasn't going to spend it, I just wanted to show it to my friends and bring it back."

Digger seized Tishan's shoulder, about to reprimand him, but Diane gave a subtle headshake and he stood down; he knew she would handle it better.

"Off to your beds now!" Tyrone had a look that suggested he was wondering why he was being punished too, but one look at his father's face and he sauntered silently to his room with his twin brother.

"Man, Shango," Digger muttered after they left, "You saved us a ton of grief just now. I knew where they were going – Mrs. Moses is the wife of the police Chief – and without a good explanation, we'd be up to our eyebrows in cops in no time. Diane and I were so panicked, we couldn't figure out a way to respond until you came in, just in time too! That was some quick thinking!"

"How did it go today?"

"Everything worked out well, picked up the horses from the stables and delivered them."

"Horses?"

"Yes, high time we start talking in code here as well."

"Real mob shit," Digger giggled.

"Oh, okay, Digger."

"All good Shango, all good. But I think we may want to focus on the big drops and let go of these airline mules – it's too risky, it's stressfu-," Digger paused and took an involuntary step back as Adigun shot him a furious look.

"Dude," Adigun hissed, "I think you are getting too excited. What do you think this is? Some mafia movie?"

"You need to calm down before you bring a world of pain down on us all! You don't make decisions about the operations, or strategy or nothing!"

"I do the planning here, not you! You just do as you are told, get it?"

"In this business, you want to learn to focus on your task, do as you are told, and keep your nose out of strategy. Patrons don't like nosey soldiers."

"That's what we are, bruv, soldiers," Digger said with a nervous laugh.

"Don't stick your head up, or your opinion can send you to an early grave. I still have to explain why I let you in, and that may go either way. I could lose my life if they see it as a slip-up or poor judgment."

"I feel you, bro, I feel you. I'm sorry. My bad. Some scotch?"

"Sure, two shots, neat, please."

Digger walked to the wooden bar and poured them single malt whiskey.

"Cheers, Padrone."

"I'm not the padrone, dude."

"Whatever, cheers anyway."

"Cheers"

4

Adigun reported to the pay phone every day at two. Sometimes he waited for hours but no call came. After seven days with no contact, he began to despair.

On the eighth day, Adigun had been out in the fields riding with Tishan and Tyrone when he realized he was almost late for his payphone appointment.

He raced through the country road to the pay phone. He could hear it ringing as he was parking the car. Trust my luck that it rings on the one day I'm late, he thought as he raced to the pay phone. But his luck seemed not to be so bad after all as he got to the phone in time. A Hispanic-sounding man gave him details of the planned meeting.

Excited, Adigun called Phoebe right away from the same payphone. "Hey, babes, the call came. It finally came, can you believe it?

"I'm to meet the fella at some warehouse at the harbor in DC…"

"Yes, that one you can see from the seafood buffet place."

"I don't know if it's the abandoned part of it but I will find out when I get there."

"Yes, Friday at 11 p.m. I'm so excited, Phibilicious." Something in the tone of Phoebe's responses bothered Adigun. "Are you excited for me?" He asked, then frowned as he listened to her response.

"Why would I have to authenticate the guy? Do pay phones just ring?"

'Yes, he also told me not to share this information with anyone…" Adigun trailed off and held the receiver away from his ear and Phoebe's strident voice emerged in tinny bursts from it.

"Typical! They want you there alone," she yelled, "So, they can kill you! I don't trust Bobby Brown, Adigun. I don't trust that man!" Abruptly, Phoebe's voice normalised as she changed tack. "Are you still riding with the twins this evening?"

Adigun, happy about the change of subject, replied, "Yes, I am. I'm looking forward to it. My game has really improved training with those two bad boys.

"Tishan has become a monster after the one week he spent in Argentina. Tyrone is more technical though, and maybe more effective. But both boys are absolutely exceptional.

"They are training for the United States Polo Association finals in Florida. It's the biggest polo event in the country and they are on the Mercedes Benz team.

"I will call you back once I finish riding."

He hung up hastily before the conversation might head back into uncomfortable territory.

In the days before he was due to meet the fellow with the code book, Adigun dived into his Spanish language books and began to brush up his skills in preparation for collecting the code book. On Friday, Adigun left Upper Marlborough early to beat the beltway traffic. He got into DC and parked in front of Noah's Bagel. He dropped a few quarters into the parking meter and proceeded into the wood-finished Bagel store.

"Three onion bagels and a medium caramel macchiato." He devoured one bagel before the coffee came out. It was the first time he was coming out in public without his security detail. Though excited about learning the code to carry out conversations with cartel members (and especially Bobby Brown), he was at ease. Speaking to Bobby gave Adigun a renewed sense of safety. He looked at his wristwatch and saw it was time to drive down to the harborfront warehouses.

He called the number he'd been given, and the Hispanic voice came on immediately.

"Yes, Amigo, I'm already at the harborfront and I can see the warehouse. There is only one warehouse."

"Okay," the voice replied, "go in there and I will meet you inside."

Adigun parked his car and practically skipped down the abandoned road and into the deserted warehouse. It was full of very derelict heavy machinery. It looked like an old printing press and there were a lot of large boxes stacked in a haphazard manner, and cobwebs all over the place. Adigun dusted off a small metal bench and sat on it waiting for the man. Within moments, he saw the man come in from the same door and his face brightened.

"*Como estas, amigo?*" Adigun greeted.

"Senor Fernandez?"

"*Si, si,*" replied Adigun. The man was in silhouette as he stood just inside the open doorway and the bright morning sun flowed in around him. Then he strode forward and into a patch of light from a massive skylight in the warehouse roof. In that instant, Adigun could see him clearly and he saw the muzzle of a matt black revolver in the man's hand, pointed in his direction.

Adigun raised his hands as the man began to speak. "I'm sorry, senor, I'm under strict instructions from the padrone. May the good Lord bless your soul." Adigun found his eyes squeezed shut as a loud crack rang out and the air brimmed with the smell of cordite. Some part of his consciousness registered the sound of the gunshot and, shortly after, the muffled thud of a body hitting the concrete. This must be what all those near-death-experience reports were about. He hadn't felt anything at all, but he was surely finished.

5

Chicago, 1995

Ada cried. She grabbed at her bulbous corn-row braids and sobbed like a toddler, a stream of tears rolling down her ebony cheeks as she patted her face with a damp wad of toilet paper. She wiped away the moisture under her small nose and dabbed at her long eyelashes. She had stormed out of the kitchen through the back door when Chike announced the arrival of his fiancé from Belgium, her mind filled with the image of a two-year-old version of the son that had been stolen from her. The abortion saga kept playing with her mind.

Chike had convinced her to go for a check-up and it ended up as an 'emergency' evacuation of a fully formed male child from her womb.

"It was a boy," the nurse whispered and cried with her after the surgery. The termination had been carried out at the behest of Chike's mother and he had let it happen. Yet, she had been fool enough to believe in his promise that he would persuade his mother to allow him to marry her when they got to America.

Ada had suffered bouts of horrible nightmares and vivid recollections ever since the abortion. Now, as always, it unspooled in slow motion. Ada saw images of her legs on the operation table and the heavy steel contraption that resembled a bicycle pump inserted into her uterus. The sting and snare of the anaesthesia and the cold metal running shivers through her spine all played back in slow motion. Half-awake she grabbed at the hands of the hairy doctor. The painful jerks from her widespread thighs and the powerful suction that pulled the life out of her. Then the sickening, meaty slap of flesh hitting the bottom of a metal bucket. This painful symphony sounds lived with Ada eternally. One thing she never got was the identity of the doctor. His face was covered by the surgical mask but she knew he was heavily bearded and spoke with an Igbo accent. The lights above the surgical table were too bright. She remembered the strange sensation she felt when he walked in and shook hands with Chike, the sharp click as they snapped their fingers to end the handshake. She had asked the nurses but they did not know; the murderer was not one of their in-house doctors, he was flown in for this crime. The nurses told her all they knew was that he arrived from America that morning.

Ada covered her ears with her palms and with her eyes closed screamed out loud. The horror of that experience had tormented her all the years since. Ada's imagination fed her images of every stage of the growth of her lost son, stoking her anguish. The anguish which contrasted so heavily against the joy and hope she had felt with Chike. She knew he loved her – he showed her in so many ways – and he was always so readily intimate with her. But that too changed after the abortion procedure: Chike never came close to Ada anymore. It was clear she had preferential treatment in the mansion and she knew he sincerely loved her, but he never mentioned his promise to marry her ever again. All intimacy ceased after the abortion.

"Abortion?" She soliloquized. "Murder! Yes, gruesome murder." She murmured to herself in a hoarse whisper. With no one to share her pain with, Ada suffered alone in silence, berating herself for putting herself up to be used by Chike. She wasn't sure what Mrs. Obidike knew but it was really strange when the woman would sometimes look at her and make cryptic statements like, "If you don't cross my lane, you are safe around me." She also constantly told her, "Remember my son is a prince; you can never be his princess." Ada was devastated to learn that Chike had chosen another bride and she was coming to live with them from Belgium. She was coming with her mother too.

In the new Obidike mansion, the household had struggled to overcome the cultural challenges they encountered. Adjusting to life in the Chicago suburb was tough. News spread on the arrival of the new 'Nigerian hillbillies' and everyone in the community was curious about the impact of this sophisticated social experiment amidst stupendous wealth. The most impacted were the Nigerian immigrant staff, many of the seventeen soon wishing they could return to their home country. Ada was the most quickly acclimated of the staff, easily adapting to the change in environment and culture. Her command of English improved in leaps and bounds, and she was always watching American talk shows in her spare time. She soon enjoyed considerable popularity in the community, though she didn't make actual friends. Many of her colleagues stayed in their African bubble, never leaving the mansion, but Ada blended effortlessly with the fashion and mannerisms of their host community. She was especially careful about her appearance and dressing, subconsciously trying to make herself worthy of her dream to be Chike's wife.

6

In the two years since the Obidike clan arrived in Chicago, Mrs. Obidike came to love Winnetka. On the surface, she had settled well into living the American life of the rich and famous. In truth anywhere away from Mazi Obidike was paradise. She had joined the Winnetka golf club, quickly made friends with many affluent residents of Winnetka, and was soon elected as the Lady Captain of the club. She was the first African to be elected to this position, overcoming many of the prejudices and misconceptions about Africans that were rife before then. Of course, their stupendous wealth helped. Doctor Obidike had planned everything well, and Mrs. Obidike marvelled at the genius of her late husband. She would often look around and just shake her head. Sometimes she cried. It had become difficult to sleep at night in a bedroom so like the one she left behind in Nigeria; she still expected her husband to walk in and toss his cap on the night table.

The Obidike mansion was an architectural showpiece. The cathedral-style mansion stood on the same topography as it did in Nigeria. Earth was moved to create hills and excavated to create the wooded valley at the back of the estate. The Italian architect, Fabricio Samueli even created an artificial lake on the east side of the property.

The interior was stunning, with furniture and interior fittings even better (and more modern) than in Nigeria. Chike and his mother had taken time to choose a more contemporary style than Dr Obidike's largely traditional, antique-leaning taste. The car park had the exact models of the cars in Nigeria. Mr. Obidike had been a collector of cars and these automobiles were a monument to his memory. A lot was done to integrate the domestic staff into the American culture, but many were bent on sticking to their Nigerian ways. As a matter of fact, most of them were unhappy and wanted to go back to Nigeria. Of the seventeen that had agreed to relocate with Chike and his mother, a majority envied Papa, their oldest colleague and personal driver to Dr Obidike, who had opted out and stayed in Nigeria. He was old and asked to be allowed to retire. The general apathy of the staff soon gave way to boredom and depression, leading to a variety of incidents.

Mmuo Ozi Beke, meaning White Angel in Igbo, or Beke for short, the young trainee chef and housemaid was arrested and charged with attempted suicide when she tried to cross the 'Chicago Autobahn', the high-speed, eight-lane highway. Beke went out of the estate to look for a market to buy pepper. Duke, who had run out of pepper, mentioned it in passing to her. Bored and homesick, Beke took money from the kitchen table and sprang out just as she always did in Nigeria. In Nigeria, Beke was in charge of the market runs. She was athletic and was always either walking briskly or running. She ran off and asked a stranger for directions to a market where she could buy pepper. Beke was a rail-thin albino and, on this morning, had tied her *Ankara* over her chest and in a knot at the back of her neck, beach-wrap style, and had rubber flip-flops on her feet. The bemused lady pointed to the Giant Grocery store on the other side of the Chicago Autobahn. This stretch of the freeway had a high-speed limit and thin law enforcement supervision, so motorists tended to travel at high rates of speed. Beke was quite accustomed to crossing highways in Nigeria as most of her countrymen were. So ingrained was this practice, that she would cross highways directly on the surface even if a pedestrian bridge was nearby – it was just faster and 'less *wahala'*. She had never even seen an eight-lane road though and had no idea what sort of risk she was taking when she dashed into the freeway like a suicide candidate, causing a sequence of screeching tires and blaring horns. Beke had a rude awakening when she got past the first four lanes and scaled the high concrete demarcation barrier. She leaped down into the eastbound section only to find that there were four more lanes of stampeding death hurtling towards her. She froze as she heard more squealing rubber, until the hollow bang of metal-on-metal impact galvanized her into action. She whipped around, turning her back on the blooming pile-up in the eastbound lane, jumped back over the concrete demarcation, and immediately produced a mirror pile-up in the westbound lane as she scuffled to safety on the shoulder. The entire stretch of freeway on both sides was littered with debris and smoke.

Beke scurried over the aluminium railing, glancing intermittently back at the accident scene. A fortuitous motorcycle highway patrolman – who had narrowly missed being clipped when the pile-up started in the westbound lane – witnessed the tail end of the disaster as Beke was crossing to the westbound shoulder. He immediately radioed in to report the incident and gave chase. Other patrol men raced to the scene from the other side of the freeway and chased after the skinny, pale girl with her blonde braids tied in black thread. She looked up and saw low-flying helicopters. Beke knew there was nowhere to run. The highway patrol riders were gaining on her. She kept running as motorcycle cops got off their bikes and gave chase. She was fast but Beke was caught crossing the baseball field just a few blocks from the Obidike mansion. She was tackled by a female officer to the turf. The officer grabbed her hands pushed her head to the ground, cuffed her and read her Miranda rights. Beke had guns pointed at her by the other officers and there was a press helicopter hovering over them. More cop vehicles arrived at the baseball field and emergency lights were flashing on the freeway, where there was now a gridlock that went on for miles on either side. It was breaking news on all the local TV stations.

Beke kept shouting, 'Pepper!'

"Pepper, oooooh!"

"Pepper!"

"Pepper!"

She was led into the police van, hands cuffed behind her and driven to the precinct station. The press followed. Officers could not get a word from Beke for hours. She refused to answer any questions or give any information about her residential address. She had no identification on her and just kept shouting, "Pepper," and tightening the knot behind her neck. The Department of Mental Health was called in and preparing emergency commitment documents when Chike arrived at the Police station. Mrs. Obidike had seen Beke on TV, captured by news cameras as she fled from the police. She called her son to inform him that Beke had made the news. As Beke looked up and saw Chike, she jumped on him and started shouting phrases in Igbo. The black thread from her nappy blonde hair was all half loose and she let go of Chike when the knot of her wrapper came undone, and she had to secure it with both hands. She looked scared and harassed.

"That's one strong and tough heifer you got there, man!"

"African turbo power!"

"Damn! what do you feed her?"

"She has the strength of a bull; it took three policemen to restrain her." Chike bore the barrage of comments patiently before responding. "I beg your pardon, officer, you shall not refer to her in any derogatory manner. The last time I checked the word heifer connotes cattle.

"I demand you stop that line of humour right away!"

"I'm really sorry, Sir," replied the officer, who seemed genuinely contrite.

Beke continued to rant.

"Oga I wan go back to Nigeria. I no do again, I no do again. I no do Obodo Oyibo again!"

She then began communicating with Chike in Igbo. It was a relief to the law enforcement officers that she finally could communicate. Soon after, Greg Mbadiwe, Chike's childhood friend and lawyer arrived. Beke tried to explain to Chike and Greg how she got to the freeway. She narrated how Duke had informed her they had run out of fresh pepper to cook. There were several minor to relatively serious injuries in the accidents caused by Beke, but none were life-threatening and Greg was able to bail her out and gave a statement on her behalf. Chike had Beke wait in the car while he hung back on the precinct steps to speak with Greg. "We have a serious matter we need to sort out," he said. Greg raised his eyebrows, saying, "What, this issue with your girl here? That's nothing, not even a blip." "Not that," Chike's expression was grave, "Something else – business . . . money." Greg grew serious in an instant. "Let's see at my office tomorrow, after hours, okay?"

Chike was already descending the steps to his waiting car. "Tomorrow, then."

Chike Obidike, heir to a tremendous fortune in excess of eight billion dollars had a great task of investing this fortune sensibly. He had bought over the largest healthcare company in the state of Illinois. He invested in funeral homes and also made some major real estate investments in the south side of Chicago. The mayor of Chicago had given Chike Obidike several community leadership awards for his philanthropy and was even given the highest mayoral award which was the key to Chicago. The Cedar Sanai investment was the largest of its kind by a single investor, made possible after an amendment in the healthcare legislation was announced by the government.

Chike had left his office and the white Rolls Royce, driven by his Nigerian driver, Ndubisi, sped through the freeway. The phone rang and he signalled to the driver to shut the dividing glass so he could have some privacy.

"G Dawg! G money," he greeted loudly, "I was just thinking about you; are you in your office? Okay, I will be with you in a few minutes.

"Ndubisi," he called, but the driver could not hear. Chike pressed the button on his armrest and used the intercom.

"Ndubisi, please drive me to the Wills Tower."

"Yes, Sir."

Ndubisi drove along the freeway for about twenty minutes whilst Chike read through a file of financial reports. The car took a turn into the downtown area and into the driveway of the tallest building in Chicago, The Wills Tower. From the doorman to the receptionist, everyone knew Chike and greeted him by his first name. Chike was loved by these people, in no small measure because he had a reputation as a huge tipper. He tipped only hundred-dollar bills. The Oxford-English gentleman's fashion never left Chike and, on this day, he strode through the lobby in a well-cut, navy-blue wool suit, and the sweet aroma of the pipe tobacco followed him through the reception into the glass elevator that took him to the 110th floor of the Wills Tower. He walked out of the elevator into the lobby of the KKM, law offices of Kohen, Kohen and Mbadiwe, the top law firm in Chicago. It was owned by father and son, Michael and Jerry Kohen with the notorious celebrity tax lawyer Greg Mbadiwe. Greg was Nigerian and had also attended Harrow School in England with Chike. Greg had gone on to Harvard Law School, while Chike got admission to Oxford University.

Greg had earned his partnership after he won the landmark tax evasion case against the State of Illinois, representing the Irish crime family, the Kilpatricks.

"Good morning, Mr. Chike."

"Good morning, Sir."

More warm greetings washed over the firm's current largest client. Greg's office was a large glass room that was a nightmare for anyone with a fear of heights. A significant section of the floor was cantilevered over the side of the building and was made of thick glass. The office was tastefully furnished and offered what appeared to be a view of the entire city. Hidden from view, though familiar to Chike, was the private recreation area with a steam room, sauna and lap pool.

"G Dawg! G-G-G money! I've told you to sell this office to me."

"Chike, buy the entire building and be my landlord; I know I will owe you rent, and you won't complain!" The men clasped arms as their familiar ritual of greeting played out. Greg was a big fella, topping out at a well-groomed six-foot-five. Like Chike, he leaned more towards British fashion than American. He pressed a button and a section of the wall opened to reveal a large humidor with wooden boxes of cigars.

"Are we doing Cuban or Dominican?"

"Do you still have that no-name Rubusto you brought from Havana?"

"At this time of the day? It's Wednesday, Chike!"

"Come on, Greg, it's already five," Chike glanced at his watch and back up Greg with a quizzical arch of his brow.

"No, no, no, bro, I'm in court tomorrow morning. If we start now, we will end up at the yacht club! Besides, I know you just want to show off the watch. Chike, you are insane! When I called Yousef and he told me he sold it, I knew you bought it."

Chike took another look at his Patek Philippe, Grand Complications, World Time Minute Repeater and grinned. "You snooze, you lose, buddy."

"*Nwane madu*, that is my watch! *Oya, comot it*, let me see."

"God forbid, Greg, I know you won't give me back."

Chike stretched out his hand and showed Greg the one-and-a-half million-dollar watch. Greg cooed with admiration. "*Biko*, when you are big you are big. How come the face has New York, Sidney, and all these cities, but they did not put Arochukwu."

"Seriously, I'm just noticing this, Greg; *na true, oh*," Chike jested, continuing, "You are mad, Greg; not well at all." The two men bellowed laughter. Still chuckling, Greg said, "If I spend half of that money you paid on that watch, not only will it have my village name on the face – *chai* – any time I look at the watch, the watch must hail me, 'G-Money! Geeeeee-Money!"

"Your head is not correct, Greg."

"*Nwanemadu*, let's discuss business quick before I bring out the whiskey."

"Bro, let's start with the London matter. I'm working on it but, as I told you, best to stay away from Europe for now. Not that it won't be sorted out, but it could create a press frenzy and you don't need that right now.

"I'm still trying to squelch the freeway pile-up caused by that silly girl. Say, has she decided what she wants?"

"It's not about what she wants, G-Money; my mum is so attached to Beke. "She's been with us since she was about ten. Sure, she wants to go back to the village – she misses her people – but mum is thinking more along the lines of a short break when the aircraft goes to Ghana next month. You know I closed that Adinkra mines deal, right?"

"Yes, Chike, but you did not use us."

"The parties insisted we should use Ghanaian lawyers," Chike shrugged.

Greg stretched to the left side of his table and picked up a large folder. He opened it. "These are the papers for the offer to the auctioneers – I am still gobsmacked about how you left Oxford University and became a sculpturist – but anyway, the statue at the Bank of England is the only one left with a lease option to renew. I have notified them that we will not be interested in renewing, but it has a penalty should they want it and we decline. All the others are straight.

"Sotheby's made an offer. Christie's also made an offer for a bulk price."

"No Greg, I'm not doing a bulk price, I want to separate every artwork. We are talking sculptures here, G."

"The logistics are a killer!"

"Bottom line is for the pieces to make it to the United States."

"Oh, yes, I put it in the offer."

"The pieces would only be sold in the United States."

667

"Yes, that's clear. They are okay with that; it's their American unit making the deal.

"Chike, you are selling these pieces far below the market price."

"Yes Greg, I want to purchase all of them as soon as they land on their auction table. In any case, this is all your idea – shouldn't I have just brought them here? They belong to me; I made them."

"Chike, trust me on this one, I'm only protecting you. You are lucky you are here in America walking free.

"Dude, you impersonated the next of kin of dead people and fraudulently appropriated tens of millions of pounds! Defrauded the probate office! That's an offence against the crown, you crazy person.

"You left an investigation behind, and we don't know what info law enforcement has… no idea what is waiting there for you.

"I have to totally wash your name off any trail. Even when you purchase it here, it would be done by a corporate entity. The name, Chike Obidike, will not be associated with these pieces.

"There has been a lot of interest in all twenty-two of these pieces because they were located in landmark locations. This made them appreciate really well. You will take a hit on the current value, but they will be in your hands soon enough.

"Next on the agenda, before the whiskey – Talatu."

"Yes, Talatu my darling."

"Her papers to move to the States. The immigration papers are all set. I spoke to her yesterday – such a lovely lady – to explain the challenges we had with her mother's papers. She is a Nigerian citizen and the American embassy in Nigeria was really funny, but it's all done now. They can both live here legally."

"Thank you so much, Greg."

"Yeah, well, please tell your people to process our payments on time. You know my partners are Jewish. They don't play with their money."

"Oh, are we not Jews too?"

"*For where? How Arochukwu take resemble Jerusalem?*"

"I've been telling you these things all these years, Greg, and you still don't believe. We are Jews, Greg, authentic Jews."

"Yeah, right! And my last name is Yom Kipor!" Greg fired up his cigar and blew a thick plume of smoke, then he asked, "*Because we like moni?*"

"Dude, bring the whiskey, and let me educate you. According to Genesis 29, verse 30, Jacob had twelve children-"

"Yes! Preach on pastor! You need ice?"

"Is that 25-year-old Glenfiddich?"

"Chike, for you, anything less is unacceptable. *Oya, bless am* – you are the oldest."

Chike tapped the cap of the bottle of whiskey, Greg opened it and poured.

"*Oya*, continue the story."

"The seventh son was Gad. Gad had seven sons, Ziphon, Haggi, Shunni, Ezbon, Eri, Arodi, and Areli."

"There was a famine in the land and Jacob moved his entire family to Egypt. Remember, this was after Joseph had been sold to Egypt and was already a governor. "

"When the pharaoh who knew Joseph died, the new pharaoh started to maltreat them. Eri, the fifth son of Gad, left with his family before the persecution began."

The intercom rang and Greg answered, "Yes, Lilly, we are okay. I will call them to lock up. Have a great trip home and my regards to the family." He returned his attention to Chike and held his glass out to him. "*Oya, biko*, top me up, top me up; I'm enjoying the story."

"So Eri left Egypt with his two younger brothers Arodi and Areli. They travelled through Ethiopia and Sudan, down the river Nile toward West Africa. They got to a place called Aguleri, through the Omambala river. This was around 1305 BC."

"You must be kidding me."

"Eri settled and lived close to the Omambala river. He was wealthy and wise, just like his grandfather Abraham, and he had five sons; Agulu, Atta, Oba, Ibo – you see that came from the word, 'Hebrew'-"

"No shit!"

"There was also Menri, the fifth son. Agulu, the firstborn, established the place known as Agulu-Eri, derived from Agulu, the son of Eri.

"Atta moved upwards to the North and established a place known as the Igala Kingdom; Do you see why their king is known as the Attah of Igala?"

"Oba went and founded the Oba Kingdom in Anambra state."

"Hebrew, also known as Ibo, or Hibo, he founded Igbo Etiti, Igbo Adagbe, Igbo Eze, all now in the Nsukka area."

"Menri founded a place known as AgukwNri, the Nri kingdom.

"Arodi moved to a place known as Arochukwu, where we both are from."

Greg jumped off his seat and raised his hands, yelling, "*Igbo kwenu! Igbo Kwenu, Arochukwu Kwesuenu ehhh!*" He and Chike lightly backhanded each other's right arms three times in the traditional salutation of the Igbos.

"I'm not finished," Chike said.

"*Ngwanu*, fire on!"

"Arodi gave birth to Nembe, Ngwa, Abakaliki, Ogoni, Afikpo, Aro-Ikot Ekpene, now known as Akwa Ibom, Aro Echie, now known as Rivers, and Arondizuogu.

"Are you aware the Aros spread all over the world during the slave trade?"

671

"Tell me."

"Brazil, Cuba and other parts of South America. Do you know they still celebrate the Aro festival?"

"What of Areli? You have said nothing about him"

"Wait, let me use the bathroom."

Chike got up and made his way into the sauna and steam room area of the luxury office, calling over his shoulder, "Dude, you may as well be living here!"

"This is my life, Chike. Since my wife passed away, I have spent more time here. What is a big mansion without a wife?" Greg's voice fell away as Chike shut the bathroom door and there was a brief silence that was broken by the sound of flushing.

"But you have refused to re-marry," Chike challenged Greg as he returned to the main office. Greg waved that away and said, "Okay, back to Areli."

"Areli had Owerri, Umuahia, Diobu, Okigwe, Orlu, Nkwerre, Elele, now known as Mba Ise, Mba Ano.

"Eri's half-brothers founded the Ijaw nation and some parts of Edo state."

"Greg, we Igbos are Jews, I'm telling you we are direct descendants of Jacob! There is a place in Aguleri called Obi Gad – remember Gad, the son of Jacob – which was the first house built in Igbo land. Now you see why every Igbo man always builds a place called 'Obi' in his house to honour his father.

"They always put a shrine in there. But before you protest about idolatry, don't forget these people left Egypt before Moses was given the ten commandments, so idol worship was part of their culture.

"Why do we shout, 'Yah' when they shout, '*Igbo Kwenu*'?"

"You tell me, Pastor Chike."

"'Yah' means 'Yahweh'."

"Oh, my God! Wow!" Greg topped up Chike's glass and then his own.

"Ol' boy, *we don finish this whiskey, oh!*"

"Thank God I don't have to drive."

"You have your limousine?"

"Yes. Lovely scotch."

"So, we are all brothers with the Jews."

"I can't wait to tell my partners. I must take them to Arochukwu to go and reunite with all their long-lost relatives."

Greg picked up the intercom. "Hi, I'm calling from the 110th ... Yes, KKM, the law firm. Please, come and lock up; we are leaving now. And tell reception to hail me a taxi…"

"Yes, the usual."

"No, going straight home this time."

Chike looked up at the mention of a taxi. "When is your driving suspension over, Greg?"

"It's been over, Chike," Greg replied with an air of resignation, "I just don't have the desire to drive anymore."

Chike and Greg, both tipsy from the vintage single malt whiskey walked through the quiet offices, past the lobby and into the elevators. The duo went down the elevators, looking out onto the city from its transparent shell. When the doors opened onto the parking level, Greg said, "Oh, good. The taxi is here," as they strode past the floor concierge and security. "Good night, Mr. Chike," they chorused as Chike and Greg approached. Chike pulled out a wad of hundred-dollar bills and gave a few to the receptionist and the security guard.

"I've told you, Chike, we don't do this in America," Greg grumbled.

"But they always take it," Chike replied with a chuckle.

"Chike's driver came around and opened the door of the stretch Rolls Royce."

Chike wound the large window down as the door closed quietly.

"G-Money!"

"*Onyeoshi!*" Greg shouted as he stepped into his yellow taxi. "Big thief!"

"God punish you," Chike laughed. "Have a lovely night, my brother."

8

Maryland

The gunshot still echoed, and wisps of gun smoke drifted across the patch of sun from the skylight. There was a rustle of clothing as someone behind the stack of boxes moved and out stepped a woman dressed in black. Long blond hair stuck out of the woolen ski mask she wore. Adigun, still standing in the same spot, opened his eyes at the sound of her emergence. The strong light made him squint at her as she returned her gun to its shoulder holster and bent to check the pulse of the man with the Hispanic accent. She dragged the ski mask off her head and looked up at Adigun.

"Time to go home, brother!"

Adigun gaped at her across the patch of light. When he had seen the blonde hair, he'd been sure it was Phoebe. Now that she'd spoken, however, he realised it was Diane.

"Diane! Wh-what…" he sputtered. "How… you saved my life!"

"Come on, Shango, we need to get out of here."

They both ran down the deserted road to Adigun's parked car.

"How did you get here?"

"Phoebe dropped me off."

Adigun's mouth was open as he drove out of the city.

"Phoebe is waiting at the red lobster down the road. Yes, here, this one. Pull up here."

They walked into the quiet restaurant and Adigun saw Phoebe sitting on a table, tears standing in her eyes as she saw them walk in, her slender fingers around a half-full wine glass. Adigun embraced her, holding her close, then spread his right arm wide and pulled Diane in as well. They stood that way for long seconds, heads touching, arms locked around each other, silent. The moment was broken when the small group was jostled by a large mass as someone tried the unlikely feat of hugging all three of them simultaneously. It was Digger.

Diane looked up at him. "You are late!"

"Sorry, darling, I was in traffic," Digger said, then turned to Adigun, saying, "So happy to see you alive, my brother."

"I'm happy to be alive."

Phoebe squeezed Adigun, whispering hoarsely, "Diggy Boo, I told you those guys were only using you. That was not your father, that was a monster!"

Digger looked up and there was a bunch of Red Lobster staff looking at them from inside the Kitchen.

"Okay, guys. Let's take this celebration to the ranch, we are creating a scene here.

"I'm happy we're back to being one happy family, but we have serious work to do. When they find out what happened to their man, they will be coming for us."

The couples drove in separate cars to the Gershom Ranch and Adigun had them walk past the stables to the woods to keep their conversation private.

As they passed the last row of stables, Adigun erupted, "This is so wrong! This is so treacherous. I called that man 'father'!

"How could a father want to kill his son?"

"Guys, I know Bobby Brown; we need to move before the news gets to him. We have a little time, but we need to be brutal and strategic or, by this time tomorrow, we will all be in body bags."

"On the upside, if we do this right, everything, I mean EVERYTHING, belongs to us! We just took over the wealth of the Edguardo family."

"We either take it over, or we die. Choose one."

He looked around the small group and they all looked back quietly. Not even Phoebe said anything in response. Good, Adigun thought, the gravity of the situation has sunk in for all of them. He continued.

"The case against the family is ongoing, with twenty-five cartel members incarcerated and more are being arrested. We have to make our move now! The earlier we can wipe out, the existing operations the better. We don't know who will start to sing.

"We will take over all the Edguardo assets and stock and make new alliances – I will try my best to break down the operations of the Family – but it means we have to take out a lot of people. Diane, you will work with me; there is more of today's kind of work ahead and-"

"No, no, no, NO," Phoebe interjected, hand raised like she was answering a teacher's question in high school. "No, Adigun, I'm not going that route! I'm not about to leave my simple quiet life and go into slinging drugs and killing people."

"Get serious," shouted Digger, "We just poked the beehive. If we don't suit up and get cover, we all get stung to death. You got *my wife* to kill this dude – what fucking simple life are you on about? There is no simple life, Phoebe!

"Do you have an idea what the consequences are?

"Oh, you are just going to just go back to your normal lives and everything's just going to be ok?

"We have cemeteries full of drugs. Chapels and churches filled with money. My freaking horses have no more hay to eat!

"My kids got caught with a bundle of money at school! Wake up and smell the coffee! We are all drug dealers and killers now. We is the freaking mob right now!"

"Don' nobody come out now and preach holy; we all have crossed the conspiracy line and are all criminally liable. Those people on the street you have been supplying drugs to, Phoebe, they know you. They will find you and take you out. I am no expert but even I know we have very little time to take them out and then we can cut a deal with their rival group and set up a new supply chain."

Adigun shook his head. "Digger is right. Phoebe, while you make up your mind if you are in or not, Diane, we are heading to the armoury at the basement of the Catholic Church in Bethesda. We need firepower.

"We will take out all the priests in the seven chapels. We will also wipe out all the buyers tonight! Digger, you will take care of the funeral homes.

"But what will we do with all the money? And our stockpile; what do we do with the drugs?

"Our goal is to get rid of the inventory we have across the country wholesale.

"We will not be continuing the business, but we have to secure our lives."

"Adigun, do you realize how much money we are talking about here?" Phoebe interrupted. "How do you intend to clean it up?"

Adigun looked pensive. "I have some ideas on how to clean up the entire system and replace it with our own trusted men. I have a relationship with a group of Nigerians that we can take this to. Digger interjected, "Nigerians? No way!"

"They are the only ones that I can trust right now. We are going to have to find some people to take over the sales after we whack Bobby Brown's men," Adigun replied.

Digger was adamant. "If we expose this secret to the Nigerians, then we are jeopardizing our safety. Then it would be the Nigerians that would get us whacked to keep all the money. Let us keep it between us and we can silently dispose of the goods and also clean the money."

Diane brushed her hair backwards with her fingers, saying, "Hmmmmm, my husband has a point. A very good point too. Something that bothers me is not knowing what our stakes are in all of this. We need to determine that now before we go any further." She looked pointedly at Adigun, who said, "Guys, my name is Adigun Komaiya! I swear to you, we will all be all right by the time we finish this project."

"My name is Didi Gershom. I swear to you that that is the most ridiculous thing I've ever heard! We risk our lives, and we don't know what our stake is? We should just jump to work on your sworn word?"

"Fair enough, I get it. We are two teams here; we divide the spoils in two. You and Diane take half and me and Phoebe the other half."

There was silence as they continued walking, reaching the lake and stopping by the row of sailboats. Adigun leaned on one and faced the other three. Diane picked up some pebbles and skipped them across the tranquil surface of the lake. When the last of them dipped into the water, she said, "Hell, no! This is crime, guys, not a marital chore. I want my share paid to me directly. Plus, I'm not waiting till after everything is over, I want mines paid to me as we go." She grabbed another set of pebbles and threw them into the clear water. "We share equally." Digger was staring at Diane with a shocked expression. She saw it and looked away, saying, "That is my take. Equal share, my share comes directly to me. There ain't no community property in proceeds of a crime, goddammit!"

"Fine," Adigun snorted, "But only after the money is cleaned."

Digger adjusted his brown scarf and tucked it into his spring jacket. Then his eyes widened, and he blurted excitedly, "Diane's twin brother works at Christie's, and he once told us how the mob used art to clean up their money!"

"Art?" Adigun asked.

"It's not just the mob either – that's the way rich white folk been doing it for ages!"

"Brilliant! Let's do this."

"Diane, we have a lot of work to do. Phoebe, you handle the guys on the east side. All our drop-off locations must be sanitized."

"I will proceed to the cemetery at Bowie and bring over the munitions we will need.

"It's a long walk back to the house – let's get moving."

The couples walked back through the woods back toward the stables.

9

Phoebe awoke from a coma-like slumber to the sound of her ringing phone. Disoriented, she let it ring. Despite all their talk yesterday of even splits, she had had the lightest load when it came to Adigun's 'clean-up'. She had only had to make two stops – and they were so close she was done in twenty minutes – but they were hard. She was used to gunfire and, in her years as a cop, she had discharged her weapon in live situations several times, but last night, she had had to do murder. Murder was hard. Both her victims were simple to dispatch – they were drunk, and their guard was down – but the act itself was traumatizing. When she had returned home, she wondered whether she would have felt easier about it if the men had been in a state to put up more of a fight, then realised she might not have made it back if they did. These were hard, bad men. Now they were dead, and she was not. She slept the sleep of the dead.

Now, she gathered her wits about her as her phone rang for the eighth or ninth time, then sat up as her answering machine kicked in. She heard her boss's voice and, from his frantic tone, knew what he was calling about. She bolted upright and picked up the receiver.

"Hello?" There was a lot of background noise, and it was hard to make anything out. Over the sounds of sirens and yelling, her boss barked, "Phoebe, get up now and make your way to the east side right way; there has been a killing spree here! You know the players, you know where. It seems like a gang war, but the victims were all in business with the Edguardo family. Meet me at Limping Lenny's place." Phoebe scrambled into a pair of khaki slacks, threw on her jacket and ran out of her house. She sped down the beltway into Washington. She knew her friends had been busy all night and cringed at the amount of bloodshed that must have occurred if they had succeeded. She didn't want to think about what might have become of her own people in this; Didi, Diane, and, most of all, Adigun.

As she approached Limping Lenny's, Phoebe had to slalom between cop cars and emergency vehicles. The entire length of the cul-de-sac appeared to have been the site of a ferocious gun battle. Bodies were still being photographed and three forensic teams were working full-tilt to mark and then secure the shell casings that littered the area like so much graffiti. She screeched to a halt at the end of the street where Limping Lenny had lived. Clearly, his limping days were over. Henry Baker, her boss was standing outside smoking furiously. He marked Phoebe's approach and began speaking without bothering with pleasantries. "There are the same style murders at the funeral parlour in Arlington." He lifted the sheet covering the body on the gurney in front of him and looked down at the bloodied teenager with the lower half of his face missing. Phoebe stifled a shudder and covered the boy's face up again.

The photographer was taking a few last shots and the ambulances rolled out leaving white chalk marks in the wake of their dead passengers. A lanky gentleman in a grey suit walked across to them from the other side of the street, where two other white outlines told the tale of more fallen soldiers.

"Hi. My name is William Brisby, DEA. Someone was sure busy overnight."

"It seems like a cartel clean-up. We have records on the guys killed in Maryland, they all have affiliations to the Edguardo mob."

"We have all the top guys incarcerated, so I think they had to clean up the remaining evidence on the street."

He looked around at the almost festive array of yellow crime-scene tapes crossing from one side of the road to the other. "This is a bloodbath."

By ten that morning, Phoebe had visited six crime scenes and recognised most of the bodies. She took careful note of the camera locations in each area and breathed a small sigh of relief each time she saw them missing entirely or knocked off their mounts and dangling by their torn cables. Adigun took care of the cameras; that was good. Yes, she was undercover, but her drop-offs to these locations had been completely off the books and she didn't want any of this coming back to haunt her later. When she had scoped out all of the scenes and determined that there wasn't anything that could lead the investigation to her crew on the ranch, Phoebe headed to the office for the briefing and a pile of paperwork. After work, she drove directly to the Gershom ranch.

The ranch seemed deserted as she rolled slowly through its gate; the Gershom's appeared to have acted on their intentions to clear the place out until the dust settled. As she recalled, they had planned to send the ranch hands off for a team-building retreat. In all likelihood, they must have sent the twins off to Diane's sister's as well. In the house, she found Adigun hosting a group of hard cases, all blond, and all smoking cigars. A thick haze hung in the air as she walked in. "Good afternoon, gentlemen. If you don't mind, I'm going to open the door and the windows."

They were silent as Phoebe drew the blinds and opened the room's windows, watching her from beneath their gelled hairlines and hooded eyes. As she turned from the last window, behind the grand piano, Adigun walked to her with open arms.

"Welcome, Phoebe-lee."

"Phoebe-lee? That's a new one; what happened to 'Phibilicious'?" She looked around the room at the assembled men whose every feature screamed mobster. "What are you doing?" Here, her voice dropped. "This is their home! You can't be bringing... strangers here; it's not right!"

"Oh, no, Phoebe, it is our home too, now. We are one happy family now, and I can bring whomever I want here." Adigun pulled her to him and gave her a warm kiss. Phoebe whispered in his ears after he broke the kiss.

"Who are these people? They look like killers out of a James Bond movie."

Adigun laughed quietly. He raised a finger to the men, signalling that he be excused for one minute, as he guided Phoebe toward the kitchen, still whispering.

"They are our new Russian partners. I know them from when they came to the East coast and offered to buy Bobby Browns California operations. They were major sponsors of all my fights. Remember the party at the Bellagio, after the fight with Ron Duvan? Their boss hosted that party."

"Oh, the old Russian billionaire?" Asked Phoebe.

"Yes, Baron Timchenko Mordashov. Remember I told you there was a war on the West Coast?"

"Oh, yes, I remember them."

"Well, Bobby Brown eventually sold the operations in the Bay Area, including San Francisco, which was especially lucrative." Now, in the kitchen, Adigun's voice resumed a regular volume.

"Yes, those people."

"They came from Russia after they fell out with the Russian government. They came into the United States on asylum with a lot of their oil cash. For some reason, they have a passion for narcotics, and they have been trying to enter the East Coast. Word is that they fear they may have to give a lot of their oil money back someday and want to multiply it quickly."

"You are talking too loud, Diggs, they may hear us," whispered Phoebe. "You guys got busy all last night."

"Very busy, Phoebe; we had to clean out the streets. Diane and Digger are upstairs, fast asleep."

"Looking at your eyes, Diggy Boo, you look like you are about to drop, yourself."

"You're right, dear, I'm very tired. I will get some sleep after this meeting."

Adigun ushered Pheobe back to the gathered men, announcing expansively, "These are my brothers from California. They are Russian Americans."

The men laughed at this quip and Adigun continued speaking, saying, "This is my fiancé, Phoebe. Phoebe this is Dimitri Turgenev, meet Igor Kuznetsova – did I get the pronunciation right this time?

"Then we have here the big, bad, Leonid Preo- help me here, Leonid."

"Try," came the languid reply from an otter-like man with what appeared to be a knife scar running from his left temple, across his nose, to his right jawline.

"Preobrazhensky," Adigun intoned haltingly. The otter nodded approval.

"Then we have here the brothers, Olezka and Oleg Smirnov." Two of the men raised their glasses to Phoebe.

"Phoebe is my business partner. There are two others, Didi and Diane Gershom. We all be in Los Angeles for the final meeting.

"Darling, our California Russian brothers have been interested in buying this business for a while now. Now it's ours, we will sell it to them. We have already had long conversations on the feasibility of the sale.

"They will purchase the cemetery operations from us, lock, stock, and barrel, including all of the inventory in the vaults. I'm working them through the angles to ensure they get controlling interests in all of the real estate too.

"The cemeteries, the warehouses in Delaware, and the containers in Long Island – we are selling our entire inventory to them. Twenty-two tons of cocaine in all the vaults and warehouses combined and we have offered it for two-point-eight billion, though we won't agree on the final price until we all get to California.

"They are offering to buy the safe manufacturing company and also the briefcase manufacturing plant.

"Let's drink to a successful closure."

They all charged their glasses with vodka and stood up. Oleg raised his glass, and spoke a few words in Russian, then, in stumbling English, he said, "To happy married life and a successful business relationship." Then he lowered his glass and fixed Adigun with a searching gaze and said, "Regarding that, how you say, wrinkle we were talking about before…" Adigun's expression changed from exultant to stubbornly defiant in the split second before he lifted his glass and downed his shot. "Not an option, Dmitri! I already told you."

"This is the only way we can have peace, brother," Dimitri quibbled. "I understand how you feel, but this man is not your father, dude – not anymore, anyway! This guy will have you assassinated any time from now. If you don't let me fix it, the sale may never take place; our big boss in California will cancel transaction." Dimitri took a long drag from his cigarette, and he continued, "Dude, listen to me carefully; I like everything I've heard here today, and I am sure we can close this transaction. Russians, we always watch our backs, but we do not like unnecessary risks, eh? I am sorry, but we will have to turn off your 'dad'. It makes no sense we buy this business and have him and his people coming after us, see?

"We have many people in the jails. Easy for us to switch him off. This is very important. Think about it!"

"We will be leaving now for another quick meeting, but we are excited for this business. To show goodwill and honourable intent, we will make immediate cash deposit, which is refundable if we do not close the deal.

"It is a lifelong relationship with our guaranteed protection. We will take your greetings to our president, Baron Timchenko Mordashov."

"We thank you and let you know Baron Mordashov will be most pleased to host you in California."

The five men in expensive dark suits filed out of the Gershom residence through the rear kitchen entrance to a black ten-seater helicopter that squatted in the meadow behind the house. Adigun waited, hunched against the draft created by the rotor blades, until the chopper was airborne, and then he loped back into the house.

"Adigun, this is a lot of blood on our hands," Phoebe said to him.

"Needs must," he replied simply, then filled her in on the major details of the deal he was arranging. The entire operation would likely be haggled down to a sale price of one and a half billion dollars. The payment included global insurance and protection for the lives of Adigun, Phoebe, Didi and Diane Gershom, as well as a business royalty of two million dollars a year for twenty years. This brought some relief to Adigun; the end of the drug business was fast approaching. He knew it was not over as long as Bobby Brown was alive but, knowing what Dimitri had told him was true, Adigun guessed that would be sorted out soon enough as well.

10

Chicago, 1997

Chike walked into the empty room that had been Ada's. The music from the swimming pool area could be heard loud even from the staff quarters. He was overcome by a strong sense of déjà vu as he felt the muffled beat through the walls. Music had been playing just like this two years ago on the day Ada killed herself. Today it was simply a gathering of friends, but on the day, Ada signed out, it had been a celebration – Chike's fiance' was arriving in Chicago. Even now, two years later, he could still feel the tension in the room like it was yesterday.

"Ada! Ada," Chike had queried, "What is wrong with you?

"What the hell is wrong with you?"

"You have not eaten in days, I heard. Look at you. Look at how sick you look!"

"You sit here sulking and being miserable, you did not come to welcome my Talatu. We are all happy and we gave a day off for all the staff to celebrate her arrival and you sit here sulking away."

"Are you sure you want to continue to work here? Are you losing your mind?"

Ada had only a bedsheet wrapping her body, and she looked frail. The veins on her broad forehead stood out in stark relief. She struggled to get up, stretched, and reached for Chike. He stepped back, bumping into the frame of the standing mirror.

"Get yourself together, Ada. Come on, get yourself together. I told you this was over before we left Nigeria. You are here, you are paid well, and you live in decent accommodations. You are free to go out, you have two days a week off… you can find another man."

"What of my virginity?"

"What of my womb?"

"I can find that too? Chike you took my most prized possession. You have ruined my life! The doctors said I would never be able to have another child. You and your wicked mother robbed me of my life and now you mock me and bring this woman from Belgium!

"Is there anything else to live for? Chike, I have never been with any other man; you are my first and only! I don't want to be with anyone else. Better I die and leave this world than let anyone else see my nakedness.

"Chike, I love you. I don't want all this. I have no desire to partake of your wealth… I just want you, Chike.

"I want you.

"I want you to make love to me like you used to.

"You showed me love I never knew, and you want to abandon me to die," she wailed.

She reached for Chike again, but he stepped away. With a bitter mixture of shame and regret, Chike recalled his feeble response. "Ada, I don't know what to say. I just want you to know I'm sorry, but you and I cannot be", he said softly. "And it isn't just about my mother's wishes, there is a great deal at stake here.

"This chapter is over," his voice became steely. "You need to get over it! It is bad enough that you and I have this open secret in this house, but you are making things worse by moping about like this. I have staff morale to think about, and I will have to take drastic action if you threaten the smooth running of the household."

"You will get yourself together and join the rest of the staff to welcome Talatu!"

"Chike, *I* am your wife!" Ada keened miserably, "I became your wife the day you and that evil doctor killed my baby!"

"I became your wife the day your evil doctor took out my womb."

"I belong to you Chike, I belong to you! But you don't have to worry about morale in your household, you hear?"

Chike had walked out of the room, not liking the ominous quality of Ada's parting shot, but not wanting to think about it. He headed back to the swimming pool area.

The atmosphere in the Obidike mansion was festive, made up primarily by the large domestic staff and a sprinkling of guests. Mrs. Obidike was dancing with Talatu to a song by Victor Olaiya when Chike joined them, and everybody had a merry time. After what he felt was a suitable period for reasonable preparation, Chike looked around to see if Ada had heeded his instructions. She was nowhere around. Chike tapped Duke on the back and asked him to go and check on her. Duke had been gone for only a few minutes, and Talatu was just asking Chike why he seemed so anxious when Duke came running to the poolside area. He bore the limp form of Ada, flopping bonelessly in his arms. "Ada! Ada!" He kept shouting as he ran. The DJ noticed what was going on and stopped the music. Chike left Talatu and ran to meet Duke and helped him set Ada down. Then he checked her pulse and yelled, "Call 911! Call 911! She has a weak pulse!" In the commotion that ensued, it was Duke who raced to call an ambulance, while Chike did what he could to make Ada comfortable while keeping the gawking, wailing staff from crowding her. Mrs. Obidike had removed her headgear and started praying in tongues. To anyone paying attention to her aggressive grunts and jerks, it was unclear whether she was beseeching God to help Ada or celebrating her misfortune.

Chike was frantic. He sent some of the staff to Ada's room to see if there were any signs of what may have happened to her. Beke, fastest by far, was the first to return but it was Duke who first reported, shouting from behind her, "There was an empty medicine bottle by her pillow! It was a small Valium bottle."

Beke shouted, "Valium ooooooh! *Na Valium! She carry am come from Nigeria!*

"Give am oil! Give am palm oil," Beke shouted. Duke ran to the kitchen and returned with a cup of palm oil. He tilted Ada's head back and poured the palm oil into her mouth. She was lifeless. By this time the siren of the ambulance was audible and drawing closer. A brief crunch of tires on gravel and then the paramedics were strapping Ada to a stretcher. Less than three minutes after they arrived, the ambulance was on its way to the emergency room. But Ada didn't make it. She was pronounced Dead on Arrival.

During the period of the inquest and autopsy, a dark pall hung over the Obidike household. For many of the staff, Ada's passing seemed to crystallize their disaffection with their foreign home, to make tangible their misery. Duke cried profusely for days, and he and seven others requested to accompany Ada's remains for burial in Nigeria. It took a while to cut through all the red tape, but Ada was finally flown to Nigerian in the Obidikes private jet. Beke was also among the mourners that flew out with Duke. It wasn't a real surprise to Chike that, after four weeks, only Duke returned. The rest all wrote long letters to Chike thanking him, but one theme was common; they could not stand the Chicago cold and found American life boring.

11

Two years after the death of Ada, Chike erected a small monument by the poolside in her memory. The vacancies left by the seven former staff members were filled by independent contractors and a semblance of normalcy returned. Rather than being aggravated by the specter of Chike's lost love, Talatu decided that understanding the story behind their relationship would help her better understand her man. During her afternoon tea at the poolside, she would often ask the domestic staff about the life of the lady that was once in her husband's life. For months after Ada's death, Chike was withdrawn and depressed, looking unkempt and undernourished. It also had a pronounced effect on his relationship with his mother, who was on the receiving end of several outbursts, casting aspersions on Mrs. Obidike's character. Chike blamed it all on her.

Despite her conscious effort to be understanding, Talatu often wondered why Chike married her at all if he was so in love with Ada. These external pressures on their marital relationship were already a strain on them both; a strain that could only be eased if Chike could wholeheartedly focus on his marriage without distraction. But, within weeks of Ada's suicide, Mrs. Obidike suffered two back-to-back strokes and was soon confined to a wheelchair. Her neurological condition deteriorated rapidly, and her eyesight soon failed. She could hear though, and she did all she could to stay in control. Chike had engaged neurosurgeons from far and wide but, after multiple procedures (two of them invasive surgery), his mother only seemed to get worse. She had a dedicated nursing staff and the grounds of the estate were comprehensively modified to allow her ease of movement in her electric wheelchair.

Mrs. Obidike was bowed but not broken and her spirit still railed against the loss of control over the household. Day-to-day management within the mansion was fast being taken over by Talatu's mum, Hadezah. Talatu and her mother spoke Fulfulde all the time, a gesture Mrs. Obidike called rude and obnoxious. Before her illness, there was a cold war between the two old women, which would often ignite over seeming frivolities, the most common of which was Hadezah and her daughter speaking in their native tongue. Something about the high-pitched gaiety of their discourse would set Mrs. Obidike off. The speaking of the Fulani dialect was the trigger, but the deeper running issue was control – of the household and of Chike, the man of the house. Mrs. Obidike had already lost her husband and, happy as she was about Chike's marriage to Talatu, she was damned if she was going to lose him too! To either Talatu or her high-and-mighty mother, Hadezah. They had several loud altercations, the theme of which was usually Mrs. Obidike calling Hadezah an opportunist and a gold-digger. The irony was that Mrs. Obidike was enthusiastic about Chike's marriage to Talatu primarily because it gave him access to the

Hausa-Fulani power block in the Nigerian political scene, a fact that was not lost upon Hadezah. So, the 'gold-digger' moniker became a double-edged sword.

Hadezah enjoyed singing her Fulani songs in the house and, whenever she sang, Mrs. Obidike would also start singing in Igbo, raining down insults and curses on Hadezah. She would also infuse her performances with mixed English and vernacular prayers, on the assumption that Hadezah was singing insults and curses at her as well. "I reject it," she would spit, "I reject it in Jesus's name.

"Any Fulani arrows shot at me in this house, return to sender!

"I am in my husband's house! Leave and go to your own husband's house!" Hadezah never replied.

Eventually, they could not be in any part of the house at the same time. Mrs. Obidike was always on Hadezah's case, and she criticized everything she did, going so far as to refuse to even allow Talatu to cook for Chike. She insisted everyone should have dinner cooked by the chef and she chose the menu.

Hadezah got fed up with the constant abuse and she openly voiced her intention to return to Africa. Then Chike's mother got sick and Hadezah found herself at considerable ease. The worse Mrs. Obidike became, the more light-hearted Hadezah appeared to be. This did not manifest in any sort of pointed malice or glee over her rival's misfortune, but more in the form of benign energy and devotion to the household. Hadezah got along very well with all the domestic staff and quickly – though unobtrusively – filled the void in Chike's life that his mother's illness created. She became closer to Chike and she was always available to discuss his problems.

It helped that Hadezah had a canny sense for business, and she was soon Chike's confidante; his first point of reference for tricky business situations. She became the silent board member of the Oben Dyke group, and Chike would rarely make any major decision without consulting her first. Though she wasn't highly educated – she never rose above a secondary-school-level education – Hadezah had worked as the personal assistant to Nigeria's richest business mogul, Alhaji Muhammed Gobir. Alhaji Gobir was a Fulani businessman whose interests ranged from oil to agriculture. He had mines in the Jos plateau, extracting precious stones for export. He was related to Hadezah through her mother and had funded Talatu's entire education abroad, giving them both a comfortable life in Belgium, where Alhaji Gobir spent most of his time, and where his African operations were headquartered. Hadezah had learnt a lot about managing a business empire and that experience came in handy for Chike.

The burning issue during the time of his mother's illness was a long-running battle Chike was having with the Jo Bore group, a holding company that seemed to be on a constant war path with Chike's businesses. The ownership structure was well-shielded with layers upon layers of offshore companies created to obscure the real owners of the business. Rumour had it that the business was owned by the Vatican. Some said it was owned by the Italian mafia. In any case, Jo Bore Holdings had become a nightmare for Chike. They constantly poached staff from Chike's group and seemed to know all their company secrets, always managing to be a few steps ahead of Chike when their interests intersected. What was clear to Chike though, was that the core of their conflict was in the area of prestige artwork. Both companies seemed to converge on the same pieces more often than was comfortable to Chike. And both went to ridiculous lengths to clinch victory in the bidding wars that ensued, usually over large sculptures.

Chike was fortunate to have Hadezah's council at this time when he was far from his best. Short-tempered and withdrawn, he was prone to overreacting when things went awry. This was the case when he learned that they had lost out on a particular sculpture he had been struggling to secure from the UK.

"What are you telling me?" Chike shouted banging his fist against the tempered glass partition of his office. "What are you saying? You had better be joking! I told you how much that Yemonja piece was worth to me." This was Chike's most expensive piece – a gigantic edifice of a Yoruba deity made of pure African brass. The piece was so large that Christie's had to move the auction to the warehouse at the port.

"Do you have any idea how much this is worth in sweat and blood? MY sweat and blood!? I spent months and months of sleepless nights making that piece with my bare hands!

"How could Christie's let this happen? I own this art, and this is the fourth time you're letting a piece slip away from me. Even the smaller pieces hurt to lose but one of this size?"

"How am I sure the Jo Bore group didn't plant you here to sabotage my business?" You know, I shouldn't even be talking to you; put Volte on right now! Volte!"

Chike's temper dialled down a notch at the sound of the placid, mellifluous voice of the new party on the other end of the line. "Good afternoon, Sir," Volte responded without the slightest hint of panic that his predecessor on the call had exhibited under Chike's withering harassment.

"This is my artwork," Chike seethed, "These are my sculptures. I sold them to you in the UK so I could buy them back from you and move them out of the UK-"

"Sir," Volte gently interjected, "I was not part of that transaction, and nothing was put into writing concerning the buyback. However, my understanding is that you were to be considered and notified whenever auctions were scheduled concerning these pieces, which I am certain we have always done.

"We are auctioneers and are bound by very strict consumer laws, we only sell to the highest bidder. I cannot be seen to be tampering with the process."

Chike was arrested by the weight of the reality Volte had just laid on him. After leaving the UK for Nigeria (which seemed like a lifetime ago), he had not had much time to figure out what to do about his statues – and the cash in them – that he had dotted around England. Arrested and locked up on arrival, then subsequently caught up in the theatre of his father's death, family trouble, and assuming control of an eight-billion-dollar empire, he simply had not had the bandwidth to attend to his assets in the UK. The tedium of renewing the leases on the art pieces and overseeing their transportation, storage and care was more than he could add to his already full plate. So, he engaged Christie's to acquire the pieces as they became available upon the expiry of their leases, and then (in principle, at least), sell them back to him when he was ready to move them out of England. He was not as thorough with the scrutiny of the terms as usual for two reasons. One was that, at the time, he was so dazzled by the magnitude of his inheritance that the value of his cash-stuffed sculptures seemed paltry in comparison. The second reason was that afraid of possible law enforcement interest in his money-laundering activities in Europe, he didn't dare travel to England to properly midwife the contract.

At this moment, he regretted the lapse in judgment. Yes, the value of the statues and their stashed cash was tiny compared to the Oben Dyke net worth, but it still amounted to millions of pounds – tax-free. Now that he was resident in the United States, he was hobbled by tax constraints and the legalities surrounding the use of corporate funds. He couldn't just dip in and do whatever he wanted, and he had big things he wanted to do. The money he had hidden in the UK would make that possible and he desperately needed to get his hands on those funds. But the Jo Bore group had proved to be a huge buyer of high-value artwork and had taken a mysterious interest in his sculptures. He had a fight on his hands, and he realised that he was burning his energy yelling at the wrong people. Chike returned his attention to Volte, who was saying, "I am really sorry about this, Sir," a statement of sympathy, not apology, that Chike ignored.

"I need you to offer any amount to buy it back. That and all the other sculptures I sold to you. I don't care what you cannot be seen to be doing, just do whatever needs to be done to get those pieces back to me." He disconnected the call before Volte could respond and pushed the button on the intercom. "Ruby, call me the Group Financial Officer right away."

In about five minutes, a compact Asian man walked into Chike's office, taking several seconds to glide along the wide expanse between the door and his employer's desk. As he drew nearer, he caught Chike's eye and glanced in the direction of the conference table by the window as if asking whether they would sit there, as was customary. Chike just shook his head and waved the man over to him. "What is going on, Park?" He asked without preamble, "Do you see what is happening to our shares?"

"I don't know precisely, Sir; the information on it only coalesced over the last several hours. I noticed the sudden increase in the purchase of our stocks, and I researched the buyer, but I was only able to trace the purchases to a shell company in the Cayman Islands. The same company that warehouses the Jo Bore group."

"Really?" Whispered Chike. "Jo Bore again?"

Park pulled out a silver cigarette case from his jacket pocket and raised his eyebrows at Chike, who shook his head. Park returned the case to his jacket without opening it and continued talking. "I knew there was something fishy and immediately alerted our broker. As of last week, the buyer had bought about twenty-five per cent of our share structure."

"Chike got up from the table and headed to the wooden shelf in the corner."

He picked up a glass and poured himself two fingers of scotch whisky, which he tossed back quickly. "Go on, Park, I'm listening."

"In the early hours of today, they started selling at a ridiculous rate and this made our share price nosedive. Whoever did this is meant no good, Sir. Also, there was a purchase offer made for the healthcare business; I traced that to the same company."

"Oh, I know where this is coming from," Chike muttered, "Do you remember the company that we bid against on the refinery purchase in California? Adenergy Inc.? I think it is the same as Jo Bore Holdings.

"Who is behind this company, Park? Lift the fricking veil!"

"I have engaged several international firms, Sir, but no one could find the people behind these companies."

"Lift it before this faceless monster destroys us!"

Chike picked up the dialled.

"The line is busy! Park, call our brokers and buy back every one of our shares for sale by these bastards, but make them think it is other parties. Let them believe they have watered down our equity. Meanwhile, we will be announcing a new patent that will put serious flesh on our shares. Maybe they will crawl back to try picking up some shares again then. Be ready.

"You know our guy in California, the one we use to do our dirty purchases? Have him send an offer to purchase Jo Bore Holdings and all the companies affiliated with that company. They want to destroy us, now let's burn the whole house down!

"When that happens, put the word out in FT, Bloomberg and every finance publication you can lay your hands on. Announce that our guy plans to take over this company."

Park looked up from his notepad, tapping his pen against his chin. "Which guy, Sir?" He asked.

"Peter Scolize," Chike replied.

"Oh, Peter? He's bad news."

"That's exactly why we will use him this time. The entire market knows he is a slimeball, and any company he buys dies. Make that move, Park. It will bring us closer to the owners of this company.

"No more of this back-foot bullshit. We are going on the offensive!"

12

Chike's asked his driver to leave; he needed to be alone. He drove slowly, processing the unfolding events in his personal life and his business. He was disturbed by the trend of things in his life and determined to turn things around. He needed to know who was behind these financial attacks and he needed to hurt them – very badly. He arrived at the Obidike mansion and walked straight into his mother-in-law's bedroom, where she was sitting in her rocking chair and taking in the view of the small pond through the open window. The fountain in the middle of the pond made a gentle gurgling sound as its jets hit the surface. Hadezah loved to sit at this spot.

"Are you okay? You don't look good." Hadezah adjusted her grey Hijab. She had finished her prayers and still held her prayer beads in her hands, rolling them with her index finger and her thumb.

"Did you greet your mum?" She frowned with disapproval as she saw the answer in Chike's expression.

"I've told you to always greet your mother before anyone in this house. She may not be able to talk, but she sees and understands everything happening in her environment. The doctor said she'll come around if we keep talking to her and treating her as we used to. I'm sure she's in her bedroom and knows that you just came in. You should go to her right away."

Chike left the room without a word and turned left in the hallway, walking to the west side of the mansion and into his mother's room. "Mama, I'm back," he said flatly. "It was a very bad day at work. Remember the company I told you about?" He would prefer to be talking the situation over with Hadezah, but he just needed to get things off his chest. "They are trying to destroy me," he continued, "And I just lost another artwork – they outbid me. Did you eat?"

Mrs. Obidike sat motionless in her wheelchair. A white shawl was draped over the white hat she wore, obscuring her face, and her chin was resting on her chest. This was her usual position lately, looking like she was carefully examining her feet. Chike sat on the chair next to her and took her hand. Such was the extent of her deterioration that he did not expect any response. Chike continued with the narrative, all the while stroking the back of her cool hand.

"Mum, I know you can hear me. You have always been my intercessor. You can't speak, but I know you can pray.

"We are sinking, mum. Our boat is sinking.

"There is a faceless entity buying up all our shares and dumping them to destroy us. They have money to burn and too much of our information in their hands. Whenever we want anything, he heads us off and gets it first, or. . ." Chike stopped, registering for the first time how truly cold his mother's hand was in his.

"Mum, should I turn off the AC? Your hand has been cold since I came into the room and it's not warming up, even while I am holding it." Chike looked up in annoyance. "This is ridiculous! We pay top dollar for three nurses to look after you and they can't even check the temperature and make sure you are fine.

"Sarah Lee!

"Sarah lee!

"Ms Bridget, where are you guys?" Chike's voice was strident as he felt himself losing his temper once again. "You spend more time in the kitchen than looking after my mum."

The two nurses hurried in and stood side by side backing the large white door.

"This room is cold," Chike thundered. "You know she cannot communicate and you leave her to suffer in a cold room? This is cruelty!

"How long have you left her like this? Here, touch her hands, feel the temperature."

The nurses didn't move or meet Chike's eyes for several beats. Then, Sarah Lee, the Philipino nurse looked up at him and said softly, "We went out to try to find you, Sir; your mother is gone. She's gone, Sir"

Chike was aghast. "Are you smoking something? Gone where? What are you talking about?"

"She's been gone for a while now, Sir. Before you came into her room."

"Are you…?"

Chike held his mother's cooling arm and it finally dawned on him that she was dead. He shouted in anguish and his voice was heard all over the house. Several members of the household rushed to the room, where Chike held his mother. Hadezah came in with Talatu and their keening soon joined Chike's cries. Then Hadezah grabbed Chike by the hand and pulled him up.

"She's gone to rest, my son. Follow me and let the nurses prepare her body. It is the will of Allah."

Hadezah led Chike out of the room and left the wailing and crying staff.

13

In the time since handing over the drug operations to the Russians, Adigun, in the guise of Adelaide Fernandez went as far below the radar as he could. It had surprised him that Phoebe did not toe the same line as Diane and insist that her share was handed to her directly. He had no way of knowing that, as a Federal Agent, Phoebe's purposes were better served if such huge sums were in someone else's name. So, while she could have just about anything she wanted, it fell to Adigun to manage the funds. Through a system of cut-outs and shell corporations that obscured his involvement, he set up Jo Bore Inc. and went legit. Nothing fancy – trade, import and export – but this offered the platform for speculation in stocks and investments in art. Digger had been right about art being a fantastic way to launder money and Adigun hired the best hands in the business to lean into it.

It was Diane's twin brother, Pascal, who worked with Christy that first brought their attention to the bronze sculptures of one Chike Onyodikara from the UK. Adigun had been given the broad strokes by his experts, approved their pursuit of the pieces and then forgotten about them. Until now. The stiff competition for the bronze pieces from one Oben Dyke organisation in Chicago had been brought to his attention within the last couple of years, but he preferred to leave the trench warfare to his staff. That way he could focus on keeping his identity hidden, himself and Phoebe alive. Now, however, he had had to get involved because the competition appeared to be trying to take over his business empire.

Giving the Oben Dyke organisation his full attention, Adigun quickly learned that it was owned and run by his old friend, Chike Obidike. At first, he wondered why Chike would be coming after him, but then he realised that Chike would not know that the man behind the Jo Bore group was Adigun Komaiya. He also better understood why there had been such a bitter battle for the bronze sculptures – Chike Onyodikara, the artist and Chike Obidike, the mogul, were one and the same. Adigun suspected that there must be a deeper reason for Chike to be fighting so hard to buy his own artwork, but the fact that they were his was reason enough.

So now, Adigun was in a hotel in Chicago, preparing for a meeting at the Obidike mansion. Since learning the circumstances behind the hostile takeover attempt on his company, he had had his people set up a meeting with Chike, without disclosing his own identity – Chike would be finding out who he was face-to-face. The prospect of the look of surprise on his old friend's face filled Adigun with almost childish excitement. Still, he was on edge about the exposure he faced on a trip like this; he still had enemies out there. He had taken the entire floor of the hotel, under an alias, and had a full security detail.

These men had been with Adigun for three years now, provided to him by his Russian friends in California as part of their deal. They were highly trained security operatives, all ex-military, and many of whom had fought as mercenaries in diverse urban conflicts. Most of them were Eastern European but two of them were ex-Mosaad. Apart from his 12-man security team, discreetly dressed in sensible dark suits, Adigun had his business staff with him. They made up a 5-vehicle convoy as they exited the hotel's private parking structure and headed for the Obidike mansion. In addition to the one driving, two of the security operatives rode in the limo with Adigun, three in the advance car, two with the lawyer and accountant, and four riding drogue in the four-wheel-drive. Every one of them was armed with at least one snub-nosed sub-machine gun (a couple of them had two) and an assortment of handguns. Adigun was also armed, but he thought little of the cold steel under his jacket, focussed as he was on the reunion ahead and the business at hand.

He planned to work out a friendly transaction that would see Chike get his bronzes back for fair market price, with the margins being adjusted as required. He would also structure a process to cease his stock acquisition in the Oben Dyke group and sell back what he already had. He could have pursued Chike's group as an investment opportunity, but he didn't want to taint his friend's business with his own. It was these thoughts that filled his mind as their convoy turned onto the private driveway that led up to the Obidike mansion, and all hell broke loose. A muffled thud broke the silence in the padded interior of the limo and it swerved minutely before correcting its course. The radios on his security detail came alive as Adigun turned to see the drogue vehicle in flames behind them.

713

"Sir," Yuri, his head of security leaned toward him, calm and steady, but urgent. "We are under attack. Unit 5 is lost, and we are boxed in here. There is no evasive action we can take, except to surge forward into the estate." As he spoke, small arms fire broke out and Adigun heard the tell-tale thumps as slugs ripped into the limo's bodywork. He ducked and reached for his weapon, telling Yuri to do whatever needed doing.

The limo sped ahead as Yuri issued instructions over the radio. A web of cracks erupted on the windshield, but the reinforced glass held intact. Two of the vehicles ahead of them, containing only his protection detail, peeled off and screeched to a halt on either side of the narrow road. They left a hole just large enough for the other two cars to punch through. As first the sedan with the business team, and then the limo, rushed through the space between the two parked cars, Adigun saw his men spilling out of them, taking and returning fire. Just as his limo pulled away from them, the car to his right was hit by a rocket and flipped into the road. Adigun hoped its occupants had been clear of it when it got hit but couldn't dwell on this thought as they were now through the estate gate and Yuri was gripping his arm. "We are going to handle this," he said quietly. "Until the gunfire ends, stay in the car."

14

"Yuri, can you read me?

"Yuri, answer me!"

Adigun sat low in the back seat of the spacious limousine. His heart pounded as he heard the muffled cracks of gunshots through the heavily insulated shell of the vehicle. The radio squawked in his hand, "This is Yuri, Sir, do you copy?

"We were heavily outnumbered, Sir, and we have taken heavy casualties, but we... we have subdued them." Yuri's breathing was labored but he still sounded as serene as could be. Adigun heard a seconds-long burst of automatic rifle fire, a pause, then the signature double tap of a pistol, followed by a single shot. Yuri himself had taught Adigun that kill sequence; two to center mass and one to the head. "Yuri? Come in, over!"

"Fucking Colombians. That was the last of them... I think, over," came Yuri's reply. Adigun did not like the way the man sounded.

"Let me come to you, Yuri. Tell me where you are, over."

"Negative, boss. Give thirty seconds, then get out of the car and keep low until you are inside the mansion. Over."

"Are you hit, Yuri? Do you need help? Over."

"There is no help for me anymore, boss. Yuri is done. Gutshot and my lungs are punctured." Now, Adigun could hear a gurgling sound as Yuri spoke. He screamed into the radio, "Hang on, Yuri! I think I can hear sirens; help is coming!"

"That… not help," Yuri coughed, "Cops! Yuri cannot be taken like this, boss. It has been an honour serving you, Sir. Now get to the house and find a way out of this place. Yuri, over and out!" There was silence for two seconds, then a single, flat report. Yuri had fired his pistol for the last time.

Adigun snatched his semi-automatic handgun off the seat and opened the limo door. He chambered a round as he ran, hunched over, toward the mansion. The gate was wide open, and one man lay dead on top of the flower bed beside it. He saw dead men on both sides of the lawn. Branches of the exotic palm trees had been shattered by bullets. Bullet holes pockmarked the cars in the driveway and the walls of the building. He walked into the hallway of the mansion crunching shattered glass beneath his feet. The walls and paintings were ripped apart by small arms fire and the giant chandelier lay smashed on the floor.

"Help," a female voice rang out. "We are here; we are dying!"

He climbed up the stairs in the direction of the voice, gun held in front of him as he proceeded. He saw the crumpled form of a woman at the top of the stairs and kept his weapon trained on it as he took in his surroundings. She was clearly alive and, as he approached, he saw that her body shielded another, smaller, older female. The young lady turned to him, arms out in a pleading gesture then she went still as she stared at his face. Faint, uncertain recognition lurked in her eyes, but the moment was broken when the older lady grunted and put a hand on her shoulder. She turned to attend to her, then froze again when she saw the expression on the old woman's face; she was staring at Adigun with naked shock and disbelief.

The old woman raised both hands to cradle her grey-haired head. "You?" She cried, then began to rant in her native tongue of Fulfulbe. She ended with Arabic.

"Allahu Akbar!

"Allahu Akbar!

"Allah Akbar!"

Adigun understood every word she said and, lowering his weapon, replied in the ancient Fulani Dialect. She shouted loud long sentences in Fulfulbe, beating her chest, then, in English, she shrieked, "Would you shoot us? Would you shoot your own?

"Adigun Komaiya! Why are you a part of this carnage? Even now, all these years later, you still clothe yourself in trouble?

"Will you shoot me now? When these are the hands that raised you?

"Will you shoot my daughter now, when you and she share the same blood?"

717

The gun hung limply at Adigun's side as he gaped at the apparition before him. "Aunty Hadezah?" He croaked hoarsely. "Can this be you?"

"Jo Bore holdings, Jo Bore Logistics and Distribution," Hadezah mused. "All this time, it was you? Why don't you wait until your real target arrives so he can know you destroyed what is left of his life?

"Why? Why?! Here in America? Two African men, the remnant of what is left of the pride of our continent, destroy each other? What could be the reason for this?"

Adigun's head hung low. "We did not know, Aunty Hadezah. I came here today to make peace, to build. I too am under attack. I am sorry that my troubles followed me to your door." At this point, the sounds of approaching sirens filled the air. The younger lady, Talatu, turned to her mother and asked, "Hadjia, how does he know your name?" Before she could reply, Hadezah saw Chike come streaking in their direction from the direction of the bedrooms.

He saw Adigun standing before the prone forms of his wife and mother-in-law and he yelled, "Talatu!" He skidded to a stop a few feet from the small group when he saw the gun in Adigun's hand. "Listen, just hold on," Chike said, edging slowly closer to his wife. He was now crouched slightly and held his hands out in a beseeching manner. Adigun just stood where he was, momentarily at a loss for words. Here was his childhood friend, his one-time hero and would-be victim, who had almost become his business nemesis. The man went down to his knees beside his wife, showing no sign of recognizing the armed stranger in his home.

Chike seemed almost unconcerned about the presence of the gunman. Now that the chips were down, he realised how much of his life he had missed out on, focussed as he had been on things other than Talatu; how much he had taken her for granted and how much pain he must have caused her with his selfishness. He pulled her to him, and all the old love filled his being as he asked her, "Are you okay, darling?" Talatu looked at her husband searchingly, struck by the strong emotion she heard in his voice and saw in his eyes. If they lived past this moment, she thought there might be a chance for them after all.

"Just my thigh," she said. Chike pulled out a handker-chief from his pocket and applied pressure on the bleed-ing bullet wound. Keeping his eyes on his wife, he asked, "What do you want from us, Sir?" But it was Hadezah that replied,

"Meet the brother to your wife, Adigun Komaiya."

Chike's head whipped up; eyes wide. "Adigun?" He gasped. The well-built specimen who stood before him was quite different from the lanky boy who had saved his life long ago, but it was the same person. Adigun squatted and said, "I have been going by Adelaide Fernandez for a long time now, brother. And I didn't come here to de-prive you of anything; I was coming to mend fences be-tween your company and mine. I only just found out who we were at war with and wanted to surprise you. But my enemies followed me here. I am sorry, my brother." "You are Jo Bore Holdings?" Chike was aghast. Adigun nodded in the affirmative. They both looked up at the sounds of tyres screeching and car doors slamming shut. Adigun leaned closer to Chike and said, "Situation is delicate for me here. The last thing I need is to be grilled by cops."

A voice boomed over a megaphone outside. This is the Chicago Police Department. Put down all weapons and come out with your hands up!"

Chike gently put his wife down and walked halfway down the stairs with his hands up. "Don't shoot," Chike yelled. "This is my house! Chike Obidike. My family is wounded. We need medical assistance. I am tending my wife, then I'm coming out!"

He ran back upstairs and hugged Adigun.

"Hadjia, this man is the reason I'm alive today. He saved my life when my uncles planned to kill me. He was the contracted assassin." Hadezah peered at Adigun with a puzzled look, asking, "Why would they pick you to do such a thing?" "Blackmail," Chike responded, looking at Adigun and continuing, "I have been searching for you. After you let me go, I asked my father's friend, the Attorney General of the Federation for a favour, that Adigun's murder case be squashed – it turned out that your victim did not die!

"Adigun, you did not kill anyone! The bursar did not die!"

Adigun's legs slid out from under him as he sagged against the balustrade.

"The bursar did not die?"

"No, Adigun. You have been a free man all this time. No one could find you to tell you."

"Mr. *Obidiki*," the bullhorn outside demanded, "We will need everyone in the building to come out with their hands, in the air. We have several ambulances and paramedics here from your hospital. They can attend to the wounded. But you must come out NOW!"

"We need to move fast," whispered Chike. "If you have police trouble, we may have a way to avoid it.

"Lay down on the floor, Adigun. Smear some of this blood on your shirt. Listen, let me take it from here, okay? Just play dead."

Chike hurried down the stairs and, after the police confirmed his identity and that he was not armed, they swarmed into the house with him and a crew of paramedics with gurneys. Chike directed two of the gurneys up the stairs with him to where his wife, mother-in-law and Adigun lay. One of the detectives ran up with them as the rest of the uniforms spread across the mansion to secure it. Chike squatted by his wife and waved one of the two stretcher teams over to where Adigun lay on his side. The other came to Talatu's aid. "We may need a body bag for this one," Chike said, gesturing toward Adigun. "He is badly wounded." The detective looked on as one of the paramedics squatted by Adigun, his view partially obscured by the paramedic's broad back as he appeared to check Adigun's pulse. "This one is gone, Sir," the paramedic said and rose to spread out a body bag.

The detective turned his attention back to Chike who was fussing over Talatu as she was strapped to the gurney. "What happened here, Sir?" Adigun, zipped up in the body bag, was lifted onto the gurney as he heard the slightly muffled voice of Chike telling the detective he had no idea what was happening – how he was scheduled to have a meeting and how gunfire had erupted outside before bullets started whizzing about. He was relieved to find that his weapon was zipped up in the bag with him – he had forgotten about it until now. He felt the undulating sensation of their descent as the paramedics took him down the stairs and Chike's voice faded till he could not hear it at all.

15

It was cold. It had been an hour since he had been removed from the ambulance and he hoped no one would wonder why the occupant of this body bag was trembling. He was hoping he wouldn't have to lie still too much longer when there was a nudge in his side.

"Get up, dead man! Welcome to the Oben Dyke Funeral home."

Adigun let himself out of the body bag and there was Chike Obidike, beaming.

"You saved my life; I have to save yours. Not only that; I'm going to give you a new life! But you will have to spend the next four days here, while I plan your funeral."

"Funeral?"

"Brother, if that kind of force is what is coming after you, I am thinking maybe Adelaide Fernandez should be laid to rest… get the heat off Adigun Komaiya, get it?"

"Makes sense, but Adelaide Fernandez is the guy with all the money. I can't let everything I've worked for go down with him."

"Two words, my guy; 'Legal Instructions'. I have the best lawyer in the business. We can work out how to liquidate your estate, where to move your wealth, and how to ensure you have access to it in your new life."

"Sounds good, but I have to get word to someone... I have a woman in Maryland."

"I understand, Adigun, but the fewer the people who know about what we are doing for now, the better. When the dust has settled, you guys can hook up again, but not in Maryland or any of Fernandez's old stomping grounds. In fact, I think you're going to have to give me a good picture of what we are dealing with, so my people can advise us properly."

The next four days were spent in a frenzy of legal activity, conducted over the phone and in the private section of the Oben Dyke funeral home. Greg let them know that, with the amount of carnage left behind after the attack at the Obidike mansion, it was inevitable that the authorities would draw a connection between the Colombians and the Fernandez persona. Since Fernandez had been declared dead, it would short-circuit any investigative efforts in his direction, but they would almost certainly insist on viewing his remains. It was also likely that they would uncover the falseness of the Fernandez identity sooner or later. This was why they needed to hurry up and stage a cremation while things were still under the jurisdiction of the local PD. But it was going to be close. The day before the funeral itself, Greg informed them that one of his contacts in the police department slipped him some information that a couple of Feds would be attending the ceremony.

Adigun was alarmed. "I don't like this," he told Chike. "If the Feds find me here, it could be a big problem for you." Chike smiled, saying, "Greg has assured me that there is no way they will be able to secure a warrant to search my premises – even if they do have reason to suspect anything – there is just not enough circumstantial evidence and no probable cause. Just stay low, stay quiet, and, once the box goes in the furnace, wait to rise again."

"I thank you so much, my brother. You have turned out to be a solid man, just like your father was. I am still sad to learn of his passing."

"The same uncles that tried to kill me got to him, yes, but he left me a lot of money so I could move his empire here. And everything was conspired to set us on this path to our reunion. My father told me that, before he died, your dad never accepted anything – not money, not contracts, not jobs – from him, but his last wish was that my dad use his immense resources to help find out what happened to his only son… and to help him. My dad told me this, and today, I can fulfil his promise.

"I am standing by you until you are safe again, Adigun."

16

The funeral of Adelaide Fernandez was quiet and sparsely attended. The small number of directors who knew of him attended, and his lawyers attended, but otherwise, the funeral parlor was empty. Adigun watched the ceremony via closed-circuit TV from his hiding place in the private section of the funeral home. The service was almost complete, and preparations had commenced for the cremation when the parlor doors flew open and a small group of dark-suited individuals – three men and a woman – strode in. Adigun squinted, and then his eyes widened as he recognized Phoebe. Alarm bells rang in his head because the men were clearly Feds and he was concerned that they had arrested Phoebe but, as he observed their progress toward the gathered mourners, he realised that she was not cuffed nor under any sort of restriction. The grainy picture made it difficult for Adigun to see her face clearly, but he was familiar with the expression of grim concentration that he could discern.

The agents approached several of the people gathered in the parlor, spoke briefly with them, and handed out cards. Phoebe appeared to be doing the same thing, but Adigun was too aghast to register that fact. What is she doing here, he wondered, and why with the Feds? His musing was interrupted by an unfolding seen on the monitor.

Phoebe appeared to be trying to get to the closed casket and two of the Jo Bore lawyers appeared to be resisting her attempts. One of them produced a sheaf of papers and held them in front of Phoebe's face. The other agents now moved in to restrain Phoebe and Adigun could now hear her voice through the walls as she screamed, "Let me see him, you assholes! Let me see him!" Adigun's instinct was to rise and rush to her aid until a glint on the screen caught his eye and froze him in place. Phoebe's jacket had come unbuttoned in the struggle and, hanging from a stainless-steel chain around her neck, her gold FBI badge swung free. Adigun's mouth hung open, and his breath stopped. He remained motionless as the scene played out on the monitor; Phoebe being dragged out by her colleagues as the assembled guests gawked. Even before they were out the door, the attendants were wheeling the casket to the crematorium.

A little under two hours later, Chike sat in the back room across from Adigun, who had barely recovered from his shock. On the table between them was a silver urn with the ostensible ashes of Adelaide Fernandez. "What was that all about?" Chike asked. "I mean, we knew some Feds would be here, and it was routine for them to canvas the guests for some information and for contacts to reach them later. But that lady insisting on seeing the body? That was a surprise. Luckily, the legalities were clear, and they weren't here with a warrant so your guys were able to hold them at bay. Phew!

"Wonder why she freaked out like that, though."

When Adigun spoke, his voice was a croak. "Remember what I said about having a woman in Maryland?"

"Oh, yes, that I said we should wait a bit before letting her know you're alive?"

"That was her. She's FBI, apparently." Adigun seemed to have shrunk into himself.

"Wait, what? Freakout Fed is your woman?!"

"I didn't know she was with the FBI… but I should have. The signs have always been there. I just didn't want to see them. Guns stored in her apartment, coded phone calls, the snooping around people's business," Adigun paused, and his eyes widened. "This is why she had leverage on Digger! How could I have been so blind?"

Chike looked at Adigun with concern. "Brother, I am not quite following you on all of this," he said softly.

"Doesn't matter," Adigun whispered fiercely. "There is nothing here for me anymore. Adelaide Fernandez really got laid to rest today, but that woman also took a huge chunk out of Adigun!" As he called his own name, his voice filled with anguish. The cycle of betrayal by the women in his life continued – his mother, Adjua, and now, Phoebe – and seemed to close his chapter in America. No way he could consider trying to stay here under a new identity; not with Phoebe out there as a federal agent to compound all of the other threats to his life.

"I have to get back to Nigeria," he said to Chike simply. "There is nothing left for me here."

Book-11

Served Cold

Okuko na-arogoro ite onu, chetekwe mma gburu ya

(The chicken frowns at the cooking pot,

ignoring the knife that killed it. – Igbo proverb)

Mazi Obidike twitched his nose in his usual way as he shuffled to put on the rusty standing fan in the corner of the shabby room. He leaned heavily on his cane and his mostly bald head wagged on his scrawny neck as he moved.

Diokpa remained seated and fanned himself with an old obituary pamphlet with one hand, while using the other to push the window wider open, looking for fresh air. The air in the room was like soup, close and stifling.

"When will you make the payment?" Diokpa asked.

Adigun looked around the house with its sagging, water-stained ceiling and patchy walls. It was clear that their fortunes had dwindled after the death of their brother. "Gentlemen, I have not come here to buy your property.

"I will not be paying for anything here; you will be the ones paying.

"But we can negotiate the price for the wickedness you showed Chike Obidike and his mother." Adigun smiled as he saw the confusion on the brothers' faces turn into looks of fear.

"We will negotiate the treachery and wickedness you have sold in several currencies to many.

"Some you sold to death. Some you leased to penury, only to finally sell to death.

"Many years ago, we sat in a room, as we do now.

"You handed a gun to a boy, to kill in exchange for a flight to America." Now the fear on the Obidike brothers' faces had transformed into terror and Mazi was gibbering.

"From this room, you plotted evil.

"From this room, you caused many people great pain."

The old men opened their mouths wide at the same time. They looked like fish, out of the v ˑter, gasping for air.

"You remember. Good.

"My name is Adigun Komaiya.

"I am from Jobore, the land of a thousand rivers, the envy of the people of Irede, the land of sixteen masquerades.

"Does that ring a bell?"

The old men struggled up from their chairs and raised their hands.

"Okoo!" They blurted simultaneously in the old Aro-chukwu fashion.

The smell of stale air was suddenly tinged with the stench of fresh urine. A gust of hot air from the window pushed the stench deeper into the room. Adigun sat at the edge of the old long table and did not move. The silence in the room was ominous and pregnant as he considered the old men before him. These men who had set him on the journey that had taken him away from his home but, ironically, whose actions had set the course for his return home. He considered them and he considered the weight of the steel in his hand under the table; not so dissimilar from the steel these same men handed him as a young boy many moons ago. He considered them as he considered the many memories in which this moment immersed him.

He considered them as he considered what he must now do to them. Adigun clenched his teeth and closed his eyes. Darkness took over his consciousness.

The End